THE TALON PRINCESS

J.C. ROSE

The Talon Princess

Accreton's Curse Book 1

Copyright © 2024 by J.C. Rose

ISBN: 979-8-218-35496-1

First paperback edition January 2024

Book Cover Illustration by Ertac Altinoz

Map of Emerion

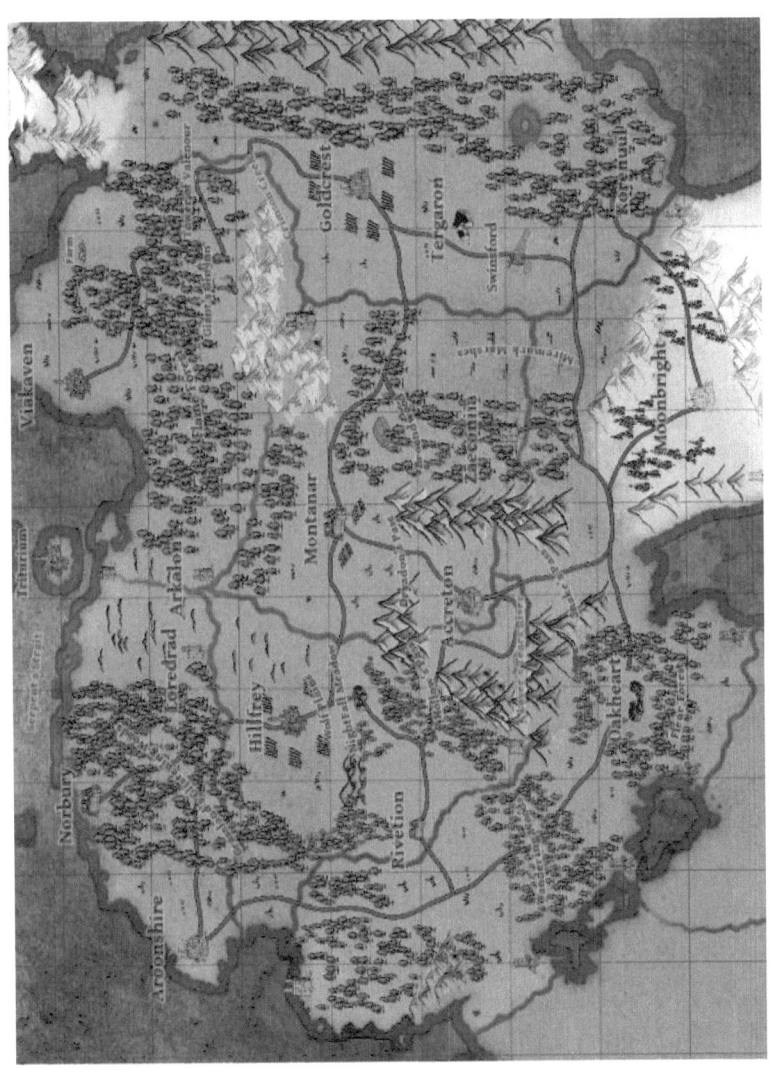

DEDICATION

This would not have been possible without everyone who helped me from day one of writing my novel. A special thanks to my mother, cousin, and sister who always told me to follow my dreams, listen to my story, and always gave me ideas throughout the process. I couldn't have done this without my editor, Michelle, whose tips helped me flesh out my novel, and she always gave more than I envisioned. A special thanks to my illustrator, Ertac, for bringing my vision to life and exceeding my expectations with his beautiful artwork. I can't thank Abraham enough for reading my novel and helping me push through those final drafts with his philosophies and interpretations of my work. Finally, I am grateful to all my friends who, in one way or another, inspired me to keep going through this lengthy process and motivated me whenever I spoke to them about my novel. And my final thanks to my readers, who take their first steps into the world of Emerion.

CHAPTER 1: THE LAST HUNT

Man is like clay, when he passes through fire, he's never the same.

"Papa, why is this hunt so important? We have walked this forest together many times, yet I have never seen you so agitated... or prepare with such haste." Isabel walked closely beside him, moving quickly in an effort to keep pace with his lengthy stride.

He stopped suddenly and turned to face her, "Isabel, do you remember much about your brother?" Isabel's large azure eyes stared blankly at him as the question surprised her.

The two had taken a ride into the forest, walking amidst the tall trees, leading the horses by their reins. Throughout the years, Isabel had taken a liking to leaving the premises of their home and traversing the forest nearby. Her fine dresses had soon been replaced by dark breeches and fitted overshirts, which aided her mobility throughout the woods and protected her fair and lightly freckled skin from injury. Isabel's brunette hair was intricately braided, the elaborate hairstyles her mother preferred remaining part of her life.

"I do," she reached for the silver pendant around her neck with the family's crest, a Pegasus. "The last time I saw him we were in these woods." *We were sparring.* Yet that much she did not say to her father, for her brother had agreed to train her in secret. With her brother gone, there was no one to teach her, nor spar with her.

Her father nodded, "I found a note from your brother in the library. The sword I gifted him, he has left it for me to find."

Isabel remembered the family heirloom sword, shattered, just as their lives had been the day Giles left Oakheart. Even when his departure had been quite abrupt, she could not help but smile at the thoughts of them sparring in their last moment together.

"It is quite late to be in the woods searching for the sword."

"It is not. It was your brother's intention for us to find it at sunset, and sunset it will be," a tear twinkled in Icas' eye, a tear Isabel had rarely seen, and he made sure it remained that way when he blinked it into oblivion. *You miss him. It is our only connection to Giles. That is why we are searching for it now. Even after your quarrel, you still love him.*

Isabel remained silent, not wanting to reopen the scar Giles' departure had left in their father. "We will find it," Isabel squeezed Icas' hand, her father forcing a smile. "What if Giles left it for you to train me as a knight?"

Her father's knight, Arot, who led the horses and was following not far behind, jumped at the idea of Isabel becoming a knight. Icas spoke briefly and firmly when he noticed the abrupt movement. "It is unfit for a woman to become a knight. To become one would imply to be a strong woman."

"I *am* a strong woman," Isabel flexed her arm, hoping to exhibit her prowess.

Icas chuckled and glanced at Arot who stood cupping his chin. "Tell her, Arot, being a knight is no laughing matter."

"That is true, Lord. It is a greater task than meets the eye, yet it is rewarding in its whole," Arot said, the shield pendant hanging on his chest shimmering with the sun's stray rays.

"It is a great task, and more so for a woman of the realm. The knife I gifted you was for protection," her father tilted his head, gazing at her hip where the embroidered knife remained sheathed. "I would have never thought it would inspire such ambitious thoughts into a young woman." He shook his head. "A knight?"

"The knife is beautiful, but I long to wield a real sword and strike down my opponents," she unsheathed her knife, raising it to the air as if standing upon a crowd in hopes of inspiring the ranks.

"A sword is not meant to strike down your opponents. Its sole purpose should be to instill justice, forge honor, and protect those you love." He smiled at her once more, "I am sure you would have been a grand knight, for we have instilled those values in your early life."

"Certainly, Father. I will uphold them," Isabel said, lowering her head and crossing her hands behind her back.

"Now why do you not partake in a safer combat skill, such as archery?"

"I have done so, Father. As much of a liking as I have taken to archery, I have reached the pinnacle of learning."

"A master in archery?" Her father removed his bow and handed her a set of six arrows with it, their alabaster fletching standing out from the wooden shaft. "If you claim to be as prestigious as you say, how about you mount that tree and shoot the six targets around the center tree before I count to ten."

"Shoot from up there?" Isabel seized the bow from his hands, narrowing her eyes at the questionable feat.

"A *prestigious* archer can make a shot from any angle. Or are you not as skilled as you previously claimed?" The edge of challenge in his tone called out to her.

"It will be done," she replied, watching as Arot leaned against a tree, ready to be entertained by the contest.

"Ready?" her father had a lingering smirk in the corner of his mouth.

"Ready," Isabel said, sitting on a branch that would hold her weight. She raised her bow, arrow ready for her father's mark for when she was to begin shooting.

"Loose," and before he finished the word she had already released the first arrow, striking down the first apple from the left tree. She swiveled to the other side, maintaining her balance and ready to fire on the remaining targets.

"...three, four," her father continued, Isabel releasing arrows consecutively in a manner that lined perfectly with his count. Two more apples dropped. Her father continued, "five, six."

Isabel lined her bow between two branches, aiming for a quick shot at the remaining three targets. The arrows struck right on target as she expected, yet the time marker was on the verge of expiring.

"Nine," her father said, Isabel switching the last arrow to her other hand and aligning it with her string and arrow rest. She did not have much time to aim, for the next number would bring an end to the challenge. Her arm moved in the direction of the tree, and before she could focus on her target, she released the arrow and sent it flying.

"Ten," her father spun towards the tree where she had sent her last arrow. The leaves at the last tree waved at them, a wave that was not caused by the wind, for the wind appeared unable to penetrate the forest due to the thick trees scattered about.

A ray of light pierced through the dense canopies, fiery streaks that lit the eerie forest now being overcome by lengthy shadows due to the sinking sun. Where the last streak of light appeared to die, so had Isabel's arrow struck, along its shaft, the last crisp apple she had aimed for.

"She has an excellent shot, or would you say otherwise, Arot?" Her father clapped as he closed in on his daughter to help her descend from the tree.

Arot uncrossed his arms, mischief gleaming in his hazel eyes as he cast a sidelong glance her way. Then he smiled and replied, "A fine shot indeed," and he left to gather the arrows littering the forest with their late afternoon snack.

"You have done it. You have completed the challenge and in record time as well," her father looped an arm around her, dragging her to his side. "Your brother would have been proud as well. All that remains is to find your brother's treasure. I cannot decipher the exact location-" His gaze dropped to the ground. "You found it. It is just as he wrote it."

"What did he write?" she asked, her brows furrowing.

"When the sun sets, and the arrows soar, under the soil will lay a true knight's sword," he read, then turned to her, "this is where we came to practice archery, but we never came at sunset."

Multiple rays of sunlight defied the dense canopies, making their way into the forest and marking the areas around them. Icas gaze was directed at the tree where Isabel's last arrow had landed, her father joining Arot as Isabel thought about the message.

That is not the tree. A second ray struck the bark of a pair of trees coming together to form an arch where the two became one, a special tree in the forest and their lives. Under it, Isabel's parents had vowed to love each other until the end of time and carved their initials on each trunk, one trunk for her father and one for her mother.

This had been many years ago, before Isabel's birth. Recently, however, this had been the place where a second event took place. One evening, Giles had not returned to the estate, and Isabel went to the forest to find him. She found him standing right where she now stood, Giles enraged at their father. With each arrow, he released his anger, and with it, his strikes tarnished the center of the arched tree. It was the last time she saw him shoot his bow and the last time she saw him before he vanished from their lives.

Isabel paced to the tree, reaching for the mark, as if touching it would send her back in time to see her brother once more. A simple circle was all that remained, her brother's precision surviving the test of time.

"I found it," Isabel called out to her father while she stared at the ground.

"Are you certain?" her father was quick to join her.

"I have never been more certain in my life." Her father raised a brow, but Isabel saw how his need to know what lay under was enough to stop him from questioning her.

They dug under the arched trees, removing the dirt that had hidden for years the treasure her brother had left after parting from the household. A low thud marked the spot they were searching for, her father passing his hand lightly over the remaining dirt, uncovering a medium-sized chest. It was intricately engraved, lined with golden leaves around its edges.

"Isabel, help me lift it," he said while reaching for one of the handles.

"Ready? Now," and they lifted the chest out of the hole and dropped it beside them, her father removing a string from his neck with a key strung in it.

The chest clicked with the turn of the key, and Isabel's heart stopped as she awaited the grand reveal. Inside lay a pearly blanket embroidered with the same leaves lining the chest. The family crest was centered in the blanket as her father laid it on his lap. He unwrapped the blanket. There it lay, shattered, the family heirloom sword.

Icas gulped when he touched the sword's grip, and Isabel's mind flashed back to the days when her brother wielded the sword for the last time.

"Father, I must have a heart-to-heart with you," Giles said, the sword's blade resting on his shoulder.

"Speak as we train. En garde," and they both raised their swords at the ready position.

The fighting commenced, and Giles blocked every strike his father sent him, remaining on the defensive, a stance he rarely took. He had become a skillful fighter with years of practice, nearly matching his father. Isabel knew he was to be a prodigious fighter as time progressed, a day not passing by when her father would not mention this to her. Icas was hopeful he might one day test his mettle on the battlefield and come to replace him in history as one of the greatest fighters to ever roam.

"Father," but he was interrupted by a strike over his head, causing him to step back to stop the blow and maintain his balance, for his words had left him unprepared.

"Watch that foot, or a moment like that could be your end on the battlefield," his father said, striking once more as his son parried his blow.

"Father, I will be marrying Bietriz," he disclosed without hesitation before the next blow came, only to send a fury-filled sword his way.

"What?" his father swung his sword down, increasing his strikes and panting with every single one. Giles continued to step back, unable to contain the strikes, awakening the younger version of his father, the natural fighter in him resurfacing.

Giles cried out in pain as his ankle turned, falling back as his father's sword followed swiftly after him. Isabel held her breath. Icas' eyes widened at the horror of his defenseless son, now susceptible to his incoming strike. Giles shut his eyes and lowered his head. Would he be able to stop in time? Isabel screamed, the sound merging with the crashing of metal on metal. Giles' sword shattered when his father struck the fuller side of the sword, breaking into three large pieces and scattering around him.

These three pieces now lay before Isabel and Icas. She glanced at her father, catching a glimmer in his eye, but he was swift to blink it away. Many years had passed since she last saw her brother, but even then, she was certain her father's pain surpassed her own when they stared at the sword.

"It is best if we take this home and have our smithy look at it. I trust he will merge the pieces and have the sword ready to be wielded once more," and he folded the blanket back around the broken shards, placing it carefully in one of the saddlebags.

While he stored the sword, Isabel could not help but admire the horse, reminiscing on how her brother would mount the steeds when he practiced his mounted archery. Unlike his, her chestnut horse was still, standing elegantly before the two, its poise mimicking those of the nobles in a king's court.

"Lord, we need to leave now," Arot returned, Isabel noting a particular oddity in his tone before she pivoted on her heel. A momentary chill overtook her body when she noticed the broken arrow shaft sticking out of his chest. Blood stained his surcoat, his voice weakened by the arrowhead digging into his body.

"Arot!" Isabel's father turned, his body coming between Isabel and Arot to conceal her from the imminent danger and the dreadful sight of Arot's injury.

"I have had worse. You must leave! There are too many of them," Arot reached for his chest.

"Who is attacking us, Father?"

"Isabel, there is no time. You need to get back to the estate and warn your mother."

"What if they capture you?" She grabbed his hand, urging him to come with her.

"Do not worry about me," he said, grabbing her by the waist and lifting her onto the horse. "Please, child, you need to warn the others."

Isabel took hold of the reins and watched her father, her eyes misting as he was to stay behind to cover her retreat. The diameter tainted on Arot's surcoat was increasing with every moment they stood by.

Then, from the height of the horse, she thought she saw a glimmer from the hole the chest had been buried in. *Is that a crown? A crown with a talon?*

But her father squeezed her hand, her attention returning to him. Before she could see what it truly was, he said, "I will care for him.

Now you must go," and he slapped the horse's buttocks, sending it speeding through the woods.

Isabel's heart sank as her father turned his back on her, disappearing into the forest. The roaring voices of men in the distance were soon met with the clashing sound of metal, sounds that were soon replaced by the silence of the woods and the drifting wind by her face.

CHAPTER 2: HELPLESS

How did they sneak up on us so swiftly?
Horses? No. They were too silent. They must have been infantrymen. They are seeking to surprise us. But why Oakheart? Why attack from the south?

What if Father does not return? What will I tell Mother? Terror rolled through Isabel as she rode towards the estate, the horse's hooves becoming louder with every stride. She passed scores of workers tilling the land, their carts full of the season's harvests. Some of them waved, but she did not see – her mind speeding through what was to come. What must be done.

She had almost reached the enormous wall that surrounded the estate. How long had she been riding? It felt like an age … and but a heartbeat. Fortunately, the gates were open, and she raced through, paying no heed to the guards patrolling the battlements.

She soon reached the stables, dismounting and handing the reins to the stableboy, who did not take long to lead the chestnut horse inside.

Carrying a basket, one of the servants halted at Isabel's presence. "M'lady, you seem troubled."

"We were attacked, Agnes. I must find Mother!" and before the woman could react, Isabel was entering the building.

Isabel entered the hall, dim shadows cast by the chandeliers and torches flickering about. The great hall had a table lined at its center, stretching over an intricately woven carpet. The timber in the fireplace crackled, but all external sounds were inaudible to Isabel. All she could hear was her heart pounding against her chest as she searched for her mother.

Isabel rushed up the steps and pounded the study door with a force she would normally not have dared to show. Despite this, there was no response. When absorbed by her work at hand, her mother seldom answered.

Isabel called out, her voice edged with hysteria, "Mother, please, you must open the door." She heard the scrape of a chair and the sound of the latch being lifted.

Peeking through the slit, a pair of azure eyes just like Isabel's appeared. They were mirror images of each other, riven through time only to stand before each other as daughter and mother.

"Isabel, you are frightening me – what has happened?"

"We were attacked in the woods! Arot was injured, and Father stayed with him."

Her mother's eyes widened as she swung the door open, revealing her study. A wooden table embellished with silver leaves on its edges stood on the opposite side of the room. Piles of books and scrolls were scattered upon it, a large scroll pinned at the center of the table by the books encircling it.

Isabel rarely entered Valaenis' study. Upon seeing a red-feathered arrow on the table, thoughts of Arot's pierced chest returned to haunt her.

"Who could be attacking us? Father had me on the horse before they could close in on us."

She remembered the shouts of men roaring all around them in the woods. As if her mind was not enough to contain them, the same sounds came back to torment her. A glint of horror flashed in her mother's eyes, but she was swift to blink it away as she rushed towards the window in the passageway. Isabel followed and glanced over her mother's shoulder.

Arrows rained from the heavens, setting everything they caught ablaze. Women and children exited houses as the thatched roofs burned fiercely. Soldiers fell from the battlements when arrows penetrated their bodies, their armor unable to save their lives.

How did they reach Oakheart so quickly? Isabel then saw the smoke in the distance and knew this was not the same group from the forest. These men were arriving from the southwest.

On the far side, the great wooden door barged open. Warriors unknown to them flung their weapons at the nearest living person. Their angry cries caused fear within the estate. Behind the frenzy-filled soldiers, two horses entered, their ebony armors and ruby caparisons catching Isabel's attention. A knight with a matching tone rode the leading horse, thrusting his lance at the nearest soldier. The second knight sat atop his mount calmly, lowering his hood to reveal his helm. He watched the slaughter in silence while holding onto the horse's reins. Even in his stillness, a crimson claw painted on his pauldron appeared to reach out to the screaming citizens.

"Find me the Valenour ladies," the second knight roared. Isabel knew it was time for them to leave.

"Come, we must find your sister," her mother snatched Isabel's hand as they hurried down the passageway. Valaenis' hand was clammy, a feeling Isabel seldom felt from her strong-hearted mother.

"Who are the Valenour ladies, Mother?" Isabel whispered.

Valaenis turned, her eyes wide and glistening, holding Isabel's hands tightly. "Listen to me, Isabel, do not worry for the Valenour ladies. Do not repeat the name. Do not ask for it. It does not exist. Understood?" There was a strength in her mother's tone she had never heard. However, there was a glint of fear when she said the name, and Isabel knew not what to make of it. "Understood?" Isabel nodded, and her mother continued to drag her away.

Screams echoed within the building, bouncing off the walls. Isabel thought she could feel them reverberating in her rapidly beating heart. A maid ran out from one of the side rooms, her face a mask of terror. It was Berta – a friend, of sorts, to Isabel. She had known of her young mistress' desire to be a knight and over the years had proven to be a trustworthy confidante. She had always buried Isabel's secrets as if they were her own. Behind Berta was a man, one of the invaders. As the Beaumont ladies watched helplessly, he stabbed her, killing her. Then he dragged the lifeless body towards the stairs. The soldier never looked at Isabel. *He did not see us.*

For a moment, Isabel's body was frozen with fear. Her legs were weak and wobbly. She nearly lost her balance and crashed to the ground. Her mother, noticing Isabel's quavering legs, squeezed her hand reassuringly. Valaenis pulled her against the wall, the shaking diminishing as the wall supported her. Her mother turned to her and said, "Isabel, listen to me. Go to your bedchamber and wait for me. I will find you."

"No, I will not leave you."

Her mother responded in a quiet, firm command, "Isabel, this is no time for debates. Now go." In an assuring gesture, her mother squeezed her hand once more and pushed her away. Hesitant, Isabel glanced back, but before she knew it, her mother had vanished. She was left standing alone while the frenzied warrior rummaged through one of the side rooms for loot.

Racing to her chamber, she closed the door behind her. Unable to contain herself from the screams and roars outside, she slid beside her bed and searched her hiding spot for her dagger. Unsheathing it, she kept it hidden beside her leg, waiting for movement from any incoming attacker.

Footsteps stormed outside her bedchamber, running to and fro but never daring to open the door. The muffled sound of men's voices echoed and bounced once more against the door, seeking to taunt Isabel's already trembling insides. She pressed her hands against her thighs, praying they would disappear and the attack had been all a dream. Inhaling and exhaling, she calmed herself. With the diminishing noise of her breathing, so did the noise outside her chambers wane.

Isabel sighed, exhaling the fear which had encumbered her body. The old wooden door groaned and the dread she had just exhaled reentered, her body stiff as a cadaver.

"Little lady, where are you?" a low voice unknown to her called from the doorway. The floorboards creaked, becoming louder and louder as he closed in on her.

"I know you are here," he lingered on the last word.

Isabel's heart sank to her stomach, holding her breath so he would not hear her over the silence weighing upon the tense bedchamber.

"Aha," the man said, turning around the corner of the bed. Seizing Isabel's arm, she remained stiff and unable to react to the incoming threat. "You *are* a pretty one. No wonder the lord wants ya," and he cackled loudly, a cackling sound that made Isabel's eyes well. Thoughts of what would happen to her flooded her mind. No woman was ever safe when captured in a raid. She closed her eyes. It seemed this was the only part of her body she could move in her petrified state.

A low thud was followed by the tension of the man's hand easing on her arm. She was frozen, colder than the lake on a winter's day.

"It is time to go," the sweet yet hasty voice thawed her body, her eyes opening to meet her mother's azure eyes. The man lay collapsed and unconscious beside them, or so she hoped, for she could not bear the thought of another dead body.

"Mother," she said, her body becoming warm as she flung her arms over Valaenis and hugged her tightly. Her mother returned the embrace, comforting her and pulling away, their faces inches from each other. "All will be well. I said I would keep you safe, but we must leave now and find your sister."

Isabel nodded, their embrace ending and her mother's gaze darting towards Isabel's dagger. "Where did you find that?"

Isabel retreated, but her mother did not wait for an answer. "Keep it, but do not use it unless you must. These men are stronger than us and can overtake us effortlessly. Now we must go."

The ladies left the bedchamber and went down the stairs. Berta's body lay unmoving and still like a wintry forest at the base. Isabel shut her eyes, turning away while her mother stepped over her.

"Isabel, do not look. Keep your eyes on me." Isabel did not hesitate to comply. Her gaze was on her mother as they passed Berta, entering the great hall. Soldiers turned tables and knocked down chairs while they plundered their surroundings. One of their cooks screamed as one of the men pulled her hair, dragging her along the floor and beating her so she would not flee.

"Mother, we can fight them. Only two of them and three of us if we help Golda swiftly."

As if the world desired to destroy Isabel's hopes of saving Golda, a group of men dragged another woman into the hall. Isabel noticed a basket fall from the woman's hand. She reached for her hair, touching gently the well-placed flower Agnes had intertwined between her braids before she had left Oakheart with her father. Isabel knew a similar fate to that of Agnes awaited Golda, the cook. The thought of it made her stomach turn.

"Not everyone can be saved," her mother said, dropping her gaze. "We must go now through the kitchen."

Isabel gulped, glancing at the women and then towards the kitchen as they abandoned them to their fate. Valaenis dragged Isabel away before they witnessed a more horrific event than Berta had proven to be.

The kitchen was now their only way out, the pair sneaking into it. Upon seeing it empty, Isabel looked towards the heavens, thanking the gods for their mercy. Her mother opened the door, quietly taking her daughter outside and into the vast garden. Men had already swarmed the area, the ladies trapped between the door and the men who awaited around them.

Their fate was sealed, or so Isabel believed. Valaenis turned towards her, handing her a colossal book in a scarlet pouch. Isabel knew what was to come, and she began to shake her head before her mother started to speak.

"Isabel, I need you to be brave," she began, but Isabel could not bear to hear it.

"I need you to find your sister in the church and give her this book. Talk to Priest Aubrey, and he will make sure you leave the estate safely. He will give you a horse and a gift that you must keep safe. Protect your sister," and a tear rolled down Isabel's cheek.

"Come with us. I will not leave you behind."

"I know you would not, child, but you must find and save your sister. That is your escape from Oakheart. I will be safe," she said, embracing her. "You are the bravest young lady I know. You have the heart of a knight," Isabel's tears fell on her mother's chest, heaving softly as she held her in her arms. "When you hear the bell, run for the church."

"No, Mother, you cannot leave," but her words flew with the wind as her mother planted a kiss on her forehead, ready to leave and ensure Isabel's safe escape.

"Be brave," and she released Isabel, their arms sliding by each other before their fingers slipped away and ceased to make contact.

Her mother turned and ran towards the bell, glancing back to take one more glimpse of her daughter. "I love you," her lips mouthed, and she turned. Isabel was left crouched, watching, wiping a tear from her cheek before she blinked the rest away with her mother. Only the bell remained to be heard, the last tintinnabulation of Oakheart.

CHAPTER 3: GLIMMERING KNIGHT

Isabel hid amongst the brushes in the garden, steering clear of the soldiers. Searching for a route to return to the stables, she focused on finding her horse and fleeing with her sister.

The men sacked the buildings around her, setting them ablaze and slaying all who crossed their path, passive or violent. Their frenzy was never-ending, barbarian-like in their way of looting and laying waste to all they encountered. Isabel had never seen such devastation and knew if she did not leave soon, she would become part of the men's pillaging.

With the stable not too far off, she noticed a group of men enter a building adjacent to it. This was her chance to bolt for the stables, still intact and unscathed by the men's raid.

Isabel dashed for it, hoping to reach its premises as soon as possible with all the items she was carrying. A roar erupted behind her, motivating her to speed up, a man's footsteps chasing hurriedly after her.

"Run all you want, I will get ya," the man said, and he did not allow Isabel to prove him wrong. Immediately, he closed the gap between them and shoved her to the ground. All her belongings spilled like water out of a bucket as she was sent sprawling out awkwardly on the floor. The soldier laughed and grabbed her leg, pulling her towards him. She flipped on her back and sent a kick straight to his face, sending him reeling. Isabel retreated on her elbows, but the man recovered and pursued her like a rabid hound.

"Oh, I was going to treat you kindly, but you asked for it." He unsheathed his sword, ready to strike her down and save her from a more miserable fate.

Isabel raised her hands, hoping to sheath her face from his sword, a helpless attempt, for she was unarmored and would be sliced like butter encountering a hot knife.

Suddenly, a choking sound brought her to lower her hands, a sword trespassing the man's belly, blood spewing from his mouth. He fell to his knees, the life within him draining as his sword slipped from his grip and danced on the floor.

The attacker who killed the man put his leg on the man's back and removed the sword. A knight's glimmering amour caught her attention. Isabel saw her reflection in the immaculateness of his shield. The knight raised the visor, and Isabel's jaw dropped when she realized this was no man, but a woman. The woman's short chocolate-colored hair was streaked with ashen-colored strands, a peculiarity Isabel had never seen for such a young woman. Only one other person had that. For a moment, she reached for a lock of her hair. Upon realizing what she was doing, she quickly scratched her neck. *Keep it hidden. No one must know.*

The knight's instructions were clear. "I cannot save you from everyone if you just stay there." With this blurted instruction, the knight turned to fight off another attacker. In less than three strokes, the attacker was disposed of.

Isabel rose, picking up the book. "I have a horse in the stable."

"Good, go get on it," the woman said, fighting off two more assailants. Isabel remained still, unable to blink at the sight of her savior. *A woman can be a knight.* "Go!"

Snapping out of the knight's induced sorcery, Isabel turned and fled inside the stables. The building had begun to catch fire, and her horse was neighing and whining, begging to be saved. She made it to her horse, still saddled and ready to be mounted for a quick exit. Storing the book in the horse's saddlebags, she hastily swung onto its back. From the horse's height, she noticed a body on the far side of the stable, the body of the poor stableboy. A blood pool had formed beside him, and she knew it was time to leave, for a similar fate awaited her if she remained in the stables any longer.

She rode out of the stables, the thatched roof's straw burning and falling around her, the heat causing her face to bead with sweat. Her body reddened and turned clammy, the smoke within the stables awakening a cough that scratched heavily against the back of her throat, barely allowing her to breathe.

The soldiers outside had fallen to the knight like wheat to a scythe. "I am ready," Isabel said to the woman.

"Then go, or you will never be able to escape," the woman pointed towards the gates with her head.

"I must find my sister. Will you not come with me?" Isabel clenched her horse's reins.

"I must find my horse. Once I do, I will be dust in the wind," the woman handed Isabel one of the dead men's swords. "I wish you might not need this, but it would be best to be well prepared." The woman smacked Isabel's horse's buttocks and sent him running. "Go find your sister," she screamed back at her before disappearing in the smoke of the burning estate.

Isabel rode through the estate, brushing past men who continued to pillage her home, carrying women out of houses. Their numbers began to thin out the further she rode, sending hope that her sister might still be safe within the church.

As she fled, Isabel thought of her parents. Do not fight anyone unless you need to her mother said. Her father's persona of helping all those who had helped him also ran across her mind. A soldier pulled a woman out of her house, alone at the far end of the estate. Isabel knew he might be too strong for her to handle alone, yet she feared the woman would face the same fate the servants in her household had faced if she did not interfere.

Isabel held her reins tightly and directed her horse towards the man, aiming straight at him without injuring the woman. The man flew, loosening his grip on the woman, allowing her to flee due to Isabel's heroic charge.

Her heroic rescue ended when she reached the church, nearly falling off her saddle in search of her sister. She took the sword, maintaining it sheathed within her grip.

The church's doors were slightly open, and she slid through the entrance like a snake slithering into its prey's nest. Dark shadows filled it, the darkness of late evening swallowing its interiors. Few candles flickered within the building, and the stained glass did not permit the remaining light outside to illuminate most of the church's interiors. From the stained glass, the god Enigma watched over her, a flower held tightly in her hands, blowing onto it, helping it grow in life and wisdom. Isabel touched the flower intertwined in her hair and murmured a quick prayer at the sight of the goddess.

The building was empty as Isabel ran through it, the frescoes on the wall keeping her company as they stared back at her and told the stories of her family, a story which seemed to be nearing its end. On the opposite wall, frescoes of Enigma plowing the earth and planting her seed ran down its length. Isabel entered one of the passageways, and removing a torch from the wall, searched deep into the church's chambers.

Investigating chamber by chamber, she found nothing, her hopes of finding her sister causing her to pace back and forth within one of the last chambers. *Where are you, Lucia? Where have you hidden?*

A low ruffling sound made her stop, wondering if the soldiers had reached the church and were on the verge of discovering her. But she quickly realized the sound had not come from outside but from within the chamber. She listened intently, hoping to catch another sound, pacing within the chamber without causing too much commotion.

Reaching the bed, she heard a whimper come from under it. She had been told dragons used to hide under their beds, but that was a children's tale, and she was certain this was no dragon. Isabel dropped abruptly to the ground, and from under the bed, a girl's shriek pierced her ears.

Behind her, the door swung open, and a loud voice boomed over the chamber's near hollowness. "Release the girl," the man said assertively, yet a drop of fear escaped his tone.

The man raised his bludgeon, ready to beat down Isabel, when he gasped in sweet realization. "M'lady, it is you," the priest said, lowering his weapon. "You are alive."

A scuffle behind her was followed by two arms wrapping around her body. She turned to hug her sister who was shivering. "We are safe, Lucia."

"We will not be, not for long," Priest Aubrey said.

"Mother said you knew a way out."

"Aye. She left you a gift, if I am not mistaken. A gift no one but you two should be able to open. It is in a chest. I will search for it," and the priest vanished as easily as he had appeared moments earlier.

"How are you, Lucia?" Isabel examined her, not a scratch on her body. The soldiers had yet to arrive at the church, but they had hidden for when they arrived.

"I am well. Where are Mother and Father?" Lucia watched her, noticing the few scratches and ashes covering her face, quickly reaching for them. "Were you hurt?" Isabel shook her head.

"I do not know where they are. Father never returned, and Mother fled to help me get here to find you. We need to leave. We will find them afterwards."

"Will they be well?" Lucia's eyes were brimming with concern.

"Aye, Lucia, they will be all right," Isabel gazed back at the azure eyes just like their mother's. Lucia's fair skin was identical to theirs, but she wore her chestnut hair loose down her shoulders, except for a single braid running down her back. Her ears poked through her hair, and if you looked closely enough, you could believe them to be slightly pointed. It was so subtle, if barely noticeable. Lucia would often pretend she was an elf, but her mother reprimanded her for it, though Isabel never understood why. After all, elves did not exist.

"I have found it," Aubrey returned with a medium-sized chest. "Let us get this on your horse. You have a horse, do you not?"

"We do. It is waiting outside."

Without much hesitation, the priest ran across the church, the girls trailing after him. Outside, the light of day had nearly waned as he secured the chest onto their horse's saddle. Isabel aided Lucia onto the horse and handed her the reins. Aubrey pushed Isabel by her waist as she swung herself onto the horse, falling on the saddle behind her sister.

"Follow this road. It will lead you outside through a hidden doorway, and you will ride straight until you reach the city of Rivetion. You must tell them what has happened here, for they need to be prepared if this is a longer campaign heading in their direction. Now go, be safe, my children," the near-bald priest bowed at them, pressing his fingers to his forehead and shutting his eyes.

With her arms around the reins, Isabel kept her sister safe in a pocket that would not allow her to fall. Isabel followed the road, which turned into a barely noticeable dirt path until it led straight to the hidden doorway and out of the estate. In the midst of the night, they would not be easily found, and their escape was perfectly opportune.

Entering the Wandering Woods, Isabel did not reduce their horse's gallop, hoping to reach the city as rapidly as possible. They rode over the long path, time drifting by slowly as the wind caressed their cheeks with the swift speed their horse maintained. Little did they know, they entered a battle between two unknown forces. *Are these the same men who attacked us in the forest south of Oakheart?*

The night's darkness clouded their vision; all they could hear was the clashing of metal, the roars of men, and the grunting of those falling with every strike of a sword. Isabel rode, evading the men running into her path, hoping not to be trapped on the battlefield. With the tree lines thinning out, she knew she was reaching the end of the woods and would soon be free from the battlefield.

Her spine tensed when she realized they would be exposed once they exited the woods if the battle raged on outside, for they were nowhere near the safety of Rivetion. *We are at peace, and no nobles in the kingdom have such an army. It is just a skirmish. It will not extend beyond the woods.*

But she was wrong. The battle was beyond her imagination. Men charged outside the woods, the sounds of battle not fading with every stride her horse took. She could see the woods ending, her hope lingering on the number of men declining as she closed in on the city. Isabel slapped the reins, holding on for their safety as the horse accelerated.

But speed did not favor them. As soon as they exited the woods, another horse struck them, sending her horse rearing. A group of spearmen attacked the horses. The two girls fell from their saddle, crashing on the ground, Isabel cushioning her sister's fall. The horse bled and reared. A second spear ended its pain, the horse wobbling. Debilitated, the horse fell on its knees before plummeting over Isabel. Trapping her under, Isabel shrieked, the pain rendering her unconscious.

CHAPTER 4: ALL GOOD THINGS COME TO AN END

Her mother held her tightly, reminding her she would never be harmed within her arms. It was a warm embrace like no other in the chilly evening as the warriors surrounded them, their presence bringing about an unfamiliar weakness in her legs. Isabel wanted the embrace to last for all eternity, yet all good things must come to an end.

Valaenis released her, Isabel yearning to be concealed within her arms and never see the exterior world of pain that awaited. The world without her family was frightening, for she had always spent her days beside them. In the worst of circumstances, she was close to them.

The scene began to fade, and even as her mother whispered, "I love you," Isabel began to panic. Darkness was descending and she knew she was alone. All alone. Her chest tightened as if a tower had been placed upon it.

Then came a familiar voice – "Isabel, please wake up." – and she opened her eyes, the world around her so dark it was as if a shadow had been cast upon the land, never to be removed. Adjusting to the night, her sister's face was buried in her chest, sobbing as she was alone amid a battlefield filled with corpses.

Isabel reached for Lucia, her sister lifting her head from Isabel's chest and smiling at her. She wiped Lucia's tears from her cheeks and the words which taunted her in her dream were long gone. "You are alone," new ghosts whispered to her. The words were soon swallowed by the darkness and a fresh pair of words came over her while she watched her sister's face light up. The world without her family was scary, but she was not without them. Her sister was with her, and therefore, she was not alone.

"You are not alone," she said to her sister as the words continued to repeat in her mind.

The smell of sweet garden flowers was replaced by human flesh and blood. Pain ran through her leg and up her spine when she attempted to stand up. Her legs were numb, and gazing down, she noticed the horse spread out on top of her. Its weight pressed against her hips and legs, her mobility limited.

"Lucia, I am stuck. Help free me. Find a tool to push this horse off me." Her sister blinked rapidly, Isabel holding her hand like their mother always did when fear struck them.

"You do not know how long I hid in those woods to avoid this horror," Lucia glanced around the battlefield. "Who knows what lays out there?"

"I understand, Lucia, but if I cannot escape, it will not be long before we are found. Fetch a spear or a sword to help me move the horse."

"Isabel," her sister pulled away and lifted her hands to cover her face. "I cannot bear to look at those corpses," her sister shivered. "They are all just butchered. I cannot," Lucia brought a hand to her mouth, heaving.

"Now, now. I understand it is terrifying, but you must not look at the faces. Just concentrate on what we need. There are many tools around here that you may use. Just search for one or two and bring them back to me," she squeezed her hand reassuringly.

Lucia gulped and left, covering her mouth while traversing the field.

The sands of time dropped unhurriedly as Isabel waited on her sister, Lucia searching for a tool to help remove her from under the horse. Isabel attempted to move, regaining a slight feeling in her legs before tiny prickling sensations ran all over them.

She ceased her attempts at escaping the horse's weight, for the pain with every turn shot up towards her mouth. Isabel bit her lip, holding the urge to scream. They did not know who could be lurking around the corpses. Silence was crucial.

Lucia returned, a spear and axe in hand. "I believe these may be of help," and she handed Isabel the spear.

Isabel wiggled it under the horse and searched for a spot where she might be able to raise it. The dead man's body beside her was a good leverage point to help her pull the spear down and raise the horse.

"Now I need you to push the spear down, Lucia. I will pull it, and hopefully, we can make sufficient room for me to wiggle out from under the horse." Lucia nodded in agreement.

"On my count. One, two, and three."

The girls began to force the spear, the body under it cracking with the excessive force they were exerting upon it. The horse began to rise, and Isabel's legs became warm as blood rushed into them, Isabel wiggling herself upward and away from the horse.

The spear began to crack, splinters rising from its shaft as it started to sever. Isabel wiggled as swiftly as she could, yet it was not enough to free her. The shaft snapped, and Lucia went soaring backward. The horse once again pinned Isabel.

"No, no, no," Isabel said, groaning as her back crashed against one of the corpses. "Lucia, did you see any more spears around where you searched?"

"No, I am not going back. Do you wish for me to hurl my last fine supper onto my dress?" Lucia pointed at her body, her dress untarnished since their escape. "There are men still alive. They were reaching out to me, all in their mutilated states. I cannot look at them any longer."

Isabel grunted, and though she needed her sister's aid, she knew her sister's horror would detain her from returning to the battlefield. She turned around, searching for a way to remove herself from under the horse. The axe did not have sufficient leverage to help her lift the horse. Only one idea remained. *It seems I will be the one hurling my insides onto the battlefield. A lady should not commit such an atrocious act.*

"Lucia, hand me that axe, please," she pointed at the weapon beside her sister.

"What are you going to do?" Lucia said while complying with her command.

"It is best if you stand back. You would not wish to be near the maniacal thing I have to do," Isabel said. "Remain near, and your dress may fall victim to my barbarism."

Lucia took a step back, and Isabel commenced the shameful process. She raised the axe, aiming it correctly to strike the appropriate area and let it drop. The axe struck the horse, tearing through its chestnut coating, the blood spewing out onto Isabel's legs. She let it fall once more, striking it and hoping not to maim herself. Blood droplets splashed on her face for selecting such a vile process. Though despicable, it was her way out.

Within time, Isabel hacked through the horse's coat, exposing its insides, the simple part finished. Isabel put the axe aside and reluctantly stuffed her hands in the horse's insides, the passage of time making its organs cold. She removed its entrails, tossing them onto the other side, eliminating the weight hindering her freedom.

It was not long before she finished the task, warmth seeping through her legs as she regained life within them. She pulled away from under the horse, its weight no longer a burden on her life, Isabel plopping back on the ground beside it.

"It is done, Lucia." Her sister grimaced at the sight, clenching the side of her dress with her petite hands.

Lucia handed her sister a handkerchief, Isabel using it to wipe the blood off her hands from the abhorrent act she had committed. For some peculiar reason, she believed it would cleanse her, but she felt grimier than ever. Isabel stretched out the handkerchief towards her sister, "Thanks."

Lucia's face wrinkled, and her head jerked back as she replied, "My gift to you, for rescuing me."

Stowing it, Isabel searched the saddlebags for the items they had carried and unfastened the chest. Lucia brought over a broken banner and handed it to Isabel. "This should help with your limp."

The banner caught Isabel's attention. Now stained with blood, it had an eagle at the center of the pale aqua background with diagonal chalk-colored lines. Recognizing the banner, Isabel said in a low voice, "The banner of Rivetion." *We have enemies heading north. We must warn the Laflammes of this defeat.* Taking what they could, they carried on through the battlefield.

"Watch your step," Isabel said. At the same time, Lucia followed closely, the pair stepping over bodies, limbs, and unidentifiable human parts left behind by the slaughter.

Banners waved in the air with the wind that carried the smell of death, the field strewn with corpses of men who fought defending the outskirts of their town, yet the reason for the enemy's attack remained unbeknownst to them.

"Why did they fight?" Lucia tugged on Isabel's overshirt, causing her pace to slacken as she wobbled, her banner piercing a man's flesh.

"I do not know, Lucia. I have pondered it since I was on the estate with Mother. These are not the same men who attacked us, however. These are barbarians," Isabel pointed at the fur outlining Rivetion's attackers. *Barbarians from the south, so far north?*

"And Mother and Father, where do you think they went?"

"I do not know, Lucia. I do not know where they could be," Isabel continued to drag forward, pushing the idea of her parents having perished to the back of her mind. *They are well.* Isabel hoped to believe it, yet her heart ached, stabbing away at her false expectations.

"Do you think they are alive?"

"I do not know Lucia!" Isabel swiveled, dropping the chest harshly on the ground. "All I know is if we do not make it to Rivetion safe, we will never learn if they survived." Shaking her head, Isabel took the chest by the handle and continued dragging it over the corpses.

Isabel stopped a couple of steps forward, and Lucia crashed behind her, looking down at the corpses, shivering. "Shh. Looters," Isabel whispered.

"Isabel, can we continue moving? I cannot bear to look at these mutilated men."

"Do not look down, Lucia. Just look forward."

Lucia pointed at the group ahead, "Perhaps they are survivors! They may help us."

"They are not survivors, they are looters. They prey on the dead or the *weak*."

"Let us hope they do not see us then," Lucia seized Isabel's wrist.

"Luck is not our ally. They are looking at us." Lucia's grip tightened. "We must turn around."

But before they turned, the looters began to flee in the opposite direction, taking their stolen belongings. Surprised, the two girls watched the couple disappear, leaving them on the corpse-filled battlefield.

"I believe they fear us. We look tougher than we seem," Isabel laughed and looked back at her sister, her smile vanishing as soon as she turned.

"What is it, Isabel?" Lucia said.

"I do not believe you look as tough as you think, lady," a group of men had emerged out of nowhere behind them.

"Lucia," she extended the *A* at the end of her sister's name. "Run!" They bolted from the three men, dropping the chest in hopes of escaping.

Isabel took Lucia's hand and fled as fast as they could. "Go, run faster," she said, skipping over the dead bodies. At the same time, the men after them trampled over the corpses like beaten grass. Isabel's limping diminished, the thought of their pursuers numbing her pain.

Isabel's heart's pounding accelerated, pushing her legs with every thump, sending her away from the men. Lucia began to stray behind with every step, but Isabel tugged at her arm. She would not allow her fatigue to hinder their survival.

"I am not an adventurer like you," Lucia said, the words being pushed out of Isabel's ear with her heart's heavy pounding.

Isabel glanced over her shoulder, "We will make one of you yet." But their adventure came to a sudden end. Glancing back at her sister caused Isabel to trip on a body, the pair tumbling onto the corpse-littered ground.

The three men reached the girls, ogling them. Unable to flee, the girls were ready to face the wrath of man's war's greed.

CHAPTER 5: SIEGE OF RIVETION

The men carried the girls into a camp with thousands of soldiers and hundreds of tents organized across the river from Rivetion. With the leader's tent in the center, the hundreds of other tents formed a spiral, facing outward. Trebuchets lined the outskirts of the camp, launching fire projectiles into the city of Rivetion, one of the major river cities granting access to the kingdom of Emerion.

The city was lit ablaze. A fiery wave extended over its walls as far as the eye could see. Its fire illuminated the heavens so vastly that the shadows of night appeared to vanish from their very existence. A lengthy bridge extended across the river, standing firmly with arches that could hold a tide change from the spring rains.

"We are too late," Isabel whispered when she realized the battles extended beyond her home.

"Ha, as if a pair of girls could ever stop us," the man who had captured her said.

"Our father-" Lucia began, but Isabel squeezed her hand, her sister stopping midsentence and glancing at her.

"What about your father?" the man leaned closer.

"Our father could be trapped in there right now," Isabel quickly added.

The man squinted, "Hm, then I am certain you have seen the last of him," and he let out a roar.

The men walked them through the tents and towards the center of the spiral. All around, warriors were drinking ale and laughing around campfires. Others knew the battle situation and sharpened their swords on the grindstones. At the same time, the remainder fixed their armor in the anvils littered throughout the camp.

A warrior took a woman and dragged her onto his lap, cackling while caressing her body. The woman pretended to be offended but then laughed at the men urging her to give them a little dance around the fireplace.

One of the men by the fireplace eyed Isabel lustily, and she quickly turned her gaze elsewhere. *I will be touched by those vulgar animals if they can lay their hands on me.* The fear of what would happen to her if those men got near her lingered until they reached the center of the tents. Her skin stood erect, the hairs on her arms and back shooting into the air as she evaded the gazes of the men gone wild by the ale running through their bodies.

They reached the center, and encircling the leader's tent, wooden cages dangled around it. Some of the prisoners within them looked down at her. Others lay sprawled about, their spirits drained from their captivity.

One of the men escorting the sisters lifted the tent flap so the pair could enter the leader's tent. Inside, men roared and laughed, drank and ate, and all who remained conscious with strength in their legs danced like savages. Pieces of food flew around them, ale spilled when the men toasted with their tankards, and drunk men wobbled before falling off their logs and onto the ground.

A giant rug sat at the center, concealing the natural ground from being tainted by the ludicrous festivities taking place within the tent. The warmth being emitted from the fireplace amplified the odors of food, drink, and warrior sweat being discharged from excess drinking.

At the far end of the tent sat a man on a throne enveloped with ashen furs that matched his beard, gnawing away at a slice of dried venison. From under his drooped eyelid, he looked up at his soldiers. A group of men sat beside him at a table, separated from the rest of the warriors at the center table.

The men dragged Isabel towards him, dropping her on her knees so she would face him humbly. A man to his left had a two-horned helmet on the table, his hand placed over it. At the same time, he gulped relentlessly as if the ale on the table would be taken from him if he did not swallow it swiftly. Rivers of the ale erupted from the side of Horn's mouth, slithering all along his chin and neck before he dropped the tankard heavily upon the table. He belched, letting out a laugh and swinging it to one of the servants so they could fill it to the brim once more.

The man with the ashen furs chastised him. "Stop acting so boorish in front of the lady," he said, and turned to the guard beside Isabel. "A lady lost in these parts. Where did you find her?"

The man who had chained her hands said, "We found them on the battlefield near the woods of Rivetion, lord."

"Why is she kneeling?" he slammed his axe on the table, a wolf carved on its side. The tankards shook in fear, Horn grabbing his freshly filled tankard before its contents were lost. "Rise, lady? Lady what?"

Isabel could not utter a word, fearful of being recognized by the men. If they were the ones who attacked her estate, they would be aware of who she was. "Answer the lord," the man beside her struck Isabel's face.

"Do you not know how to treat a lady?" Wolfax narrowed his eyes at the man beside her, Isabel grasping her cheek.

"Forgive me, lord," the man retreated, his limbs shaking.

"Strike her once more, and I will have your hand removed and hung from our camp's entrance," Wolfax took a sip from his tankard.

"It will not occur," the man took another step back. At that moment, Isabel feared Wolfax would jump over his table and strike the man down.

"Where is my drink?" Horn shook his tankard as it remained empty for the second time since Isabel had been in the tent. Horn pulled on a rope beside him, and out from behind them, a man was summoned, bound at his wrists and ready to serve his masters.

The man's disheveled chestnut hair matched his bushy beard, a worn brigandine armor adding to his battered state. Scratches covered his face, and streaks of dried blood tainted his neck, injuries of the battle that had taken place before she had arrived. He poured ale onto the tankards, Horn turning to speak with him. "Next time, make haste, *Lord* Odo."

Odo's face wrinkled, and he turned his head as if he had not heard. Isabel could see that his right ear was swollen and clotted with blood and matted hair. Horn pulled sharply on the rope. "I do not care how much damage I did to that pretty head of yours. I detest repeating myself. You will come when I summon you."

Wolfax continued. "What is your name, lady?"

Isabel was hesitant but reassured herself that it might save her for a few more hours. "Lady Isabel."

"Lord," the man next to her murmured.

"Lady Isabel, lord," she repeated louder.

"Lady Isabel. Now that is a pretty name. How was it you ended up on my battlefield, Lady Isabel?" Wolfax leaned back on his throne.

"It-it was a mistake. We were riding, and we happened to fall in the midst of it," Isabel replied, attempting to contain her emotions as her legs wavered.

"*Happened* to fall in the midst of it. Are you sure you were not looting these valuable men off their war trophies?" his eyes narrowed at her.

"No, lord. I would not dare." Her legs were ready to give way and drop her to the ground.

"And if you were not looting, where were you riding to? Rivetion?"

His question was left in the air with the scent of sweat trapped within the tent's closed flaps. A group of men entered carrying a second prisoner and brought him forward to Wolfax. Isabel glanced from the prisoner to Wolfax, catching Odo's eyes widening in a flash.

"Lord," the newly arrived soldier began. His body was concealed by plate armor lined with spikes. A row of spikes went from ear to ear in his helmet, a crow crest cast onto the center chestplate of his armor.

"Why am I being interrupted?" Wolfax smashed his fist against the wooden table.

"Forgive us, Lord. We found a spy lurking in our camp."

Wolfax's tension towards his soldiers eased. "Release the lady and have her serve drinks here at the table with us. Send the little one to the other tent." Isabel's heart accelerated when she saw the men tug Lucia away.

"She may just teach Lord Odo something," Horn cackled as Isabel strode in their direction. With his tankard between his hands, he had taken a respite from his indulgent drinking.

Isabel made her way around the table, Odo glancing at her as she passed around him. At the far end of the tent, the group who had brought her in settled the chest Aubrey had given her in a corner, along with her other belongings.

"Did you believe you would escape my defenses, *spy*?" Wolfax taunted him by lobbing his drink at the man kneeling before him. "Tomorrow we will show the people of Rivetion that not everything should be seen. Gauge his eyes!"

"Gauge me?" the man shook his head, "have mercy!"

"Mercy is weakness. Weakness is death. Take him away!"

The men dragged the prisoner out of the tent. Yet, before he turned, Isabel noticed a hardly perceptible signal he sent to Odo. Isabel feared he would be caught and his gauging would instead be turned into an execution before he dropped on the hay that night.

Odo avoided Isabel's gaze when he noticed her glancing at him, searching his face for a sign that would give him away. However, Wolfax and his men, intoxicated by the alcohol they were consuming, did not perceive the signal. The man was well on his way towards his cage.

Where are they taking Lucia? Her sister was not strong enough to defend herself against the brute men littered between the tents, their drunk state sending them pillaging any town or grappling any woman they could lay their hands on. She shook her head and shivered away the fear.

Wolfax turned from the men and stared at Isabel's body. He pulled his chair back and said, "Sit," and he patted his thigh.

Isabel's eyes widened, his face turning sour when she did not comply with his immediate request. She had never sat on any man's lap, and this was the slightest way she had expected it to occur. Odo watched from the corner of his eye, awaiting her response to the leader's request.

"I will not repeat myself. Sit, *girl*." The anger glimmering in his eyes was enough to make her comply, Isabel sitting gently upon his solid lap. He removed the flagon from her hand, setting it on the table before them.

"Now why did you really come to Rivetion? A lady such as you should not be traveling alone," he dropped his tankard, the contents spilling around his hand. His ale-filled breath struck her face, a scent so strong not even drunk men could bear it without tumbling to the ground.

"We were going to the market," she lied, her gaze unable to match his.

"A market so late. Any lady like you would know it would be closed by the time you arrived." He paused. "I detest liars. Are you a liar, Lady Isabel?

"No, I could never. We were to stay with our uncle and head to the market the following day," she extended her lie, her heart racing while searching for ideas to send him off her trail.

"Then the chest my men brought to the tent must be what you were to sell at the market. What does a lady like you sell in Rivetion? What is inside the chest?" A wicked smile slipped from the corner of his mouth.

"I-I do not know. I was never told," she dropped her gaze. His thigh was beginning to tense.

"Now, is that not odd?" he turned towards Horn. "A girl going to a market at night, unguarded amidst the roads and with a chest in which she has no idea of what it might contain."

"It is a wonderful tale," Horn laughed, and so did Wolfax, his laugh tense and unreal, his fingers curling into a fist before him.

"Goatshit," he slammed his hand on the table, then sent his hand flying for her neck, clenching it harshly. She gasped as he squeezed the air from within her windpipes. "I despise liars, yet I despise even more those who attempt to lie to my face."

Isabel's hands clutched his wrist, but her effort to remove them was to no avail. A tighter squeeze and he would undoubtedly kill her. With the tightening pain in her throat, her eyes welled, warm tears strolling down her cheeks.

"Fire!" the words came from outside while the ground under them rumbled. Wolfax released Isabel, nearly dropping her on the ground as a man entered the tent, yelling once more, "Fire!"

CHAPTER 6: AND ANOTHER

Isabel clutched her throat, coughing as she heaved heavily, struggling to recover the air Wolfax had stolen from her. Snatching his axe, Wolfax stomped away to inspect the camp, his men trailing.

Horn dragged Odo with his rope, standing at the group's rear, peeking around the mass of soldiers. Odo glanced at Isabel, then back at the rope. Isabel nodded, hoping she had understood his gesture.

Once they were the only three remaining in the tent, Odo commenced his plan. Lifting his hands, he circled them around Horn. The barbarian choked, Odo kicking the back of his legs, Horn dropping abruptly on his knees. Amid their scuttle, Isabel snatched an axe from the center table. She raced towards them, seizing the opportune moment of freedom before her. Stretching his hands and pulling away, Odo created enough distance for Isabel to cut his rope. Without hesitation, she dropped the axe upon it, Odo stumbling back as the rope snapped.

With Odo free, the heavy man remained on his knees, choking and gasping for air, mimicking Isabel when Wolfax had clutched her throat.

"We must leave now before he regains his strength," Odo said, seizing her axe and handing her a sword. Jerking her head back while cocking an eyebrow at him, Odo swiftly answered her gesture. "It is a more formidable defensive weapon. I hope you know how to wield it."

Odo began to head for the entrance's flaps, Isabel dashing in the opposite direction. "Where are you going? We must leave now."

Horn groaned and rose gradually as Isabel reached the chest, her bow beside it. *They found my bow*. Isabel believed her bow had been lost after she fell from her horse. The men must have seen its quality and brought it as a gift for their leader.

"Leave it. You cannot run with it," Odo's gaze darted from Horn and back to her. Gripping the chest's handle, she began to drag it with the rest of her belongings.

"I cannot, but perhaps if you were of aid, we may flee with it." She continued to tug at it, the chest scraping along the ground. Shaking his head, Odo ran back. Together, they dashed with the chest towards the tent's exit. Horn had risen and began to swing the rope that had nearly taken his life, adapting it as his new weapon. Slapping it in their direction, he struck Odo's back as he shielded Isabel. He winced as it cut his skin through the tear on his gambeson, the man nearly losing his balance as they exited the tent. Nevertheless, the abrupt movement caused the chest to smack Isabel's heel, the pair stumbling onto the ground.

The fire had been no false warning. Amidst the center of the camp, tents were lit ablaze and burned to the ground, Isabel's eyes flashing with the flames. Men bolted from the nearest troughs and carried buckets to douse the fires. A helpless effort, for new flames ignited all around them. The sound of hoofbeats instilled fear in the ground, trembling and intensifying with every passing moment.

Roaring men and horses charged around them, slicing down the barbarians rushing to extinguish the flames. Isabel shielded herself from the charging horses, leaping behind a trough to avoid being trampled. Between shadows and fires, she could barely discern friend from foe.

"Ambuuuuush!" one of the barbarians yelled, unsheathing his sword and waving it before being squashed by an incoming horse.

Shrieks pierced the air, Isabel scrambling across the battlefield. She was quick to forget the chest she had dropped. Her sole focus now was on the screams, hoping they would lead her to her sister. A horse galloped by, rearing as the knight riding it struck an enemy soldier in the chest with its lance. The man fell and groaned, the rider slapping his reins and continuing his charge through the field.

Isabel's eyes widened at the ongoing event, a gush of wind blowing past her as the horse continued its onslaught. With her mind returning to the task at hand, Isabel continued to sidestep the battling soldiers, following the shrieks piercing between the shouts of men and the clashing of metal against metal. The shrieks increased with every step she took, Isabel certain she was gaining on her sister. A man tussled with a figure, the streaks of fire casting long shadows upon it to the point where she could not distinguish its identity.

"Let me go," the voice was perfectly recognizable. Isabel reached for her dagger. Her heart hammered into her chest. If not struck at the opportune moment, the burly figure grappling with her sister would overpower them with ease. Isabel sheathed her dagger and took out her bow.

"Just think it is an apple," she murmured, placing the shaft on the arrowrest. She had never killed anything, not even hunting with her father. He had promised to take her one day, but she had not yet been of age for the day to arrive.

She pulled on the bowstring, aiming at the man's back, hoping to release at the right moment and not shoot her sister. Her pulse accelerated, her hands wavering as she inhaled and exhaled. Ready to let loose, an arrow struck the man.

Except it was not her arrow. Glancing back, a man and woman mounted on a pair of horses stared in her direction, the man lowering his bow. The chestnut-haired woman glanced at him before riding her horse forward. She raised her sword, and the burly man turned to confront her. Timing, however, had not been his ally, for her sword swung down and spilled the life out of him.

Isabel rushed to her sister, embracing her tightly as she sobbed inconsolably. She took one of her daggers and pressed it against Lucia's hand. Her sister shook her head, pushing the dagger back with trembling hands.

"We must leave. It is time to flee this place," Isabel said as the battle roars diminished. A horn blew in the distance, and a group of men rode toward Rivetion, ready to leave the encampment to the fate of the flames.

Lucia spotted an unsaddled gray horse and pointed towards it. "Sharp eye," Isabel said as they scampered towards it and claimed it as their exit from the skirmish.

They mounted the horse and rode out, watching the disordered men fighting for survival. Others fled from the attack which took them by surprise. The horse galloped from the encampment as if it desired to leave the field of death. With his anxious gait, they soon joined a group of riders crossing the bridge to Rivetion.

The two wooden doors were slightly parted, permitting the riders to rush through and enter the city while allowing the guards to close it quickly in case of retaliation. Retaliation, however, was impossible, for they had caught their opponents completely on their heels.

The horses galloping ahead speared through the gate, but when the guards spotted Isabel, they stood in the center, their spears rising to meet the two sisters. The archers on the battlements aimed their bows at them, preparing to eliminate them if they stepped towards the city. Salvation, so near, yet it had become complete damnation in the blink of an eye.

"No, no, it cannot be," she said, her shoulders tensing. Regret overtook her instantly when her sister spoke.

"They cannot leave us outside. We are allies," Lucia said, her hands seeking comfort in the horse's mane.

Circumstances took a turn in that instant, the archers relaxing their strings and the soldiers standing away from the entrance, permitting the sisters free passage into Rivetion. She passed the doors and heard the clinking chains, the drawbridge lifting behind them. Guards encircled the entrance, standing ready for the worst of moments. One of the guards halted them, grabbing their horse's bridle.

Hoofbeats behind them reduced to a trot, and beside them, the two riders who aided in saving Lucia appeared. "They were prisoners in the camp. I saw them fight for their lives. Let them take refuge in the city," the woman said to the guard.

"Aye, Jolecia," the guard replied, releasing the bridle.

"May the gods bless you for saving my sister," Isabel could only remember how she nearly lost Lucia.

"You cannot hesitate as you did on the battlefield. Next time, shoot," and Jolecia rode out with the soldier beside her.

The great doors behind them closed, and the guards yelled over the gatehouse to each other as they put the city in lockdown. Isabel glanced at the horse's flanks. They had lost the chest that Aubrey had insisted they cared for, and with Lucia's empty hands, Isabel knew the book was gone too.

"Where may we stay?"

"If you have coin, there is an inn near the River Market District," the guard eyed her bloodied outfit. "Flamehouse Inn."

"And if we do not?" Isabel's words caused the guard's head to jerk back.

"There is a refugee camp near the eastern city gate."

"That should not be necessary," Lucia pulled out a pouch filled with coins, bouncing it with pride as they jingled inside.

Isabel nodded approvingly and rode the horse towards the market, searching for the inn. It was the moment of the night, the building easily recognizable with the average drunk falling outside on the streets while conversing with their traveling counterparts.

Isabel and her sister stood together before the inn, hesitant to enter another world unknown to them. *Ladies alone in an inn. Not the best place to be.* Decided, Isabel swung the door open, and they entered the heavy aroma-filled building, an aroma quite similar to the one they had encountered within the tent.

The sisters sat at one of the corner tables, evading much of the commotion and hoping to stray from the men's sight. A difficult decision it was, for the building was brimming with men. Men with that much liquor in their bodies only had one of two thoughts in their minds: violence or women.

A lively tune played from a table close to them, the strumming of strings catching Lucia's attention, Isabel watching as it seduced her, luring her away. The culprit was a lovely fair-haired woman with skin so smooth you would be afraid to touch her for fear of blemishing it. Her fingers strummed at the cords, quickly and naturally, as if she had been born with the lute in her hands. The woman sang:

The great king of Emerion, the raiders he fought back,
Away from th'land he forced them, fighting from horseback,
To him goes all the glory, the triumph of his attack,
Men in horror would flee, when they saw him on 'is horse in black.

The travelers followed her words, elevating their tankards in the air to support the historical richness of the days of the grand king. They drank and sang, raising their spirits as the city underwent the siege. Lucia plopped her chin on her palms, watching as the jade-eyed woman strummed her fingers upon the lute and continued to produce a beautiful melody. When the song came to an end she bounced from her chair and went to talk to the fair-haired woman.

"Lucia, stay," but Isabel's words were helpless as her sister abandoned her to converse with the singing lady, the barmaid snatching Isabel's attention as she arrived at their table.

"Is there anything we could serve you?" the barmaid carried a flagon and flashed them a smile.

"No drinks, but we would like a chamber," Isabel kept glancing towards her sister. *Do not be reckless, Lucia. I cannot lose you again.*

"We have one chamber vacant. How many nights will you require it?"

"Just the one night," Isabel smiled weakly, her gaze fixed on Lucia.

The barmaid looked in Isabel's direction, "Do not be concerned for her. Faylinn is a friend of the inn." Isabel stared at the woman by her side, her lips parting but words not escaping them. "Well, we will show you to your chamber when ready. You must pay before you stay. Innkeeper's rules," she shrugged.

"I will head back when we are ready. Thank you," and the barmaid was on her way to serve the table beside them.

Isabel strode to Lucia, avoiding the gazes following her within the inn. Faylinn's music had taken a turn, and the somber, melancholy tunes somehow reassured Isabel. "I got us a chamber but we must first pay the barmaid," she said as she reached Lucia.

"We will pay her in a moment. Let us hear Faylinn play another tune," Lucia begged, shooting pitiful glances at Isabel as she would do with her mother. They were never enough to convince Isabel and they would not be now.

"It has been a long day. We must rest. How can you be so cheerful after losing our home, our family?" Isabel tugged at her wrist, tired from the unrestful and eventful day they had endured.

"It *has* been a long day. But Mama and Papa are strong. I trust they still live. Mama always said, be strong and keep a cheerful heart in trying times," she paused and looked down. Whispering, she continued, "Isabel, I fear sleep. I fear what may become of my dreams after this dreadful day." Isabel wrapped her arms around her sister. There was truth in her words. *It has been a long day. Lucia is terrified. What would Mother do?* "Could we please listen to one more song?" Lucia was relentless, her words tearing into Isabel's tired soul, causing her to shrug and close her eyes as she agreed to listen to one more tune. One more tune soon turned into another.

And another. And another. That night they stayed by the tables watching and humming until the last drunk had fallen, the last tankard had spilled, and the last tune had been played.

CHAPTER 7: DEFENSIVE LESSONS

"Are you ready?" Lucia was up with the first streak of sunshine peeking at them through the window. Its warmth kissed their cheeks, attempting to burn past night's events.

"What time of the day is it?" Isabel turned on her bed, shielding the sunshine from striking her eyes. A few strands of hay were inferior to the feathered beds in her estate, her body aching from the uncomfortable beds.

"It is time to go to the market. Make haste," Lucia jumped onto Isabel's bed, shoving her sister abruptly, Isabel groaning.

"I will head down in a moment," Isabel turned over on her bed, pushing her sister off.

"We are famished. We will wait for you downstairs."

"We?" she murmured, but Lucia was gone, and she was left all alone. *What are you up to, Lucia?* Isabel sat up on her bed, her impressions of the past day flying across her mind. In one day, she had lost her family. Her estate had been burned to the ground. Isabel was held captive along with Lucia. They were both in a strange city. Lucia was in her care. *How did this all happen? In one night, life is not what it once was.*

With the anticipation of who her sister had meant by us, Isabel readied herself and made her way downstairs promptly. She glanced at her sleeves, tainted with blood from the preceding day's atrocities. It was the odd occasion when she went to bed under such horrid conditions without a bath. Still, it was a novel situation for her to sleep with blood on her clothing.

She swung the tavern door open, Isabel raising her arm over her head to block the rays of sunshine as she left the dim ambiance and entered the brightly lit outside world. Faylinn, the lute player, awaited outside with Lucia, the pair turning in unison to greet Isabel.

"I thought you would never leave that bed," Lucia said. "You remember Faylinn? She has been kind to guide us around the city."

Isabel was dubious at the apparent generosity of the stranger. Still, her facial expressions did not give way to her true sentiments. "And your sister was generous enough to pay a coin or two to guide you around," Faylinn smiled. "She mentioned you wanted to go to the market. May I suggest we see a bathhouse beforehand? I believe it would suit your appearance," Faylinn glanced at Isabel's sleeves and blood-filled clothing.

"We could certainly use a bath," Lucia pulled on her clothing, demonstrating its filth, dirt, and blood, now indistinguishable.

Reluctantly, Isabel followed Faylinn towards the bathhouse. She had never bathed publicly and only had her servants aid her back in their estate. An uneasiness overcame her when she removed her clothing and entered the wooden tub, her stomach tight. Her sister joined her while Faylinn waited for the sisters outside of the bathhouse.

"How did you come across such an ample amount of coin?" Isabel dipped herself in the tub. Taking hold of a ball of soap, its smell was unnatural to any of the olive soaps used at her estate.

"Those men that attempted to touch me, well, they were not quite careful when I slipped the coins out from under them," Lucia smiled, washing up.

"Soft touch. It was the least I imagined from you," Isabel laughed, her sister shrugging and rolling her eyes. Without the aid of their servants and unwilling to receive any assistance from strangers, Isabel began to wash herself. "Now Faylinn. We cannot trust her like that. We do not know where she is from or what her intentions may be."

"Faylinn is a good person. She means well," Lucia mimicked her sister's movements.

"What if she is a thief and steals what little we have?" Isabel was startled when one of the bathhouse girls entered, believing that Faylinn may have overheard and rushed in. She turned back to

Lucia when she noticed it was not her, the woman leaving quickly when she was called away.

"I do not believe she is ill-intentioned. You will see. Nevertheless, we should be vigilant. If we do not want her, we can refrain from using her services," Lucia continued with her bathing.

Isabel nodded. They needed a tour of Rivetion, and having Faylinn take them where they needed was safer than being lost in an unknown city. The sisters bathed, and once they were finished, they met with Faylinn outside.

"I see the dresses fit you well," Faylinn said when she saw the pair in the dresses she left for them to use while their clothes dried.

"Indeed. Now we must go to the market," Lucia said after mounting the horse they found in the encampment, Isabel leading it by the bridle.

Faylinn walked alongside the opposite side of the horse, guiding the girls towards the market when the sound of hoofbeats began to approach them. They stood to the side of the road, a group of knights riding past them, heading into the city's lower levels. One of the knights strayed from the cavalry unit and turned towards the young ladies.

The rider halted beside them, his ashen horse standing erect with the family crest on its peytral, a charcoal sun. The knight's golden brigandine armor wore scratches along its length, pride of its past battles, the same charcoal sun from the horse painted on his armor's center.

Lifting his visor, a gasp escaped Isabel, "Sir Odo," she said when she saw the friendly face.

"*Lord* Odo, Lady Isabel," he corrected her. "Thank you for saving my life yesterday." Odo bowed lightly from his horse.

"It was the respectable thing to do," she returned the bow.

"It was an act of bravery. Anyone could have forgotten about me and left. I have your belongings in the castle. One of my men will escort you so you can regain them," he whistled at the cavalry unit, two horsemen riding towards him.

"She is the lady who risked her life for me yesterday. Escort her and her friends to the castle, ensure they are well attended," Odo said to one of his cavalrymen.

"Aye, Lord," the cavalryman said.

"You may just take her with us," the voice from the knight riding towards him sounded bitter with the suggestion. When she joined them, Isabel recognized her instantly. *Jolecia.*

Odo's expression sharply turned, and he gazed back down at Isabel. "You seem adventurous and have proven your bravery. How would you like to join us at the battlements?"

Isabel's face beamed, and Jolecia's soured, shock being replaced by a wrinkle on her forehead. "We cannot do that."

"Who said I cannot take her?" Odo glanced at her, Jolecia's auburn eyes meeting his gaze, her horse whinnying as she pulled on its reins with her scarred hands while attempting to control its strong temperament.

"Are you certain?" Isabel said, yet her insides jumped at the thought of heading to the front lines.

"But we were going to the market," Lucia murmured, a murmur that was not low enough to prevent Odo from overhearing.

"Aye, I am certain, Lady. And little lady, the markets in the lower levels are closed," Odo said, pulling on his reins and turning his horse.

Faylinn nudged Isabel, raising her eyebrows and mouthing, "We will care for her at the castle."

"Aye, but my sister-" she began before being cut off.

"My men will ensure they are safe," he extended his hand towards Isabel. She hesitated, then reached out to him. Odo pulled her onto the horse with such force she was left in awe at his strength.

"Escort the ladies," and Odo rode to the battlements with Isabel and Jolecia.

At the battlements, Odo instructed the men, positioning them strategically and preparing the castle for another day of siege defense. A knight wearing plated armor had joined them and followed Odo as he issued orders across the battlements. Like Odo's, the knight's plated armor wore dings with pride of its past battles, his helmet's aqua plume matching with the paint on the family crest, a majestic eagle on his armor's center. The knight's tousled blond hair cascaded beneath his helm, and his deep brown eyes shone like polished chestnuts. The knight narrowed his gaze upon Isabel, a thoughtful expression running down his face and vanishing as Isabel walked beside Odo.

"As you can see," Odo stood upon the battlements next to the main gate, "We have only one bridge for them to enter. All their units will be bottlenecked, permitting our archers to rain arrows upon them as they attempt to attack our castle."

Odo sent the knight to issue the orders on the defensive system they had organized. "Our drawbridge here will not permit them to enter our castle. They would need to gather ladders or siege towers, scale our walls, and bring it down from the inside, a not-so-simple feat given the bottleneck effect I explained earlier." Odo could not contain his pride in their defensive system when he presented each component.

"If they were to scale the walls and drop the drawbridge, how would you defend it?" Isabel questioned, wondering if they would abandon the walls or concentrate on maintaining the entrance.

"Already strategizing," Odo shot her a quick grin, Jolecia shaking her head unapprovingly of the exchange between the pair. "If that occurred, they would still have to manage against the dropped portcullis, complicating their opportunity of entering the castle so swiftly. We have heated oil and rocks stored to drop upon those who assault the castle through our main entrance. As a last remedy, if they were to overcome that defensive measure, batter down our doors, and raise the gate, we would have no alternative but to meet them along the city and fight them."

"And your last defensive measure?" Isabel remembered her estate's hidden escape route. "Do you have any means of fleeing the castle?"

"If I did not know better, I would fathom you were an enemy spy," he squinted at her. Isabel's eyes widened, afraid she had pried too much into the affairs of the castle's defense. "I am jesting with you, My Lady. If it occurred, we would fight and hold them at the upper levels of the city."

Isabel felt her question go unanswered and was left wondering if he was concealing their escape route or if they were trapped and had no route of escape if the worst were to come. "Our archers have maximum vantage points and will allow us to defend vast castle areas with reduced numbers if that ever occurs. Our trebuchets would also aid in defending against the incoming troops."

"Who are these people attacking our lands?"

"Barbarians from the south, I would say. They seek new land."

"These barbarians, they are different from the men attacking my home. Those knew our names, our family."

"Barbarians rarely know the names of those they attack. Your attackers… they want something… or someone." Odo stood silent.

"They want us. My sister and I," Isabel said, fidgeting.

"Enemy lines at the horizon," one of the soldiers from the battlements called out.

"Defensive positions," Odo yelled across the battlements, a repetitive wave of his voice bouncing over and over from soldier to soldier, its sound waning as the distance grew between them. "Strategy lesson is over. Jolecia, escort Isabel to the castle."

"But my place is by your side at the battle," Jolecia gripped her sword's handle.

"Do not fret, Jolecia. The battle will not end so swiftly. Now go," and Jolecia followed Odo's orders.

CHAPTER 8: SCALY OVALS

A rumbling sound erupted around the trembling castle, fear instilled within it by the hellfire being dropped upon it. Relentless projectiles shook its walls, the servants within the court fearing a breach. A fourth of their army had been crushed outside the Wandering Woods, and word was spreading that it could hinder their cause. Those who had lived there for decades knew it would withstand what was to come their way, or so they hoped. Isabel could see they kept a calm demeanor, but their solemn expressions were testimony of their concern for the siege they were undergoing.

Making her way around the castle's lengthy passages, Isabel detained one of the guards she had previously spoken to. "Any word on my sister?"

"She was spotted in the archery range," he said, staring at the other soldiers. All men were being called away towards the castle's entrance.

"The archery range?" she said, her brow furrowing. "Why would she be at the archery range?"

"Relieves the tension. Distracts her from the battle."

Isabel nodded. "Where might that be?"

"Enter the great hall, turn left, and that passageway will lead you to her," the soldier directed her with his spear.

"Thank you," she bowed, and the soldier rushed off, Isabel following his guidance.

Exiting the castle through the passageway the soldier had mentioned, the gentle strains of the lute resonated in the distance. Unlike the night at the inn, the lute's sounds were less fluid and followed by abrupt stops. A thud followed a whistling sound, and right as she turned the corner, Isabel spotted Faylinn and Lucia.

Faylinn readied a second arrow, aiming swiftly while her elbow went back. Releasing the string, she sent the arrow flying straight forward. Thud. Faylinn struck the bullseye from fifty feet out. The target was cluttered with arrows, her precision unmatched.

"Isabel, where have you been? We were concerned you may have left towards the battle," Lucia said while placing the lute on her lap.

"I feared the same for you," Isabel crossed her arms.

"Lucia was feeling unwell. She feared the men would come and capture her again," Faylinn said.

"That is why Faylinn swore to teach me to use a bow. However, she insisted we wait for your blessing. While we waited, she has been teaching me how to play her lute," Lucia smiled, but as the castle trembled, she looked in its direction, shivering. Faylinn winked at Isabel, and she understood she was attempting to distract her from the battle. The previous encounter had certainly left its mark on her sister. Isabel preferred her sister to focus on other activities, hopefully forgetting the preceding night's events.

Faylinn lowered her bow and shrugged while raising her eyebrows. "I said it was best to wait and hear your thoughts on the matter."

"Thank you," Isabel nodded approvingly. "I am certain it would be no harm to anyone if she were to learn." *It will serve to protect her if the time may come.* But Isabel kept this to herself, for she knew Lucia did not enjoy combat.

"Precisely what I said," Lucia shrugged and rolled her eyes. "I am no longer a child. Besides, only two winters separate us."

"I am aware, Lucia. That is why you should learn," Isabel agreed. Hoping to put the argument to rest, she added, "You have much to practice if you wish to be as great as Faylinn."

Lucia's enthusiasm extended into her joyous fingers as she strummed away on the lute a not-so-pleasant sound. "There is still some time I must dedicate to the lute," she chuckled. She jumped off the haystack, spun to place the lute upon it, and plucked away the strands of hay that had become one with her beige dress. "However, I must not leave a challenge unattended," and she looked at Isabel, narrowing her eyes defiantly, then smiling playfully.

Lucia stood beside Faylinn, taking the bow from a pile of hay next to them. Squinting to reassure herself of what she was gazing upon, Isabel realized Lucia had taken *her* bow. Faylinn placed her vambrace on Lucia's wrist to prevent the bow's string from striking her delicate skin. The vambrace, although loosely slipped, was enough to protect her.

"Now aim through here," Faylinn put her hand loosely over Lucia's. "Keep that elbow high and pull the string like this," and she demonstrated with her bow. "Now release your fingers without causing too much movement on the bow." Lucia did as she instructed, and her arrow soared through the air. It flew and flew, the distance growing between them as it continued to fly lightly over the air.

Lucia was in awe at the flying arrow, and Isabel could see she was confident it would strike the bullseye on her first attempt. Only it did not. The arrow's speed waned, and it plummeted to the ground, not reaching its target. Lucia's glee faded and turned into a frown, disappointment flushing her face.

"That is typical," Faylinn chuckled. "It occurred to me on my first attempt at shooting an arrow. You are not accustomed to the tension you must create to shoot and you may pull it too weakly or strongly. Now, if you remember how much tension you applied to it, you must pull the string farther, and you may just hit the target."

Lucia repeated the process, pulling the string slightly farther back so her arrow would not plummet and strike the ground as it had previously done. Releasing it, the arrow flew once more. This time, it struck her target, although not at the bullseye, and Isabel could see the frown on her face not fading.

"Great shot. You might have not hit the bullseye, but you hit the target during your first shots, and at fifty feet, that is some feat," Faylinn patted her back.

"I must stay wary, or you may defeat me at an archery competition one day," Isabel said, then chuckled, the girls joining her in dissonance, her words washing away Lucia's frown.

Lucia handed Isabel the bow, "Oh, I borrowed your bow," she smiled. It was her technique to prevent Isabel from scolding her mischievous ways.

"You have some sneaky hands," Isabel shook her head, smiling softly.

Lucia took Faylinn's bow, and the girls continued to practice their archery in the range. Without her bow, Faylinn sat upon the haystack and took her lute, strumming along while Lucia bounced with every shot her arrows struck the target. Unlike Isabel and Faylinn, her arrows were scattered throughout the target. By the time the sun kissed the horizon, her arrows had begun to land closer to each other, yet there was much training to be done. After finishing, Lucia stared into the sky, and Isabel knew her concern for the battle had returned. Archery had merely abated it momentarily.

The sisters and Faylinn entered the castle, four figures coming their way. A man with ashy hair, similar to the streaks in the knight Isabel had encountered within her estate, approached them. A silky, pale aqua robe hung loosely around his body. *Why does he seem familiar?* The woman walking beside him had similar porcelain skin, yet unlike him, her obsidian hair was crowned with a silver diadem. Draped over her, she had a loose ivory dress, its silk so thin you could see the secondary layers under it. The two guards remained back, and the nobles stepped forward for an introduction.

"Good evening," the man said softly, "You must be our guests. I am Lord Layne of Rivetion, and this is Lady Cicely. Who are we to have as our honored guests?"

"Good evening, I am Lady Isabel. This is my sister Lady Lucia and our friend Faylinn," the three of them bowed for them, Lord Layne staring at Faylinn as they did a reverent bow.

"It is our pleasure to welcome you to our grand castle, even under such dire circumstances. Who is your family?" Layne continued speaking ever so calmly as his gaze returned to Isabel.

"Our family name is Beaumont," his eyes widened as she finished her sentence.

"The Beaumonts? The Beaumonts of Oakheart? Previously of Accreton?" The girls nodded, though their visages displayed disquiet at the mention of Accreton. Cicely touched his arm lightly, and Layne's excitement abated, returning to his calm demeanor. "Why it is an even greater honor to have your presence here. Your father is a brave soul. I still remember fighting alongside him in the War of the Ancestors."

It was difficult for Isabel to imagine Layne as a fighter, for he was so peaceful in his expression, and his body fit well under the exclusive fashion of silk attires. His slim body did not correspond to that of a warrior's, and he seemed too delicate to survive the harsh reality of war. Nevertheless, she nodded once more, avoiding hostilities.

"Walk with us and inform us, how is your father?" the words struck Isabel's heart as they walked beside them towards the great hall.

"I fear we do not know of him. Last I saw him, we were out in the woods," Isabel felt the words choking her.

"Oh, it is heartbreaking to hear of such a dire situation," Layne glanced at her, his eyes glistening as if he too sensed the girls' pain. "And your mother, if I may ask?"

"Lost to us, My Lord. We were separated from her while our estate was being razed," she lowered her voice, the thoughts of her mother leaving her raiding her mind and causing havoc, just as the soldiers had caused havoc to her estate.

"Was it these heathens that lay outside our walls?" Layne's tone took a more aggressive turn yet somehow remained passive.

"They were not. These men were different. A pair of ebony armored knights led them," Isabel held back the tears.

Cicely placed a comforting hand on her back, "Do not fear, child. Your family is a strong and brave one."

"Lady Cicely speaks the truth," Layne continued. "Your lineage has proven to be resilient through the most adverse circumstances. I can only believe they will continue to demonstrate it. Let us take you, for instance. Two young ladies who traversed treacherous roads teeming with barbarians, rescued Lord Odo, and breached the enemy's siege lines to reach our castle," Isabel and her companions smiled at his remark.

"I just cannot come to understand, who would attack you? These barbarians attacked my lands, and we attempted to ambush them as they came from our southwestern border. We sent riders to warn your father. Did they ever arrive?"

"They did not. We had not heard nor seen anyone from Rivetion until we came upon the battle by the Wandering Woods."

"Terrible. If only your family had not needed to leave Accreton. I always wondered-"

The great doors opened, the group's attention shifting towards Odo entering the castle, Jolecia and the knight from the battlements closely beside him. "Good, you have returned," Layne said, smiling. Then he turned his attention back towards his guests. "Why do you not all return to your chambers and prepare so you can join us for supper?"

The girls nodded and bowed, leaving the great hall and going to their chambers to prepare for the evening's meal. As they left, Isabel was gladdened glances could not pierce human flesh, for if they could, she would not have left the hall unscathed from Jolecia's gaze. *Why does she seem to dislike me? It cannot be over the arrow I never shot. Did my family hurt her? Is there more beyond Accreton that we have yet to know?*

CHAPTER 9: SIEGE FIEST

"Will you just spend the rest of your days gazing at that chest and not open it?" Lucia shook her head while staring at a group of dresses she had acquired without Isabel's aid.

"I would, except I was not given the key for it," Isabel watched from her bed, hoping the chest would magically open.

"A chest without a key. Now that is the most peculiar matter, would you not say?" Lucia reached for one of the dresses, raised it through its sleeves, and then dropped it back on the bed while shaking her head disapprovingly.

"Most certainly. What has it got inside?" Isabel said in a near murmur.

The chest in her chamber seemed to laugh at her, watching her intently through the keyhole as she could not open it. They had forgotten to provide her with a key. Any attempt to pry it open would be of no avail. She pulled it close to the bed, vastly superior to the one she had slept on the previous night.

Dirt littered the chest, the grime of time sliding between its protruding designs. Isabel wiped and carved away at the chest with her dagger, the dust falling on the ground, the designs appearing as if she was carving them herself. The obscured images did not permit her to identify the symbols. She could discern what appeared to be three skulls, with flames and spikes in the background. Ovals lined the borders, the same scaly oval replicated all around. A rune-like scripture was at the bottom, a familiar scripture, yet she could not remember where she had laid eyes upon it.

"I will not be able to read this, let alone open it," she murmured as she dropped back down on the bed, her hands on her face. "Why give it to me without the means to open it? This is incredibly frustrating," Isabel said, then sighed.

Lucia's footsteps in the background followed a silence as she sauntered across the chamber. Silence overcame it once more momentarily when she stopped behind Isabel and hummed. Isabel glanced from the corner of her eye at Lucia.

Lucia plopped beside the chest, tracing her fingers across the chest. Her finger moved rhythmically over the dragon egg designs. Abruptly, she halted, fixating her gaze on a particular spot. Isabel followed her gaze. Upon reaching the corner, the protruding egg had transformed into a tree carved into the chest. A mirrored pattern adorned the opposite side.

Lucia glanced at the scriptures at the bottom. "Where the two trees meet, a new world awaits."

"How could you read that?" Isabel turned towards the chest, staring at Lucia wide-eyed.

Lucia tutted. "If you had visited Mother in the evening as she said instead of hunting, you may just have learnt yourself."

Isabel rolled her eyes. "Even if you can read that, how will we open this chest?" She leaned towards the edge of the bed, squinting at the scripts as her necklace dangled from her neck.

Lucia's gaze remained fixed on Isabel. "What?"

But before Isabel got an answer, her sister snatched at her neck. Clank! Lucia yanked Isabel's necklace.

"Ow! Have you gone mad?" Isabel nearly leapt at her sister, but then she noticed what she was doing.

Lucia turned the Pegasus' wings, transforming the pendant into a tree. Isabel's necklace fit perfectly in the slot. Lucia slid her necklace over her head and placed it on the opposite side. Turning the pendants with the tree emblems, the chest clicked, the sound of creaking hinges following it soon thereafter. *Lucia was always one to enjoy a puzzle.*

Lucia grinned at the contents within the chest, Isabel lurching forward.

Lucia reached for the objects, scaled oval eggs huddled together for warmth within the chest. They were no ordinary eggs, for their scales caused them to shimmer like metal under torchlight. Touching the pasty one in the corner, her sister winced as though burned when she touched the egg.

It appeared as if Lucia was attempting to pull her hand away, yet the egg seized it. She writhed and let out a scream. Her body was thrust away from the chest, her head striking the edge of the bedpost.

"Lucia!" Isabel leapt and knelt beside her, placing Lucia's head onto her lap. Her sister was unconscious, her body limp and unmoving. The warmth of blood from her scalp touched Isabel's hand, the young noble shivering at the sight. "No! No! Lucia, stay with me." Isabel's sudden touch awoke her, Lucia blinking rapidly.

"Talk to me, Lucia," Isabel searched her scalp, inspecting for the sight of the wound. Somehow, even with the blood, she could not find a wound injury.

"My head is pounding," Lucia felt for it," and your screaming merely aggravates it." Isabel chuckled, sighing with relief. "What happened?"

"You-you touched that egg, and it sent you soaring," Isabel could not comprehend what had just occurred. She led Lucia to her bed, her sister groaning. Lucia stared at her hands, a few drops of blood staining her skin.

A knock at the door startled Isabel. Her heart pounding, her attention darted to the chest. "Who is it?" she pounced on the chest, closing it tightly and shoving it in a corner between the two beds.

"It is Lady Cicely," she heard the gentle voice from the other side. "May I come in?"

"Aye, My Lady," she said, dropping a pile of pillows over it in hopes of concealing it.

Cicely entered the chamber, a lady's maid standing behind her. "Are you ladies well? I thought I heard a commotion come from your chamber."

"All is well. Lucia had a fainting feeling overcome her, and she is feeling out of sorts." Isabel glanced nervously between Cicely and her sister, hoping they would not discover what had just occurred.

"Oh no. Must we take Lucia to the infirmary? Or must I bring the healer to her chamber?" Cicely's sincere concern did not calm her stomach.

"I believe she is in demand of rest. I fear the day's activities and the sudden turn of events have caught up to her," Isabel knew she had swayed them.

"I will have the servants bring her supper," Cicely said as she sat at the edge of the bed, touching her head. "She is scorching," then looking at her lips, "she is parched. It would be best if we douse out the torches while she rests. I will get my lady's maid to bring her damp cloths and water." She spun towards the lady's maid accompanying her. "Leave that here and bring me the cloths."

"Thank you. We appreciate your generosity," Isabel bowed lightly.

"Now, I was hoping the dresses I had brought Lucia were suitable." She shook her head. "It matters not now." She turned to Isabel. "I have brought you some as well. I reckoned that in your swift escape from Oakheart, you did not have the opportunity to arrange a set of clothing for your travels," she pointed at the dresses now lying atop her bed. "They belonged to my youngest sister," there was a pause while she caressed the silk, her gaze drifting for an instant as if she had forgotten the girls were in the chamber with her. "She was very lively. Your presence brings her to mind vividly." She paused. "Now where is Faylinn? Will she be attending the feast?" Cicely sat by the edge of Lucia's bed, resting the back of her hand on her forehead.

"Faylinn? Are you or Lord Layne acquainted with her?" Isabel stared at her. "She left for the town to search for her things before supper."

Cicely looked at her silently, but her eyes did not give way to any emotions. "We have heard she sings for the men at the inn. Her voice is as enticing as a siren. Why?"

"I just," Isabel began, the woman eyeing her intently. *Why did Lord Layne look at her like that?* However, Isabel remained quiet. "I was just curious." She turned her attention to the dresses and said, "Your sister certainly knew how to grasp a court's attention."

Isabel admired the dresses, and although she seldom wore any, she knew these were amongst the kingdom's most luxurious.

"It was rare for a spectator to not look when she arrived at court," Cicely glanced at Isabel while stroking Lucia's arm. "I must go. Maple will return to care for your sister," she rose from the edge of the bed. "She will aid you in preparation for the feast."

"I cannot leave Lucia here while she is feeling unwell."

Lucia glanced at Isabel, "You must not miss the feast. I merely need to rest."

"Are you certain, Lucia?" Isabel said, Lucia nodding.

"Then it is settled. Your sister will be in good care," and with those final words, Cicely abandoned the chambers.

Isabel watched the embroidered edges of the silk dresses spread out on top of her bed. The emerald dress piqued her interest, but she could not stop thinking of Lucia and how the egg thrust her away even while staring at it. *Is Lucia truly well? Will she be all right without me?* As if Lucia had read her thoughts, she nodded and smiled once more when Isabel glanced at her.

Maple returned and sat by Lucia's bed, dropping a bucket of wet cloths beside it. She wrung the cloth and placed it gently upon Lucia's forehead before turning to Isabel.

"M'lady, have you picked the dress you wish to wear?" Maple stood from the bed.

"I have. The emerald one."

"A beautiful choice," the servant picked up the dress from the bed and aided her in getting dressed.

"Lady Cicely says your name is Maple. What a beautiful name," Isabel slid into the dress.

"I am most grateful, M'lady."

Upon Isabel's arrival at the great hall, the diverse aromas of food were strung together in the air and caused her stomach to grumble. Hams, sausages, black puddings, and a wild boar lay at the center of the table. Spreading from its center, nuts, wild cherries, and grapes extended the length of the tables around them. No one was close enough to hear the monstrous beast in her belly calling out to be fed.

How could these people have a feast amidst a siege? Layne and Cicely sat at the great table, an ashen damask draped over it, representing their house's color.

"Our guest of honor, Lady Isabel of Oakheart," the herald seized the crowd's attention and nearly startled Isabel with the unexpected introduction. A couple of men from the crowd spun their attention to the newly arrived noble, yet most indulged in the need to warm their bellies and raise their tankards in song.

"Join us," Layne pointed at the empty chair beside him. Lady Isabel sat next to them at the elevated great table. "I have been informed that your sister is feeling unwell and will not be joining us."

"Indeed. Our journey appears to have worn Lucia down," Isabel noticed a servant stand beside her with a basin and a jug. The servant let the chilly water stream down from the mouth of the jug and onto Isabel's outstretched hands. She removed the napkin from the servant and dabbed her hands dry.

On the other side of the great hall, Faylinn entered and joined a group of men at the far end of the perpendicularly lined tables before them. Isabel flashed her a grin when their eyes met and felt a slight ease when she realized she was not alone. She thought of how Cicely had inquired about Faylinn. *Why is she so curious about having a lower-class female musician attend her feast? Is there more to Faylinn?*

The minstrels played a lively tune, creating a festive ambiance amidst the siege they encountered. The battle had ended, and so had the trebuchet fire, yet their enemies remained across the river, hoping to defeat the defending forces and capture the city.

"Lord, if I may ask, why have I been proclaimed the guest of honor? There are so many important guests here."

"Because you saved my great friend Odo. I would believe a more horrid question would plague your mind. You might be questioning yourself, what vile man would celebrate a feast amidst a siege?" Layne chuckled while raising his eyebrows.

"Not at all, My Lord," Isabel answered, and he gave her an appreciative nod.

"Let it be known that this feast had been organized months ago. It was not until the guests arrived that we were caught under this siege. I cannot help but wonder if such circumstances are of any benefit. We have grand generals and warriors who might aid us in our defense but... Oh, who am I to bore you with the details of war? Such talk is of not fit for a lady."

"It is of no bother to me," Isabel desired to learn more, but he spoke of it no more.

"Drivel. It is no conversation for a noble to speak to a lady. A lady must be spoken of songs and dance, not war," he turned to have his servant replenish his goblet with wine.

"Let it be known, I take quite an interest in all subjects."

"I would be careful to address them in court, for it could drive suitors you might have come your way," he turned to Cicely, "would it not, dear?"

"I would be careful," and she winked at Isabel, "but I am certain Isabel has suitors lined and waiting for her hand. I would not let the mind of men be of any bother to you. You are looking beautiful in that dress, if I may say."

"Was that not Seraphina's dress?" Layne drank from his goblet.

"It was, but it will be of no use to her now. I reckoned it would serve a better purpose if Isabel wore it tonight instead of building up dust and wearing away."

The servant poured Cicely's wine and approached Isabel's goblet. "I rarely drink, and I wish to stay vigilant amidst the siege."

"There will be no battle now. Let us not make any haste decisions. You must try this extraordinary wine from Swinsford. One will not hinder you," he said. Upon hearing the word Swinsford, she nodded. The servant poured her wine. "It will not disappoint."

Pressing the goblet against her lips, Isabel remembered when she last visited Swinsford and tried the wine for the first time with Robion. She smiled while she thought of the happy memory in the fields, the pair watching as the sun's last rays raked over the vineyards, the wine similarly warming her chest as the last rays of the day had done with Swinsford.

Her eyes lit up, Layne's enthusiastic expression awaiting her reply. "It is quite good," Isabel let the soft wine slide down her throat once more.

"We serve quality here at Rivetion, particularly to our honored guests."

"Mm indeed," and Isabel had her goblet refilled by the servant. "May I ask, where is Cicely's sister?"

The lord's smile faded, his eyes glancing back at his wife and the men. "Is there anything else you would like to discuss?"

The air around them felt heavy, Layne's veins protruding as his hand tensed around his goblet while sipping. Isabel recalled their first encounter and his words about Accreton. "You mentioned Accreton and my family. Could you describe it?"

His face came alive once more. "Why there is not much to recount."

"You mentioned my family was from there before Oakheart, is that not true? My father never spoke much about it to us."

"Indeed it is," he put his goblet down. "It merely does not exist anymore, or at least the city that was once Accreton. All which remain are ruins."

"Why? What happened?" Isabel nearly spilled the goblet on the table as she closed in on Layne.

"Dragons, my dear. Dragons scorched it to the ground. All that remains are the ruins that could resist the fierce fires of a dragon's breath. In the second Dragon Age, the wars dragged on over the area, and it resisted, its location vital to secure the kingdom. One day, however, the dragons that roamed freely within its mountains were furious at man's endless warfare and decided to settle it once and for all. They flew down and laid waste to the poor people who lived there, and no one ever returned. After the dragons vanished, people said it was cursed, that the fire and death that overtook it was so fierce that anyone who laid foot on that land would burn upon arrival. Some even say," and he lowered his voice, watching the eyes around him, "that a dragon still lurks in its mountains."

Isabel was unsure whether to be fearful or excited with the story she had been told. Raised eyebrows were all that remained on her face after the tale, for she knew over time, stories changed. Only the corpses who no longer roamed Emerion could confirm it, and by now, she was certain not even bones would remain.

Layne was quick to turn to his wife and join her in some intricate conversation she was having with a noble, leaving Isabel with her wandering mind. Soon Isabel let the story drift to the back of her mind, the young noble of Oakheart taking her time to savor her venison stew. While taking a drink from her goblet, she watched the walls filled with Lord Layne's banners, an eagle at the center of the pale aqua background with diagonal chalk-colored lines.

She admired the guests around the tables, laughing and enjoying the feast while forgetting the danger lurking outside their walls. Finishing her stew, she left the table, heading towards Faylinn with her wine-filled goblet.

"Faylinn, I am glad you arrived," Isabel nearly tumbled with the length of the dress.

"Is that Lady Isabel speaking or her wine-induced body?" Faylinn pouted while questioning her.

"Is that any way to *address* a lady?" Lady Isabel waved her goblet.

"Is that any way to *behave* as a lady?" Faylinn could not contain herself and giggled, Isabel joining her.

"You should try this wine. It is from Swinsford," Isabel said as she pushed the goblet towards her, Faylinn tasting it and returning it.

"From Swinsford. They say the best wines originate from there."

"The claims are true," Isabel could not help but continue to drink as a servant replenished her goblet.

Faylinn stepped back, and Isabel, although with her senses slightly dulled, questioned it, "You do not intend on leaving me here?"

"Lady Isabel," a voice said, approaching her unexpectedly. She swiveled on her heel unhurriedly, hoping to maintain her composure and not embarrass herself. Before her, in a beige cotehardie, awaited Odo.

CHAPTER 10: A QUEST OF SORTS

"Odo. How have you faired?" Isabel bowed at the man who had nearly surprised her.

"Remarkable, considering days ago I was a prisoner. Who knows where I may have ended if not for my brave heroes," he raised his goblet. "Now, how are you being treated in the castle?"

"Good, great, I must confess. Lord Layne and Lady Cicely have been quite the hosts." Isabel felt lightheaded. "And your ear? I remember your neck was tainted with blood in the tent."

"I can still hear you amidst this commotion, can I not?" he laughed. On the other side of the great hall, men cheered along with the minstrels while singing about one of their most remarkable exploits.

Isabel could not help but laugh, exceeding her ordinary laugh. *Faylinn is right. I may have had enough drink for one night.*

One of the men rose after their song had ended, raising his tankard, "Now a toast. To all the brave men manning the walls and to our beloved guest, Lady Isabel Beaumont of..."

"Of Oakheart!" Layne completed his statement.

The men roared in unison, cheering and taking a drink.

"Those murderers!" The celebration was short-lived. A man stood out from the crowd. A bulky figure he was, with a lengthy wet beard littered with scraps from his food.

"Forgive my brother. It appears he has had enough ale, too much for one night," Layne said gently.

"They are all murderers. You know it. I know it. Everyone knows it," the man yelled, nearly tumbling when he moved about the hall, his wine spilling over his attire. "They are murderers!"

"She is not a murderer," Layne raised his voice at his brother.

"You know what they did to our people, to their people, to everyone," the man continued. He grabbed onto a noble while pointing at him and the rest of the crowd, emphasizing his point.

"I will have no disrespect in my castle," Layne slammed his goblet on the table. "Guards, escort my brother to his chambers."

"You dare betray your kin like that?" the guards dragged the man away while he attempted to free himself, but his drunken state did not permit him. A profound silence fell over the hall, the guests glancing at each other perplexed.

"There is no need to end the festivities over a minor commotion. Minstrels, play," and the minstrels brought life to the great hall once more.

Layne regained his composure, and as if the events never occurred, he made his way from Cicely to Odo and Isabel. "I hope you will forgive my brother Osbert. He can become quite *passionate* when inebriated."

"No resentment will be held against him," Isabel replied. Yet, she wondered why he had called her family murderers.

"Thank you for your indulgence, Lady Isabel," he replied and marched away to attend his guests. Two men quickly joined Odo and Isabel, cheerful with their tankards to the brim.

"Odo, we know you are one for quests, and we would like you to join us," said the first, a giant, brawny man with a clean-shaven face and full cheeks. His cheeks had been built through time by indulging in feasts, and Isabel held no doubt about it as he carried about a trencher.

The second was a firm man with a scruffy face and defined eyebrows. Bright blue eyes hid under them, the man well groomed, unlike his slightly unkempt counterpart. His strong jaw and broad shoulders contributed to his confident stance as he spoke. "In truth, it was all Rustplate's plan, at least the part where we were to have you join our company."

"What is this *quest*?" Odo replied, raising his eyebrows.

"Lord Layne told us of a special wine in his cellar. Said he wished to grant us a barrel," Rustplate said, placing the empty trencher on a table beside him.

"Why were you sent by him then, Rustplate?" the other man crossed his arms.

"Look at these arms," and he flexed them. "Why he sent *you* would be the appropriate question," Rustplate let out a roaring laugh.

"These knights have been tasked with an important quest and would like me to join them. If you have not yet made their acquaintance, this here is Sir Baenlorn, renowned in most circles as Rustplate," he pointed at the brawny man. "This is Sir Sehan, his brother-in-arms," he said, pointing at the firm man. The bright blue eyes appeared to freeze her body with each glance, her heart coming to a halt.

"It is a pleasure to meet you, Lady Isabel," both said in unison as if they had rehearsed it many times over.

She bowed lightly, and Odo continued, "So where does this adventure lead?"

"To the castle's cellar," Rustplate straightened his body as if the world's survival lingered on their ability to consume the wine that night. "For us. We merely need you to keep watch."

"Keep watch?" he raised an eyebrow. "It has been long since I had guard duty."

"No need to worry. Leofwin will signal us if you spot someone," and he pointed with his head toward the cellar.

"Let us fetch it."

Leofwin's squire joined the group, lingering in one of the passageways outside the great hall. A slender youth, his frame hinted at the burgeoning athleticism cultivated through his training within the castle walls. Nevertheless, he had not yet blossomed into the knight society hoped he would become.

"Henry, fetch us some ale," and the group returned to one of the tables while Leofwin accompanied Rustplate to the hall in search of the barrel.

"Is Isabel the young woman who saved your life?" Sehan leaned the wooden chair back against one of the columns.

"She is indeed," Odo said, keeping a watchful eye, ensuring no man approached the passageways.

"You are telling me, this lady right here, can wield a sword better than you?" Sehan challenged him, smiling smugly.

"That I do not," Isabel shook her head. "I have not wielded a sword. At least not a real one."

"A hero without a sword. That must be a new tale for history," Sehan said, cupping his chin and pondering.

"It is not fitting for a lady to brandish a sword. It exposes her to unnecessary danger," Odo said.

"After rescuing him, Odo has not spared a moment to instruct you?" Sehan continued, steadily feeding wood into the fire.

"I will have you know, Odo, danger is one thing I have been unable to escape these days. Danger, I do not fear. I merely fear being unable to defend myself when the circumstances arrive. I think it is a matter of time before I am granted defensive lessons," Isabel pouted.

"And the lady has the soul of a warrior," Sehan laughed. Rustplate soon arrived alongside Leofwin, joining the group at the table.

"I hear laughter, and I am not involved. What have I missed?" Rustplate argued.

"You enjoy gossip more than Viakaven's bar wenches." Sehan took one of the mugs from Henry as he arrived, Rustplate placing the barrel of wine on the floor. "We are merely wondering how it is possible that Odo was saved by Isabel, and she has not yet had the opportunity to wield a sword."

Rustplate chugged his ale and slammed it hard on the table. "Well, I will be damned. A fighter without experience saving a lord. She deserves to be taught. Even Enigma knows this is her path."

"It can be quite difficult to train a warrior while you are manning the defenses," Leofwin argued, shaking his head at the troublesome knights.

"All I have heard are pretexts. If Odo truly wanted to train her, even if *he* could not, he would have found her someone," Sehan concealed his smile behind his mug.

"Henry here could have trained her," Rustplate added.

"Me? I do not believe that would have been suitable," Henry sat wide-eyed, Rustplate smacking him across the back, the young squire nearly choking on his drink.

"We are jesting with you," Rustplate said, cackling.

Sehan remained silent while looking across the hall. "Is that? It cannot be. Is that who I believe it is?"

The group turned without dissimulation, staring across the great hall at the huddled figure with a cobalt robe. His straw-like hair was as white as the winter's snow, his face withering with age and the experiences that burdened them over the years.

"Norman," Rustplate said, unbelievingly dropping his mug on the table, the drink sloshing within it as if a quake had stirred the world.

"Any other pretexts awaiting you, Odo?" Sehan straightened his wooden chair so he could take a closer look at the man on the other side of the inn.

"Do not agitate him," Odo said.

"Isabel, you wanted to be a warrior and it seems your moment has arrived. Come with me," Leofwin said, placing his mug on the table, Lady Isabel following closely behind him.

The pair walked over and stared down at Norman while he sat alone. A servant had just handed him a tankard of ale, the man holding it between his hands as if its sight could bring consolation to a desolate heart.

"Lord Norman," Leofwin began, but Norman raised his hand to him, urging him to stop. Norman met his gaze, jade eyes reflecting the turmoil and strength earned through a century of experience.

"Lord Norman has ceased to exist. You may leave," the man lowered his hand and drank from his tankard.

"We only wish to know if you would be willing to train-?"

His gaze rose to meet them, squinting at the two from a pair of jade eyes oddly familiar to Isabel. "Now, why should I undertake such a task? Why devote myself to training others? What efforts have others expended on my behalf?" Norman took a gulp of his drink. "I am here on Lady Cicely's request. I intend to pass the night in tranquility."

Ignoring his remark, Leofwin pried on. "We are willing to pay for her training."

"Payment? You nobles believe your coin reigns supreme in this world. Allow me to enlighten you, it is not everything," he shook his head. "Train her? Training a woman is a burden I would certainly not wish to shoulder in these tumultuous times."

"Let us go, Lord Leofwin. We should not have meddled with him," Isabel could feel the wine seeping into her head, the world starting to spin. Norman stared at her, anger flashing in his eyes. For a moment Isabel believed she saw something beyond the anger, but all thoughts were soon washed away by her drink's effect.

"Be gone," the man's eyes flashed once more. The stern look demanded Isabel not pry in a place she was not wanted.

The two spun and left, Isabel not glancing back. Her head felt woozy, and maintaining her balance became a more significant ordeal than before they reached him, Isabel nearly tumbling over one of the guests. Never having a drink in her life, she was convinced this was what people meant when they spoke of reaching their limit. It had been a long night, and she certainly had more than her fair share.

"Lord Odo, I think it is best if I retired to my chambers." The group bowed, Isabel leaving carefully to avoid seizing the crowd's attention once more.

CHAPTER 11: DAGGERS

The following day was not one of happy sorts for Isabel. With her head throbbing from the excessive wine drinking, the Swinsford wine she had consumed appeared as if it desired to destroy her. A pressure in her stomach awoke her, a pressure followed by piercing tiny daggers digging deep into her flesh.

Isabel let out a shriek. Her eyes flung open with the pain, and what lay atop her was horrendous at first sight. Unlike the tales she had heard, a little face stared back at her. However, the longer she looked at it, the less it reminded her of the stories. The stories portrayed them as savage creatures that would consume what came their way without hesitation.

Its almond-shaped eyes were bluer than the day's sky, its scales whiter than the winter's snow. The creature snorted, exhaling warm air onto Isabel's face, its horns jutting behind it, seemingly piercing the air. With a quick sniff, the animal lunged back in distaste. The pressure on her body eased slightly. It stood on its hind legs, its dagger claws stabbing Isabel's thighs as it flapped its wings. Isabel screamed, the dragon soaring into the air. Immediately, it lost control and plummeted to the floor.

"Why are you screaming?" Lucia turned on her bed, rubbing her eyes and sitting at the edge before noticing the beast that had invaded their chamber.

The sprawled-out beast straightened itself out, and using its wings as forelimbs, vaulted on all fours towards Lucia. She leapt on her bed, cornering herself as the dragon jumped onto it and decelerated. Its wings stepped one in front of the other, inching closer and closer. Lucia's arms clung to the wall as if claws would grow from her hands, allowing her to climb away from the beast. The beast sniffed, and Lucia shut her eyes. She was helpless, helpless to the tiny, mighty beast on the verge of devouring her.

Isabel would not stand to watch her sister become the helpless lamb of a newborn dragon. She unsheathed her dagger, prepared to defend her sister. Isabel was ready to strike it down. Suddenly, the beast stopped before Lucia. Lucia must have sensed it, for she opened her eyes, peeking at the creature ogling her. The beast lay before her, gentle as ever, innocent to the commotion it caused. With her dagger high in the air, Isabel stood behind it, ready to strike it into oblivion.

"Wait!" Lucia's voice prevented her sister from lowering the dagger on the animal. The dragon turned to meet Isabel's dagger, fright overcoming it as it dropped its head, ready to succumb to its fate. "It means us no harm," Lucia dropped next to it.

"You cannot know that," Isabel remained ready to strike it down if it dared to have a change of heart.

"I feel like I do," Lucia reached for the dragon, the creature lowering its head in fear, its snout burying into the sheets under it. "No harm will come to you," she said, her tone having a calming effect on the beast. It raised its head, Lucia's hand meeting it halfway, its rigid, knife-edged scales welcoming her touch.

"Careful, Lucia. You do not know what it may do," Isabel said. *Could it be? Is it the dragon from the chest?* She bolted towards it, opening the chest and realizing what she feared was true. One of the eggs was cracked open, the shattered shells littering within and around the chest, remnants of the beast's emergence.

"Were dragons not extinct, Isabel?" Lucia continued to caress its scaled body.

"I fear not. You have awoken it from its deep slumber," Isabel turned and watched the dragon flap its wings as it nestled itself between Lucia's legs.

"Me?" Lucia rested her hand on the beast, glancing at Isabel while she stared pensively at a wall. "How? I have done nothing."

"Yesterday, you touched the egg, and it thrust you away. Have you no recollection of it?" Isabel dropped the dagger beside her, pressing her hand to her temples.

"No. I just remember yesterday we were in the chamber and today waking up."

"You hit your head. It must have caused you to forget."

"It explains this throbbing pain," Lucia rubbed her head.

"What have we done?" Isabel shook her head. "We have awoken a monster."

Lucia laughed, "Does this look like a monster to you?" The dragon looked at Isabel, tilting its head, requesting her compassion with its blue eyes.

"It may not now. Yet it will grow. And when it can no longer fit within these walls, it will devour the world around it, it will burn castles, it will make ashes of us all."

"You are being theatrical, Isabel. You would make a great bard."

"This is no jest, Lucia! Can you not see what we have awoken?" A knock at the door startled the girls. "Quickly! Hide it! Make it disappear. I will distract the maid."

"I am not just some mage who can swing my staff and cause it to vanish," Lucia held onto the dragon.

"Do something. I care not what you do. No one must learn of this," and Isabel leapt towards the door. Opening it slightly, she stared through the crevice. "Hi, Maple," she said as the familiar face raised an eyebrow.

"Is everything well, M'lady?" Maple attempted to peek into the chamber. Isabel pressed her body against the slit, concealing any movement behind her.

"All is well. My sister is merely changing her attire."

"Oh! Does she require assistance?"

"It will not be necessary, Maple. She likes to tend to herself when we are away from home. She can be, shy, if you may," and Isabel exited the chamber, closing the door behind her to prevent Maple from spotting the dragon.

"Lady Cicely sent me to get you for breakfast," Maple crossed her hands before her, patting down her dress.

"Aye, let us go and join her," Isabel started walking away from her chambers, hoping Maple would follow along beside her.

"The matter is, breakfast is over. You slept through it. We managed to stow away your rations so you could eat once you awoke. Lady Cicely imagined the night's revelry had taken its toll on you and wished to spare you from being roused."

"How kind of her. Let us go."

"And your sister, M'lady?"

"She will join us," and Isabel continued walking until they reached the bottom of the stairs. She came to a halt, feigning a moment of contemplation. "I left one of my belongings in my chamber. I will join you in a moment."

"M'lady, I can go and fetch it for you." Still, Isabel was long gone, vanishing within the spiral staircase, leaving Maple alone in the entrance to the great hall. "The odd lot," she said and continued to grab their breakfast.

Isabel hurried to her chamber, only to find it deserted. She searched under the beds and chest, but the dragon was nowhere to be found. *Where did she go? Where did you run off to now, Lucia?*

Hiding the chest once more and careful not to touch any of the eggs, Isabel walked to the door and closed it. She turned abruptly and collided with a stern figure, her body crashing down on the ground.

"Pardon me," the figure said to her, a young man standing before her, slim, yet his clothes were tightly trimmed to his figure. Outstretching his hand, he assisted her, his eyes widening at the young woman who stood before him. "Lady Isabel."

"Lord Robion? I was not aware you were in the castle," she said as she patted her dress, straightening it as best as she could after her fall. Her gaze met his, and she was in awe at Robion. Even though it had not been many moons since she last saw him, it had felt like ages. Robion had tousled blonde hair and a finely edged face, his lively coffee eyes enchanting her every moment their gazes met. Her stomach tightened, yet this time the culprit was not the dragon's claws that attacked her.

"Nor I of you. I was to travel to Oakheart to visit you," Isabel blushed at his words, tearing away from his gaze. "If not for the siege, I would have been there today."

"Why did you not write? I would have told father..." but the thoughts of leaving her father came rushing back.

"I was to send a letter when we arrived at Rivetion." He paused, "What bothers you?" He reached for her hand. His touch sent a shock running through her body. How she missed his gentle, warm touch. *Robion. How I have missed you. If only we could return to the fields of Swinsford. Reminisce of the past. Think of our future while the sun sets on the horizon.* Yet she dared not say this. The time they spent apart had made her somewhat reserved in his presence.

"Lucia. I cannot find her," Isabel fiddled with her hands.

"I did see her spend an awful lot of time yesterday at the archery range. Did you search for her there?" *And you never inquired to her about me?* But Isabel knew it could be frowned upon if he approached her sister while the two were unchaperoned.

"I did not. I will see to it."

"Allow me to join you."

"No need, Robion. I reckon you have matters of import to attend to."

"I insist. Searching for your sister is as important as any other duty. Besides, we have been apart for far too long." His words melted her heart, and her legs grew weak to the point where she nearly wobbled. She knew he was the one she longed to marry.

"Let us search then," she said.

"I hope Lord Osbert did not ruin the feast for you last night," he crossed his hands behind his back as they paced along the passageway. "I was told he insulted House Beaumont, but I was not made aware it was because you had attended the feast."

"With my cheerful state last night, his remarks left me unbothered. Besides, I was not quite sure what he was speaking about," Isabel shrugged away the idea without glancing at Robion.

"He tends to be over-expressive when he sinks into his cups, particularly at feasts. He brought disorder to our court once, but it now lies buried in the past," he decreased the length of his stride to match Isabel's shorter yet swifter one.

"If I may ask, what disorder did he bring about in your court?" Isabel glanced at Robion, her pace slackening when their gazes met.

"The simpler account of the story began with my sister. She was to marry, and he sought to dissolve her engagement to offer his daughters to my sister's intended. The union was meant to bolster his standing within the kingdom. Nevertheless, it did not transpire. My father uncovered his nefarious intentions and confronted him. Blood was nearly spilled, yet we managed to weather the storm diplomatically. If not for my father's ways, who knows how many lives would have been lost," he stopped himself.

"That is a most noble path to take. Noble houses rarely forgive so easily. It is the reason for all these blood feuds," Isabel went off, then contained herself. "Forgive me, Lord Robion. I did not intend to come off so passionate."

Robion laughed, "Your passionate ways are what has made me fond of you, Lady Isabel," he said, stopping before her and stroking a lock of her hair behind her ear. As his fingers traced their way gently over her ear, a warmth blossomed within her. Isabel glanced down, crossing her hands behind her back.

"Easy it was not," he shook his head, readdressing their previous conversation. "Forgiveness is never a simple task when ill-willed attempts are taken upon your family. My father taught us, however, that if no harm was done, why should we allow ourselves to be consumed by such resentment." He paused. "Perhaps this is the way we create a better world."

"There is truth in your father's words," she was unsure if she should add to the matter, even when Robion was fond of her passion.

A squire bolted over to them, joining the two as they stepped out of the castle and overlooked the archery range. The squire panted before finally speaking. "My Lord, your father has summoned you. You must join him immediately."

He turned, yet before he could speak, Isabel said, "I understand. Do not let it burden you. I will find my sister."

"I do hope you find her swiftly," he bowed, joining his squire at his father's request. He glanced at her before vanishing into the castle, "Will I see you this evening?"

With a broad smile, Isabel replied, "It would be disheartening if you did not."

CHAPTER 12: NOT ALONE

The clashing of metal in the distance led Isabel to stray in the direction of the archery range. To her surprise, it was desolate. She soon found herself in the battlements, staring down upon a courtyard at two men fighting. The pair of leathered armored men slashed and parried, alternating blows while moving swiftly around the courtyard.

Isabel watched, forgetting the world around her: the troubles she had encountered, the sudden disappearance of her sister, the dragon. It was a sort of enchantment she could not shake away, and even if she wished to, she would certainly not be one to fight it. Leofwin would strike Henry, instructing him when he committed a mistake or praising him when he fended his attacks appropriately.

The men finished their session, and Leofwin caught Isabel staring down upon them from the battlements. "Lady Isabel, care to join us?" his words broke her spell.

Making her way to the base of the stairs, Isabel noticed Henry sheath his sword and plop down in a corner, expelling exhaustion with every breath he took. Without hesitation, she sped down the stairs like a young girl running to her father bearing gifts. Except this time, it was not her father, and this time, there was no gift.

"Interested in your first sword fighting lesson?" Leofwin grinned while sheathing his sword.

"It is no noble act to play with a young lady's emotions," she crossed her arms, attempting to pout. Yet she was beaming inside, her enthusiasm evident in the smile she could not hold back.

"I would not dream of it. Henry, hand her a sword," and Henry unsheathed his sword, ready to hand it to her. "No, novice's sword. We do not want her cutting away and causing herself any injuries. At least not yet, for we are all aware that even the greatest of warriors bear scars." Henry nodded and sheathed his weapon, disappearing within the garrison's barracks and returning with a pair of wooden swords.

"Now, are you knowledgeable of the appropriate stance, your dominant leg slightly forward?"

Taking the wooden sword, Isabel positioned her right leg forward, the sword slightly ahead. "Aye."

"Good, now swing at me. I will parry your blows," and so they began, the first lesson in Isabel's long journey of knighthood. He parried all her blows, Isabel unable to find an opening to strike him down. Her body, nevertheless, was bolting with energy, enthusiasm keeping it alive with every strike.

"Now that is good. It is time for you to parry my strikes," and they continued their training. Isabel parried a couple of his slower strikes, missing the swifter ones. Leofwin's experience allowed him to detain the sword before he was able to strike her, preventing Isabel from taking mementos of a failed parry.

The fighting session extended beyond what Isabel expected. Her movements began to slacken, her stomach grumbling as they came to a stop. The short-lived work hours by others were deemed pure enjoyment for her.

"Has all that grueling work finally taken its toll on you, Lady Isabel?" Leofwin asked. Isabel was certain he heard her stomach's monstrous grumblings.

"I may have forgotten to eat my breakfast," she stated as she threw herself on the ground, the day's lesson causing her to perspire.

"Henry, would you care to share our rations with Lady Isabel?" Henry handed her a piece of dried boar meat, remnants of the surplus food Layne served during the feast.

"Now, this is some ration," Isabel said, satisfying the ever-groaning beast within her.

"One can never be sure if we may end up near the battlements or, even worse, stealing away to some deserted forest. Is that not so, Henry?"

Henry nodded, devouring his midday meal before beginning a second sparring round or heading to the battlements for the remainder of the day. That decision rested on Leofwin, and Henry was to follow him step by step, ensuring he learned every piece of knowledge cast his way.

"Isabel, are you certain you have never wielded a sword?" Leofwin sat next to her while eating his share of the rations.

"It is true, Lord Leofwin. My father was never fond of the idea that I dreamt of becoming a knight," she paused, noticing Jolecia's arrival.

"I must say, you have a natural talent to grasp new movements quite swiftly. Nevertheless, you have much to learn. With the proper swordmaster, I am certain you will become a grand swordswoman," and he turned to Jolecia. "Any news? You seem quite concerned."

Jolecia raised her eyebrow, "Odo requests your presence at the main gate."

"We must not keep him waiting. Lady Isabel, our next lesson will have to wait. Remember what I told you," and Henry leapt to his side, the three disappearing within the castle towards the lower city levels.

A group of soldiers arrived, sparring with each other while Isabel finished her midday meal before retiring to her chambers. She wondered if Lucia had managed to rid herself of the dragon and finally decided to return. Patting her dress, she entered the castle without a backward glance.

The walk back proved quite lonesome, the halls now barren, not a single guard where she had spotted them earlier on her walk with Robion. *They must have relocated to another section of the castle.* She hoped to encounter Maple on her way to her chamber, but not even the ghosts of the castle's past generations dared step into the passageway. Not a single servant in sight to fulfill any requests she may have. Though she rarely requested servants to do her bidding, the thought of them vanishing lingered in her mind.

Her chamber door was slightly open when she arrived. *Lucia is back!* Isabel's face came alive, hoping to learn how her sister had rid them of their burdening dragon. But stories she would not hear, for the chamber was silent when she entered. The chamber was untouched, everything perfectly placed where it had been before they departed earlier that morning.

A quick hand slipped across her lips, grasping her hastily. A hard body crashed against hers, its warm breath beating against her neck. Isabel's knees buckled, the figure pinning her hand when she reached down.

"Lady Isabel," the voice whispered, a voice unknown to her. "It appears you are trouble to this world. Fortunate for me, I can earn my cut for ridding you of it."

His words sent shivers down her arms. Without anyone to save her and with her hand pinned, she whimpered. The man unsheathed her dagger, rendering Isabel defenseless. He pressed the dagger against her ribs, gradually making his way up her body until he reached her throat.

The knife bit her neck, ready to slice where Wolfax nearly choked her to death. Isabel squeezed her eyes shut. Any sudden movement would make her death quicker and more painful.

"If you wish to be spared, you will avoid such a rash decision." Faylinn's voice caused her heart to leap, the man spinning to meet her. Isabel blinked away the tears welling in her eyes, grateful for Faylinn's arrival.

"You would not dare, girl," the assassin said. "It would be unwise for you to tempt me," the assassin added as he reached for his back, a mistake that would cost him.

His grip around Isabel loosened when he searched for a second dagger. One moment was all it took, Isabel elbowing his stomach and overpowering his dagger hand against her throat. Isabel spun, the assassin unsheathing his other dagger to strike her down. Amidst his movement, he exposed himself. Faylinn let her arrow loose, a thud followed by metal clanging as he dropped his dagger. His limp body reached for Isabel, and she jumped onto her sister's bed when she sensed it.

Isabel glanced back to find the assassin sprawled on the ground, motionless. Faylinn darted towards him, twisting the arrow, which struck him laterally across the ribs. She unsheathed a dagger and stabbed him in the heart. "The Beaumonts will not suffer, not under my guard," and she removed herself from the lifeless body, cleaning the dagger with a cloth.

Isabel huddled in the corner of the bed, burrowing her head between her knees and chest. Warm tears streamed down her cheeks, tiny streams of fear from nearly losing her life.

"Why? Why does everyone want to kill us? What have we done to deserve this? My family has never been cruel."

"You have done nothing," Faylinn wrapped her arm around her. "Though you may have yet to see it, the world is a cruel place. Harsher to those who are kindest."

"I certainly have. The assassin said it himself. I am trouble, and someone is out to destroy me."

"Do not listen to him. You are safe now, and no one will ever get through to you. Be strong, be brave," Faylinn said, the last words striking her at the heart. *Mother. Where are you? Why can I not be safe by your side?*

Those questions tore at her, reminding her of the pain of losing her family and nearly losing herself. "What if I cannot do that?"

"You can. You have kept your sister safe. You have been strong by her side. You must continue to fight for her, for the two of you. I will be there by your side."

"I would not be alive if not for you. How did you even find me?"

"I was searching for you when one of the guards by the courtyard said he saw you entering the castle. I reckoned you were heading back to your chamber."

Isabel wiped one of the tears rolling down her cheeks. "I do not understand. Why do you care for us? What is in it for you?"

"Nothing," Faylinn said, pausing for a moment. "I would not want to see either of you live in a world where you are alone."

"But we are alone. We lost our parents to the raid."

"That is certainly untrue. You have each other, and now, you have me," Faylinn said while wiping a tear rolling down Isabel's other cheek. Isabel wrapped her arms around her, unable to contain the vulnerability running through her body, the fears escaping with every tear, the pain dissipating with every shake.

"Do you know who might be responsible for this deed?"

Only one person came to mind. "I believe I do."

CHAPTER 13: ERRATIA

"Where have you been? I have been searching all day for you," Isabel said as she met her sister at the spiral staircases leading to the great hall.

"I was doing as you asked. Then I may have taken a slight detour," Lucia joined her sister and Faylinn on their way to the meal in the great hall. With Layne as King Ulron's brother, Rivetion's great hall perpetually bustled with activity, welcoming constant visitors throughout the year.

"You mean the dragon?" Faylinn interjected.

"It seems secrets are no longer between two," Isabel shook her head.

"It was not my intention. Faylinn caught me when I was trying to rid myself of Erratia." Lucia trailed her sister, careful not to crash into her, when Isabel halted abruptly to scold her.

"E-what? Do not name it. It will only create attachment. We seek the opposite, to detach ourselves from it."

"I called her Erratia. Why could we not just keep it?"

"This cannot be happening. How did you rid yourself of it?" Isabel watched her step, careful to not trample over her dress and plummet down the stairs.

"I might not have," Lucia cringed before her sister even had the opportunity to react.

"What have you done with it this entire time?" Isabel stopped at the end of the staircase, which met the archway into the great hall.

"It is in our chamber. It will not be a problem. I stowed it inside the chest."

"Have you gone mad?" Isabel reached for her temples as they began to pulsate. She felt she could faint at any moment. She searched her surroundings, seeking anything for support if her body were to betray her.

"It is *in* the chest," Lucia emphasized, yet her sister could not believe it remained within their care.

"It is still *in* the castle."

"What is still in the castle?" Cicely joined the ladies. Isabel nearly jumped out of her dress when she sensed the familiar voice behind her.

The three glanced helplessly at each other. "The meal, Lady Cicely. I was telling my sister it was in the castle. She wished to remain in our chambers for safety, yet both are within the castle. We are equally safe whether it is in our chamber or the great hall."

Cicely nodded, "Indeed. Safer amongst friends in the great hall, particularly considering your last encounter. How do you fare after the attack?"

"The attack?" Lucia cocked an eyebrow.

"Aye. An assassin attacked your sister, yet Faylinn eliminated him before he could harm her."

"Why was I not told of this?" Lucia closed in on her sister. "Were you injured?"

"I am fine. As dire as it was, I remain unscathed." *Should I confide in Cicely who I suspect may be scheming against me?* Layne summoned Cicely to entertain their guests, and the opportunity vanished before she could inform her.

"I hope you are not planning on speaking to her about who may be plotting against you," Faylinn shook her head. She did not wait for Isabel's answer before expressing her disapproval.

"It was him, I am certain. I must inform Cicely. If not, how will we stop him from striking again?" Isabel had an edge of determination building within her. All her fear had drowned within the pool of tears she had shed earlier that day.

"You lack evidence, Isabel. You cannot accuse a man who is scheming against you without it. You will expose yourself to ridicule." There was reason in Faylinn's words, and Isabel knew it was best to bury her accusations until there was evidence.

Searching the great hall, she spotted Robion, the young man pacing in their direction, silence weighing heavily upon the group.

Lucia broke the silence with his arrival and said, "Robion, we thought you would never visit our estate."

"Lucia!" Isabel's eyes flashed at her sister. "If you will forgive my sister, Lord Robion."

"I have pardoned worst crimes," he smiled at Lucia. "Swinsford has demanded much of my time, Lady Lucia. I was going to visit Oakheart when we were trapped in this siege."

"If that is indeed true, then we will let you two be," she winked at her sister, hooking Faylinn's arm and dragging her away. Lucia blended into the masses at the feast, evading her sister's gaze.

"Lady Lucia is quite-"

"Considerate?"

"Considerate beyond imagination."

Lord Robion gestured in the direction of a group. "My family is here. My father has heard of Lord Layne's guest of honor and is eager to speak with you."

Robion's father, John, was a man with tousled blonde hair, his face littered with battle scars, an oddity to Isabel, for his son had emphasized him to be quite diplomatic during their time courting. His face had lost the tightness of youth, the years having left their mark, and the toll of countless restless campaign nights evident in its lack of rigidity. Isabel knew the stories of her father's campaigns and the tensions such would yield upon any man.

Robion's mother's lengthy blonde hair stretched down to her back. Unlike her husband, Ada's skin remained taut and unblemished, a testament to a woman wed in the bloom of her youth, for she retained the vivacity of her childhood.

Their daughter Leticia was a woman who bore a resemblance to her mother, the lengthy blonde hair and thin figure causing her dress to drape over her shoulders and hang loosely around her body. Her hair was intertwined into a braid cascading down her back before ending shortly below her waist.

"Lady Isabel, my family," and they bowed to each other.

"I have yearned to visit your estate," Isabel said.

"I pray it was for us and not the wine," John said. His voice emitted happiness, yet his facial expression remained calm, as if his body was tired from all the problematic years it had experienced.

"I commented to Lady Isabel that we sympathize with her on behalf of Lord Osbert's vile treatment. She is aware we have had our fair share of experiences with him and that, ultimately, they will come to pass." She hoped they did come to pass. Osbert seemed driven by his words, and she hoped he would not come to act upon them in any way to harm her family.

"Now, Robion. You should not burden others with our matters, particularly if they are ill-willed," John shook his head at his son's comment.

"I just wanted her to not feel at a disadvantage. To know she is not an enemy here, for our true enemy stands outside these walls, not within," Robion stepped forward and Isabel smiled. Even when she wished to be a knight, it warmed her heart to know Robion was there to protect her.

"Well said. There is no need to destroy ourselves within these walls when we face a common enemy outside," John nodded. "Lord Osbert can become quite spirited. I am certain he meant no harm."

Isabel, however, believed otherwise, and the attempt on her life had brought her to question all those who surrounded her. Her adversaries lurked where she least expected, and she understood she must keep a wary eye wherever she journeyed.

"I hope you did not intend to carry off with my guest of honor," Layne interjected, having skillfully navigated through the gathering crowd to join the conversation. "After all, she is a hero of Rivetion. Saved my dear Odo after he was trapped behind enemy lines."

"Living off to your warrior dreams, Lady Isabel?" John cocked an eyebrow in amusement.

"Not quite," Isabel enjoyed the word yet refrained from using it when referring to herself.

"It is not ladylike to be a warrior. However, we must raise our cups to celebrate her remarkable courage, for she cast aside the judgement from the realm to save those in need. She is as valiant as any knight, placing herself in harm's way for the sake of others." Layne drank from his goblet, beaming while he looked at his happy guests.

"A man or woman can become a great knight. One cannot live to satisfy the wishes of all in the realm," he remarked. John and his wife watched Layne eagerly drain his goblet, a servant promptly coming to his aid when it had been depleted.

"Well said," and he glanced at Isabel, raising his goblet in tribute. "Who knows, perhaps one day it will be Isabel who sets a new standard, reshaping the world's perspective on the women of the realm."

Isabel and Robion withdrew from the group, putting some distance between themselves and the crowd so Isabel could speak more privately with him. "Robion, there is an incident I must share with you, one that occurred after our morning banter," Isabel began, casting a cautious glance around them, "let no one hear of this."

"Your secrets are mine," he said, leaning into her, and she knew she had his undivided attention.

"An attempt on my life was made."

"What?" he nearly spilled his wine. "Were you harmed? Did the guards capture him?"

Isabel felt her cheeks flush. Though she knew he cared deeply for her, she had never seen him demonstrate such distress over her well-being. "I remain unharmed. My friend killed him. Nevertheless, I must confess it gave me a fright. I cannot indulge you in the details at this moment," she tapped her foot lightly, "yet I believe Osbert sent the assassin."

"Osbert?" Robion questioned, his brow furrowed. "Do you have any evidence to support your suspicion?"

Isabel sighed and shook her head. "No, Robion. But you must believe me."

Robion's expression softened. "You know I will always trust you, Isabel. However, you are aware accusing a lord without evidence can bring about significant consequences." Robion ran a hand through his hair, staring at the floor. "Without it, your accusations will likely fail in trial. Are you certain it was him?"

"You have mentioned he has been ill-willed in the past, and with what he mentioned on behalf of me last night-"

"This will not suffice. However, there is reason for him to have acted accordingly. Nevertheless, we must discard other possible culprits if we wish to be certain it was him," he glanced across the hall at Osbert.

Layne joined his wife amongst the grand table, observing the lively crowd below as if they were stationed on a castle's watchtower, gazing down at the world unfolding before them. He whispered into his wife's ear, Cicely chuckling. Meanwhile, Osbert made his way through the center hall, his glance flickering towards Robion and Isabel. He stopped five paces from the great table and commenced, "I would like to make an announcement."

The crowd around him ceased their chatter, their attention centered on him. A pang in Isabel's stomach prepared her for another eventful night. Deep within her, she hoped it would not involve her or her family. An aura in the air sent shivers down her spine. Isabel glanced around the great hall. Unfamiliar faces began to emerge, faces that had not been a part of the meals tonight nor the previous night.

"Brother, I know we have had our disputes, and at times our perspectives may not have aligned. There comes a moment when it is time to bring the world to terms to make it right," Osbert said with conviction, yet Cicely remained unconvinced. "That is why I must ask for your forgiveness."

Isabel, however, sensed that something was amiss. The crowd was captivated by Osbert's speech, yet she could not shake the feeling that this was merely a distraction from the actual event unfolding around them. Isabel surveyed her surroundings carefully.

Her keen eyes discerned the subtle movements among the cloaked figures nearby. Osbert's resonating voice masked the hissing whispers slithering through the crowd. Men in cloaks stealthily unsheathed their swords and daggers, their actions accompanied by an almost inaudible hissing. Isabel knew something was wrong.

A glimmer of light caught her eye, emanating from beneath the men's cloaks. It was a light glimmer, not of hope, but rather the ominous flash of steel right before impending doom. The air seemed heavy at that moment, weighing down on Isabel's shoulders. It was as if the horse that trapped her near Oakheart now pressed down upon her once more.

The life of a noble was not as glamorous as many imagined - a world of dances, of exquisite fashion, of lavish feasts. No. The life of a noble was tinged with fear, tainted by greed, and in this chilling moment, death. The world she had come to know was ceasing to exist, her parents' disappearance plunging her into a domain of desolation and treachery.

I must warn them! She thought desperately, but a dreadful realization washed over her as she moved to take action. It was already too late.

"Father," a voice yelled, a voice which instantly felt as if it was fading in the distance, a voice she could barely recognize. Except it was all real, death had come for them; death had marched right up to their door, hitting them while they were enjoying life's ultimate moments, and thrust its dagger into their hearts. Death had thrust its dagger, and the life it had struck slowly started to wither away, marching with Robion's father's soul.

Guests all around her began to fall to the weapons of their attackers, stabbed to death before they could realize what was happening. Isabel froze. Death had come for them all. Isabel could hear the pain in Robion's voice. He witnessed his father fall to his knees. Fate was cruel. His father's fate became an ill omen. Wherever she went, death became a relentless, unwanted companion.

CHAPTER 14: BLACK FISH FEAST

The music within the great hall ceased, replaced by the screams of those who fell upon death's door and the roars of those carrying out death's wishes. Nevertheless, the world had turned into silence for Isabel. Her eyes flickered from deed to deed, unable to react to the dire situation before her.

Chaos erupted as men in chainmail slashed away at the unarmed guests. Panic spread like wildfire, many of whom stood frozen in terror, like a deer caught between a hunter and his bow. Robion bolted towards his father, yet time had not been his ally. He lay on the ground, gasping for air, overwhelmed by the amount of blood spilling from his grievous wounds.

Leofwin, Sehan, and Baenlorn struck their attackers with the first weapon they could muster, from table knives to plates and tankards. An axe was swung against Layne's closest guard, striking him in his stomach. Layne sprung on the attacker, not permitting the soldier to remove his axe and strike his wife down. Having indulged in Layne's wine, the remaining men were too intoxicated to fight the attackers.

Across the great hall, Lucia was exposed, a man bolting towards her with a sword. Isabel snapped from her frozen spell, her sister's imminent danger setting her on course to protect her. She roared like the warriors who had embarked on the castle's massacre, the sound of her incoming voice causing her sister's assailant to turn. He was slow to react in his bulky armor, Isabel bashing into his hard body. Her momentum was enough to send him off balance, Isabel saving her sister's life.

Not too distant, Odo watched as the brave young woman saved her sister. Taking a table knife and striking his attacker's eye, Odo stripped him of his sword and eliminated his imminent threat with a thrust to the chest. Without hesitation, he bolted towards the young woman in need of aid. The chain-mailed soldier swung his axe down on Isabel, Odo reaching her just in time to parry his strike. Odo swung his elbow at the man's face, sending him to the ground with a perfectly timed blow.

Isabel snatched a sword that lay around the few littered enemy corpses. She searched the tumultuous scene desperately for her sister, who, to her realization, was gone. Amidst the chaos, she must not have seen it was Isabel who saved her and fled. *Where have you gone off to Lucia?*

The great hall's doors swung open, and a barrage of enemies entered with excitement to join the festivities. A castle guard garrison entered from the adjacent passageway. Though vastly outnumbered, their duty pitted them against their enemies to the very end.

Odo finished slaying the man who had attacked Isabel and swiveled to confront the enemies, overpowering them. Slaughter was imminent, and their survival lingered on fleeing. They must live to fight another day. The great hall caught fire, archers releasing their arrows at the banners hanging on the walls. Lord Layne's eagle banner descended upon a group of fighters, setting them ablaze.

"Lady Isabel, we must leave. Only death awaits us here," and she nodded. In a matter of moments, the group of enemy troops had almost overrun the great hall, the defender's numbers dwindling dangerously.

"Follow me," Isabel snatched his hand, leading him towards the spiral staircase. At the top, the enemy's infantry had overtaken the area before they arrived, fighting the few remaining guards. Faylinn was amongst the guards fighting for their lives. "Swiftly, we must help them."

Odo trailed her, charging at the enemies fighting the guards. Isabel parried the men as best she could, recalling the limited lessons she acquired during the day. While she parried, Odo attacked, their teamwork allowing them to endure against the group of men who previously had the advantage.

A shriek not so distant caught Isabel off guard. Amidst the sudden distraction, one of the soldiers managed to graze her ear with his sword. She winced, the energy building within her and sending her into a state of survival. Isabel ducked, narrowly dodging the infantryman's strike. Seizing the opportunity, she thrust her body against his, sending him stumbling backward and reeling as he lost his balance. Evading the fighting group, Isabel ran to her chambers, searching for her sister.

A man had managed to slither by them. He was prepared to kill Lucia, who was pinned in the same corner Isabel had dropped against earlier during the day. The memories flashed within her, sending a dash of fear and pain. Isabel's fear transformed into energy to retaliate. Unaware of her presence, the attacker groaned as Isabel thrust her sword through him.

Lucia's shriek pierced Isabel's ears, and the dead man fell weakly before her. "You-you killed him," Lucia shuddered at the sight of the dead man. Her eyes were wide with horror, yet Isabel knew it had to be done.

"It was the only way, Lucia. It was you or him," Isabel removed the sword, the blade stained with the man's blood. She stared at the still face of the first man she had deprived of life, his mouth falling agape while memories flooded into her head. Isabel had heard many men speak of war with her father. They mentioned how those faces never disappeared from their minds, and after this moment, she was certain it must be true. The man mumbled at her, but his words could not be made as his weakened body became lifeless. He remained staring at her, a blank stare Isabel could not shake away.

"They are everywhere. What are we to do, Isabel?" her sister's eyes flashed with fear, pleading for help, hopeful her older sister would guide her away from this horror.

"I do not know, but we cannot stay here any longer. We are vastly outnumbered," Isabel searched the chambers for Giles' sword.

"You are bleeding," Lucia pointed towards the streak of blood running down Isabel's neck.

"It is nothing. We must go now." Amidst the chaos and frenzy of the battle, she had not felt the warm blood descending her neck until her sister mentioned it.

"Let me clean it swiftly."

"I said it is but a graze, Lucia. Now gather your belongings and let us make our escape. Do not forget the book," Isabel slung her bow over her back.

Faylinn and Odo entered the chamber, aiding the girls with their packing. With Faylinn's help, Isabel dragged the chest out into the open, its secrets sealed away from the outside world. As Odo's gaze settled on the chest, his expression tightened, and he shook his head in disapproval.

"It would be best if we leave the chest, or we may not escape," Odo said.

"The chest comes with us," Isabel felt a surge of power spring within her, her eyes darting at the man. Her voice's strength caused Odo to raise his eyebrows, and he did not insist.

"Very well. If it will slow us, it is best if we leave now," and the group nodded. They entered the passageway, escorted by the two remaining guards who survived the previous enemy encounter.

At a corner near the end of the passageway, the rushing of footsteps brought the group to a halt, the party ready to confront any enemies that may appear before them. Dropping the chest hastily on the ground, Isabel shielded her sister with her body. She prepared to strike down those who had raided the castle.

Her muscles relaxed when the familiar faces turned the corner. Layne, Cicely, and Maple joined them, their clothes tattered and burned from the great hall's conflict. The surprised gaze on their faces matched those of Isabel's group, relief overcoming them when they realized they all remained alive.

"We presumed the worst of fates came upon you when we did not see you in the hall," Cicely hugged the ladies.

"I always said she was resilient. I was not mistaken," Layne walked over to Odo. "You are well, my friend. I am forever grateful to you for taking care of these ladies."

"It has always been my duty to ensure the realm's safety," Odo replied, bowing lightly.

"Now we must go," Layne placed a hand on Odo's shoulder, pointing with his head in the direction they were to head off to.

"Time is of the essence, and more men were following close behind us," Layne said as he led the way.

As they fled through the passageways, Cicely mentioned to the ladies that the castle was home to secret passages that could lead them out unnoticed, passages which were now heavily guarded and inaccessible to them. However, there was an entrance that would lead them out of the castle. Though not a secret exit, their guards knew to clear it if the secret passages became inaccessible. *Does Osbert know we may use these to escape?* Isabel hoped not. It was their only way out.

The guards had cleared the enemies right before they reached the door, but Isabel could hear the distant footsteps increasing swiftly. It would not be long before they caught up to them.

Out in the battlements, trebuchet fire lit the skies while buildings were smashed and set ablaze. The vivid images of Oakheart plagued Isabel's mind, instances of her moments fleeing her home coming alive with the balls of fire that rained upon them. Hordes of infantry and cavalry flooded the streets, vastly outnumbering the units besieging Isabel's estate. Despite the vast difference in numbers, the destruction and carnage were equally devastating.

As they sprinted across the battlements, the thunderous roars of men charging towards them filled the air. Layne fell back, Odo and the guards joining him to cover the ladies' retreat. Isabel joined their ranks, hoping she could be of aid to fend off the men. However, they were outnumbered as enemy troops continued to pour from the castle.

"There are too many of them. We must retreat," Layne yelled as one of the guards by his side fell to the enemy's sword. "Odo, go with them. If we do not leave now, there will be no escape."

The group started withdrawing, Layne and the other guard covering their escape. In the distance, a man with a wolf pelt around his neck and a giant axe charged at them. *Wolfax!* The remaining guard received a blow to his shoulder. His opponent's sword sliced through his flesh, the remaining links in his chainmail preventing his arm from becoming severed from his body.

Isabel bolted to Layne, protecting him from a second soldier charging at him. "You must go," he yelled while dodging the incoming blows.

"I will not leave you. Not after all you have done for me," Isabel blocked a blow from an attacker with an axe.

Amidst the struggle, Layne struck down pairs of opponents with ease. Isabel aided him with the third man, preventing Layne from being overwhelmed. The group of men was soon replaced by Wolfax, the barbarian swinging away at Layne. The Lord of Rivetion parried his relentless strikes, Wolfax swinging with fury every moment his axe did not hack through him.

Their encounter was short-lived, a ball of fire lighting the sky and plunging towards them. Isabel and Layne evaded in unison, the projectile destroying the battlement, disrupting their escape. Debris from the crash dropped around them, Isabel covering her head to prevent further injuries.

Layne opened his eyes, their gazes meeting as footmen around them screamed in pain. His ashen hair was now stained with his blood, a long gash spreading down the length of his cheek. The battlement under Isabel started to crumble, Layne snatching her hands before she went down with the collapsing battlement. Her legs hung as she glanced at the ground below, Wolfax groaning and starting to rise behind Layne.

"You have always been a warrior," Layne said. "No one will take that from you. Forgive me, Lady Isabel, I only hoped to protect you." Isabel's heart clenched at his words. *Do not do this, Layne. Do not do this!*

A dazed gaze overtook Isabel, words fleeing her lips for a fleeting moment. She regained her composure, "Do not do it, Lord Layne," but the moment to retaliate had passed. He released her hands, Isabel plummeting with the crumbling battlement. She reached for the wall. The jagged edges burned and tore into her palms, Isabel decelerating her descent, but it was all for naught as she failed to grab on.

Thud! From the ground below, she watched Layne raise his sword once more to face Wolfax. He dodged, swung, parried, and swung. The group watched from the opposite side of the battlement in horror. Wolfax was a bigger foe, and his strength was beyond Layne's, his strikes sending Layne back with each blow. Layne seemed weak. Weak from the explosion, weak from watching his city being ravaged by opponents who had managed to enter it without him realizing. Wolfax struck his hand, Layne's sword flying as Wolfax swung for his chest. His axe struck deep into his flesh, tearing through and then out his back. Isabel's heart pounded against her chest, her mouth agape. Her heart ached for the man who had shown her kindness, now losing his life to Wolfax's brutality.

Cicely's cries echoed through the burning city, unable to help her husband and watching him lose his life right before her eyes. Layne dropped onto the battlement, his eyes dismissing the world as he uttered one last sentence to his wife.

Odo glanced down at Isabel. "Go," he said. "I will meet you on the other side," and Isabel nodded, the group leaving her behind amidst the city streets.

Alone in the streets, Isabel evaded the enemy troops while searching for an escape route. While on the battlements, Cicely had explained where they were heading. Isabel was sure to recall the details of the escape's location, but the thought of Layne falling before her kept intruding on her thoughts, challenging her focus on her escape plan. The heavy smoke within the city made it difficult to discern the direction she was heading. When she believed to be lost, she glanced at the castle and located her position swiftly.

Swords clashed, and Isabel was surprised the people were still fighting back. Except they were not. The few that remained battled in the alleys with pitchforks and cleavers, falling like wheat to a scythe versus their better-armed opponents. Only one caught her sight: a man in the street fighting two armored soldiers. Even though he was unarmored, he proved to be a suitable match for his opponents. With every step she took towards them, a familiarity crept into this unknown figure.

The man's feet danced with every parry, with every slash. His snowy straw hair and cobalt robe allowed Isabel to identify the figure. *Norman!* Isabel was confident he would outmaneuver and defeat his opponents, all except one.

A knight on a horse with ebony armor and a ruby caparison charged at Norman, an armor identical to the knight that had asked for the Valenour girls at Oakheart. Afraid he would fall to the rider, Isabel aimed her bow at the charging knight, her hands trembling on the bowstring. Pain jolted through Isabel's hands, her skin torn from reaching for the crumbling battlements when Layne had released her.

"Steady, Isabel, steady," she repeated to herself. However, the pain while pulling the bowstring prevented her from maintaining a firm aim. She aimed for the center of the chestplate, hoping it would not stray so far as to make her miss. *You cannot hesitate as you did on the battlefield. Next time, shoot.* Jolecia's words echoed through her mind, Isabel pulling the string further with assurance.

Norman slayed the men fighting him and turned to see the charging horse. The rider was now too close for Norman to lift his sword and strike him down. The knight's sword was raised high, falling upon Norman. At the last moment, the knight recoiled, and his horse changed course abruptly.

Norman's eyes bulged, noticing the arrow that had penetrated between the knight's pauldron and his chest, the ruby fletching on the shaft matching the knight's armor. He turned to meet his savior, Isabel, who was now rushing towards him.

"Come, follow me," she said. Without hesitation, Norman pursued her, a group of footmen heading in their direction.

Making their way around the tavern, Isabel found Sehan, Baenlorn, and Henry. Having just defeated a group of men, they stood guard while Isabel and Norman approached them.

"Where is Leofwin?" Isabel searched among them.

"He was defending a group of serfs with Jolecia. We are heading their way now," Sehan said.

"It appears as if we have more friends coming our way," Baenlorn raised his shield when a group of enemy soldiers turned the bend.

"Henry, go with Isabel. Ensure her safety," Sehan raised his shield, standing side by side with Baenlorn.

"What of Leofwin?"

"Those were *his* orders. Leave the city. Cicely is waiting at the secret exit. Go!" Sehan and Baenlorn charged at the incoming men, covering their retreat. At the same time, Henry led the way towards Cicely and her secret escape.

It did not take long for them to reach Cicely, where she awaited with the remainder of the group at a doorway. Odo had his arm around her, comforting her while she wept at the loss of her husband. Lucia jumped at the sight of Isabel, and Cicely raised her head, wiping away her tears.

The pair embraced Isabel, content that she persisted in finding the exit and escaping the tumultuous city streets. Lady Cicely gulped and said, "Isabel, you made it. It is time to leave the city. We are short of time."

"Forgive me for not saving Layne," Isabel said, Cicely sniffling.

"You are not at fault. You are not a warrior, not a full-fledged one yet. He always wanted the best for everyone, and he did it until his last breath," she wiped away a tear before it ran down her cheek. "Now, make haste before we are discovered."

The group passed the door and down a passageway, walking beneath the battlements until they were outside the city. Once in the city's outskirts, a deafening metallic crash echoed behind them, causing them to pivot simultaneously. The grim realization that they had not all stepped outside caused Isabel's heart to sink to her stomach. Cicely had let down the portcullis and separated herself from the group.

"What are you doing?" Isabel held onto the gate, her eyes welling.

"Just as my husband, I will not leave my city," Cicely held Isabel's hands across the gate.

"The city has fallen. Come with us," Isabel could not bear the idea of losing two people on the same day.

"It is my duty. Lady Isabel, remember you are a warrior, yet you will always look beautiful in those dresses. Wars are won on the field and in court. Only the strongest warriors dominate both," she whispered with a faint smile. Her hand slid along Isabel's as she took one last look. Isabel squeezed her arm, reluctant to let go, but Cicely shook her head. Isabel knew what she must do. Releasing her, Cicely vanished into the shadows under the battlements, leaving behind a sense of duty and sacrifice that weighed heavily upon them all.

CHAPTER 15: AN OATH OF FAITH

Not long after they escaped from the castle, the group located the pair of horses where Cicely mentioned they would be. The four ladies mounted the horses, taking turns riding to prevent themselves from tiring too swiftly. Amid the night, they had encountered a company of carts filled with survivors. Joining them, they marched without rest. Isabel knew what they were all thinking. *Are there enemy patrols?* If the enemy spotted them, they would at least have acquired more distance before an attack could come upon them.

Across the fields, the city ignited like a giant torch in the middle of the night. The raining trebuchet fire resembled falling stars upon it, crashing and causing sparks to fly into the air. The procession was teeming with the loss of many of its members' close kin, the few sounds escaping the survivors being prayers and soft sobs. Women's shrieks and men's roars were soon exchanged by murmurs and the silence of the woods.

Odo and Norman strayed near the group's rear, their words unheard as the soft winds blew by them and strung their murmurs along. "Why did you not train her?" Odo's voice was firm.

"I will never train another soul. What ails you folks, burdening me with the task of training others, particularly a young woman like her?" Norman's lip curled, his grip tightening on his sword's hilt.

"Being such a skillful swordsman, nearly retired from your lifestyle, one would ponder at the idea that you would like to pass on your expertise to the next generation," Odo said, focusing intently on the man beside him.

"I wish for no such thing. I bear no interest in training anyone. As long as I roam this land, I will not," Norman matched Odo's gaze, his eyebrow twitching.

"Her skill with a bow kept you alive. You should be grateful. Any other soul would have let you rot after such treatment at the feast. Still, Isabel, she was kind enough to stray from her path and save you," Odo saw the effect of his words on the man, whose eyebrows relaxed momentarily as he exhaled.

The refugees came to a halt and set out to camp in the woods, shielded from being spotted by enemy patrols. The ladies tied the horses to a nearby tree while Odo and Henry searched for timber to start a small fire. It did not take them long to gather a few twigs. Norman started the fire and warmed his hands over it.

Lucia plopped amongst one of the logs and grabbed the book Isabel's mother had given her. Maple, ever attentive to Isabel's needs, inquired, "Is there anything you need, M'lady?"

"All is well, Maple. Rest. It has been a long day." Maple nodded and raised her dress as she dropped beside her, the pair watching the fire crackling.

"Henry, you have first watch," Odo ordered while joining Isabel in front of the fire, sitting on one of the logs. "I have the second watch."

"Lord," Henry nodded and was off, wandering around the camp to ensure their safety.

"Lady Isabel," Odo stared straight into the fire. "I have an inquiry for you."

"What troubles your mind late at night, Lord Odo?" Isabel stretched her hands over the fire.

"Are you Lord Beaumont of Oakheart's daughter?" he turned to watch her. Lady Isabel continued to stare into the fire.

After a brief silence, she replied, "Indeed I am." She finally turned to face him, watching as the fire revealed an approving smile behind his pronounced beard.

"If I may," and she nodded, waiting for him to continue, "he is one of the greatest men to ever roam Emerion."

"How did you know he was my father?" Isabel pulled her cloak around her neck.

Her facial expression must have triggered his memory because Odo smiled lightly before replying.

"You are alike in your expressions when you battle. Within the great hall, when you saved your sister, you reminded me of him and our days, our days long ago. They are days I would soon not forget."

"How did you come to know my father?" she hoped to forget the day's events. Her sister, who seemed to be reading, though she had a confused expression, peeked over her book attentively at the conversation about their family.

"I was a knight under your father's command. He was one of the greatest lords I ever served. He was brave, loyal to all his subjects, and caring to the furthest of his extent. Years after the war, my services were no longer required, and he released me from my oath. Why are you ladies not accompanied by your father?"

Isabel glanced at her sister, hesitation tying her tongue before replying. "Our estate was razed to the ground, our father straying behind to allow us time to escape. Our mother vanished as well. We have no knowledge of their whereabouts."

"We can only hope they are well," Odo scratched his beard. "Time has passed since I pledged my oath to your father to always stand true to his side in sword and estate, yet most importantly, to protect his family. If it were not for my services no longer being required, I would have served him until I became one with the land."

"Thank you, Lord Odo," Isabel nodded. "Your devotion is most admirable. I see why my father kept you by his side as long as he did."

His eyes appeared to come alive, and for a moment, there was silence while Isabel stared at him. The man's eyes flickered from the ground and back towards her. "Though I was released from my oath, I feel my duty to protect your family never ended. I wish to be bound once more by my oath," Lord Odo rose, the ladies watching him when he unsheathed his sword and knelt, his hands over the pommel.

"You must rise, Lady Isabel," Norman watched them. "Do you have a sword?"

"I do not," she replied, and Norman unsheathed his, handing it to her. "Now you must gently place the fuller side over his right shoulder, then over his head, and finally down upon his left before returning to his right side after his oath. Begin, Lord Odo."

"I promise on my faith that I will be loyal to Lady Isabel, never cause her harm, and will observe my homage to her completely against all persons in good faith and without deceit. My sword is your sword," Odo lowered his head, Isabel passing Norman's sword over his head as instructed.

"Your oath is your bond. Rise," and Odo rose, removing his sword from the ground and sheathing it. Isabel remembered the tales of knights pledging to their kings, and today, her body tingled as if she were true royalty.

"Father truly was loved in the realm," Lucia said, the book now placed by her side.

"He stole the hearts of people and warriors alike. The bards still sing of his most famous battle in Triturium," Odo added.

"Triturium?" Isabel's eyes narrowed, "he never told us of Triturium. Can you tell us this song?"

Odo shook his head, "Forgive me, Lady Isabel. I am no bard. And this story is one your father should tell you. I am certain he would love to share it."

Lucia tugged on Isabel's arm, urging her to sit beside her. "Soon, we will hear all about it, Isabel. Soon, when we find Father. I am certain he will tell us all about it."

"Soon," but Isabel could only smile weakly at her sister. Who knew when soon would be, if soon would ever be genuinely so near? Isabel returned Norman's sword and settled by her sister, wrapping her cloak around them as they faced an uncertain future together.

Odo rested on the opposite side of the fire, the flames flickering in the space between them. After a while, Isabel broke the silence. "It stays with you, does it not?" Her gaze remained fixed on the dancing flames, and her words carried a weight of shared experiences and burdens that they all bore.

"What stays with you?"

"The face of all those whose lives you take away?" her voice was solemn.

Odo sighed. "It is the harsh reality of warfare. With its great instilled honors, the horrors one must carry are a formidable burden for any person to bear. With time, one learns to bury it far from one's thoughts, yet death is always knocking on a warrior's door," Odo said as Faylinn placed an arm over Isabel, comforting her.

"It is best to remember," Norman said, "it is your life or theirs. That tends to ease my burden," he mumbled some words afterwards, but Isabel did not hear them. She wondered if even that was enough to ease her burden. She would do anything to save her sister. *Perhaps Norman is right. When you must fight for the ones you love, who knows how far you can go to save them?*

"Taking a life is no simple manner," Faylinn joined the conversation, her eyes narrowing at Norman. "With time, however, the mind hardens. It does not get simpler; you simply learn to live with it."

"Melee combat is an art not made for the faint of heart. Some men are born to do it, while others simply adapt when they are thrust into battle for their first kill," Norman picked the fire with a twig.

The fire crackled until it died out, the trees casting a shadowy blanket around them while they slept within the forest's shelter. The trees danced with the chilly wind, and the fire's warmth vanished with their movements. Isabel shivered, her eyes flinging open before the first light of dawn. The remaining twigs in the fireplace resembled dragon eyes staring at her, their gazes red. They beckoned to be reignited, but they had served their purpose, and now they lay watching with a cold and dying gaze as if they had one more story to tell before fading into ash.

Lucia had snuggled between her and Faylinn just as Erratia had once buried herself when seeking protection from Isabel's dagger. Henry had joined them by the fireplace, and Odo lurked nowhere within range.

Isabel walked away from their circle of bodily warmth, straying away from the sleeping bodies and their horses, leaning onto a tree. The man's icy body lingered in her mind, lifeless, gone with the thrust of her sword. Flashes of Layne's death at the hands of Wolfax's axe and his final words of apology continued to haunt her like a relentless specter. *Come with me. I will fight beside you.* She longed to say these words to him instead of becoming mute. *You have always been a warrior. I only hoped to protect you.* His words echoed through her head, reminding her of the friend she had lost.

"Do you have a sword?" a voice behind her caused her heart to leap.

Noticing the straw hair, she said, "You gave me a fright Norman."

"It was not my intention. Do you not own a sword?"

"I fear not. The only sword that remains with me is the shattered pieces of my father's sword."

"You were gifted your father's sword?" Norman's head jerked back.

"It was originally intended for my brother. He had renounced it, and we found it a few days ago. It was the last moment I shared with my father," Isabel said, watching the horizon when the first streak of light slipped into the sky.

"You will need a sword then," Norman admired the horizon with her.

"Why is that? I still have my bow and daggers to defend myself," but as she said the words, she searched for the true meaning of his words amidst her sleepy mind.

"One cannot learn to sword fight with a dagger."

"There is no one who-" she turned, a shaky, disbelieving voice overtaking her. "You are going to train me?"

"If you acquire a sword." She jumped at his words and wrapped her arms around him. "You can release me," Norman swallowed. "The only instance in which we will make contact is when our swords strike each other."

"Forgive me, Norman," Isabel stepped back, smoothing out her dress. "The excitement overtook my emotions," she said, pursing her lips while attempting to contain her excitement.

"Nevertheless, I will require a favor from you."

"What may that be?"

"There is a task I must fulfill. Afterward, I wish to return home," he said, pausing while looking distantly. There was a moment of sadness about him, and Isabel almost pitied the man. "And you wish me to aid you in your task?"

Her words seemed to wash away his sadness, "I do not." He turned towards her, "When I decide to return home, I will require a group to escort me. Will you escort me?"

"A warrior requiring an escort?" Isabel raised her eyebrows, but Norman remained serious. "Aye, Norman. I will escort you home. Where is your home?"

Norman was glancing at the campfire when she asked. Turning towards her, he stared silently before answering, "Far, far away, Lady Isabel. It is a dangerous trip. For now, it would be best if you did not know of this place." But telling her she should not know merely sparked more curiosity. Isabel, nevertheless, remained silent. If it had been Lucia, her curiosity would have gotten the better of her, but Isabel knew when to remain silent.

"Very well. When the time comes, I will be a part of your escort."

"Then it is settled," and they shook hands.

Isabel turned, her eyes fixed on the castle at the end of the valley, long forsaken yet erected mightily for all who would dare approach it. "That is Accreton, is it not?"

"Precisely. Leading towards it is Hollow's Pass, one of the most feared entrances in the entire kingdom. The building perched atop the mountain is the long abandoned and scorched keep of Accreton, though below it stands an enormous city." Isabel watched the rays of sunshine beaming behind it as if the gods had come to illuminate this mysterious and foreboding place.

Isabel's gaze beamed brighter than the rays rising from Accreton's towers and said, "My ancestral home."

"Aye, indeed," Norman repeated. "Your ancestral home." *How does he know?* But Isabel did not ask. The less people knew of it, the better. That is what her parents always said. At times, discretion regarding their heritage and lineage was the difference between survival and danger.

CHAPTER 16: RELIVING MEMORIES

Isabel and Lucia sat on a cart, Lucia cleansing Isabel's ear wound from the previous day. Though it had been a mere scratch and Isabel had been fortunate not to lose her ear, an infection could alter the situation quickly. Lucia believed it worse for the blood trickling down Isabel's neck. With the calmness of morning, she offered to aid in cleansing it, Isabel eventually complying.

"Thank you," Isabel said as her sister wiped her ear with the cloth. "Forgive my impolite behavior when we left Oakheart and were out on the battlefield. I am aware you were worried about Mother and Father. I should not have disregarded your concern for them as swiftly as I did."

"You were quite boorish," Lucia said thoughtfully, then, unable to contain herself, smiled. "We are sisters. Is that not bound to happen?" she embraced her, Isabel's body relaxing at her sister's mercy. "You have done your best to care for me, and such situations can be quite distressing."

"And I will continue to do so. I swear to care for you until we find Mother and Father," Isabel held her hand.

"You better, or you will not have anyone to cure your battle wounds," Lucia squeezed her ear lightly.

"Ow," Isabel tightened her grip around her hand.

"It will hurt much worse if I cannot help you," Lucia winked at her and twisted away from her grip, leaping off and bolting away.

Odo rode beside the cart, decelerating his horse's gallop into a light trot. "Lady Isabel, I will ride ahead of the group and scout the town the guards spotted."

"I will join you," she jumped off the cart, Faylinn swiftly replacing her. Henry, who had taken his turn riding the horse, dismounted and aided Isabel in mounting the saddle. Odo and Isabel galloped ahead of the group, riding until they reached the village of Nightfall Meadow, the words carved into a broken sign out on the city's outskirts.

While they rode, Isabel asked Odo, "Are you aware of what happened to Cicely's sister?"

There was a moment of silence before he finally spoke. "There are some folk who say bandits took her. Others say it was a ransom, yet that idea does not sit well for me, for there has been no message from her captors requesting coin. There was a trail after her disappearance, and a group of knights had gone in search of her. They were attacked and, amidst a storm, lost all direction to where she might have been taken. The idea of her disappearance is wretched, for she was the kindest young woman I ever laid eyes on, yet hearty regarding matters of import to her. I searched for her with a group of men, but it was to no avail. I will not forsake my duty to find her, but I fear the scent has been lost."

The sight of the town impeded Isabel from inquiring further. A crooked sign and broken fences welcomed them into the village, herds of cows on their outskirts. Chickens and ducks roamed the streets while the two descended the muddy path. Few people roamed the streets, the villagers diligently gathering their harvests throughout the surrounding fields.

At their sight, an elderly man bolted towards them, his smile quickly fading. His ragged clothes were filthy, his feet bare while his toes hid in the grass as he returned from the fields to meet them.

"M'lord, M'lady," the man was barely able to speak.

"Good morrow," the pair replied.

"You must help us. There are these men, these *barbarians,* at our tavern, and they will not leave. They eat all our food, and they are boorish with our people. You must make them leave. If you save us from this disgrace, we will pay for your efforts with what we may scavenge."

"Do they pay?"

"That they do, M'lord. That is why we fear asking them to leave. They are strong men, mercenaries, I might even say. They are the rowdy ones in the tavern. Difficult to miss."

"We will relinquish you of your burden," Isabel said, pulling on her horse's reins when the elderly man glanced behind them.

"Thank you, M'lady. The tavern is in that direction."

"Lady Isabel," Odo leaned in her direction, whispering, "you are not trained in melee combat. I must protect you from harm. If they are as the villager says, we are bound to exchange more than words. We cannot accept."

"Lord Odo. I know what it is to have your village invaded by foreigners. I will not have these people suffer as I did. Nevertheless, you are right," she looked at him, then back at Norman and Henry as they arrived, the villager taking a step back. "I am not trained in melee combat, but you are. How blessed I am to have you pledged to my cause," and she shrugged, leading her horse in the direction the elder had pointed.

"It seems we arrived at the opportune moment," Norman said.

"It seems we may just need you two after all," Odo turned his horse, following Isabel.

The tavern, the most prominent building in Nightfall Meadow, had a pair of chimneys creating a cloud above it. A team of six horses was tied to several posts outside the tavern.

"Are you certain we should confront them?" Henry turned to the pair on the horses.

"It is the noble deed to do," Isabel glanced over her shoulder, Odo nodding lightly, though she could see he did not quite approve.

The warmth from inside the building snugged their bodies as they entered. Four tables with benches were spread evenly across the tavern, four rowdy men sitting in the furthest one from the entrance. Huddled around, they sang and roared, unaware of Isabel's company's arrival. The brewer stood behind the bar, eyeing them fearfully, and Isabel could see he was hoping they did not belong to the band of intruders already in their town.

"Let us avoid bloodshed if necessary," Isabel began to move forward, Odo stepping quickly to her side.

"My Lady, are you certain you wish to proceed? Once we confront them, we may be unable to step away if a fight occurs."

"It is the least we can do for this town," she replied. Odo released her as she strolled straight for the men. Clearing her throat as she reached them, Isabel began to speak before they could turn.

"Gentlemen, the townsfolk have been complaining of your extended visit. I believe it would be best if you paid your coin and went on your way," Isabel said bluntly, standing before the group.

The burly man with his back to her was the first to speak. Clad in a burgundy gambeson, a cuirass, and coif, he began to talk without turning. "The town can kiss me arse. I have paid my fair share of coin, so why can I not stay here until I tire of sitting on me behind?"

"They would say it is more a manner of your behavior."

"Well, I be damned. Who is to tell us how we are to behave? It is a tavern, after all, and these people are not me mother," the burly man said, finally turning to face her.

"Let them take every last coin we pay them. We are not going anywhere," the man with a dirty blonde braid, shaved sides and complementary full beard said. His sapphire eyes widened when he saw the man next to Isabel. "Odo, my dear friend, is that you?"

"Uthred?" Odo said, clearing his throat.

The group huddled around the table turned, their faces sharing the same surprised expression as Odo's. An elderly man with rosy skin and a frosty beard made his way around the table, the man quickly embracing Odo. "The thought that I would never see you in my life crossed my mind. I am glad to see you in great health, my old friend."

"Beavis, it is good to see you."

"In good health? Odo has seen better days, that is certain," remarked a figure shrouded in chainmail armor and a barbuta helmet. He stood from his bench, swinging his axe over his shoulder. His helmet was personalized, a plate added across his face to conceal his identity. Draped over the chainmail was a charcoal surcoat and cape, frayed at the edges. From the man's chestplate, a stone stag stared at Odo. The mysterious figure approached Odo, looming over him from inside his armor, a penetrating gaze fixed on his old friend.

Odo matched him, and the two watched each other momentarily before shaking hands. "You would be one to speak, Merek," Odo's expression turned cheerful while glancing over his friend's attire.

"It suits me. You are a man of the court and should not be prowling in such conditions," Merek dropped the axe's eye to the ground.

"Could you be careful with the wooden floor?" the brewer called from across the inn.

Merek's helmet swiveled towards the man, a fire burning within his eyes even when their sight was unnoticeable. The brewer averted his gaze, fearful of further provoking his customer.

"Why are you tattered? Your lord did not abandon you now, did he?" the burly man squinted at him, analyzing his complexion.

"He has not, Fulk. My lord has passed, and now I have returned to serve the family I once served," and he pivoted towards Isabel. "I now serve Lady Isabel."

"Well, Odo. Here I believed that with your lord's death, you had come this far to join us, but her? Now I think you have dug yourself a real pit," Fulk leaned back on the table.

"Do not speak ill of Lady Isabel," Odo stomped the plank before Fulk. Fulk's head jerked back, though his facial expression did not reveal if it was due to fear or instinct.

"Still commandeering as ever, I see," Merek leaned onto his axe's pommel.

Rough warriors. Dangerous roads. They do not carry themselves as knights. Mercenaries perhaps? Who knows what we may encounter? Odo is a nobleman; they must be great warriors if he knows them. Are they loyal to their subjects or the coin?

"Odo," Isabel pulled him away from the other men and continued to speak in a whisper. None of the men paid much heed to them when she dragged him away, except for Merek, who continued to stare intently from behind his helmet. "Who are these men?"

"We go back to battles before I fought by your father. When I joined Lord Icas, they came to our aid in several battles."

Isabel crossed her arms over her chest and thought for a moment. *If they fought for my father and Odo, they must be loyal.* "Would you deem them honorable men?"

Odo raised his eyebrows, "Loyal and great warriors they are. I cannot say they may all fall as honorable, for they are not knights and do not live under the code of chivalry. They are mercenaries but good friends since I have come to know them."

Isabel nodded. *A band of warriors is what we need. They can protect us. They may be of aid while we find Mother and Father.* "If you trust them, I will do so as well. Tell them to fight for me."

Odo acknowledged her request and turned to the men. "You men still seem like formidable fighters. Lady Isabel would like you to join her party and fight for her," Odo crossed his arms.

"Her?" Fulk and Uthred said in unison.

"You see here," Beavis commenced, "I do not want no woman being my leader."

The thought of Lucia's deep pockets had Isabel speaking before she could consider the consequences, "I have got the coin."

"Well, the coin *is* my friend," Uthred gave in.

"I would have to weigh my options, but I have become quite weary with this place. You can be the leader," Fulk chipped in behind them.

"Beavis, Merek?"

"Once more roaming the land with an old friend," Beavis shrugged, "Why would I discard such an offer?"

"You know my mind better than most. If there is killing, I will follow the trail," Merek swung his axe over his shoulder.

"Lady Isabel, it appears we have our first band of men," Odo turned to her.

"I will join too," a feminine voice from the opposite side of the tavern called out. Her figure remained shrouded beneath a robe, though hints of her leather armor were visible beneath the cuffs. With a graceful motion, she drew back her hood, unveiling her tanned complexion and disheveled chestnut hair. A few fresh scrapes littered her neck, and Isabel knew she was not a newcomer to adventure.

"On Malefic's sword," Beavis boomed from across the inn. "She has a staff. What is she to do with that? Beat me senseless like a mother scolding a child?" The mercenaries with him roared in laughter.

"Can you fight?" Isabel ignored Beavis' remark.

"My father taught me the fundamentals when I was a young girl," the young woman said.

"Using crafted staffs from besom brooms for sweeping tavern floors is not deemed fundamentals in melee combat," Uthred added. The mercenaries' laughter grew louder with their banter.

Isabel, unfazed by the jests, turned to the source of their mockery. "And what might your name be?"

"Lunet," the young woman came forward, Isabel eyeing her over.

"Welcome to our company, Lunet."

"Twenty Emerion Silver says she will not make it a day," Fulk turned to his friend Uthred.

"She will at least make it three," and they shook on it, Odo shaking his head at his companions and their gambling habits.

"We will need additional horses," Isabel turned to Fulk.

"I got them," he winked, "but it will cost ya."

CHAPTER 17: WHO'S THE LEADER?

"That city ahead is Hillfrey, ruled by Lady Katinee Loup, sister of Cicely LaFlamme and Seraphina Loup," Odo led his horse beside Isabel. The city was double the size of Rivetion, rising higher up on the hill it sat, aiming to reach for the clouds, yet its stature did not meet its ambitions. A moat surrounded it, not permitting past and future tunnel diggers from collapsing its walls. Enormous farmland extended around the surrounding plains, numerous carts with the seasonal harvests leading towards the city.

The thundering gallop of a horse behind them drew the pair's attention, and they turned to see a rider approaching on a snow-white armored steed. It did not take long for Isabel to identify the rider, the tousled blonde hair and charming coffee eyes increasing in size as the horse closed the distance.

"It is Robion," Lucia said. Beside her was Faylinn, who glanced back. Before they left Nightfall Meadow, Faylinn and Lucia had caught up with the caravan and joined them.

"Robion," Isabel shouted, the men allowing him to pass through to her. It did not take him long to reach the front of the team of horses, the noble matching their pace. "I hoped the worst had not occurred to you. My condolences to your family."

"Thank you, Isabel. I cannot believe I could not protect them after being so close."

"You must not burden yourself with harsh thoughts. How could you have known that was to happen?" Isabel could not help watching those lively eyes in such a melancholic state, Robion's gaze dropping to his steed's mane.

"I may have been able to defend them. I feared the worst had occurred to you as well when I left you for them." Robion's eyes glimmered when he met her gaze. Isabel was pleased to know he did not meet his family's fate. Isabel, however, could sense the hurt within his eyes, and it shook her down to her bones, for the pair had come to live similar fates.

"It was just for you to return to your family." Isabel pointed towards Odo. "I must be grateful for Odo. Who knows if we would have made it out of Rivetion without his help."

"Indeed. Odo has proven to be a great warrior throughout many battles," Robion nodded in acknowledgement at the man leading with Lady Isabel.

"How did you manage to find us?" Isabel said.

"Cicely told me you had ridden towards the caravan. When I reached Nightfall Meadow and did not find you amongst them, I went towards the tavern. The brewster described a group there, and I knew it was your party heading towards Hillfrey. I should have known," he raised his hands while holding his horse's reins, "Katinee was the nearest and most logical place to seek aid."

A dust cloud formed from the forest and moved into the clearing. The dust stormed through the air, making its way towards a caravan and a group of carts riding into the city.

"Bandits," Norman called from the rear.

"It seems we arrived at an unsuitable time," Fulk told Uthred.

"Unsuitable? We have arrived at the adequate moment," Isabel readied her bow.

"This matter does not concern us," Fulk called towards her.

"It does if I am here," Isabel called out. *Lucia cannot fight. She should not be a part of this nor see more bloodshed than she already has. We must strike first to prevent Lucia from becoming a part of the skirmish.* "Maple, stay back with Lucia. If you can make it to Hillfrey, then move swiftly." Maple nodded.

"What are you doing, Isabel? Do not endanger yourself," Lucia said, tugging at her arm.

"Lucia, no one should live the horrors we lived. I must protect them," and Isabel turned to her men without providing further explanation, "Ready?"

"So long as I am getting compensated for my troubles," Uthred waved his axe.

"You will not do much with it when I win me bet," Fulk cackled, swinging his Warhammer and roaring.

"Time to paint the soil," Merek joined Isabel and Odo, prepared to lead the charge.

"On me," Odo led the way, Isabel maintaining pace with him while readying her bow.

They charged at the enemy, aiming to intercept them before they reached the caravan. A new cloud formed with their galloping horses, dust picking up around them as if they, too, were a storm to be reckoned with. As they drew nearer, Isabel could discern the armed bandits more clearly. Though incomplete, most wore chain mail with pieces of plated armor, with only a few being wholly clad in plated armor. They were heavily armed with swords, axes, and even maces. It did not take long for them to intercept the bandits, their weapons clashing, horses neighing, and the roars of men eclipsing the screams of fleeing serfs and merchants.

Isabel remained on the outskirts of the fight, selecting her targets with her bow and setting arrows loose upon them. With their heavy armor, her arrows were rendered useless. *Their armor is impenetrable.* Then, Isabel altered her aim towards the gaps in their armor. With quick movements in their horses, it was nearly impossible for her to strike her targets. It was a rare occasion for Isabel to unleash her bow from horseback, and unfortunately, her arrows failed to find their mark as they soared through the air. They served as a testament to her lack of experience, and she realized there was much training to be done as her archery skills failed to excel while riding the saddle.

One of the bandits charged at her, Isabel ducking as he swung at her. The man grabbed her dress and dismounted her, dust rising as her back crashed onto the ground below. Isabel's horse reared and fled from the battlefield, leaving her to her demise.

The mounted enemy turned and charged at her. He was prepared to strike her without hesitation. Isabel attempted to flee, yet the bandit's speed outmatched her sprint. Her heart slammed onto her chest to the rhythm of her feet. Isabel dared not glance back. With the beating hoofs getting louder, she glanced over her shoulder. A wooden staff intercepted him, striking his chest and dismounting him. Realizing the pair were now on even ground, Isabel unsheathed her dagger and dashed towards the man. He did not have an opportunity to rise when she leapt on him, sending her dagger to his neck, the man's warm blood spilling over her hand.

Isabel's second kill had been bloodier than her first, a personal execution with her dagger. She removed herself from his body, unable to gaze at his face, fearing she would never forget it if she looked. The dust around her settled with her kill, and the remaining bandits fled the battlefield, their fleeing gallops met with her men's celebrations.

Odo rode towards her and dismounted his horse. "Are you injured, My Lady?"

"I am well, Odo, thank you."

Beavis galloped towards her, leading her horse and handing her the reins. "M'lady, if I may."

"You are free to speak, Beavis."

"You need a sword. Close encounters such as these are dangerous when fought with a bow. I would say you were quite fortunate today."

Norman nodded at the observation, "It is not merely for your training but for your survival."

"Beavis was a skilled blacksmith in his time. I am confident he can fix your father's heirloom sword," Odo added.

"Odo, my dear friend, I am out of practice," Beavis maneuvered his horse as the men circled her.

"All you require is a good forge, and your lifetime of work will make certain it is as the first day it was forged from its fire," Odo nudged his friend, urging him to accept.

"I will speak with the smithy here at Hillfrey," Beavis said.

Isabel mounted her horse, and Odo leaned into her, "What is your command?"

"Let us continue to the castle."

"On behalf of the loot," Odo pointed at the littered corpses while Uthred and Fulk trotted around them desperately.

"The loot of your kill is your welcome payment, excluding any jewelry," Isabel shouted at her men. "Fulk," she said while handing Odo her horse's reins.

"Aye, M'lady?" Fulk feigned to raise his head attentively, mocking Isabel. She had now crouched beside the man she killed and inspected him. She jiggled a pouch she found, coins clinking from within, Isabel smiling. Pouring it onto her hand, a silver necklace was intertwined within the coins.

"Here," she turned to meet him, handing him the pouch after counting the coins. "It will be my first payment towards the pair of horses you sold us."

"Aye," and Uthred pursued him as they fought over their loot.

"It seems I am leading this bet. Your coin will soon be mine," Uthred reached for Fulk's dead man's loot, Fulk glowering greedily at him.

"Those were no ordinary bandits," Odo said, Norman nodding.

"They were not. The armor they donned exceeded the measures of any bandit in these parts. It is best if we report it to Lady Katinee."

The group rode into town, the cathedral's spire reaching further into the sky than the surrounding buildings. Halting them at the entrance, the guards lowered the spears between them and the undrawn bridge.

"Your business in town?"

"We are here to speak to Lady Katinee on behalf of Rivetion," Isabel led the group.

"Lady Katinee is not granting an audience. Nevertheless, news of the Black Fish Feast has already reached the castle. There is nothing more to be discussed," the guards crossed their spears between the entrance, continuing to impede their passage. *The Black Fish Feast? Why the Black Fish Feast?*

"We seek lodging for the day while we replenish our supplies and we will be on our way," Odo added.

The pair of spearmen glanced at each other, and after a moment of silence, they glanced at the group. "Very well. If we hear of any trouble from your party, there will be consequences." The guards lifted their spears, allowing the group to enter the city.

Purple banners hung along the front of the buildings leading into the city, demonstrating the people's high regard for their homes. The stench of human dung struck their noses, mixing with the raw meat and a diversity of fruits from the vendors. A band of children ran towards them, screaming and reaching for their feet.

"What are you looking for?" said the first.

"You should try our meat," said another.

"Watch your horses," Fulk yelled at the group, "There are thieves amongst the bunch."

"The inn is all we require," Odo flicked a coin at one of the boys. "Lead us there."

One of the tattered boys guided the group to the inn, the party securing their horses to the posts and entering with their hard-earned spoils. The inn was of a greater magnitude than the one in Rivetion, its expansive interior featuring roughly ten tables and individual seats scattered about. Chaos reigned within, the brewer and barmaids rushing around the inn, diligently serving the countless patrons who poured into the inn shortly after the recent skirmish.

The group enjoyed a warm leek soup, the newly hired men laughing as if the world around them was nonexistent. Killing had no effect upon them, their lives impervious by each life they took from a breathing man.

"What worries you?" Robion reached for Isabel's hand, Faylinn and Lucia's gazes darting towards them.

"How can they kill and go about their day, their minds filled with such peace?"

Robion sighed. "It is not a simple task, yet once you take more than one man's life, the feeling of guilt tends to disappear. My father once told me, rest his soul, that if it is to save another man's life, it is worthwhile to carry the burden."

Isabel stared at her hands, wondering when such day would come. "I will make do. Over time, I hope," she replied, pushing the imagery away.

"Here is your share," Fulk dropped a filled pouch before Isabel, joining them at the table.

Isabel spilled the contents onto the table, revealing jewelry and a few coins. She swept them into the leather sack, hoping to avoid unnecessary attention. Maple's eyes briefly flickered towards the coins before returning to her soup. Isabel took the coins and handed them to her.

"Here, Maple, in case you need any supplies."

"You must not, M'lady."

"You deserve them for all your aid," Isabel pushed them closer, "take them."

There was a look of hesitation in Maple's eyes, but she swiftly removed them with a quick swipe. "Thank you, M'lady."

Sitting beside her eating was Lucia, and Isabel leaned into her ear. "Where is Erratia?" she whispered, Lucia looking up from her leek soup while blowing on it. The firm, pungent aroma struck Isabel, and after sipping on it, Lucia answered her.

"She is still in the chest. I only let her out to eat at night," Lucia said while dipping her spoon in her soup. "We do not wish to attract much attention." Isabel nodded. *Lucia is right. The less people know, the better. We should order her meat before we head off to sleep.*

"What is the matter with you, boy?" Fulk turned towards Henry. "You have not stopped tapping that foot since I got here. Last time I saw, there is no music to dance to."

"It is nothing," Henry stared down at the table, his face pale.

The door to the inn swung open, and a pair of guards entered. Glancing about the inn, they moved toward Isabel's party, halting before their table.

"Who is the leader here?" the guard's voice boomed, silencing any other chatter within the inn, his spear looming over them.

"She is," Fulk gave Isabel away swiftly, Isabel glaring at him. "What? You said you wanted to be the leader," he shrugged.

"Lady Katinee requests your presence at the castle," the guard said. "Come with us."

CHAPTER 18: WOLF'S DEN

"Lady Katinee Loup of Hillfrey," the herald announced. Lady Katinee entered the great hall and sat on her elaborate wooden chair, a wolf pelt draped over it.

Her chestnut hair contrasted against her fair skin, a golden leaf comb averting it from her face. A dusky dress with golden streaks concealed her body, exposing one of her shoulders and her arms.

"I have been told you have uttered my name in the streets. You are a woman unbeknownst to me. Who may you be?"

"I am Lady Isabel Beaumont. A friend of your sister, Lady Cicely."

Lady Katinee was silent, the indigo banners over her flowing as a shadow was cast upon the city, the weather outside taking an eerie turn. A wolf was centered in the banner, a pair of swords crossing behind it. Braziers were lined along the walls and appeared to urge the external world's shadows to flee from the horrors that could lie within the castle. Even then, the flames' glows were too dim to usher them away.

"Your family name was once of great import, yet that time has passed, and with it, the recognition of your name. My sister has failed to mention you the few times we have met in recent years," a scraggy man in a robe joined her.

"It was a novel friendship."

"Ah, I see. I must say. I am grateful you and your ragged soldiers destroyed the band of bandits, yet it was a waste of men for a worthless group of serfs." Isabel was bothered by her remarks, her head jerking back at her callousness.

"It was not just serfs. There was a caravan of merchants heading into the city that would have fallen prey to their efforts. Regardless of who they are, all individuals of the realm deserve our protection, be it merchant or serf," Isabel hoped to unveil her sympathy. Katinee, however, looked up towards the ceiling, and Isabel knew her efforts had been fruitless.

Her words were meaningless to the woman, "Serfs, merchants, are they not all the same rubbish? They perish, and more come to replace them. There is no ridding yourself of them."

Shaking her head, Isabel knew there was no longer need to dwell on the matter. The group was safe, and she needed to focus on more pressing issues. "I have come to inform you of the siege of Rivetion."

"The Black Fish Feast?"

"Why are they calling it the Black Fish Feast?" Lucia spoke before Isabel had the opportunity. Isabel could not contain her curiosity any longer, but Lucia's curiosity surpassed hers.

"It appears there was treason amongst my sister's warriors. Those who remained loyal to her were poisoned with fish during their supper by the traitors," she said, looking at the scraggly man beside her. Katinee shrugged, "Treason lurks even in those you feed."

"Why would they do this to her? Your sister is nothing but kind to her people," Isabel took a step forward.

"Lady Isabel," Katinee turned slowly to face her, "you will come to learn that even some dogs bite the hand that feeds them. There will always be that greedy beast hungry for more. Have you not experienced a similar fate?"

"Never. Our people are beyond loyal."

"It would come to explain why the Beaumont name has vanished in the wind during the past years. The world is a dangerous place, ladies. You have secluded yourself from the realm, making you forget how cruel it can be. No matter how far you flee or how silent you attempt to be, it is a vicious hound sniffing, sniffing, until it finds you."

Oakheart! Does she know? "Have you any news of my home, Oakheart?"

Katinee remained silent, looking at the wolf pelt on her throne while sliding her finger over it. Her gaze then met Isabel's, "I fear the only news of Oakheart is that there is no news," she paused, "the town was torched to the ground."

Lucia's breath caught, and Isabel wrapped her arm around her. "Are you certain?"

Katinee raised a hand, "My scouts know what they saw."

"And survivors?" Isabel brought Lucia closer to her chest, rubbing her back gently.

"There is always a serf or two who escape. However, the estate was barren. Dust, bodies, and the stench of death is all which remains."

"You hear that, Lucia? Mama and Papa may yet be alive."

"Even if they were alive, I would not advise returning. You have no knowledge of who you are fighting."

"On the contrary. I have met those leaders outside Rivetion. We were captured. They are barbaric men, foreigners to our lands."

Katinee shook her head, "Lady Isabel. The attackers who attacked Oakheart are not those who attacked Rivetion. Their methods are different. In Rivetion, it was a massive siege. In Oakheart, they sneaked up on your family and razed it all to the ground. I believe you would have noticed. You were there. Did you not notice any differences?" *The ebony knight versus the barbarians. They could not have been the same. Their armor and tactics were different.* She had remained silent, and Katinee cleared her throat.

"They did ambush us."

"Perhaps they are not as loyal as you believed them to be. Perhaps you had a greedy dog in your people."

"Impossible."

Katinee tapped her finger, "At times, the greedy hound is right before your eyes and feigns as the victim, allowing it to escape justice." *Arot. No. Arot could never betray us. It was all chance. Arot is as noble as a knight can be.* "I hope I may have shone some light into those shrouded memories."

"They may not have been the same attackers, but we were not betrayed. As much as I am certain our parents are alive. The enemy was merely better prepared." Katinee pursed her lips when Isabel replied so optimistically. "And your sister, any word of her from your scouts?"

"She survived. Cicely was a prisoner for returning to her castle, but she survived. A fool if you ask me," Isabel felt a wave of relief wash over her as she learned of Cicely's survival. *How can she speak of her sister with such regard?*

"Even then, your sister needs aid. You must send help," Isabel's words bordered on a plea, her concern evident.

Katinee stared at the ceiling, tapping her finger in a moment of thought. "It burdens me to say I have not the numbers required to aid her at my disposal," Katinee turned to her servant. She opened her mouth, and the servant fed her wild grapes. *Heartless.*

"You must send aid to your sister. Abandoning your own blood? How can you leave her to fend for herself?" Isabel stepped forward.

Katinee's gaze darted towards Isabel, her tone rising slightly. "There is nothing which I must do. Blood or no blood, the men and resources are currently not at my disposal. I know you are no cartographer, but any simple soul would know the next line of defense is Hillfrey. A word of advice: it is unbecoming to see conceited children in court," she leaned forward. Isabel's blood boiled as Katinee persisted, "Will that be all, Isabel?"

"That would be all, Katinee. If you will excuse us," Lady Isabel was turning when the woman called her. Standing still, Isabel eyed Katinee over her shoulder.

"Though I cannot provide support to my sister, Lady Isabel, I have accommodations for you and your retinue. It is unjust for even conceited children to sleep amongst serfs. Make use of them as needed and consider yourselves welcome to Hillfrey. And if you would be so kind, can you invite Henry into my hall upon your departure?

"Your generosity is most appreciated, Lady Katinee," Isabel turned and left, Lucia closely behind her. "How can she not help her sister? I would aid you if you were in such a dire circumstance," she murmured without glancing at her sister. "Would you not do the same?"

"Certainly," Lucia answered instinctively, Faylinn and the men merging with them at the doors as they swung open. "Henry, Lady Katinee requests your presence," she said, and Henry nodded.

Settled within the castle, the men went out to the town to resupply for future trips. They were to sell their loot and be ready to move once Isabel instructed, for she was not to sit idle while innocent people died once more. On a gloomy afternoon, she sat on her bed while the sky's darkness crept into her chamber.

What should we do? Gather an army? Retake Rivetion? Return to Oakheart? Katinee says all that remains is ash. If she is correct about the party who attacked us not being barbarians, then who did? Why did they attack us? They called for the Valenour. Who are the Valenour? Perhaps I should send a scouting party. Is it truly worth our time? What of Mother? Father? We cannot live in Hillfrey all our lives. We must move. But where?

A loud rap snapped her thoughts, stirring her attention towards the door.

"Enter," she said. Odo made his way inside.

"What is it, Odo?"

"How are you fairing?" he sat on a wooden chair by the table next to the window.

"Do you want the honest response or the ladylike one?"

"I am here to aid you, My Lady. What burdens you?" he watched her intently.

"I just cannot imagine how she will not assist her family. I will not stand idle for it. Can you recruit more men?"

"More men? More men will not suffice to recapture Rivetion."

"To save Lady Cicely, we will need numbers."

"Indeed, yet it will require more than numbers. You will require a true army. May I ask, are you ready to lead these men?" Odo seemed hesitant with his question, staring at the young noble as her brows furrowed.

"Why would I not?" she crossed her arms, her gaze fixed on him.

"You cannot bear killing a man," and Isabel winced slightly as if his words had poked at a painful wound within her that had yet to heal. "Forgive me, My Lady. When you lead men, they will bring victory with the strike of their sword, but many will not see the next dawn. My question is, are you ready to lead men and watch them perish?"

The question felt like a warhorse charging into her chest, his dagger jabbing deeper into her wound. Isabel gulped, clearing her throat to reply to such an inquiry. "You speak truly, Odo. I am yet to be ready. With time, when we have our men, I will be certain to be. *You* will make certain I am."

"Very well. I will prepare you as best I can." Odo rose from his chair, wiping his leather armor. "What you did today was brave."

"And what would that be?"

"You faced one of the most feared women in the kingdom and decided to be a noblewoman by staying within her castle. Yet now you are in the wolf's den. Exercise caution."

"I will."

Odo nodded and opened the door, ready to exit, when Isabel called him back. "Odo."

"My Lady?"

"Thank you," and Odo bowed lightly, abandoning the chambers.

Isabel watched from her bed as the door closed, the chest on the other side of the chamber calling to her just as it called her sister. The grime had appeared to fall with their travels, its designs reflecting the candle's light.

Thoughts of Lucia touching the dragon egg and her subsequent expulsion flooded her mind. The dragon had been quiet, not stirring within the chest and garnering attention to itself. Unsurprisingly, such a feat had come about even for an untrained beast. The chest seemed to beckon to her once more, the idea of the dragon wanting space coming to her mind.

How odd. The chest was unlocked. Isabel sat before it. She opened the lid and peeked inside it. The dragon was nowhere to be found. Lucia undoubtedly took it, for she could not resist the allure of the untamed creature.

The chest, nevertheless, was not empty. Inside lay a pair of eggs, unscathed by humanity. The eggs seemed to urge her to lay her hands upon them. She read the inscriptions or pretended to do so, for the past days had not allowed her the opportunity to learn how to decipher them. Curiosity placed a quill pen in Isabel's hand, and soon ink stained the parchment her sister had left on the table.

Her writing lessons lessened with her coming of age when she began to spend a great time in the woods. Isabel's hand was not as steady as her sister's, and it took her a couple of strokes to get the inscriptions onto the parchment. She folded the writing and hid it within her clothing.

The chest called to her once more, and she could not help but watch the jade-scaly egg at the center watching her. She believed she could hear its whispers screaming for her.

Her hand reached for the plea for help, hoping to aid the whispers in their call for freedom. Isabel touched the egg, but assisted it she had not. Whispers turned to deafening screams. The egg's scales hardened, becoming tougher than any metal or diamond. Its color shifted into deep ebony as if the shadows had now enveloped the life within it.

"What have I done?" The egg went silent, no longer calling her. Isabel withdrew, reluctant to touch the other egg, fearing it might suffer a similar fate.

Her touch would not bring it to life, and unlike her sister, it did not appear as if she had the gift to allow such dangerous creatures to hatch into the world.

"I killed it," she whispered to herself.

Isabel closed the lid, walking away from the chest and pressing her back hard against the wall. The thoughts of the man she had killed were now replaced by the creature inside, either withering away or trapped inside its egg for all eternity. To kill a guilty man was one matter, but a vulnerable, unborn creature… that was just beyond cruelty.

The world of dragons that existed centuries ago had ended, with their species considered extinct. After the passing of such time, it became evident they had not yet vanished entirely. There was hope for their kind, except when brought upon the hands of Isabel. Perhaps it was for the best, for the destruction wrought by dragons centuries ago had been immense.

Mankind had pitted these animals against each other, turning them hostile toward their race. A predisposition for destruction did not mar their legacy; rather, it had been spread upon the frescoes of history by man's ability to tame them and exploit them for their vile purposes.

"It is for the best," she interlaced her clammy fingers.

The door swung open, and Isabel leapt backwards, but the wall held her from going any further. She yelled, "I killed it." Her sister stared at her wide-eyed while closing the door behind her.

"What did you kill?"

"I killed it. The dragon, I killed it."

J.C. Rose

CHAPTER 19: ILLEGAL LANGUAGES

Isabel and Lucia strolled down the dusty city streets, rain unseen upon them for months. Traders and serfs congregated to sell their goods as the harvest season approached, their purses growing heavier with each transaction. Enrichment came only for the traders, however, for the serfs spent every coin on necessities needed for their daily existence.

"Do not believe it to have perished," Lucia said, glancing at her sister.

"You need not tell my burdens to the world. Speak more softly, and let us avoid the spread of rumors." Lucia's eyes widened as she stepped back from Isabel.

"I am merely trying to help. You have worried dearly since you last saw it."

Isabel shook her head. "Forgive me. The strain of the past days must be taking a toll on me. I ought to calm myself," Isabel said.

The pair joined Beavis and Maple in the market. Maple overheard her while they were approaching, for she quickly said, "I know just the remedy for your ailment," and she turned to the merchant.

"Beavis, are you aware of where I may find a scribe?" Isabel recalled the inscriptions on the parchment she had inscribed earlier in the day.

"Aye. Further down the road, a book is drawn on one of its signs outside," Beavis answered. "Are you a literacy enthusiast?"

"Not quite. I was merely hoping to discuss a translation. Thank you."

"Oh. Certainly cannot help you there. The art of writing was not a privilege my family had the pleasure of indulging in," he shook his head. "Nevertheless, strength is all we needed."

"I can teach you to read if you ever find yourself dawdling about with nothing to do," Lucia interjected, glancing briefly at Beavis. He returned her a quick nod with a smile. Isabel always admired how her sister was prepared to aid and educate others.

Isabel turned, reaching for her coins to pay for the remedy. Crashing onto a plump body, she nearly dropped the pouch Fulk had handed her at the tavern. The man wobbled, regained his balance, then knelt to gather the pouch he dropped, its contents now spilt. Isabel crouched beside him, assisting the man with his troubles.

"Forgive me, My Lady."

"Do not burden yourself," she handed him a ring and necklace from the ground.

"Forgive me," he repeated. He looked up, meeting her gaze, Isabel cocking an eyebrow as the man smiled and continued, "For not thanking you after saving our lives outside the city."

Isabel stared at the man in silence before replying. "It would have been dishonorable to stand idly by while those bandits took your life."

"Few nobles would risk their lives for us common folk," he peeked in the castle's direction. Isabel nodded, for she understood not all nobles were created equal. Her father had always been one to help his subjects, and though it might not be a universally held belief to all those higher in the hierarchy, it was a trait that ran deep in her family's veins.

Isabel reached for an emerald that fit snuggly in her hand, averting her gaze from the castle and the thoughts of Katinee's denial to assist her sister. "Wow, it is beautiful," she watched the gemstone, wanting to keep it forever before handing it to the man.

"It is a fortunate one, for emeralds, though strong, easily chip, and that one remains intact," the man scrutinized it in his palm. "Here, a token of our encounter."

Isabel's eyes widened. "I could certainly not. It is a costly gem. I will ruin your business."

"If not for you, there would be no business to run now. The emerald stone and your dress are one and alike, harmonizing beautifully."

"Now, are those not the words of a suitor?" Isabel said, raising her eyebrows. The plump man's face went pale at her inquiry. "I am jesting with you," she laughed, "I will forever cherish this gift."

"Nearly gave me a fright. My wife would have my throat at the thought of me flattering a woman out on the market."

"Your wife is fortunate to have a kind man like yourself." Isabel admired the gem momentarily before looking at the merchant. "I must take my leave. I did not catch your name."

"Bokli, My Lady."

"Lady Isabel. It was a pleasure making your acquaintance. Your kindness will not be easily forgotten," and the two were on their way.

Lucia and Maple were chattering, their gazes darting at a nobleman on the opposite side of the market. Beavis lagged not far behind, waiting for Isabel. Joining him, she handed Beavis her newly acquired gem.

"A beautiful stone, M'lady. What is the purpose of this?"

"My family heirloom sword, I noticed it has a slot for a gem on its pommel. Is it possible to fit this gem in it?"

"Hmm. It may be a feasible task. I will attempt to place it at the forge," Beavis said as he grasped the gem and departed.

Isabel joined her sister and Maple, the pair chattering away as they observed the man they had been watching earlier. He was a fair-skinned man, his straight ashen hair resembling that of Layne's. The young man wore an emerald surcoat, a gambeson of matching color underneath it. With hair and family colors like those, Isabel recognized him instantly. He noticed the ladies watching him, and without hesitation, he approached them.

"Greetings, fair lady," he directed himself towards Lucia. "The name is Daeron LaFlamme." *The King's Son. Here in Hillfrey? Has he heard of the battle in Rivetion? He seems so calm. It is improbable. However, royals and nobles are always taught to remain calm even in dire situations.* Isabel watched closely as the guards stood firmly by his side, prepared to interject if any assailant dared to strike the King's son.

"A pleasure, Your Royal Highness. I am Lucia Beaumont," and Daeron took her hand, planting a kiss upon it, Lucia's cheeks becoming ripe as tomatoes. "This is my sister Lady Isabel Beaumont and-"

"Maple," he finished her sentence. "A noble servant of my uncle's wife, Cicely." He turned to her, "How have you come to serve the Beaumont sisters? I always believed you were treated fairly in Rivetion." Nevertheless, he did not wait for an answer, his attention returning to the sisters. "The Beaumont sisters. I see why your father has you hidden away from the world," he addressed both, yet his eyes remained fixed on Lucia.

"Your Royal Highness, what brings you to Hillfrey?" Isabel interjected.

"Please, call me Daeron."

"King Ulron's son should not be called upon merely by his name," Isabel added.

Daeron nodded, and after pausing slightly in contemplation, he added, "Agreed. Lord Daeron will suffice." Without dwelling on it further, he continued. "Now, on behalf of your previous inquiry, it is the beauty of Hillfrey that lures me to it! Is this place just not marvelous?" the three women watched him, perplexed, their gazes shifting back and forth between each other. The city was far from marvelous, and here he stood admiring the nonexistent. He laughed and said, "It was a mere jest. I am here on account of my father. I was sent to meet with Lady Katinee."

"Does that imply we will see you for the evening meal?" Lucia asked, and if her cheeks had not betrayed her, her eyes now certainly did. They shined more than she had ever seen them. Isabel knew the years of being locked within their estate diminished their encounter with men. Still, she would have not imagined her sister bewitched so swiftly by the King's son.

Daeron looked at Lucia, "It appears the evening meal will not be dull after all." The bells rang, his words being drowned by their incessant tintinnabulation. "I must be on my way, Katinee awaits. I hope to see you throughout the castle, ladies. Good day," he bowed, the ladies curtsying him. As he left with his guards flanking him, a servant appeared from the crowd and scurried after the group.

"We should go with Daeron," Lucia swiveled to meet her sister and Maple.

"M'lady, we are not yet done with our daily tasks at the market," Maple began.

"Lucia, you will see him soon enough. You must calm yourself, or your eagerness might not please the Daeron," Isabel glanced and noticed a book sign in the distance. "I will go to the bookshop. Go with Maple to the castle once you are done. I will join you for our meal."

Maple continued assessing the market while Isabel held Lucia back. "What have you done with the dragon?"

"It is safe."

"Where is it?"

Lucia opened her robe, the little creature clinging to her clothes. It had doubled in size since Isabel last laid eyes on it. Soon, its rapid growth would inhibit it from being stowed inside the chest.

"We must rid ourselves of it. It is growing too swiftly."

"We cannot. I will care for it."

"How will we be able to feed it when it grows?" Lucia gave her no answer. "It is too much of a burden. Do not be seen with it. I will see you at the castle."

The pair parted, and Isabel weaved her way through the crowd. She arrived at the nearly empty bookshop as the scribe scribbled away in a corner. Monasteries managed most books, and even she found it odd that Hillfrey would have a bookshop. A rare occurrence, she thought, for few people in the realm read.

Watching the scribe, she saw a mortar and pestle lying behind him, filled with charcoal, which he had ground to create his ink for inscribing the parchment that now lay sprawled on his table.

"Good evening, My Lady. How may I be of service?" he said without looking up from his work. "Are you searching for a compendium of poetry for yourself? Perhaps a book of the Ancestor's War exploits for your father or brother is the luxury you seek?" The lengthy-haired man had tucked his hair over his ear, continuing to write on the parchment while awaiting her reply.

"I do not seek to buy any books. Do you know how to read?"

He dropped his quill, his face bewildered while gazing at Isabel. "My Lady, it would be difficult for a scribe to write if he knew not how to read."

A flush of embarrassment overwhelmed her cheeks. "My inquiry was to be, what other languages are you well versed in?"

"Ah," he continued with his quill. "The common tongue, the ancient tongue, and a few of the outlying kingdom's tongues. Is there any that interests you?"

"I am not quite certain which tongue this may be," she pulled out the parchment concealed within her clothes. "I was hoping you might translate it," and she placed the parchment before the scribe.

The scribe's eyes grew wide, incoherent mumbles escaping as he searched for the words that fled his tongue. "This is an ancient and forbidden tongue. I fear I cannot translate it."

"Why not?" she reached for the parchment, hoping he would not seize it and report it to the authorities.

"I-I just cannot. You must leave. At once."

"Let me take a look," a masculine voice behind her called, the wooden floorboards groaning with the man's approach.

The scribe and Isabel turned towards the man, his robe concealing his violet cotehardie and lengthy tunic. His slick ebony hair framed a clean-shaven face, and his eye bore the mark of an old slash. He leaned onto a wooden stick, limping on his left leg and stabilizing his body upon the opposite leg.

"Lord Loup, having you in my bookshop is an honor. I did not mean to break the law. Forgive us, My Lord," the man stuttered, unable to find the words to continue. "She just barged on me-"

"I am not here to apprehend you," Lord Loup replied to the scribe, placing his hand gently yet firmly on the table. He turned deliberately towards Isabel. "I am Lord Terrowin Loup. Lady Isabel Beaumont, are you not?" Isabel was surprised he knew her name. As if he read her mind, he continued, "I saw you when you and your band of men left my sister's hall. What is that you have there?"

Isabel hesitated. *Why is it forbidden? Why is it so terrible to know this language?* His hand remaining outstretched, she surrendered to his request and handed him the parchment. He glanced it over and murmured to her:

By the touch of the first three siblings, the egg will commence its sizzling,

Through the failure of precise imprinting, the egg will hatch a sickling.

128

Let it bear the touch of the right master, to prevent further disaster,

As its shell begins to shatter, become its master, not its captor.

"Now that is poetic, would you not say?" Lord Terrowin returned the parchment to her, the scribe staring at him wide-eyed.

"How do you know how to read that?"

"My father was an academic. He taught me to read ancient scrolls, and I learned a variety of Ancient Script runes. Where did you acquire this?"

As she concealed the truth, Isabel's thoughts raced through different possibilities, saying, "A warrior had it stored in a satchel during the siege of Rivetion. I searched it after the man was killed, and I found this inscribed."

"It is quite fresh ink," the scribe noted. Isabel's eyes locked onto him, almost daring him to say more. He gulped. She could almost... "a couple days old, I would say," and he turned away, continuing to scribble away.

"You were at the battle of Rivetion? How did you manage to escape?" Lord Terrowin leaned against the scribe's table.

"Lady Cicely, your sister, I believe, aided us in escaping the city. I requested Lady Katinee to send troops to Rivetion, yet she did not have enough at her disposal."

"My sister can be quite protective of her people. She must fear the worst is coming for us if she cannot spare any men for Cicely." *If only that were true. Katinee does not seem to lose sleep over her subjects' welfare.* "I wish I could help," he looked down at his leg, "but my state is useless to me."

"You could convince Katinee," Isabel urged.

"My sister has the mind of a rock, unchanging and unable to see beyond what it desires."

"Not even for her family?"

"It goes beyond family, but it should be of no concern to you. If she said she could not spare the troops, you must take her word for it. As I said, she seeks to protect our city, for we are next in line in defense of our kingdom." Lord Terrowin turned and headed for the door. "I will see you through the castle, Lady Isabel," and he vanished from the bookshop, stomping with his departure Isabel's hopes of finding aid for Rivetion.

J.C. Rose

CHAPTER 20: TURMOILS OF WAR

A week passed, and Isabel's men grew restless, the local ale insufficient to maintain their spirits while waiting for their next travel. Fortunately, a clue on Cicely's youngest sister had been found amidst the inn's chatter, and the group had assembled to find the young lady per Odo's request. She could see his sense of duty, or more accurately, that of guilt in his words, making it evident how Odo believed he failed Seraphina and her family. Against her better wishes, Isabel gave in. However, the news of her last location was unsettling, for her location had been pinpointed towards the feared Hollow's Pass.

Isabel wished to continue their hunt for reinforcements and her family, but numerous enemy patrols had kept them locked away within the castle. Though their party had slightly increased in Hillfrey, she was uncertain if searching for Seraphina now was the best course of action.

The weather had turned chilly since their arrival at Hillfrey, and Isabel's dresses had soon returned to her dark breeches and loose overshirts. Over her attire, a heavy fur cloak now aided in maintaining her body's warmth, and a leather armor protected her from the dangers of her travels.

The men at the camp rested while Isabel finished her sparring lesson with Norman, a task he had decided would be best if they commenced with wooden swords. With the sudden temperature drop, their bodies failed to perspire while they trained.

"That will be all," Norman lowered his wooden sword, sitting over a log. "We must reserve our strength, for excess training could hinder us should we encounter any foes."

"I think that is just your age talking," Fulk said.

"I bet he could wipe your ugly arse even with his age overtaking him," Uthred elbowed Fulk, teasing him.

"You should listen to your friend. He speaks more sense than any words I have heard escaping your lips," Norman rubbed his weathered hands. "It would be inappropriate to teach a veteran soldier a lesson in melee combat."

"He certainly has you with that one," Uthred laughed.

"That is it, old man. Pick up your sword."

"No one will be fighting today," Robion rushed between the men. "Enemy patrols in the area have thinned in the last couple of days, but we must conserve our strengths. We never know when we can encounter one."

"Who made you the leader, *lord*?" Fulk could not contain himself.

"That is enough. As Norman said, we do not know what lies ahead, and we must maintain ourselves ready," Odo's order was sufficient to silence the men. Isabel could see it was not his words nor tone that silenced them, but instead, the high regards in which they held him.

I long for the day men will respect me as they respect Odo. Is it so difficult for men to push aside their pride and look up to a warrior woman? A future knight of the realm? I would not desire to be born a man, but it seems one must be one to receive their respect.

Leaning against a tree trunk, Isabel drank from the waterskin Maple handed her, the liquid sloshing through her throat like a springtime flood. Beavis joined the ladies, sitting across from them.

"M'lady, I have not forgotten. Your sword," and she took the sword wrapped in a blanket.

Unwrapping the blanket, the family heirloom sword was revealed. The bastard sword now included her emerald gem at its pommel, Isabel admiring the inscriptions she was unable to read along its blade. She slid her finger delicately over the edge, the sword so sharp that she nearly cut herself even with her light touch. Though its touch was cold, the sword warmed Isabel's body, for she knew the history and greatness it carried within it. Passed down for generations, only the greatest in her family had come to wield it.

"A sword fit for a warrior queen," Beavis admired it.

"I would never be queen. A warrior, nevertheless, that I strive to be," she rose and swung the sword through the air, feeling its perfect balance as it garnered a power of its own, seeking a fight without her intention.

"Now, this is excellent craftsmanship," Robion strolled over to admire the sword.

"Speaking of swords," Fulk turned towards Lunet, "How did you acquire such a sword? Were you not happy with your stick?"

Lunet rolled her eyes at Fulk. "I would not have imagined you being resentful over loot."

"Extremely unlikely," but their conversation was interrupted by Isabel's command after sheathing her sword.

"We ride," and the group mounted their horses, lining up and ready to depart once more on their journey.

Odo led the group, and Isabel fell back to speak with Beavis. "Thank you, Beavis. As Robion stated, the sword is of excellent craftsmanship."

"That is of no thanks to me. The sword had already been crafted. I merely restored it to its original form. Now, it must be tested to ensure it does not shatter into its original three pieces."

"I am certain it will not fail," Isabel nodded while making her way towards the front of the group.

Traversing the roads, the group remained close. Few travelers were encountered, the chilly weather keeping them at home by their families around the fireplace. Isabel thought of Lucia, who remained at the castle with Faylinn. She was certain they were huddled around a fireplace, Daeron nearby to flatter her with his words as he had done the past week. Isabel had closely watched them, and his intentions did not seem ill-mannered. Faylinn had told her that she would maintain a discreet watch over them, caring for Lucia as she had done since they first met.

It was not this which troubled her peace of mind. Instead, Katinee's final words before her departure continued to plague her: *A sister for a sister.* Indeed, it was her way of stating she would care for her sister while Isabel searched for Katinee's. Nevertheless, every time Katinee spoke or even looked at them, Isabel's stomach tightened. If she could care so little to help Cicely, why would she care for Lucia? Was it indeed because Isabel was on the hunt for Seraphina?

Pay no heed to it all now, Isabel. Katinee is a lady of the realm. She is a woman with power. She must rule with fear, lest she wishes to lose her seat of power. After all, how many women truly have power in this realm? It is all but a mask. Lucia is safer in Hillfrey than out on the roads plagued with barbarian armies. But the words continued to haunt Isabel. *Is it truly a mask?*

The group marched for hours, Isabel immersed in her thoughts when hoofbeats in the distance snapped her from her wandering mind. Her group rode over the hill, watching the battle that ensued.

A battle it no longer was, for one of the armies had already been crushed. The attacking army's cavalry overran them. The few surviving men attempted to escape into the woods, deep within Hollow's Pass.

The attackers showed no mercy, thrusting their weapons into the wounded and helpless who attempted to crawl away. Isabel saw the waving banners of the victorious forces, a rider leading the cavalry group. He retrieved a fallen banner from the field and tallied it to his collection, securing it to his horse's saddle.

Carts rolled into the field, men lobbing onto it the loot they had won. Over a thousand corpses littered the field, a field now irrigated by the blood of men. The remaining few fought tenaciously for their lives as the warriors surrounding them pressed relentlessly.

"They are part of the group who attacked Rivetion. We must help the men," Isabel pulled on the reins, prepared to lead her horse towards the executioners.

"I fear the time has passed for us to change the course of this battle. We must leave," Odo shook his head, turning his horse in the opposite direction.

"We cannot just let them die."

"My Lady, those men are already dead, and if we attempt to go down there, we will only be corpses amidst the ones already littering the ground."

"That is the barbarian dubbed Bannerlord," Merek rode to the hill. "His enemies' banners become his trophies. As you may very well see," he pointed while the horseman continued to retrieve banners.

"My Lady. You asked me to teach you to lead men and their lives. Men who you lead will die, yet their deaths must be meaningful. There is a difference between leading men into battle and leading them into certain death," Odo whispered to her.

"Oh, he has spotted us," Fulk aimed at Bannerlord, who was instructing his men.

Horsemen around Bannerlord galloped and then charged in their direction, their pace slackening once they ascended the hill. "M'lady? What is your order?" Fulk watched the men while retrieving his warhammer.

Isabel watched the cavalry, her men anxious while awaiting her orders. She watched the group of survivors around the battlefield, crawling and meeting their end. Gripping her horse's reins tightly and locking onto its mane, she held her breath. Odo's words ran through her mind, yet her need to save the souls from their suffering lingered like a foul taste on her tongue. Her decision was made, and hesitantly, she replied, "Let us go. Only death lurks here."

"As much as I want to fight, Isabel speaks reason," Uthred pulled the reins on his horse as the group galloped away. They bolted towards Hollow's Pass, where they would seek refuge and continue their quest for Cicely's sister. The cavalry charging up the hill reached the crest, but Isabel's party was already beyond them, approaching Hollow's Pass. Only the sane avoided the place, Bannerlord's men standing watch from the hill. *That battle would have been the end of us, but is Hollow's Pass not a similar, or better said, a crueler fate?*

Isabel's men entered the pass, ridding themselves of their pursuers. The valley was just as men mentioned it to be. It reeked of death and was barren of all life. No animals ran, no plants grew, and dead branches were all that remained. It was as if a thousand men and a thousand dragons fought in this valley, for its ashen dust and ebony ground were all that remained.

"I never believed myself to enter this place," Robion said while riding beside Isabel.

"I think he is frightened," Fulk said to Uthred.

"I would if I was at the lead. Back here, I can turn and scurry off if need be," Uthred answered.

"I believed you were brave men," Lunet laughed and rode past them. "I will allow you to have your escape route free. At the first sound, the two of you will flee with your tails between your legs," and Lunet left the two, riding until she reached Norman.

"Are you certain this is the last place she was seen?" Isabel inquired without turning her head.

"Aye. It is what the men at the inn reported," Odo kept his eyes on the path ahead.

A horse galloped in their direction from within the valley, fleeing while men shouted at it. Robion caught the horse's reins, the war horse rearing as he pulled on it. The group unsheathed their weapons and prepared for the potential danger lurking ahead. Their suppositions were unmet, and a potential threat appeared to be the least of their concerns.

Injured soldiers littered the ground before them, groaning as the few uninjured came to their aid. The wounded men caught sight of Isabel's party. Although they seemed weary from their previous battle, they unsheathed their weapons. The limited number of abled men stood to fight for survival, hoping to fend off the riders that located them.

"We are not in search of a skirmish. Whose men are you?" Odo yelled to the group.

"We are Lord Bullion's army. Who is inquiring?"

"It is Lord Odo. Where is Lord Bullion?"

One of the heavy knights came forward, his plated armor filled with dents. A gash on his arm tainted his chainmail, but he marched on, seemingly unbothered. "Lord Odo. Lord Bullion has been wounded. Come."

The group followed the knight, Isabel watching as men groaned in pain after their crushing defeat. Their bodies lacked limbs, had bleeding gashes, were missing eyes, and some were even pierced with arrows. Her men might have reached a similar fate if Odo had not been there to guide her. They might have even met their death, yet here they were, watching the turmoil of war, realizing there were fates similar to those of entering the Hollow's Pass.

CHAPTER 21: ACCRETON

Lord Bullion lay sprawled out on the ground, his body drenched in blood while he clutched his ribs tightly. His thin, filthy hair clung to his scalp, his face rough and littered with battle scars from his years as a warrior. A scruffy beard concealed the remainder of his face and scars, the man in the chainmail armor and gashed surcoat nearly unconscious.

"Odo," the man from the ground saw through slit eyes as Odo approached him. "You missed the festivities."

"Lord Benedict, old friend. If only I had arrived earlier to aid you."

"Do not lay the burden of this battle on yourself. We were meant to aid Layne when we encountered these men," he coughed, blood spilling from his wound while Isabel stood behind Odo watching. "Cicely dispatched a plea for aid, but it seems we were too late. The city has fallen."

"Maple," Isabel called. "Do you have any experience tending battle wounds?"

"Nay," Maple joined the lords. "I reckon one of Odo's men knows.

"Fulk saved a couple of men in our days," Odo added. Isabel called him over, the man approaching her. Isabel would have never considered him a field surgeon.

"May you tend to Lord Benedict Bullion here? If he will allow it."

"An old fool like me who is near his deathbed. I reckon it is not worthy of an attempt," Benedict coughed once more, his fingers drenched in blood.

"Fulk, attend the lord. He is delirious," Odo made way for him to kneel beside Benedict.

"There is a familiarity about you. You bear a striking resemblance to your mother. Lady Beaumont's daughter, are you not?" Benedict leaned forward to get a closer look. As Fulk looked into his ribs and applied pressure, Benedict groaned. Isabel saw as he stopped breathing momentarily, and when Fulk eased the force, he gasped.

"Remain still," Fulk pushed the man gently against the ground. "You will merely aggravate your injury."

"She is indeed Lady Isabel Beaumont, Benedict," Odo stepped aside for the injured man to inspect Isabel.

"Indeed. I have not been mistaken," and the man stared into the sky when Fulk reapplied pressure, Maple handing him a clean cloth while he cleansed the wound.

Clouds merged above, blocking the sunlight from being cast into Hollow's Pass. They became heavy, carrying the tears of all the women and children whose fathers and brothers had been lost in the battle that ensued hours earlier. Droplets fell upon the barren valley, its water enough to wipe away the agony and renew the lives of those whose bodies were riddled with pain.

"Water? In Hollow's Pass?" the plated knight gazed at the sky, lifting his visor to feel it drop on his face. "Muster what you can," he said to the men around him. "We will use it to tend our wounded for the night."

"Norman," Isabel said, Norman walking towards her, leading his horse by his side. "Is Accreton able to fit the men we have here?"

Norman watched his surroundings, the men around them alleviated with the water dripping down their bodies and washing away the pain. "Accreton was one of the major cities in Emerion, if not the biggest. I have yet to visit it. If the structures are intact, they may serve a purpose and accommodate these men."

"Then we will ride ahead and inspect them." Isabel turned to Odo, "Will you join us?"

"If it means sparing these men pain, then without hesitation. Let us ride."

"May I join you?" the knight stepped forward. "If it is to aid Lord Benedict, I would like to be of assistance."

Odo and Isabel looked at each other. "Any abled man would be of aid."

"If I may, I will remain here to aid Benedict back to health with Fulk," Maple replied without turning while tending Benedict's wounds. Isabel agreed, and Maple wrapped Benedict's ribs with a cloth while Fulk pulled him forward.

The group mounted their horses, riding through Hollow's Pass, the rain beating against their clothes. Before long, they were completely drenched, and the water-soaked clothing weighed them down. Isabel was certain their movements would be hindered should they encounter enemies. With the heavy rain obstructing their line of sight, the path ahead was unclear while they galloped through the barren land.

"Henry," Isabel called him over, Henry riding towards the party's front.

"You summoned me?"

"Henry, how swift is your steed?"

"Swift to compete with the best of stallions."

"I will need you to scout ahead. If you see anyone, you must remain unseen."

"Aye," and Henry bolted in his steed, disappearing from their line of sight while the rains continued to pour about.

The day darkened, Isabel quivering, her body shaking like a wet hound as it hides under a canopy to conceal itself from the rains. Without cover from the rain, their unrelenting purpose was to locate Accreton and seek its shelter swiftly. *How far is Accreton?*

As they continued, the rains began to subside, the shadowy silhouette of Accreton rising on the horizon. A vast field lay between them and the city, mountain ranges surrounding the area on three sides while a river flanked its remaining side. The mountain ranges were lined with trees, abundant resources for an isolated city. Accreton stood on the far end of the plains, beyond the river, which created a natural barrier to protect it from invaders.

Accreton must have been unconquerable, surrounded by mountains, rivers, and Hollow's Pass. Just having a dragon swoop from above could decimate an entire army, leaving them nowhere to flee.

The keep rose above the city, reaching towards the sky from its perch on the hill, three towers stretching like fingers hoping to catch the heavens. The city was as prominent as Norman had described it, for it spread far and wide, its massive walls guarding it from any opponent who dared attack it. Towers were evenly spaced throughout, and a network of vast bridges interconnected the city like a maze as it spread through the plains and ascended the slopes of the mountains.

The passing of time had turned the city into one with nature, for creeping vines had overcome it, scaling its walls. Towers and walls were beginning to erode, a few towers beginning to crumble. Most of the structures remained intact, the masons who had brought about its construction taking into calculation the weather and the city's enemies. To Isabel, it was impressive how such a structure had become one with the land around it and how it remained a separate entity entirely. *Is this what will become of Oakheart if we never return?*

Henry bolted towards them, his horse coming to a halt before Isabel. "As far as I could see, the castle is occupied with at least forty men."

"Did you see any prisoners?"

"Aye. There are various prisoners. They hang from gibbets, yet I failed to locate a lady."

"The rains will allow us to enter undetected," the knight said, watching the portcullis. "Is there a section of the wall that has been weathered down?"

"I noticed an area where we may climb," Henry aimed his horse in the direction he had spotted.

"Then that is our entry point," the knight said.

"The area is overwhelmed with guards in that area. We will require a distraction," Henry pointed to the area filled with the most men.

"They have double our numbers," Isabel murmured to herself, then turned to the men. "If we can distract them, as Henry mentioned, we may find our way into the castle. Henry, you must call them at the portcullis while we clamber around."

"*I* will be the distraction?" Henry's face paled.

"The boy will be scurrying away from there before we can cross over," Uthred cackled.

"I may believe that if it were you riding to the gate," Lunet glanced at Uthred.

"We will need an archer to take down the enemy before we reach the walls," the knight with the great helm turned to Isabel.

"I will make it rain arrows upon them." She removed her bow from her horse, swinging it around her body.

"A few extra arrows. In case you require them, Lady Isabel." The knight with the great helm removed a heater shield from his horse. He plucked the arrows that had penetrated it, giving Isabel the functional arrows.

"Thank you-"

"Sir Bryce."

The plan was set in motion, the party positioning themselves against the walls, awaiting the signal of Henry charging to the gate. The muffled hoofbeats splashed over a puddle as the rains continued to beat. Isabel's back was firmly pressed against the wall as she observed Henry ride towards the main gate. Henry halted his horse, calling to the men stationed on the battlements, "Hey! Who is in charge here?"

A man over the battlements met him, the guards turning in his direction. "Who do you think you are?"

"I just want you to return the woman you stole."

"Stole a woman? We have no woman here, only smelly goats and you," the men by the battlements roared in laughter, most abandoning their posts near the crumbling wall.

Isabel readied her arrow, quickly stepping back from the wall and pivoting towards it while Henry distracted the men. She aimed her arrow and let it loose. Instantly, she knocked one of the men from the wall. Uthred and Merek started the climb with the group of men Odo had managed to hire at the local Hillfrey inn.

Uthred hurled his axe towards one of the guards while Merek stabbed one of them through the neck. As they kept watch, the rest of the group crossed behind them. They heaved the lifeless bodies over the battlements to avoid detection. Uthred and Merek stayed vigilant, awaiting Isabel's signal to launch their assault.

Isabel was joined by Robion and Odo, the party counting the men in the streets. Henry's distraction had managed to amass them all to the portcullis, their backs to Isabel and her men. Realizing no men were behind them, she raised her sword, signaling the attack to begin.

Isabel's sword met its first opponent, the first test of its freshly mended steel. Her party closed the distance between the enemy, catching the first group by surprise. At the same time, Uthred and Merek ran the battlements, executing any man who stood in their path.

She parried the first blow deftly and followed with a swing aimed at the man's legs, but he skillfully countered her strike. Isabel quickly adjusted and swung toward his vulnerable side, her sword slicing through his leather armor and cutting into his shoulder, causing the man to cry out in pain. It was clear that Norman's lessons had proven effective.

While the fighting ensued amongst the groups, a man from an outlying tower spotted the skirmish. He rang the bell, its tintinnabulation echoing across the desolate city. A second gate's chains began to rise, the men lifting the bridge to prevent Isabel's party from charging into the city's interior. Merek and Uthred struggled to lower the other bridge to allow Henry to enter the city.

Isabel watched helplessly while the bridge rose, her mind brimming with ideas that Odo would disapprove of. Her moment was now, and Isabel reacted accordingly. Sheathing her sword and retaking her bow, she charged towards the bridge. The arrow release was executed perfectly. Isabel's arrow struck the torso of one of the men raising the bridge, bringing its close to a halt. The chains slackened, followed by the clanging of metal. Isabel jumped onto the rising bridge and slid down to the other side.

Only one man awaited her on the opposite side, Isabel battling him while watching a man run with a woman in a mud-filled crimson dress. They were going up the hill to the keep's courtyard when Isabel was detained by the man she was fighting. The man became Isabel's sword's next victim before she swiveled to strike a man approaching from behind.

Her downward strike was met by a man snatching her wrist, her eyes locking with him. She recognized them instantly. Robion. "That was not a clever decision," he said, releasing her hand.

"And yet here you are, chasing after me," she smiled and turned toward the hill. "Follow me. I believe I found Cicely's sister."

The two arrived at the castle's courtyard, a monumental church standing near a collapsed drawbridge, its doorway guarded by a pair of statue knights. Isabel and Robion bolted towards the church. The rain continued to pour around them, the grip on their swords slipping.

Inside the church, the heavily armored bandit leader held the woman in the crimson dress, a pair of men at his side. "Kill them," he ordered, and the two men charged at them. Isabel disposed of her attacker swiftly while Robion handled the more aggressive attacker. Free of her opponent, she charged toward the bandit leader, who, upon seeing her rush in his direction, threw down the woman in the crimson dress.

He sent his sword down towards Isabel's head, and she blocked it, yet she sensed his superior strength. Every strike she parried exhausted her further. She was unprepared for an opponent as powerful as he was. Isabel grew weary, her parries mistimed, and she stumbled as the man delivered an elbow to her face. Falling on the church floor, her sword slipped away as she struggled to grasp the wet grip.

The man loomed over her. He was ready to execute her, Isabel clenching her jaw. His sword came down, Isabel rolling at the last instance. She seized her dagger and cut the man's leg, weakening his stance. The man plummeted to the ground, groaning in pain. Wounded, he attempted to strike Isabel with his sword. But the time to strike back had passed. Isabel's sword was pressed against his throat. Robion stepped onto his hand, restricting the man from retaliating.

A group of bandits burst into the church, tipping the balance of the fight. "Finish them," the leader screamed from the ground. The bandits rushed towards Isabel and her companions, but they stopped abruptly when the door swung open once more. Odo had arrived with the remainder of the group, the turn of events leaving the bandits outnumbered.

"We can spare your lives," Sir Bryce said, "Or if you attack the lady, you can meet your graves." His words carried weight, and the bandits dropped their swords, realizing that a fight was a feeble attempt at victory. "Wise."

The men seized the bandit leader and the remainder of his men, Isabel and Robion swiveling to meet the woman they had liberated.

"May I know the names of my heroes?" the young woman wiped her crimson dress.

"I am Lady Isabel. This is Lord Robion. You must be-"

The woman interrupted her, "I am Lady Seraphina Loup. The honor is yours."

CHAPTER 22: A CASTLE'S SECRETS

"Lady Seraphina should not be a burden to you," the pale, scraggy man said.

"Isabel is on her way to find her. My sister learned the family secret my father had taken to his grave, Nalthok." Katinee paced around the chamber, the fire crackling in the fireplace while the rain outside beat against the stone walls.

"Do you think she would come to mention such a fact?" Nalthok fiddled with his hands.

"I will not wait to have her reveal her knowledge to the entire kingdom." Katinee stared into the fire, its resemblance burning within her eyes. "It is not a fact if none learn of it."

"What if they do not track her to the precise location?"

"She sniffs like a hound. Isabel will find my sister. It is not a matter of if, but when." Lady Katinee continued sending her vivid imagination of probable situations into the fire before her, hoping to find the right solution to incinerate her crisis.

"You cannot be certain she will speak," Nalthok sat on the wooden chair with carefully carved wolves upon their arms.

"Whose advisor are you?" she spun towards him, nearly causing him to climb over the chair and seek shelter on the other side.

"You, My Lady, you. I would serve no other," he gripped the chair's arms as if he sought moral support.

"Another word favoring my sister, and these flames will be the last sight you behold," Katinee turned her back to the scraggy man.

"She has a murky past. Your sister is not as pure as she seems," Nalthok interlaced his fingers mischievously.

Katinee swiveled on her heel, a smirk creeping slowly. "You may still serve a purpose to me after all, Nalthok," her voice softened, "you may still serve after all."

Lucia had come across the scheming voices in the passageway, her ear pressed against the door, listening to the secrets known only to those who lurked behind it. Though the secrets had not been divulged, she was more aware of the situations roaming through the eerie castle of Hillfrey and the potential danger her sister could soon come to be in.

"Eavesdropping is not taken to kindly," Lord Daeron crept up from behind, her heart leaping into her throat.

"You gave me a fright, Lord Daeron. I had not expected to see you until our meal," she turned to meet him.

"Now you have the advantage to see me before it. I promise not to tell of your mischievous ways," and he winked at her. "You look lovely this evening."

Lucia's cheeks flushed, snatching the attention of the dress complimenting her eyes. It was of the finest silk, bought in the ladies' market trip. She beamed at Daeron, "Thank you."

"Would you like to go on an excursion around the castle with me before our meal?"

"A lovely idea," and the two went through the gloomy castle, exploring while sharing stories.

"That was a dangerous deed you went about," Odo joined Isabel. Shortly after, the party set camp within the castle's courtyard, for the castle was nearly uninhabitable. Above them, the bandits replaced the prisoners in the gibbets. Bryce was right. They were spared but not allowed to roam freely.

"If not for that, Lady Seraphina may have very well not been by our side now," Isabel glanced at the courtyard, the azure and ruby banners filthy on the ground while the rains buried them with dirt.

"I am merely worried for your wellbeing, Lady Isabel. Nothing more."

"Thank you, Odo, yet I need not be saved," Odo sighed at her words, but he nodded in acknowledgement. "Where is Bryce?"

"He rode out in search of Benedict and the remainder of their men."

"Did any of our men accompany him?"

"No, My Lady."

"Did we lose any men in the skirmish?"

"I fear only two of the newly recruited men lost their lives, and one was severely wounded."

The first two lost under her command. It was merely two, but two lives fighting for their cause. "Odo, I do not have sufficient coin to continue maintaining such a party."

"I understand. Do not fret. It was for my cause in search of Seraphina that they were hired. I will oversee their wages for your protection."

"When we come upon more coin, I will make certain to return the favor," Isabel said. He was going to refuse, but Isabel shook her head before he could continue. "I insist. You have done much for our family." Then, gazing at the city once more, she said, "Have five of our men search for carts in the city to carry Benedict's wounded men. I want three men rotating on the inner walls watching, rotating them every two hours. Have them drop the closest portcullis to the castle. That will be our defensive perimeter."

"I will make certain your command is seen through. I must say, your knowledge of defensive command is brilliant."

"A good master taught me well during my stay in Rivetion," and Odo smiled at her.

"I see. Rest, you deserve it. You led well today," and Odo departed in search of the men.

The doors into the great hall were slightly open. Isabel entered, setting foot inside her ancestors' castle for the first time. If the exterior was magnificent, the interior would leave her imagination searching for adequate words to describe it.

Upon entry, the great hall stretched far and wide, an eerie feeling overcoming Isabel as long shadows were cast along its length, the hairs on her nape rising. A pair of statues flanked the entrance, much like the guardians of the church. The statues portrayed a man and a woman, standing firmly with their swords pointed downwards, hands gripping the pommels, and shields resting against their legs."

To her right side, filthy windows lay shrouded beneath the encroaching wilderness outside the castle walls, the light entering limited. The rain intensified, battering the glass with unwavering determination, streaks of lightning torturing the mountainside. To the left, an expansive wall with tattered banners lined down its length carried a coat of arms unknown to Isabel. Frescoes behind the banners held the secrets of a bygone era, a story Isabel was unable to interpret. Layers of cobwebs veiled the story of her past, keeping the story out of reach, a story she desired to learn.

Isabel traversed the heart of the hall, envisioning it bustling with people seeking the castle's lord. The hall's center had been seized by the dust and greenery that entered through the windows like a plague upon the stone floor. Isabel stepped over the vines, hoping to not become entangled by their ongoing growth.

At the far end of the hall before the grand stairs, two spiked braziers had lost the flame that once burned within them, the fire of Accreton, the fire of life. Beyond, elevated high above the stairs and sheltered beneath a majestic thirty-foot archway, loomed an elaborate throne, silently observing the void of the hall. Even though it stood there, it felt like an uninvited guest in its own hall.

Isabel walked up the stairs, the coat of arms banners hanging behind the throne, the top of the dragon-scale wall crumbling. The quartered ruby and azure coat of arms was visible. At its center, at the plateau's crest, a dragon released a mighty blaze from its agape maw, unknown inscriptions of the forbidden language adorning the bottom. It was the only banner that remained untattered, unharmed by the passing of time or the unknown history to Isabel. *This is not our family coat of arms. Did another family live here after ours? Were the Beaumonts driven out of Accreton?*

Beneath the banners, a pair of statues guarded the throne. Clad in plate armor with great helms, they carried a pair of lances and bore sturdy heater shields, the shields bearing the same dragon as the banner. On opposite shoulders, the pair of guards proudly displayed a dragon each, reminding Isabel of the snowy creature her sister would not abandon.

The throne stood before her, its arms fashioned in the semblance of dragon's legs, while its backrest bore scales reminiscent of the creature. At its apex, a fearsome dragon skull, jaws agape, presided in solemn grandeur. Isabel imagined once upon a time it must have blown fire into the now nonexistent crowd, and its flame, like the life around it, extinguished. Dust and webs had conquered the chair, preserving the seat and ruling over the vast emptiness of the great hall. The elaborate wooden throne's azure paint had cracked with the years left in solitude. *Does it truly belong here?* Though intricately carved, the throne did not seem as lavish as the castle's walls, frescoes, and glass.

Isabel wiped her hand over the throne, the dust and her becoming one. She turned and sat gently upon it, an uncomfortable throne nonetheless. The past rulers on this throne would have no hassle remaining awake in moments of dullness within the great hall, alertness their ally when their foes would enter to exchange courtesies or stories of the vast unknown.

The expanse of the great hall could be seen clearly from where she sat. Isabel envisioned grand feasts, the melody of dancers and minstrels filling the air, diplomats locked in heated debates over matters of alliances and war. Those days had long since faded into the annals of history. Nevertheless, this was not Accreton's last chapter. *One final battle, or treason, poison perhaps, that is what must have occurred here in Accreton's final days. Why else abandon a place like this? What happened? Is there justice to be found on their end? Who, or what, did this?*

The thoughts of her family's past drove Isabel to seek answers, compelling her to rise from the throne and continue exploring the castle. A concealed archway emerged behind the throne, and Isabel was prepared to vanish into its obscurity when a voice startled her.

"Mind if I join you?" she swiveled to meet the man in the cobalt robe.

"That would not be an intrusion, Norman," and he carried the lit torch beside her.

The adjoining passageway was filled with puddles, water trickling and seeping from the roof and walls. Numerous chains and portcullis lined the passageway, areas of the roof crumbling. Unlit torches were spread evenly along the walls, and Norman handed Isabel the torch.

"It was a custom for a Beaumont to light Accreton when it was first inhabited."

"Thank you," and Isabel lit the torches as they traversed through the passageway and into the adjoining room.

Broad columns adjoined by many arches split the room, the marble columns adorned with dragon carvings and depictions of the deities. At the far end, a rotunda with stained glass was crowned by a domed ceiling. Tapestries, once grand, hung from the ceiling, now tattered and frayed, their forms blending with the spider webs.

Within the dome, five statues graced their pedestals before the glass windows. Isabel whispered the names of the gods, "Aphrodicia, Phobedio, Vraedron, Enigma, and Malefic."

"This must be the worship room," Norman watched the statues, the figures wrapped in robes. Aphrodicia, however, stood proud, holding a vine of grapes, her body exposed for all to admire. With one of her hands resting on her hip and the other intertwined within her hair, all could see why she was the goddess of love and beauty. *The human figure has always been a focal point of worship for our people. If we neglect its care, we disrespect the sacred temple that the gods have bestowed upon us.* Phobecio, the god of fear, quivered at all that may strike him, yet he held tightly onto a dagger to stab away at fear and end it once and for all. Vraedron, god of life and war, was sought by his followers for his prophecies. He held a lyre, representing the arts of life for which people lived. *Enigma guides me. Perhaps Vraedron will guide my way in the battles to come. Would Enigma be furious if I sought his guidance?* Enigma was the god of reason and lost paths. She was the world's wisdom and held a flower in her hand, for the proper knowledge could help one grow into the future. The final god was Malefic, the god of death with a snake encircling his neck, carrying a golden spear for all those to fear or accept in their dying moments. *Long ago, did they worship them all equally, or would they choose one to guide most of their life as we do in Emerion?*

The pair proceeded down a second passageway, the path dry and in a better condition than the previous one. Windows lined one of the sides, permitting the entry of natural light into it for only one chandelier lit it throughout its darkest moments. The chandelier was positioned near one of the corners, where a dragon figurine rested on an altar adorned with countless candles. Carved onto the walls were dragons and riders, depicting stories of triumphs and the ultimate downfall of the dragons, who eventually met their demise after years of war.

On the opposing side of the glass windows, the walls were lined with an array of candles, their multitude so extensive that Isabel could not count them. Miniature dragon figurines were placed on niches along the wall, alternating between dragon bodies and carved human heads.

"It is The Hall of the Fallen Dragons," Norman watched in awe. "For every dragon and rider that has perished, a candle was lit in its remembrance."

A stairway descended at the passageway's center, the catacomb's entrance. Isabel led the way into the catacomb, yet Norman's feet behind her became silent. She turned, spotting the man as he shook his head.

"The catacomb is a sacred place for the Beaumonts. Until here my company, My Lady."

"Before I leave," Isabel looked up at him from the entrance to the catacombs, "how do you know so much of Accreton? It is so old, and none speak of it."

"Just because it is old does not imply it is forgotten," he said. "At times, that which is old is what brings the most intrigue," he looked into the flame burning in her torch, "though perhaps, at times, the past is best left forgotten." Isabel could see he was no longer talking about Accreton.

When his gaze drifted back in her direction, she replied, "Perhaps. Or perhaps, it is from the past that we learn of the present, or even of what is to come." Norman stayed looking at her blankly. "A story for another time," and he nodded, turning away as Isabel entered the catacombs.

Inside, the air was heavy, a damp smell spreading within the catacomb. Isabel ignited the torches mounted on the walls, their flames casting flickering light upon the three sarcophagi in the center of the catacomb. She approached them. The center sarcophagus bore a carving of a woman, while the other two depicted men. The inscriptions were illegible. Within the secluded chamber, Isabel felt a calm and deep connection to her history - the only family who were near her.

The silence within the catacomb and the crackling fire reminded her of her days at Oakheart beside the fireplace. Few were the moments when her family sat around the fireplace, yet they lingered in her mind as if she had lived them countless times. The chamber transported her through time to the past, the days when it was not necessary to flee to survive, where being home with her family and eating by the fire during winter was all the survival she required.

Her peace was short-lived, for rapid footsteps in The Hall of Fallen Dragons made her turn and leave to join the murmuring men.

"Isabel is in the catacomb. I cannot go in to tell her that this instant," Norman said.

Isabel reached the stairways and walked up, Henry and Norman turning towards her. "What has happened, Henry?"

Henry was pale, and she could see he was struggling to find the words to begin speaking, his gaze shifting from candle to candle.

"Speak, lad. Inform the lady of what has happened."

Henry snapped from his shocked estate, blurting helplessly, "It is Odo. He is dying."

CHAPTER 23: RUNNING BLOOD

"How did his health deteriorate so quickly?" Isabel inquired while watching Odo lying near the great hall's entrance.

"It appears he was injured during the battle," Robion demonstrated the gash on his leg, the injury plagued by a shadow spreading across it. "Necrosis. The weapon was poisoned."

"Do any of the prisoners have the remedy?"

"I fear not. We must return to Hillfrey for a healer. It is the closest one for us," Robion washed the wound.

"We will never reach the city promptly with this storm," Norman added, observing the water seeping into the great hall through the shattered glass windows.

Seraphina's eyes lit. "We may not need to stray so far."

Seraphina had a thin nose and almond eyes, a lively chestnut color that emitted energy to those who encircled her. Her wavy chestnut hair harmonized her eyes, the sapphire circlet and earrings situated gently upon her fair skin. A gold necklace and a sapphire ring added to her collection of jewels, her value soaring beyond her high status to the bandits who once captured her.

"What is your plan, My Lady?" Henry turned to her.

Isabel's gaze lingered on the wound, Odo's health deteriorating. The world had a wicked way of treating her, appearing to turn on her, for one life saved had meant the quick loss of another. Odo's eyes were closed, the poison spreading and sapping the life of Isabel's closest advisor. *Odo, you cannot die on me.*

"I think it is dangerous," Robion added. "Do I not speak the truth, Isabel?"

Isabel looked up at him, then Seraphina. "What did you have in mind?" she turned towards Seraphina, Odo's life resting on her hands.

"When the bandits captured me, they spoke of a woman near the mountainside. She is a herbalist and may have a cure."

"Under this storm? It is madness," Robion shook his head, his eyes wide as shields.

"If we do not act, Odo will succumb to the poison," Isabel spun towards Seraphina. "You say she is near?"

"Aye, I will guide you. I saw it while we passed."

"Then we must go before his state worsens," Isabel followed Seraphina.

Robion, hesitant upon their decision, pursued them. "I will join you."

Seraphina halted, swiveling towards him gracefully like royalty. *Did she grow up in the palace?* "I heard she does not take kindly to visitors. I am afraid I may only bring Isabel."

"What if you encounter more bandits along the way?"

"In this storm? Only a madman would ride into it for a pair of young ladies," Isabel winked. "All will be well, Robion," she said, touching his arm. Robion was hesitant, but after a pause, he took her hand gently and nodded. Isabel pursued Seraphina, the pair exiting the castle.

"She can care for herself," Odo grabbed his heel, awakening from his weakened state.

"I cannot leave her alone," Robion sat beside Odo.

"I am aware you care for her," Fulk added once the women exited the great hall," but if you may forgive me bluntness, I believe you were the madman she was talking about." Robion's head jerked back at the remark.

Lucia sat at the table beside Daeron, the two waiting for Katinee and the remaining nobles within the household. From the moment Daeron had snuck upon Lucia, they had remained together, conversing within the castle's passageways, speaking of pleasantries only nobles enjoyed. Faylinn entered the hall, joining them at the table while maintaining herself isolated so they could continue their banter. Daeron's gaze shifted towards Faylinn, and for a moment, Lucia believed his face twisted at her sudden appearance. Before she could analyze it, his attention had returned to her, and his honeyed words had all but caused her to push the thoughts to the back of her mind.

Katinee entered the hall, followed by Nalthok, and soon after, her brother. As dinner progressed, Lucia's mind wandered off into the whispers of conspiracies she had heard within the castle's walls. Her curiosity longed for the details, why Katinee feared her sister's knowledge, and what it was their father had done.

"You did not answer my question Lucia," Lord Daeron said, enjoying the mutton placed before him while awaiting her answer.

"Forgive me, I did not mean to disregard your words. I was just plagued with sudden thoughts."

"I pray these thoughts concerned a particular lord of the realm," mischief spread upon his lips.

He had been bold, bold since his arrival, Lucia was most certain of that. Lucia, however, was not intimidated by a man's rank and spoke her thoughts freely, at times causing uneasiness within her mother.

"If I may be bold, not all my thoughts revolve around you," she lowered her voice, murmuring the ending, "At least not now."

"So I hold a place in your mind at times? Is that what you are murmuring?" he leaned closer to her.

"I must say, you are unrelenting in your search for my thoughts." Lucia leaned towards him, paused slightly, then retreated swiftly.

Lady Katinee watched over the rim of her goblet, irritation overflowing from her body and into the goblet as she nearly spilled it onto her clothes. She banged the goblet on the table, garnering the table's attention.

"It is the dinner's story time," she set her food on the table abruptly.

The group continued eating, waiting for Lady Katinee's story to commence. She sipped her wine, ensuring the attention was solely on her before she began.

"My father used to tell me this story when we were children. Ages ago, there was a serf's farm teeming with every animal you could imagine. It was a vast farm, brimming with happiness, the animals living about it roaming freely.

"One day, the rabbit was prowling about and spotted the wolf. This particular wolf was not wicked, for it never attacked the farm, restraining itself from entering its perimeter. The wolf and fox met as they casually did, sharing tales about the recent events in their lives.

"They kept to themselves, never meddling in the affairs of those within the farm. After all, what reason did they have to create any disturbance?

"Yet not all thought as they did. The day came when the rabbit stood upon the fence, prying with its large, thick ears upon the fox and wolf's conversation. The rabbit believed the fence would protect it, for the wolf never dared enter the farm.

"You see, the rabbit was mistaken, for though it listened with its large, thick ears, it did not spot the chickens watching it. Chickens, oh, how they enjoy chattering about all the animals on the farm. The chickens clucked so loud that the wolf overheard from the opposite side of the fence of the rabbit prying into its private affairs." Katinee's gaze moved steadily from guest to guest, watching their expressions intently before moving on to the next.

"The wolf was a friendly wolf, and it meant no one any harm. Nevertheless, the wolf despised prying ears, and the rabbit had pried far into her private life.

"The day came when the rabbit went to sleep blissfully with its large, thick ears. The chickens clucked their last cluck, and the sun on the horizon snuck. The night turned gloomy, the silence of night so vast, so great, the rabbit slept happily.

"But slept too happily it did, confident in its ears. Deep in the middle of the night, the rabbit was stirred awake, its ears perking up, searching for the sound echoing, disrupting the silence. Its eyes opened wide, and it realized the night was still dark. The rabbit was aware there was much time left for slumbering and should not be spent worrying," Katinee's gaze seemed to become fixed upon Lucia.

"Except she was misled, for the night had not truly been dark. The wolf's mouth had cast a shadow over her face. Before the rabbit could squeal, the rabbit was no more. In one swift swoop, the wolf devoured it for prying whence it should not," Katinee's gaze turned to meet Lucia's, her body frozen.

Lucia's heart raced at the words devoured, pondering at how Katinee must have overheard she eavesdropped. The one person who had caught her was Daeron. He had spent the evening with her. He did not leave her side once. She had not noticed any servants, Lucia's mind racing as she recalled the day's events, searching for an answer to her question.

A slow clap made Katinee turn her gaze. Her brother tilted his head and said, "Beautiful story, dear sister." Her lip curled slightly, and Lucia's tensed shoulders relaxed when the woman's threatening look was shifted elsewhere.

"A gloomy story," Faylinn added, "does not sound like a children's tale to me."

Katinee's gaze narrowed, focusing on Faylinn, "The world is not a joyful place. Children must be taught early on that it is cruel and not all stories have happy endings. A fable, or so the bards call it." Faylinn shrugged, Katinee sighing. "You would not understand." Smiling, she added, "That is all. Now, let us continue our meal."

The beating rain soaked Isabel's cloak, absorbing every drop of rain as if it were to live the remainder of its life in a desert. Seraphina's icy horse now bore a russet layer, the dirt that had splashed it on their ride stealing it of its majestic glimmer. The ladies dismounted, avoiding the mud puddles in hopes of not drowning within their endless pits.

A hut of various indiscernible animal skins hid within the trees at the mountain's base. The ladies entered, a warmth overcoming them as the fire flickered within its center, the flame luring Isabel. Dead ravens hung from wooden sticks forming the framework inside the hut. Various animal skulls littered the ground, several easily recognizable to Isabel, such as those of a cow and a horse, yet others remained mysterious to her eye. A woman with her back towards them stood by a pot, a strong scent radiating towards them. She removed a pair of raven feathers hung on a string and dropped them into the pot, the cloud of smoke rising and causing the hairs on Isabel's nape to rise.

"Lady Seraphina. You have arrived just as I envisioned," the frail voice said, the woman not turning to greet them. "You have brought a friend. *That* I had not foreseen."

The woman turned to meet them, her bony body cloaked by a shadowy robe. She had a crooked nose with a shadowy scar implanted upon it, her thin hairs attempting to leave her head in search of more fertile lands. Her eyes were cloudy, her gaze searching for the ladies as they were hesitant to close the distance.

"Do not fear. I will not curse you. Sit, you must be famished." The ladies hesitated, then sat.

"How do you know of my name?" Seraphina watched the boiling pot.

"I did not, yet here you have acknowledged my claim on a fortunate prediction," the old lady snickered, turning to the pot and stirring it. "What has brought you here?"

"We have a friend, and he is injured, poisoned. We were hoping you might have a remedy," Seraphina peeked into the pot.

"A friend of yours he is not," the old woman said to Seraphina while turning towards to Isabel, pointing her curved finger. "Would you illuminate my frail senses on behalf of his ailment?"

Isabel swallowed, the bony finger a nail away from touching her nose. She feared the woman's touch would curse her and twist her nose. "After he was cut, it spread quickly, like a plague. Like murky rivers flowing within his leg."

"Nekrotu Elvmen. That is the poison," the woman identified it without much thought. Searching the racks, she displaced the containers in search of the cure. Her crooked fingers reached for a russet vial, the frail woman returning to the girls.

"What is its value?" Isabel searched her coin pouch.

"It is free. A gift for your first visit."

"Are you certain?"

"If I may, I would like to know who you are. This will suffice as your payment."

"That would be all?" she looked at Seraphina, who merely shrugged. "I am Lady Isabel of House Beaumont," Isabel stored the pouch, the frail woman cackling and sitting before them.

"No, my child. That is not the way for me to learn who you are. Place your hand over mine," Isabel's gaze darted towards

Seraphina. After much hesitation, Isabel conceded to her request timidly.

The woman set her palm over Isabel's. Her brow furrowed upon the old woman's touch, her soft, wrinkled hand covering hers. The woman's cloudy eyes turned murkier, her sight reaching into a realm far from theirs.

"Mhmm," she began. "Ah. I see." She paused, then looked up at Isabel. "You wish to be a warrior, perhaps a hero. You may become one, but not all will see eye to eye with you. Lady Isabel, to what lengths would you go to save the realm?"

"I would do anything."

"Spoken like a hero. Would you go to the lengths of killing anyone, or anything, to save those around you?"

"If it meant saving the world, in a heartbeat." *All heroes must destroy their foes to save those they love. Naturally, I would do it.*

The woman laughed. "That is what all would say until they learn it is the person within them who must die. Would you kill her? Would you kill the woman in the mirror?"

Isabel's eyes widened, and she found herself unable to reply. *Me? How can killing me save the world?* "A heartbeat has passed, and yet no answer. You see, every person wishes to make the world a better place until they realize it begins with them. I fear for the future, young Beaumont. Dark days are coming. Fire will Reign."

She is speaking senselessly. This cannot be true. How can she be certain? If anything, it is the barbarians killing our world. She knows nothing. Who does she believe she is?

"Your heart, it hurts. Your family you have lost. Pain. Death. That is the price you must pay, Lady Beaumont, while you continue to walk this realm. Heavy is the crown of your family. Arduous are the decisions you will face, yet their outcomes remain cloudy. Your world, fire will incinerate it, or the flame will be its salvation. From the ashes, you will rise, or beneath it, die. Children you will bear. Their fates, in your judgment, lie. Not all, you may save." The woman shook her head, "My sight will only permit me to see so far into your future." The frail woman held Isabel's hand tighter, hoping to console her, Isabel's hand trembling with fear. "Forgive me, child. No lady should experience all this pain. A Beaumont should not die before their last breath."

Isabel twisted her hand from the woman's touch, whose once soft hand now had taken a turn to the chilliness of the weather outside the hut. Her bony fingers had appeared to reach for her dreams, pilfering them before they had been realized. Isabel trembled, not from the cold weather but instead from the cold future which awaited her.

"We must go, Seraphina," and Seraphina glanced back, snatching the vial the frail woman presented with outstretched hands.

"Lady Isabel, we will meet again," but Isabel and Seraphina were long gone, riding into the rain, fleeing into the future.

CHAPTER 24: JEWEL CALLED RARITY

The ladies had risked their lives amidst the storm. After they entered the castle, the bridge collapsed behind them, trapping them within its perimeter. Isabel and Seraphina returned to Accreton's keep, watching Odo as he drank the poison's remedy.

Odo turned and continued to rest, his body drained from the plague that consumed him from within. Isabel could only hope he would recover, her thoughts consumed with the question of whether they had reached Accreton promptly. Odo had endured while they were gone, yet if their arrival had been ill-timed, there was no assurance the remedy would serve its purpose.

Isabel strolled towards the braziers near the throne, lighting it with her torch and lingering around it, warming her drenched body. Seraphina joined her, the two staring into the fire, seeking its warmth.

"Who sent you to find me?" Seraphina watched her from across the flame.

"Your sister, Cicely, and Layne were kind to me while I remained in Rivetion. I overheard about your disappearance, and they never illuminated me on the manner, though Cicely seemed heartbroken about your disappearance. After I left Rivetion, or may I say, escaped, Odo heard of your recent whereabouts at a tavern. Odo, dutiful as he is, urged us to search for you, and we decided to find you. I was indebted to them and reckoned it was a suitable way to repay their kindness."

"You said escaped? Why did you escape?"

"The city was under siege. During a nightly feast, they reached the keep, and your sister aided us in our escape."

"And my sister. Did she... survive??"

"When I last saw her, your sister was alive and well. Layne, I fear, did not meet a similar fate."

"Impossible. You cannot say Layne has passed away."

"Forgive me. The fates were unkind to him."

"How? Why?" Seraphina raked her fingers through her hair and went around the brazier as if the shortened distance between the two would bring her closer to Layne's final moments.

"It was a brave death. He died with a sword in his hand, saving the rest of us in our escape. I fought beside him in his final moments, yet he did not allow me to assist in his salvation, for he dropped me from the wall. I tried."

Isabel's eyes welled, her throat turning dry. Seraphina's eyes glimmered when puddles built up within them. "That is the Layne I knew and cherished. Always brave and risked all for those who encircled him. My sister must be brokenhearted, for their love was profound. Where is Cicely?"

"I fear she remained at Rivetion. She would not leave the city to burn, not as long as her heart continued to pound against her chest."

"They were made for one another. Their loyalty to that city... I... I cannot even begin to understand."

"It seems so," Isabel's thoughts flashed to Oakheart and how her mother remained there while the two sisters fled from the flaming estate.

Benedict waved at her, Isabel leaving the brazier and joining him, the man resting with his men along the wall. Maple had managed to bandage his wounds, the men returning to the castle after Seraphina and Isabel had left to find Odo's remedy.

"Benedict. How are you fairing?"

"I must say, your mercenary and servant have the hands of a mage. I was certain I had seen the last of my days."

"Quite the pair," Isabel glanced along the lines of Benedict's soldiers. "Where is Sir Bryce? I have yet to see him after my arrival."

"He has returned to our home to send aid."

"In this tempest?"

"That knight can weather any storm. He is as resilient as a bear in a long winter." He looked around the great hall. "I am in deep admiration of your castle."

"I must say the same myself. I never believed my ancestral home to be..."

"Say it. Brimming with grandeur. Declare its beauty."

"Brimming with grandeur," Isabel smiled, gazing at the banners on the walls. It was not just Isabel who recognized the magnificence of Accreton, for even in its deteriorating state, she knew it still exhibited the qualities of when it was the pinnacle of civilization.

"It is indeed true then," Benedict added, admiring his surroundings before looking back at Isabel. "This was the home of the Beaumonts, before the end of the Fall of Fire Era." He pointed to the banner above, "That was your banner. House Valenour."

House Valenour. The name the knight who attacked Oakheart said. Valenour girls. He is truly after us. Why? Isabel shuddered at the thought.

"What is it?"

"Nothing."

"Few dare to enter Accreton. Less know it is truly the Beaumonts who were the Old Valenours. It is in the restricted books of Viakaven where the old histories lie, away from any who may seek its knowledge. Sadly, that is all I know. The knowledge is merely kept amongst those with access, the King's family. All others are forbidden from its knowledge." *That is why Layne and Cicely knew.*

"Why?"

"To prevent the feuds from returning and ravaging the land. The old names are dangerous. To wear the colors of the Valenour is a brave yet foolish act. Who knows what perils await if the old House names return." *I fear the perils have already knocked down our walls. If the knight continues his quest, soon all will know we are House Valenour.*

"Can it be proven? That we are House Valenour?"

"Only the ancient book states it. As long as it remains hidden, none can know. It is a capital offense to enter Viakaven's restricted library. You are safe," he gazed at the broken glass. "No man will rebuild Accreton. It is feared. Lost territory. Will you reconstruct it?"

"Reconstruct it? It was never my intention. I intended to return home to Oakheart. Rebuild it after the attack."

"How could you risk letting such a grand castle wither within these mountains? I have heard the news of your home being razed, and it would only be fitting that you return for your people stronger. Accreton is your place to return for them. To garner strength. The perfect reason to rebuild it without drawing attention to the fact that it is your birthright. Few will question it." *Lord Benedict may be right. This is our chance to restore it to its former glory.*

"Forgive me, Lord Benedict. I have not the resources, subjects, or knowledge on how to reconstruct a castle to its former glory."

"My city has an excess population. The floods have left many on the streets. I will take it upon myself to send them to Accreton if you assure me of their safety and well-being. They are laborers, and the scarcity of work in my estate will send them swarming your way. Refugees have established an encampment in my city and nearby lands after Rivetion. Many lost their homes. If I were to send messengers, I am certain they would come to Accreton in search of a new home."

Isabel glanced at the men by the entrance of the great hall. "That is very generous, yet I fear I lack the resources."

"The land is all you need. I will have my people come to your city with a fresh supply of grain and stone to aid in the reconstruction of your city."

"And what is it you covet in return?"

"You saved my life. I am merely grateful for you and your people." Benedict smiled, "Nevertheless, Accreton sits on a mine of rare metals. I am willing to receive that as payment. I will pay, yet I am certain we may agree on a fairer price for its high value."

"It is a much generous offer. I will give it thought. As of now, my focus is to build an army to save Cicely and her people. I am indebted to her."

"I understand. What of Oakheart? What of your estate?"

"As you stated, our land lies in ruin. Left to rubble and ash. There is not much to return to if the people are no longer there. I intend to send scouts to Oakheart. I must find and reunite my family. Together, we may rid ourselves of the men who attacked our home."

Benedict looked at her in approval. "Find me when you have decided, and if there is anything I can do to aid, send a messenger my way."

"Thank you," and Isabel left the man with his comrades.

Isabel's journey throughout her castle continued, discovering a spiral stairway behind the throne. She ascended the stairs and followed a passageway leading to a vast chamber. The chamber was adorned with a wall filled with glass windows that had endured through the ages. The pitter-patter of the rain brought calmness to Isabel's life amidst the days of turmoil she was experiencing.

A banner hung along the wall beside the windows, a symbol that had been seen throughout the entire castle. Chandeliers provided dim lighting, creating an aura of rest in the chamber.

A stone mosaic in the center of the chamber's floor depicted a three-headed dragon on a plateau, spreading its flames within a circle. A bed, chest, and wooden table remained within the chamber. Isabel did not pay heed to them, her mind finding solace in the serenity of the window and the rain outside.

Isabel was certain the castle's creator had built the chamber for its solitude and escape from the demands of society. The mountain landscape was teeming with a broad assortment of colored trees, the coming of winter causing them to shed their leaves slowly. The rulers who once occupied this chamber must have cherished the peace it offered, and Isabel could not help but imagine the life that had thrived within these walls.

"May I enter?" Robion stood by the chamber's entrance.

"Aye. Join me," Isabel said over her shoulder, continuing to admire the rains as they facilitated the trees into shedding their leaves.

Robion joined her.

"My family would have truly been at peace here. I could have never imagined that, through the generations, the love of nature would be passed down in our lineage."

"It is a sight for generations to admire," Robion watched below, the howling winds causing the trees to quiver.

"Is it not satirical how I am brought into the world of my past generations, permitted to revive them, yet I have lost the present generation?"

"You have not lost them," he looked at her, "your parents may be out there, breathing still. Your sister, she remains alive."

"And yet she is not here."

"I would give all that I have to spend a moment with my family once more, to see them alive, even if not by my side," he added, shaking his head.

Isabel turned to Robion, the heavy weight of his family's death lingering within her chest. "Oh, forgive me, Robion," she hugged him unconsciously, feeling the warmth of his body amidst the chilly weather besieging them. His body tensed, Isabel quickly retreating from the instinctive movement that had taken over her.

"I did not mean," she began to turn away, embarrassment flushing into her cheeks.

Robion reached for her hand, preventing her from straying any further. "It is all right. You need not leave like that. Recent events have put me under tension. It is not you," he paused, focusing on her. "On the contrary, your presence has made me feel at ease."

Isabel could not match his gaze, her hand enveloped by his. Her gaze searched for a distraction in the natural world outside the window. Though her eyes sought elsewhere, Isabel's thoughts remained fixed on her hand trapped within his, or as she desired to envision it, safe within his.

"My mother had a belief, one where we live in a world in which we must marry out of obligation," Robion began. "We would never be allowed love. That was a rarity within our way of life. I must say, I believed that to be true, that I could never attain this jewel called rarity. Until now."

Isabel's hands grew clammy, her gaze shyly meeting his as her heart raced. They were feelings she had never encountered before. Fear overtook her in the form of a swift shiver, even though her hand remained securely entwined in his. Her instincts urged her to pull away, yet her heart yearned to be drawn closer to him. As if he sensed her uneasiness, he squeezed her hand gently.

However, it only made her mind plunge into chaos. *What are you saying, Robion? Marriage? Us?* The more they met and exchanged letters, the more Isabel hoped they would marry. However, their parents had never spoken of any formal arrangement. They had shared moments together throughout the past two years, but matters of the realm had kept Robion away. Nevertheless, he always managed to write to her, and she could not have been more excited when a messenger carrying one of his scrolls arrived in Oakheart. Marrying for love was always on her mind, but as nobles, their duty could alter the circumstances. Her father was not against them. She could not help but think what her father would say if Robion asked for her hand.

Isabel's uneasiness grew, and the thought of marriage caused her to scurry. She withdrew from his grasp, and Robion, noticing her unease, relaxed his hand and looked at her. "Those are beautiful words, Robion. I must say, it is a luxury indeed, and I feel as if I could never experience them either," she said without looking at him. "It is truly a rarity." Her heart felt as if it was to leap out of her chest. Robion's grin faded. *What are you saying, Isabel? Robion nearly professed his love for you now.*

Isabel looked at him shyly from under her eyebrows. "It is a true rarity. However, we may have found this rare gem." Robion smiled at her remark. Isabel's heart beat so fast, she could feel it pounding in her throat. She stared out the window, hoping to ease the tension, Robion's gaze following hers.

"It is heartbreaking to realize that in life, we occasionally lose things, only to be met by new ones. It is like those trees," she pointed at the tree being whipped by the wind, "just like the leaves upon them, as winter comes, they must let them free. This allows it to survive through winter, only to be reborn after the harsh times pass. It enlightens us to understand that for new life to grow, the old one must be shed."

Robion's confusion was evident as he raised his brow. "Isabel. A family and its legacy live through its home. Do you not see it, feel it?" Isabel hesitated before nodding. "You are standing here, and you can feel your family's long love for nature. Their history, their lives. They are enriched by this place. Your family remains here with you, regardless of the distance or ages which separates you from them."

Robion swiveled on his heel, unsheathing his sword while shielding Isabel from the entrance. "Come out. Lurk in the shadows, and I will have you found." Isabel watched the entrance, unsure if Robion had gone mad or if there was truth in his words.

To her relief, his words held true. A man appeared in a beige robe, his clothing taking the form of his plump body. "I mean no harm," the man stepped from within the shadows and into the dim light, wooden staff in hand. "I reckoned the voice was familiar."

The man lowered his robe's hood, revealing a bald head with stray hairs limp along its side and a broad nose.

Isabel could not believe her eyes. She circled Robion and sprinted with open arms towards the man who had lurked in the shadows, exclaiming, "Priest Aubrey!"

CHAPTER 25: OLD FRIEND

"Lady Isabel," the priest hugged the young woman, "it is so great to see you are well. I imagined the worst of fates came upon you after the incident in Oakheart. Your sister, where is she? Did she… survive?"

"She is well. A friend is caring for her in Hillfrey."

"Hillfrey?" his eyes darted from side to side. Without commenting further on the matter, he continued, "And your parents?"

Isabel shook her head, "I have not known of them since Oakheart."

"Forgive me, child. I pray you kept the gift your parents bestowed upon you and your siblings safe."

"We did. Were you aware of its contents?"

"I fear not. It was unknown to us all. Your mother said it was a family secret, and it was best if it were to remain so." Isabel, however, knew Aubrey well enough, and she could see he had lied. Whether it was to conceal it from Robion, she did not ask, but it truly was meant to be a closely guarded secret.

Robion raised his eyebrows, and Isabel noticed, instantly turning to him. "Aubrey, this is Lord Robion. Robion, this is Priest Aubrey."

The pair exchanged greetings, and Aubrey added, "I have a newfound friend I would like you to become acquaintance with." The priest turned and called out towards the passageway behind him. "Dunstan, join us. Stop lurking in the shadows."

A rosy man in leather clothing approached them, the thick snowy hair and complementing bushy beard concealing his face. Two lengthy scars stretched from his left temple and ended at the center of his nose. A pair of pince-nez glasses stood still upon his face, and Isabel found them intriguing. Dunstan had modified them, leather strips running the length of his temples before looping around his large ears, preventing them from collapsing.

"Hello, My Lady," he said. He quickly glanced at Robion, "Lord."

"Hello, Dunstan. How did you meet?" Isabel looked at the man.

"We happened to be trapped here in the castle before you found us," Dunstan said.

"Aye," Aubrey continued the story. "After Oakheart, I could not find a safe escape and became trapped upon entering Snake's Pass. There was no other route except to flee to Accreton. I thought the tales would suffice in keeping others away. Unfortunately, a bandit group arrived and used it as their hideout after I had been hiding away for a couple of days."

Dunstan chuckled, "His misfortune was my fortune. Aubrey spotted me upon our arrival and liberated me from the captors. They paid no heed to an old scribe. Nevertheless, we could not escape the castle and have been here ever since."

"Though the food was scarce, it has not been a dreadful time in Accreton, particularly for a scribe like Dunstan. He is rich in knowledge about the history of Emerion," Aubrey mentioned, "he has fallen in love with the castle's archives."

"It is a striking view. One could live there for centuries and not finish half of the ancient books and scrolls," the man's cheeks rose in excitement.

"I have not yet had the opportunity to visit it," Isabel pondered momentarily. "How have they not been looted?"

"It is an intricate system which locked the entrance to it. Nevertheless, it would not deter a pair of scholarly men," Aubrey paused and winked, "with private knowledge of Accreton." *It seems Aubrey knows more about Accreton than I imagined.*

Isabel crossed her arms over her chest, narrowing her eyes at them. "It seems there are secrets better left as just that, secrets." She looked at Dunstan, "Do you have a home?"

Dunstan touched the base of his neck, "I had a home. That was until these heathens razed it to the ground before I was sequestered."

We have a couple of warriors, who knows how many scrolls, and the aid offered by Benedict. Perhaps there is more on the Valenours. Perhaps within, there is a reason for the attack of these men at Oakheart. It may be just what we need to understand why we are being attacked, why they are doing this to our family. If there is as much knowledge as they state, and without Oakheart, this could truly be a haven for us. With time, it could even become our home once more.

"Would you consider making Accreton your home if I offered you the archivist position?"

Dunstan ran his hands through his hair, "Is this castle not abandoned?"

"Was abandoned. With Oakheart scorched, we need a home. There is not a better time to inhabit Accreton than now. With time, we may restore this grand city to its former glory. It would be my honor if, as Priest Aubrey has revealed, a man with such vast knowledge of history and books were to oversee our archives."

Dunstan was left speechless, Aubrey nudging him with his elbow. "Um, aye, it would be an honor, My Lady."

"Then may I suggest you gather your books if you are to read them all before your time has passed," the man's cheeks rose, happiness overflowing from within his body into his jittery fingers.

The group abandoned the chambers and returned to the great hall, Isabel searching for Benedict. He stood on the other side of the hall, tending to his men. The thought of her father overseeing his men seeped into her mind while watching him. *Is he alive?*

"Lord Benedict."

"Isabel, how may I be of service?"

"I have given careful thought to your words, and there is not much time if I wish to save my family and people. I will restore Accreton to its former glory, and with it, I accept your offer."

"I was hoping you would."

"Why is that?"

"I had already sent my men to carry out the preparations," he shrugged, then smiled.

"What would you have done if I had decided otherwise?"

"Let us just say I am glad you did not," and the man nodded with a wink.

Isabel joined Henry and the group of men gathered around Odo. They were chattering, eating supper as evening appeared to have closed in on them earlier than the previous days. With the storm winding down, Isabel planned to return to Hillfrey in pursuit of her sister.

"Henry, have half the men stay tonight with the wounded and the rest ride with me. I must return Lady Seraphina home."

"We will ride tonight?" Henry asked as Isabel pulled him apart from their men.

"Armies are roaming and looting the land. It is the safest way. I must return to my sister as swiftly as possible."

"As you wish. I will have the men ready to ride out on your command."

Odo awoke, leaning onto the wall, and waved for Isabel to join him. "I see you are planning to leave without me."

"Odo, you are hurt. You must rest. There will be other adventures for you to join me."

"You require me out there, My Lady. I cannot have you alone in this perilous world."

Isabel shook her head and placed a hand on his shoulder as he attempted to rise. "Odo, what I require is for you to rest. You will not help me if you are under the ground. It is a long journey, and it will hinder your healing. I am not alone. I will take half the men. I will require you to manage the castle on my leave. You are and will be my most trusted advisor."

Odo winced at his pain, smiling weakly in acceptance of her words. "I will keep an eye on your home while you are gone. However, I know you wish to reach your sister swiftly, yet patrols are emerging from Rivetion. Ride north, take Dryadon's Pass, and go through Montanar. It is safer."

"I will heed your advice. Heal swiftly, my friend," and she touched his knee lightly, Odo nodding. Isabel rose, eager to bring her sister home.

The crackling of thunder in the middle of the night awoke Lucia, the lightning strike that had provoked it tearing through the sky.

She glanced across the chamber, the cold bed where her sister slept days ago now vacant. Isabel had left Lucia behind while she searched for Cicely's sister, stating that the world beyond was unknown and dangerous. The young sister wondered, however, if the natural world could be less hazardous than being stuck in the wolf's den of a woman who did not take a liking to them.

Erratia had cuddled between Lucia's arms, sleeping and unbothered by the dangers lurking in the world. There was truth in Isabel's words, for the beast was now peaceful, yet what was to occur when it grew was certainly in nature's hands. They were known to be wild and untamable, but every time Lucia gazed into Erratia's peaceful face, a warm feeling crept into her stomach and told her otherwise. For now, she decided to enjoy its peace, hoping to not burden her mind with these dire contemplations.

Lucia slipped away from the resting dragon, crouching by the chest and opening its lid. The middle egg was now conspicuously missing, Lucia's heart leaping with hope and trepidation, praying Isabel had taken it on her travels. She remembered Isabel's stern instructions to safeguard the chest with her life, and Lucia furrowed her brow in contemplation. It was odd that they continued to carry the eggs, yet once they hatched, Isabel would want to rid herself of them.

A light rap on the door startled Lucia, her head jerking in its direction, almost causing the lid to crash onto her fingers. Her gaze shifted between the door and the once slumbering dragon, the animal now staring at her with drowsy eyes. A second rap had Lucia on her feet and peering through the door. Her eyebrows rose when Faylinn's face appeared between the crevice. Faylinn pushed her to the side, entering the chamber. Her swift entry was met by a quick retreat at the sight of the dragon, the woman nearly tumbling on Isabel's bed.

"I had forgotten you were carrying such an animal, if it may be called such."

"Erratia is of no harm," Lucia closed the door and sat on her bed, caressing the dragon's scales. "What has happened? Why have you come in the dark of night?"

"We need to leave this castle."

"I would love to, yet my sister has not returned. She urged us to remain here."

"We must leave now. I did not take a liking to how Katinee spoke at that table. Did you manage to upset her?"

"I did nothing of the sort."

"Are you certain, Lucia?"

Lucia did not meet her gaze, a sigh escaping her. "I may have overheard her speaking within her chambers. However, I have not said anything."

"Did anyone witness this?"

Without hesitation, she exclaimed, "Daeron, yet he never left my side. I reckon he was unable to reveal it to her. He would not."

Faylinn's brow furrowed, "It is difficult to trust in court."

"As I said, he would not, and he could not."

"It does not matter. We must leave. She is seeking blood, and I am certain she may achieve it. Now is our moment to escape the castle."

Lucia knew Faylinn's word held truth, and they must leave the castle. Katinee's suspicious secret, unknown completely to Lucia, was a secret she did not want disclosed and would go to the lengths that she must to preserve it.

Lucia and Faylinn snatched their belongings, moving through the hall swiftly to avoid detection. They were able to escape the upper levels of the castle promptly, as there were only a few guards patrolling the area.

The ladies reached the entrance to the great hall, a pair of guards standing by the door. They were stiff as a board, the ladies watching them from the safety of the shadows. One of the guards tore through the silence with a yawn.

"If you succumb to slumber, Katinee will have your eyes gouged," the second guard said.

"I will not succumb to slumber, not with you bickering every night about it. 'Sides, I am famished, that is all."

"Not even your mother would believe the falsehood of your words."

"It a dull duty standing here all night doing nothing except staring at that ugly face o' yours."

"This is the prettiest thing you will probably see in your life. You are fortunate you do not have to stare at that ugly arse of yours all night."

There was a silence as the two men stared at each other before erupting into a roaring laughter.

"Let us go," Faylinn said before she whistled.

"What are you doing? We will be caught," Lucia said, snatching her wrist. Faylinn merely smiled. She pointed towards the guards, and when Lucia glanced back, they were gone. *They just disappeared?*

Faylinn rushed by her and approached the main entrance, the doors left unguarded. Lucia could not comprehend what was occurring as they exited the castle, the pair reaching the stables. "What did you do?" Lucia finally asked as Faylinn helped her mount her horse.

"Let us just say you owe me a couple of coins," and she winked at her. "Now, I do not wish to learn if Katinee has any compassion for guests who know her secrets. Ride," and the two rode out, the ladies bolting towards the descended bridge. It began to rise, and Faylinn glanced back. "Quick, the guards I paid said we would not have much time." Faylinn jumped first, Lucia trailing.

Lucia's horse hesitated as the bridge's gap increased. The intensifying incline frightened the steed, causing it to slacken its pace. Lucia flicked the reins. Squeezing her heels into the horse's flanks, she urged it to save their skins. She was certain worst fates awaited them if they were to remain in Hillfrey. Her horse whined as Lucia flicked the reins and squeezed her heels once more. Her heart became still as it leapt over the bridge, Lucia watching the gap below.

Landing on the opposite side, Lucia's horse sprang to life upon seeing Faylinn and her steed. It was not long before the ladies made their escape, abandoning Hillfrey and the conspiracies of Nalthok and Lady Katinee.

CHAPTER 26: EQUALS

After two days on the road, the group halted on a hilltop, where they could see a castle erected on a taller hill across the vast plains before them. Around the castle entrance, hundreds of tents were arranged in orderly rows, soldiers sauntering about. The group descended towards the tents and rode in the castle's direction, Isabel admiring the serfs while they harvested the season's crops.

"My Lady," Dunstan rode beside her, "the grand castle of Montanar. It is renowned for its surplus salt mines and thousands of animals freely roaming its fields, awaiting slaughter and preservation for trade. Some men have come to say there are more cows than soldiers in the lord's army," Dunstan chuckled.

"Remind me, lady, why is we carrying this sack of potatoes with us?" Fulk called from the rear.

"I am on an important quest if you must know," Dunstan replied, adjusting his glasses.

"And what may that be? Are you here to acquire a book for your archives? Is that your mission?"

"I will have it known: I am here to find my apprentice," Dunstan raised a finger as if he was a king who could smite the world with one swift hand.

"Sounds like a quest given by the king himself," Fulk rolled his eyes.

"Are they constantly cruel and uncivilized?" Dunstan turned to Isabel.

"In time, you will learn to disregard them. If you do not, insanity will come for you," Henry said while trailing Dunstan.

"They snicker at your ears until they drive you mad," Norman added. "I have begun to see them in my dreams, or better said, nightmares."

"Norman, as unpleasant as your words may be," Fulk mocked, "you know we have a grand time, old man." Norman grunted, ignoring Fulk and urging his steed closer to Dunstan.

Seraphina rode until she was matching Isabel stride by stride. "We should stop at Montanar. They may be of aid to you. Your sister is in Hillfrey. She will not go anywhere."

I do not wish to keep Lucia alone. However, we need all the help we can muster. One stop will not kill us. "We are here. A quick stop will not hurt us."

The party reached the tents aligned on the outskirts of the castle. Lacking a moat, Montanar relied on its imposing hill and curtain wall for defense. The towers remained under construction, men operating treadwheel cranes to lift the massive stones. Carts loaded with stones were positioned beside the cranes, laborers loading the stones into them and maintaining a steady pace.

The group traversed the castle's gates, Isabel expecting to hear children's footsteps, reminiscent of the eager children who greeted them in Hillfrey. Nevertheless, her anticipation was in vain, for children did not rush to them at Montanar. She searched for them amongst the population and was surprised when she found many were working. The children aided in the restoration of the castle, and those who were too young stood by, watching and learning from their elders.

Carts were aligned by the masses, men carrying their crops, others guiding their animals to be sold. The voices of criers and merchants urged all to come near, Isabel recalling the man who had given her the emerald, her hand reaching for the pommel. Disregarding the activities of a bustling market, the group pierced through the masses, directing their horses towards the castle.

Upon arrival, the lord's guards sequestered their weapons before they entered the great hall. Inside, amber banners hung from the ceiling, an ebony raven at its center with its wings spread wide, ready for flight. The hall was brimming with soldiers, merchants, and serfs, men searching for an audience with the castle's lord.

The lord's soldiers carried round shields, spear in hand, and were clad in mail armor. At the far end of the great hall, the lord sat upon his throne, listening to a pair of merchants who sought his aid. As the group approached and drew nearer to the lord, Isabel observed him watching over his subjects. He was a lean man with bronzed hair and a close-shaven beard. One of his eyes was cloudy, mimicking the woman from the hut near Accreton, a prominent scar crossing over it. Sympathetic, he was not, for his face was wrinkled and demonstrated his lack of interest in the merchant's news.

Seating beside him was a woman, her ashen hair matching Layne's, her delicate features contrasting those of her husband, whom the wars had left torn like his castle. She had a fair complexion, her eyes as grey as the skies of Hillfrey. Unlike her husband, who was armored while in his hall, she donned a silk tunic, her neck wrapped by lynx furs.

Beside them was a plated armor knight wearing a cape with the family's amber color. His sugarloaf helmet concealed his face, the knight standing high and wide, his hand on the pommel of his sword, ready to protect his lord should the need arise.

"Lady Isabel. Are you acquainted with Montanar's lord?" Lady Seraphina grasped Isabel's arm, her muscles tensing at the sudden touch.

"I am not. However, if I am not mistaken, that is Lord Rulf Courbet, and beside him, his wife, Lady Catrayne Courbet. I must not forget the great knight standing beside them, Sir Laedor, one of the greatest knights in the realm." Isabel narrowed her gaze. "Does Lady Catrayne not remind you of Layne?" Isabel could not contain the words racing through her mind.

"You have a sharp eye," Seraphina beamed, yet it was quick to fade. "The familiarity has roots, for she is his sister... or was." A silence befell Seraphina, but her noble posture did not betray her, Seraphina staring forward with a high chin and shoulders back.

Their moment to speak with the lord had arrived. "Lady Seraphina, it is good to see you alive and well," Rulf leaned forward from his chair, "news had spread of your disappearance. It seems to have been tall tales."

"I see you remain in good health, Lord Rulf. Nevertheless, I must say, tall tales they were not. I found myself in the clutches of bandits, as one group defeated another and took me as their prisoner. It was not until she came to my rescue that my fate took a different turn."

Rulf's eyes narrowed. "This is Lady Isabel Beaumont," Seraphina announced to the great hall as if she were the herald at a great tournament. Rulf's eyes flashed momentarily at the sound of her name, Isabel catching a glimpse of it yet not paying heed to it after he blinked it away.

"Lady Isabel Beaumont. Welcome to Montanar," Rulf said before returning his attention to Seraphina, "how may I serve you today, Seraphina?"

"I have brought Isabel here, for she is the one who requires your assistance."

Rulf swiveled his attention once more to Isabel, his forehead wrinkling. "Is that so? What has brought you here, Lady Isabel Beaumont?" his words lingered on her family name, Isabel's stomach turning.

"I am certain news has reached you regarding the siege of Rivetion."

"They have," his expression remained unaffected. His wife's expression, however, soured. The woman shuffled in her chair, awaiting Isabel's next statement.

"I am gathering an army to lead them to Rivetion and recapture the city. Will you join us to liberate it?"

The man cackled, the hall silent as he leaned back onto his unadorned throne. "How do you intend to do this?"

"My Lord, we will gather all the men and nobles who will stand for the kingdom and free ourselves from these barbarians."

"We? I have not joined you. Barbarians they are not. They are trained, organized men who will fight for their lord. Why would we fight for you, *girl*?"

"Lord, if we can rally the men and recapture Rivetion, we may rid ourselves of these warriors. If they are left to stand in Rivetion, they will march to the next village, the next city, the next castle. Yesterday it was Oakheart, today it is Rivetion, tomorrow it may very well be Montanar," his lip curled at her words.

"These men are not the ones who attacked Oakheart. My scouts report their armors are different. Your family must have upset a lord, and they seek vengeance." He shook his head and cupped his chin, "Regardless of this, you speak of war to my people, my people who seek a respite from all this bloodshed. You have no military knowledge. Can you fight? Certainly not. You are a girl! There is no logical reason for me nor my men to join you in what will be a slaughter. Rivetion has fallen, and the resources required for a siege will kill our men through the winter. May I say, my men, for I have not seen your army." *Just a girl? Being a girl does not imply I cannot fight.*

"Even if we cannot choose every war that comes our way, we must fight for our allies, those who guard our doors, those who are our gracious neighbors."

"They may be our allies, yet the city is lost. We choose our wars, and I have decided to stray from this unnecessary bloodshed. Is that all you seek? If it is, this audience is over. There are more important matters I must attend to," Catrayne remained wide-eyed, and Isabel could see her disbelief in Rulf not aiding her brother's city. She reached for his hand as if the touch of her thin fingers would seep compassion into his heart. His heart, however, was unaffected, cold as the amber ring on his hand.

Isabel's skin boiled, the young noble turning away as a serf swiftly took her place, requesting the lord additional time to pay his tithe. Seraphina chased after Isabel while Norman, Robion, and Henry remained close.

"I sense your discomfort, Isabel. I am certain other lords will join your cause," Seraphina grabbed her wrist.

"They will not. I am a woman, and men will not follow a woman into battle. My own men do not want to follow me. They seek and chase after my coin purse."

"They fear you as a woman. They fear you will accomplish greater deeds than they ever could. They fear your prowess will undermine them," Seraphina squeezed her hand, Isabel coming to a halt. "Odo follows you, Robion follows you, Henry follows you. I am certain they are not men who seek your gold. They are good men. I can see it within them."

"She speaks the truth," a feminine voice crept behind Isabel. She turned to meet the woman, her mouth agape and her muscles stiffening. Isabel stammered, "It is you."

The chocolate-colored hair woman with the ashen strand who had saved Isabel at Oakheart now stood before her. Her shiny armor was concealed by her cream cloak, a pair of knights with sugarloaf helmets standing stiff as statues one pace behind her. "You may leave us," and her guards left the three of them. "Lady Isabel?" Isabel nodded, unable to speak, recalling her hero's aid when she was in need. "I am Lady Alaehrayne."

The King's daughter?! How had I not known? "Thank you for saving me that day," Isabel regained her composure as best she could, but knowing she was in the presence of *the* Lady Alaehrayne made it all near impossible. "I pondered at the idea of your survival."

"I was bound to survive," she smiled, her gaze shooting into the sky boastingly. "*You* were bound to survive. It demonstrates, as Lady Seraphina said, men fear us."

"You are King Ulron's daughter," Seraphina chimed in.

"Men have a reason to follow you into battle," Isabel added.

"You need not mistake my lineage with men following me into battle. My men were reluctant at first, yet I gained their respect by leading the few who joined me, and with time, word spread of our victories, and more sought to join us. At first, it may be a daunting task. You must do the same, Isabel, and you will see how your name will be renowned, how it will be whispered through the halls, how it will be sung at taverns, and how it will travel across the land for men to be inspired, or feared by your presence."

"How will I be renowned when men will not even follow me?"

"Mercenaries. Pay men to follow you, and more are sure to come. Where there is victory, there is power, and if I have learned anything in my life as King Ulron's daughter, it is that men cannot resist power."

"If my father has taught me anything of warfare," Seraphina rejoined the conversation, "it is that mercenaries have no loyalty unless it involves the shine of a coin."

"That may be so," Alaehrayne nodded, "yet you will find that even men, once they discover a formidable and respectable leader, they will continue to follow them. If you can prove you care for your men and bring them victories, you will inspire more men to follow you, ones whose loyalties extend beyond the coin."

"Will you be willing to join us in our fight to aid in liberating your uncle's city?" Isabel gazed upon the figure she most admired.

"Who would I be, a king's daughter, to follow a minion into battle?" she winked at her. "I am only led by distinguished leaders or fight beside equals." There was a slight pause, Seraphina watching as Alaehrayne stared at Isabel before placing her hand on her shoulder. "Isabel, become my equal." Isabel's heart leapt as she nodded. "Men are fools. They often underestimate us. Most will value a woman merely for her beauty and believe that we have little else to offer. However, that is their weakness, not ours, and it is a weakness we can exploit."

"What do you mean?"

"You are a beautiful lady, and your beauty may prove to be one of your greatest allies. You may discover that you can use it to your advantage." Isabel's eyes widened, but she knew Alaehrayne was right. *What a terrible society this is in that this is the only way women are seen as people of worth.*

"Seraphina. We will require coin to build an army. I must say, I do not believe I have the amount needed to raise one."

"That can be arranged. Nobles always have valuables to offer. I am certain you own a couple of boxes filled with idle jewelry you may utilize to begin raising your army."

Isabel paused, then said, "Jewelry I do not have, but I believe I have something of greater value."

"Then let us not spend another breath," she said, "for I know an individual who has all the coin we will require."

CHAPTER 27: GREED OF THE COIN

"This is no place for a lady," Seraphina said as the party entered the local inn.

"I believe it was your suggestion to search for mercenaries willing to fight for me," Isabel turned to her, frowning.

Seraphina pouted and crossed her arms. "There is some truth to that. Let us be done with it swiftly. I would not want any loose tongues uttering my name for visiting a local inn," Seraphina threw her hood over her head, hoping to keep the people's gazes away from her.

"The man in the plate armor," Merek pointed at a man surrounded by warriors with chain mail armors.

Isabel and Robion went in the direction of the man, the man turning towards them when they interrupted his group's chatter and laughter. The man in the plate armor had a clean-shaven face, short hair, and a bumpy nose. His lips were far from a smile, his mouth crooked at the sight of the unwelcomed guests.

"Why are you interrupting our gathering?" the man with the bumpy nose said.

"You are mercenaries, are you not?"

"Who is asking?" the man remained hostile, narrowing his eyes at Isabel.

"The woman who wishes to offer you coin to fight for her."

"*The woman?* You?" the men cackled. "You make it seem as if you are important. You are merely a girl, a child." The man leaned forward, "Nevertheless, you had me at coin. How many men do you require?"

"How many men are in your command, and what would be the weekly wage to maintain them?"

The man's head cocked back, glancing at the two men beside him, "Aspiring young lady. I can put the word out to the surrounding towns and villages. My name is known around these parts, and, for the right price, I could secure around three hundred men if it was worth their while. Say, one coffer every four weeks for their wages?"

"Gather your men. I will have your coin," Isabel watched the man's eyes widen. He leaned forward again.

"Half the payment first, and I will gather the men."

"A quarter of their wages, and you find me my army," Isabel said, Robion raising an eyebrow at her serious expression.

"A hard bargain, the lady," the mercenary shook his head, "where is my coin?"

"I will have it for you by day's end."

"You mean to say you do not have my coin? Lady, you are wasting my time," he dropped back onto his chair, shaking his head while crossing his arms across his chest.

Isabel leaned forward, planting her hands on the table, "I said I would have them. You have my word."

"Ha!" the man clucked his tongue. "Only the coin speaks the truth. Let it settle this matter. You fetch my coin, and I will fetch your men. When you have it, ask for Barda. Who is it that requests my service?"

"Lady Isabel."

"Well, Lady Isabel, I hope the word of a woman is worth more than that of a man's, and you return with my coin by day's end," he seized his mug.

"If I were in your greaves, I would be gathering the men before I return," she turned, leaving the men behind as Barda snarled at her remark.

Men had poured into the inn swifter than the brewer could pour ale into their tankards. Merchants, serfs, and warriors had gathered within it, some arriving from distant lands to trade within the castle's bailey, others arriving in search of work. With the winter season approaching, an abundance of work filled the castle, men rushing in and out of the building to continue about their day.

"I had yet to admire your aggressive bargaining skills," Robion walked beside her.

"I would not be so swift as to call it aggressive. Lady Alaehrayne understands my men must respect me if they are to follow me." Isabel and Robion reached their party, who were gathered at a table drinking the establishment's honeyed ale.

"It is not always better to be feared than loved," Robion sat at the table, watching Isabel while she remained standing beside him.

"It is always better to be feared than loved," Merek brought his throwing axe down upon the table, the men leaping at his rapid motion. "My point is made," and he cackled.

"Will you not join us at the table?" Robion patted the seat beside him.

"Seraphina and I have business about the merchant's district. We will return once we finish with our trade. Is it not time, Seraphina?" the young noble jumped at her name, the lady immersed in thoughts amidst the roaring men at the table. She bowed, leaving the men to their laughter and joining Isabel. "Inconspicuous, were we not?"

"What can I say? They are a jolly bunch. A moment longer, and I may have been confused for a madame if they caught me dancing upon the tables," Seraphina laughed, pacing beside Isabel.

"M'lady," a voice interrupted them, the two turning to meet the person calling them. A brunet man with lengthy, straight hair and a bushy beard stood behind them. He wore a cloak that appeared to be blended with his hair, their colors indistinguishable, and a pair of onyx leather boots. The man was armed with a sword and quiver, and his bow was slung over his shoulder.

"Who might you be?"

"The name is Jarin, M'lady. I overheard you are in search of men for your army."

"Did you seek to enlist?"

"I did, M'lady. I would need a favor in return."

"A favor?" Seraphina appeared just as confused as Isabel, the pair exchanging glances.

"I would like for my friend to join your ranks."

"Is he a warrior?" Isabel said, Norman rising from the table, approaching them.

"He is, and a skilled one."

"Then he is welcome to join us."

"He needs a favor before he can join."

"She is paying you coin," Norman joined the conversation, the man spinning to face him, "is that not enough for you men? Are you to pickpocket her at night while she sleeps?"

"Nay. It is not my intention to pickpocket the lady."

"Isabel, I have seen men like this in my days of war. They will cut your throat to acquire extra coin while they ride with you. It is best if you leave. I will rid you of this vermin."

Isabel nodded at Norman and shrugged at Jarin, his shoulders slumping as he looked around in confusion. Isabel and Seraphina left the inn, Henry waiting outside by the entrance. He was leaning against the wall, drinking ale from his tankard, while Lunet sat on the ground, sharpening her sword with her whetstone.

"My Lady," Henry set aside his tankard, "will you need me to escort you?"

"Join us, Henry." He abandoned his post by the entrance, following Isabel and Seraphina.

Isabel unfastened a sack from her horse's saddle, shielding it from the world with her cloak and carrying it to their destination alongside Seraphina. She felt the gaze of onlookers, as if the sack and its precious content captured the attention of those who surrounded her in the bustling streets. Isabel, however, was aware that her concerns were a mere whisper amidst the clamor of a world absorbed in its own troubles, unaware of her striding to her destination.

"Is it indeed as you described it?" Seraphina cast a fleeting glance at Isabel's cloak, as if her gaze could pierce through it and discern the sack's content. Nevertheless, she quickly averted her eyes, Seraphina maintaining her gaze ahead to prevent prying eyes from wandering toward the sack.

"It is. It is solid as a rock. The life within it lost since the years when the last one roamed freely," Isabel whispered, wondering if her words stood true, and life within it did not lurk as it once did in Erratia's egg.

"Its value will extend beyond a couple of coffers. I am certain. You may acquire an army and much more. If you had more than one, the riches instilled within it may have lasted you a lifetime." Seraphina's words intrigued Isabel, imagining the amount of gold she may have amassed if she traded the remaining pair. Even in a world where power was measured in gold, gold would never amount to the power wielded by a dragon, for in their times, dragons had destroyed the riches of kingdoms, the most powerful of men. However, she would not dare part with the other two. She would not sell an egg that could regain life, just as her sister's egg had done. She had readied herself to part with this one only because it had encased itself and ceased to live, or so she hoped.

"If only there were more," Isabel replied. "One should suffice, for I only need an army, and wealth is not of my interest."

Seraphina shrugged, "Some folks can live a bountiful life without much coin to their name. It is marvelous, and perplexing," she eyed her glimmering ring.

"How is it that a refined lady such as yourself, knows how to sell goods on the black market?" Isabel asked her companion.

"There is much you have yet to learn about me. I lived a whole life before you rescued me."

"Now that is a story I would like to hear."

"And I may even tell you some day, but for now we need to find this merchant."

As they arrived at the marketplace, the clang of blacksmiths' hammers rang out, shaping iron into tools to build the fortress and weaponry for the guards of Montanar. Tapestries depicting tales of Montanar's history and exotic fabrics were brought out onto the dusty streets by their merchants, urging the travelers to buy their wares. Baskets of colorful fruits and vegetables littered the ground near carts and stalls, while the aroma of roasting cattle lured any hungry passerby who could spare the coin.

Amidst the bustling marketplace, Isabel searched for the merchant who was to purchase her dragon egg. "There he is. Follow my lead," Seraphina led her towards a man with a carriage.

The man in the stall resembled an ordinary merchant, unlikely to dwell in illicit sales. He wore a golden coat with trimmed fox furs along its edges. Upon his belt, a purse hung with the coins of his daily sales, the man bowing when the ladies reached his stall.

"Lady Seraphina, we have long awaited you. May we interest you in this fine horse and carriage?" the merchant said.

"Peronelle, it is quite the steed. How could I reject it?" Seraphina smiled cheekily, Isabel's forehead wrinkling in confusion.

"Good. One of my men will befit your second horse. Join him, and he will be of aid." Seraphina and Isabel walked to an alley's entrance where a man in a cloth overshirt and trousers stood awaiting them.

"Welcome, M'lady. I reckon you have our payment. The merchant aligned the horse to shield their transaction from the masses. Seraphina gave Isabel a nudge, indicating it was her turn to reveal their item for sale. Isabel opened the sac, the ebony egg concealing within its shadowy scales the dragon that once could have lurked within, the man's eyes glimmering with greed. He reached inside, his fingers brushing over the scales. He nodded in approval, satisfied with their offer.

A horse whinnied, and Isabel closed the sac, glancing over her shoulder to glimpse her surroundings. In the market, she noticed the ebony-armored knight from Oakheart, riding atop his ruby caparisoned horse. A shiver ran down her spine. Behind him, the other knight she had seen when they scorched her estate trailed along, much like he had on that fateful day.

The men perused the market, except Isabel knew their search went beyond the goods the merchants were offering. She shuffled to the side, seeking refuge behind the horse the merchants had brought, attempting to shield herself from being spotted.

Even as she remained concealed from the knight, the man beside them watched their every move, his eyes burning with greed once more. "This is worth every coin your friend requested," he said.

"Where is our coin?" Isabel's heart quickened, the hairs on her arms rising like the towers in Hillfrey.

"It is the cart with the tarp. The horses are yours to drag it along." Seraphina glanced back at Henry, the squire raising the tarp to inspect the cart and its coffers. He lifted the lid, the gold coins and goblets shimmering within as promised. Isabel was stunned at how Henry had been informed while she remained lost within the exchange, wondering how Seraphina had been discreet in organizing the entire trade.

Isabel handed the man the sac with the egg, "It is fortunate your friend's promise has been fulfilled," he said while she peeked over her shoulder in search of the ebony knight. The knight had vanished. As Isabel turned to reply to the man, he too had followed the knight's steps and disappeared, leaving the ladies in the streets with a wagon brimming with gold.

CHAPTER 28: FRENZY

"Barda, I have your coin," Isabel's men dropped a coffer of gold upon the inn's table.

Barda's head jerked away, watching the men around him as they laughed. "It seems, My Lady, that you have taken your time bringing my coin. The high demand for our services has led to an increase in our price if we are to join you. An extra coffer should suffice."

"An extra coffer?" Isabel squinted, crossing her arms while shaking her head. "You gave your word on one coffer."

"I gave no word," he leaned forward, "I presented you with an offer, lady. Now you may take it, or you may fetch your little feet and leave my sight," he roared, his men echoing his sentiment.

Isabel was struck by how Barda failed to fulfill his word. She continued to shake her head, unable to agree with his steep price. Her hand tightened around her pommel, Isabel demanding her respect.

"I will accept your steep price," a smirk spread upon Barda's lips.

"Have you gone mad?" Robion whispered, Isabel ignoring his inquiry.

"We will settle it with our swordsmanship. If you emerge victorious, I will pay the price. However, if I defeat you, you and your men will follow me, a quarter off on the remainder of our payments."

"You wish to fight me?" Barda roared, slamming his hands on the table, "a woman?" the men joined him once more in laughter.

"Are you so frightened to fight a woman that you can no longer wield a sword?" Isabel stepped forward, Barda's brows furrowing.

"You will regret the day you challenged me. You will pay me my two coffers and leave Montanar with shame," and he pushed his chair back, the group leaving the inn.

"You *are* mad," Robion followed Isabel outside, a group of men huddling to watch the fight.

"We will have our army," Isabel tugged on her leather gloves.

"You will be killed. You have no armor. Barda's plate armor will protect him. It will be impossible to kill him."

"Precisely! I will be faster, and my victory will not require his death. Mercenaries never fight to their death," Isabel dared not glance at his expression of disbelief, Robion keeping pace with her quick strides. "I will survive. I will win," and she was gone, entering the circle to confront her opponent.

"Place your wagers with me," Fulk yelled across to the group of men. "Will you stake your coin on the veteran mercenary or favor the novice lady?" Isabel shot him a frown, but Fulk merely shrugged.

Merek leaned into her, "It is his way of winning more coin. He means no disrespect."

"You mercenaries and your coin," Isabel rolled her eyes.

"My bet is on the girl beating the mercenary," Merek yelled, Isabel glaring at him. "Once again, pardon me," and Merek roared in laughter, turning to a man beside him. "What, are you frightened to bet against a girl?"

The men in the inn placed their bets, Isabel unsheathing and swinging her sword, warming her body for the duel awaiting her. The mercenaries roared upon their leader's arrival, Robion rubbing his forehead with fear. Aubrey prayed while Norman called out to Isabel, "This is madness." It was evident she would not yield, and the fight would ensue. Norman shook his head and added, "Remember all I have taught you."

The men encircling them managed to enlarge the circle, Alaehrayne standing amongst them, Isabel unaware of her presence. Uthred stood in the center of the circle organizing the unforeseen entertainment that awaited the crowd.

"Sword sharpened?" he turned to the mercenary. He nodded. "Boots tightened?" his head rotated towards Isabel. She nodded as well.

The two duelists stared at each other, ready for Uthred to issue the command. Isabel's pulse rushed within her veins. "Fight!"

The crowd's roars boomed. The duelists made their way around the circle's rim, searching for the moment to strike. Isabel raised her sword, charging at the man, the metal clanging of her sword against his sending the crowd into a frenzy.

She struck down upon him twice, Barda ducking on her second strike. He took the offensive, and Isabel stepped back. With each of his swings, his strength caused her to reach the outer rim of the circle, the men seizing her and shoving her back inside.

"Fight you monkey," one of the mercenaries who pushed her in yelled.

Isabel watched Barda's movements, analyzing him before striking again. For a plated armor mercenary, he had more speed than she had anticipated. Nevertheless, she was swifter and nimbler within her moves, intending to use it to her advantage. Years hunting near Oakheart had made her a nimble warrior.

The man sent his sword down upon her head. Isabel seized the opportunity and charged at him, colliding with his body. His stance was rigid, his body reeling only a couple of steps. Pain rushed from her shoulder and down her arm from the crash into his cuirass. He elbowed her, sending her away. Isabel coughed from the blow which landed on her ribs.

Barda charged at her, Isabel parrying his strikes, yet his elbow to her ribs had left her aching, her blade slackening with every move. The ensuing fight caused her strikes and parries to become sluggish, and fatigue set in. Isabel deflected his sword and landed a blow. The metal clanged upon his plated armor, only to tally another dent into his cuirass.

"It would have been simpler if you had just paid me, little lady," the mercenary swung at her.

Their swords clashed, their faces inches away while their swords searched to overcome each other. An experienced soldier, Barda trapped her crossguard with his and gained control over her sword. In one cohesive movement, he brought her sword down. Barda struck her face with his forearm, Isabel tumbling back a couple of steps before regaining her balance. The crowd roared with Barda's strike, Isabel tasting a metallic flavor, her lips numb. He struck her once more while Isabel remained unable to defend herself, still stunned from the previous attack. Their swords clashed, and Barda kicked her, knocking her to the ground. Isabel gasped for air, her sword falling beside her.

Barda turned his back to her, bellowing into the crowd while raising his arms. The onlookers joined in with their cheers. The noise reverberated inside Isabel like an incessant bell. With the relentless roars in her head, Isabel looked up. Barda remained elated in his cloud of victory, forgetting Isabel in her entirety.

"Women should not fight, especially those ill trained by their families," Barda yelled into the crowd. Isabel coughed and spat the blood pooled within her lips, catching her breath before snatching her sword. The frenzy that had built in Barda now overtook Isabel. It was sufficient to aid her to rise, Isabel charging at him. Her battle cry echoed just as it had at Rivetion, Barda turning to confront her.

Barda timed his parry, yet the strength amassed within Isabel had the power of a hundred horses, and she sent him staggering. Isabel raised her sword and swung it upon him as he continued to parry. She repeated the pattern, Barda continuing to stagger with each blow. Her constant strikes broke his defense, his sword tilting slightly enough to allow her to disarm him with a swift strike.

The man crashed to the ground. Isabel's sword slashed his face on the final blow, blood gushing onto his face and staining the dirt around them. Silence befell the crowd, Isabel consumed by her frenzy. She was ready to strike him down when a sword intercepted her, preventing her from removing him from the face of the kingdom.

Isabel panted and spun to meet the sword's wielder, Robion, standing at the opposite side of the blade, shaking his head. "The duel is over," Robion said, Barda's face twisting, the fear slowly disappearing from his face with Robion's words.

Isabel stretched her arm, regaining her senses, her frenzied state dissipating. They stared at each other, Barda wiping the blood from his cheek while wincing. He rose, disregarded her hand, and walked away until he vanished within the crowd. Isabel stood in the circle's center, the crowd still silent from her victory.

One of the mercenaries in chain mail approached her, "M'lady. The men you ordered are gathering to fight for you. Our men will accept the payment you have offered," and he departed, pursuing Barda.

"You cannot kill your generals," Robion whispered as they strode away towards their group. Isabel's men patted her when she rejoined their party, Norman and Henry glancing at each other wide-eyed by her preceding battle rage.

Alaehrayne waited by Isabel's party with her arms crossed over her chest, her two knights standing beside her. "Did I not mention to keep that pretty face unharmed?" she laughed, Isabel matching her smile with a bloodied one, her lip throbbing at the reminder.

"You also mentioned I must gain respect from my men," the two ladies were deserted as the crowd dispersed hastily.

"That I did. You have taken the path of fear in doing so. That frenzy overwhelmed you, yet it favored you in this duel. Beware, for this may be detrimental. Losing control of your emotions can be reckless," Alaehrayne and Isabel paced towards Isabel's horse.

"I will keep your counsel if it were to repeat itself."

"It will," Alaehrayne's voice was solemn, her gaze searching the scattered crowd in the distance. "My men are having a feast tonight at our encampment. You are invited to join us, for tomorrow we ride out to the capital."

"We will join you," Isabel nodded.

"It is best if we part now. The guards are approaching," and Alaehrayne vanished into the scattering crowd with her men.

"My Lady," Henry handed her a charcoal robe, "this may be of use to you."

"Thank you, Henry," and Isabel's men dispersed, agreeing to unite once they had traversed the crowd.

The guards rushed into the inn, Isabel reaching the marketplace while Robion trailed closely. The group gathered gradually until they had entirely assembled before a crowd. The people threw tomatoes, rocks, and any object they could gather in their surroundings upon a man locked within the stocks, his head drooping.

A man from the crowd caught sight of Isabel and bolted towards her, his hood concealing his identity. Robion and Merek intercepted him, the man halting and removing his hood. Isabel recognized him swiftly.

"M'lady. It is I, Jarin, from the inn."

"Did I not order you to keep your distance, lad," Norman rode to the front.

"You did. You see, that is my friend, the one who needed the favor. Could you free him?"

"We do not take criminals," Norman interjected before Isabel could respond, her gaze shifting between Jarin and the man in the stocks.

"He is no criminal. May you release him?"

"What is his crime?" Isabel's eyes narrowed while she glanced at the man.

"He just cursed before a noble. He is no criminal, M'lady."

To be humiliated before an entire crowd for foul words? That is no way to treat any soul, regardless of their societal position. It is cruel to lock him up, to be shamed before an entire town. Warriors like him should not be condemned for their language, especially when their service is needed for the kingdom's defense. I reckon half the folk taunting him would not dare to stand in his stead and safeguard these lands. Men like him are essential in these times. He deserves a second opportunity.

"Is this all?" Isabel glanced at Jarin. He nodded, and Isabel continued, "How much is his penance?"

"Ten silver coins, M'lady."

"You cannot be considering it?" Norman spun towards Isabel.

"Norman, would you risk losing a skillful warrior over a pair of wrongful words?" Before Norman could answer, Isabel turned towards Jarin, "I pray he is as skillful as you stated."

"He is, M'lady."

With his confirmation, Isabel called over the crowd to the guards standing by the stocks. "I will pay this man's penance." The crowd rotated towards her, rotten vegetables in hand. The sight of her men's swords restrained their urges to toss their ill crops, the crowd cleaving with their passing.

"Are you certain?" the guard asked while his gaze darted towards her party.

She pulled her coin purse, counted the coins, and handed them to the man, the silver speaking for her silence. "Release him," the guard ordered.

"Meet us outside the city, Jarin," and the party continued their march towards Lady Alaehrayne's encampment.

CHAPTER 29: FEAR OF THE WEAK

The sun's last rays were soon replaced with the light from the numerous campfires littering the encampment. With the traders abandoning the roads as night fell upon the land, their chatter was soon replaced with the roars of drunken men dancing and loitering around their warm fires. Isabel's men had fused with Alaehrayne's, the warriors sharing stories of days past and those to come.

Alaehrayne's men had numbered around six hundred, but now that they stood outside Montanar, her numbers were halved. Isabel saw the wounded soldiers and asked her, "Where was your last battle?"

Alaehrayne sharpened her sword with a whetstone, Isabel finding it quite peculiar to see a king's daughter working on her sword. She looked up at her, stopping her work on the blade. "In the outskirts of Rivetion. Father sent me to Aroonshire to find horses for our men, and on our way to Rivetion, we found a party of Layne's fighting. We went to their aid, but we were vastly outnumbered." One would believe Alaehrayne's men would be the best in the realm.

"With six hundred men?"

"No. We had fewer by then. We fought a band of barbarians arriving by ships after departing Aroonshire," Alaehrayne continued, tending to her sword before resuming. "We razed their ships to the ground once they landed on the beaches near the Lover's Tears River, but by then, many of my men were gravely injured. I foolishly sent my men to fight in the second battle."

"Foolish or brave? Did you not save Layne's men?" Isabel inquired, but Alaehrayne did not look up.

Alaehrayne remained silent, then replied, "Some, but not all. I lost more than I saved. Even if we charged to save his men and serfs."

"A bloody battle indeed. But an honorable one," Isabel added, "for you rushed in to save those who may not have been able to save themselves. Is it not what a true princess would do?"

Alaehrayne stopped working on her sword yet remained staring at the blade for a moment. Looking up at Isabel, she said, "Perhaps. What knights are we if we do not protect those who require our aid, even when the odds are pitted against us?" She smiled at her.

"One unworthy of the code," Isabel smiled. "How did you make it to Oakheart?"

"My party was separated, and when I saw the flames, I bolted towards it. If I had more men, perhaps we could have saved your estate, but our little party did not suffice." *Even with a small party, she came to our aid. What noble, what princess, would ever do such deed when outnumbered? She is a true knight, a true queen if she ever became one.*

"Word has spread of your encounter with the mercenary," Alaehrayne added, joining Isabel as she watched the men.

"Words of blabbering men can be quickly disremembered as tall tales," Isabel met her almond eyes.

"But a scar will not be so swiftly forgotten. A woman defeated a mercenary. She sends fear into the ranks of cowardly men, even if it is fear only in the eyes of few."

"What is fear if it disturbs only the weak?"

"Fear is everything. Even if it touches cowards, it can spread through your enemies' ranks like a plague. If you can nourish the fear within the enemy's ranks, their will to fight you will dissipate before you swing your sword. The bulk of your enemy is the weak, for they will only fight when directed by their leader, who conveys strength. Without a leader, or with fear, they will fall like wheat to a scythe."

Isabel turned to watch her men, "What if it is not fear that I wish to be my resolve?"

"It is not what you wish," Alaehrayne watched the men jumping about, "it is what you nurture that you will acquire."

"What if I fear it for what it does to men?"

"Fear is like a flame. Once you light it, it will spread. You must learn to control it, for if you supplement it with ample timber, it will burn and overtake you."

"It sounds like it is best if it is not used."

"Believe as you wish, yet now you have reaped what it sowed for you," Alaehrayne noticed the mercenaries marching into the camp. "Or is that not your fruition?" she pointed at the men.

"I must confess, it has given me what I require. Nevertheless, I do not wish to be known nor remembered for being feared. I have never desired to rule, but if it were so, I wish to rule and be loved, just as my father before me."

"At times, it is best to be feared than loved." There was a pause, Alaehrayne's gaze lingering in the air. "Your father, did he excel with this method?"

"He did, although he is not here anymore to remind me of it." Isabel and Alaehrayne had come to sit down on a log away from the fireplace. Isabel lowered her head at the reminder of her father, and Alaehrayne placed a hand on her shoulder.

"I cannot speak on those ideals, for my father as king, and the kings before him, have ruled with fear. Love is not a luxury kings may afford, for love may lead to a knife twisting in their back. Fear, in turn, proves to stabilize a kingdom. You are no queen. For this reason, your methods may alter, and if you follow this path, I will pray it may serve you well. You need not your father to learn from him, for his memory, if it serves you well, will be enough to reawaken those days and lessons you acquired by observing him."

"Spoken like a true princess," Isabel tilted her head, a smirk on her lips.

"I am no princess. I renounced that rank the instant I grasped my sword, the instant I fought for my father."

"It must not be simple to relinquish it?"

"Simple?" Alaehrayne replied without hesitation, her voice filled with calmness. "It has been the simplest decision I have made in my years roaming Emerion. From the moment my brothers held a sword and I crawled to watch them, I knew it was where my life lay. As soon as I walked, I sparred with them. I even bested my own brother, the prince," she boasted, her eyes staring into the night, as if the stars themselves held the tales of her past. "That is a story I should not tell, for it would disgrace the prince if the kingdom learnt his own sister defeated him wielding a sword," Alaehrayne laughed, Isabel joining her. "You must promise me you will never tell a soul."

Isabel covered her mouth with both of her hands. "How can I tell a soul what I do not remember?" Isabel winked, and Alaehrayne smiled, returning her wink.

"You appear to be a true friend, Isabel. That much, I must say. It is not a simple word for me to hurl around, for my family is bound to the word treason more than friend by those who wish to usurp our power. It would have been remarkable to have a friend like you at the castle while I was coming of age. As my brothers matured, it became quite lonely."

"The roots of loneliness spread far and deep throughout this kingdom. I as well, lived the same. My sister and I did not spend time with each other, not nearly as much as we do now. That is partly my fault, for I was after Father and his adventures."

"It is the burden of the woman who carries the sword."

The pair remained silent, the long shadows of men dancing around their pavilions while the intoxication of ale and the bard's tunes turned them blind to the world around them. "How did you survive Oakheart?"

"I fought my way out and found my horse," Alaehrayne replied. "A few of my men arrived after you left. We fought the enemies we could, yet there was nothing we could do after their arrival."

Isabel envisioned Oakheart, where timber and stone once rose, now ashes seizing its place. She could not imagine if she had the heart to return, if she could absorb all that occurred to her home. Was it like Accreton when she arrived, or had the outcome been worse?

"Where will you march now if not to aid our cause in Rivetion?"

"My father has sent word that our men must return to the capital. He has not neglected his kingdom. He merely wishes to amass his army before it is to march."

With the entire realm gathering and his nearly limitless resources, his army would amass in the thousands. Isabel's and Alaehrayne's troops' tents, gathered before Montanar, numbered in the hundreds. It was impressive, and Isabel could not imagine what an amassed army would look like for the king. The tents reminded her of the siege of Rivetion, an army multiple times bigger than the one amassed before them.

"Ladies," Robion had left the dancing shadows and joined them, "Lady Alaehrayne, may I seize this lovely lady?"

Alaehrayne nodded, and Isabel was certain her gaze had given her away, Alaehrayne nudging her lightly towards him. "And here I was wondering how I would rid myself of her," Isabel gasped, turning to be met with a wink from Alaehrayne when Robion glanced away, Alaehrayne's intentions pure.

"Now, Isabel, dance with me," Robion took her to the fire, where men sang and danced with the local ladies who had escaped the city's walls to enjoy a night amongst knights.

Robion extended his hand, taking Isabel's with a gentle touch. His other hand settled at the small of her back, Isabel arching her back at the sudden touch as if it singed away at the night's chilliness. Robion's eyes widened, but Isabel exhaled, calming her pensive mind, for time had passed since she last danced with another man. They glided around the fire, drawing closer with each graceful step. Alaehrayne watched them from a distance, a knowing smile playing on her lips as one of her knights joined her by the log, diverting her attention elsewhere. Isabel's body warmed with every step they took around the fire. Soon, her feet loosened more than ale could loosen a man's inhibitions.

Time escaped them, Isabel imagining how the sands of time could dissipate so swiftly while he held her close. Their faces were so close she could smell the mint of his breath. It was like a winter dragon's breath with every exhalation that appeared to kiss her neck. Shivers rushed down her spine, Isabel attempting to remain calm. That was possible, until she looked up and met his coffee eyes. Her heart raced. She could feel her palms becoming moist. She wanted to pull away and wipe them, but in doing so, Robion would take notice. *Just breathe, Isabel. He is a man, like any other — a man you have been attracted to for a couple of years.*

As night waned, the men around them dropped when the ale within their bodies prevailed over their conscious minds. Isabel's mind drifted like a mastless ship in the ocean until the remaining song was that of the howling wind, caressing the tent's flaps and kissing the mouths of men who slept.

"Would you fancy a walk?" Robion pulled away from Isabel, Isabel nodding while the temporary midnight darkness weighed upon her body. Isabel yawned, the two leaving the encampment and Robion leading her to a minute lake.

The pair sat by its edge, the moon peaking over the clouds and glimmering upon the still waters. Away from the encampment, away from the city, the world had a tranquility to it Isabel could not explain. The sound of men, the hoofs of horses, the clashing of swords, they all ceased to exist in this moment. Isabel sat beside Robion, his hand reaching for hers, his touch no longer strange upon her body.

"Is it not beautiful?" Isabel watched the grass shivering with the night's winds, the moon gazing upon them and the lake, illuminating their worlds.

"It is indeed," Robion said, then turned towards her while saying, "and the moon. It is beautiful as well."

Isabel's cheeks flushed like ripe strawberries, uncertain of the beauty he was admiring, yet certain it was that which her heart longed and swelled for with every beat. His gaze turned to meet the moon, Isabel's trailing after his.

"The night, even in its darkness, has such a serenity to it." Isabel admired the moon.

"Its power over man, to tranquilize it, to pacify it, is simply overwhelming," Robion added. "One may merely wonder if it affects in that manner all who encounter it, who admire it. If it makes it fall in love with its beauty, with how it illuminates the darkest of nights, and how even when it vanishes, it always appears to return."

Isabel was perplexed, cocking an eyebrow while turning to him, certain his words had escaped the subject at hand. Robion turned, matching her gaze. "Can the world live without its moon?"

The whites of his eyes glimmered with the moon's water reflection, the moon being cast into her own. Isabel's heart quickened, her body boiling like a fever even without his touch there to inflame it. Her breathing accelerated, the moon in their eyes widening as the distance between them decreased.

Their lips parted, and Isabel could feel his warm breath upon her lips. She closed her eyes, prepared to immerse herself in the moment. Then, he paused before her, and with it, so did her heart.

Why did he stop? Did I do something wrong? Isabel began to open her eyes, unsure of why he had stopped. But before she could fully look at him, his lips met hers. She kept her eyes closed, immersed in the moment, in the sensation. Even with winter approaching, Robion's presence made it seem as if it was not so. Isabel's stomach felt nature's butterflies flying within it, her body burning like a flame igniting her from within. Her first kiss with Robion, she could not have asked for anything better.

The moon's soft radiance graced their sight. Isabel opened her eyes to meet Robion's, the pair locked in a loving gaze. The world around them had momentarily ceased to exist, happiness beaming within their gazes.

It was a light that was no more, short-lived by a shadow that overwhelmed her. The scuffling sound and low groans from Robion were met simultaneously by a rough sack scraping down her face. Isabel heard a *thud* followed by a body dropping on her leg. Arms wrapped around Isabel, her mouth concealed by a leathery, icy, metallic arm around her face as the sack failed to descend onto her lips.

Isabel pushed and pulled, striking the body that crashed against her back, a body she could not overpower. A pair of arms looped around her body, preventing her from retaliating further. The accelerated breathing returned, this instant not by a moment of peace. A pressing sensation against her stomach stole her breath, Isabel attempting to wriggle free from her assailant's grasp.

The shuffling of feet around her hastened, heavy steps approaching as the man wrapping his arms around her struggled to keep his grip. Isabel wiggled her arms, and with sufficient space between them, she elbowed the man. Striking him blindly and freeing herself from his grip, she tumbled onto the ground. With her vision obscured, she attempted to run. A second pair of arms managed to loop their way around her body, restraining her once more.

"You cannot escape this time, princess," the man behind her grunted.

"She is no princess," a familiar voice said, yet Isabel could not identify it. "I will demonstrate how it is done," the person added. She could hear stomps approaching, becoming louder with each step. The feet halted near her. A *thud* was heard, pain erupting through Isabel's head. The world plunged into darkness, and not even the moon's light could remove its shadow and awaken her from it.

CHAPTER 30: FEAST OF VULTURES

The rough road returned Isabel to the land of the living, rocking her until her head struck wood, resuscitating a throbbing pain from the night's scuffle. Wooden bars rose around her, holding her captive within the long fingers enclosing her. Isabel sat on the hay, men in chainmail armor preventing her from escaping as they surrounded the cart traversing the woods.

The sun's soft rays vanished below the horizon, a few rays piercing through the sparse trees. One of the guards glanced at her, his hood concealing his identity from Isabel. He murmured words she failed to hear, the throbbing pain erupting into her ears with each heartbeat.

A rotting smell made Isabel reach for her nose, turning for the culprit who attacked her nostrils. For each tree in the woods, an impaled body stood. Some bodies were severed, legs and arms missing, heads gone, others with their eyes gouged. The party's presence did not frighten the vultures, their hunger surpassing their need to flee the newly arrived men.

Isabel turned to watch the head of the group, the ebony and ruby knight, leading them into a wooden palisade fortification. Uncertainty twisted her stomach as Isabel wondered if she would rather become a feast for the vultures or meet an undesirable future within the wooden walls. Nevertheless, decide she did not, for the cart rolled through the wooden doors, the guards closing them as the last of the men entered. The groaning doors tightened the knots within Isabel's stomach, the young noble lowering her head as her escape was closed off.

"Escort the Beaumont lady to her luxurious palace," the knight ordered, the soldiers erupting in laughter, for even Isabel knew captivity offered no luxuries.

Her lavish palace was made of straw and wood, slightly grander than the one she had just been transported by within the woods. Grander by size, for its luxury had not improved, Isabel dropping within it, a man snoring weakly on the opposite side of the cell, as if each breath snatched a moment of his life.

A foul odor crept about him as if he had been dropped in a pig's pit and dragged upon the rotten field of dead men. His beard was scruffy, a brunette beard which reminded her of a beard she had not seen, not for the length of years. Yet, there was a familiarity about it she could not discern. The man appeared frail, weak from living within the cell, a fate Isabel might soon face. She dared not approach him for fear of draining the poor soul of the last air of life remaining within him.

Isabel sat in the corner, her feet tucked, watching the man move and grunting in pain. *How long have you been here?* The yells of men brought her gaze to the battlements, men leaving their posts to be relieved by the fresh guards who would ensure Isabel would not escape without being perceived. *How am I to escape this time? Will Robion and the mercenaries follow my trail, if there even is any?*

The man grunted once more, the few rays of sunlight making their way past the trees and striking over the cage's thatch roof and onto his face. The man's sound was familiar, and Isabel peeked over, hoping to catch a clearer glimpse of his filthy face. His eyes opened, the man shielding his face from the sun's last rays, his mouth agape as if searching for food.

Certain she would meet the man's fate, Isabel sobbed into her cloak, concealing her face as the man had. Upon hearing her cries, the frail man sat upright, leaning onto the bars and scratching his eyes to take in a clearer view of the girl before him.

"Isabel?" the man's voice was all too familiar to her. Isabel peeked over her cloak to glimpse the man whose voice she would never forget over time.

"Father?" her knees shook, her body regaining strength at the sight of her father's weak smile. *It cannot be. You are alive?* She sprung towards him, thrusting her arms over his neck and digging her head into his chest.

"Not a day passed where I wondered if you or your sister escaped alive." His hand was frail, Icas dropping it over his daughter's back. Isabel hoped his gesture would suffice in consoling the wailing cries escaping the deepest trenches of her heart and drowning within his chest.

"I believed the worst had come about you, Father, yet I merely prayed for the best," she said between sobs.

"I know my dear, I know my dear," he repeated softly, his arms shielding her from the dangers of the outside world. "Where is your sister, your mother?"

"Lucia is safe, Father. Mother, she is as gone to me as you were moments ago. She fled to save us."

"Oh, Valaenis, always sacrificing for our family. My dear, where may you be?" he appeared to speak to the wind, as if it were to carry his message across the kingdom to his wife.

"Do you believe her to be alive, Father?" Isabel wiped away a tear before she shed a second to take its place.

"Your mother? She taught you to survive, and within my arms, you rest. I would not deem her capable of anything less," his words brought comfort, and his arms wrapped her with peace.

"The Beaumont family, or should I state, Valenour family, united," the ebony and ruby knight approached them with a wicked smile, though his helmet shielded it from them, "the idea of it resting in my hands would have never crossed my mind."

"If it were not for you, there would be no need for a reunion, Morkath," Icas held Isabel tighter as if protecting her from Morkath's words.

"Icas, you may shed your anger upon me, yet you cannot blame me for the horrors your family has caused in the past. I will rid your disease-causing lineage from this world and all the scrolls where your names may be written," Morkath swiveled and walked away from the cage.

"Why his hatred for our family father?" Isabel gazed into his eyes.

"It is best if you remain ignorant of the past. It should not define us."

"I will not remain oblivious to it. It has defined us and continues to define us," Isabel pulled away. "What has our family done?"

Icas lowered his gaze, shaking his head, and she could see he was hesitant for the words about to escape him. "Our past generations were riders, dragon riders. With the skill they had acquired, they brought great turmoil to the land. Their control over them was utilized to scorch those who opposed them, their obsession with power causing them to do inconceivable deeds, deeds which have marked our lineage undesirably."

"Why is he after our family now?"

"Priest Aubrey," he whispered, "did he not give you and your sister a chest?"

"Aye," a glint of fear twinkled in Isabel's eyes.

"The ancient prophecy said dragons would one day rule the land, ushering a new era and much destruction caused by the three-headed dragon. Those who could ride would once more have the ability to rule over our world," his words caused Isabel's eyes to glimmer, the realization of his fears being cast from her gaze as he became silent momentarily. "It has begun, has it not?"

Isabel only nodded, "There is, however, no three-headed dragon."

"There is none. The three-headed dragon represents the three siblings who will hatch the eggs."

"And it will grant them power?"

"It can, but with it, great danger lurks. Isabel, I must know, who hatched the egg?"

"Lucia. Mine has perished."

"Perished? Perished how?"

"It darkened. I heard its screams, Father. I killed it."

"Where is it now?" her pleas went unheard.

"I have sold it to amass an army and rebuild Accreton."

"Accreton?" he ran his trembling, thin hands through his hair. "It is real. Nevertheless, there is a fault within the prophecy. Your egg should not have died, not unless," his gaze was unfocused, Icas scratching his jaw.

"Unless what father?"

"Unless it was not your egg. Unless your egg is lost in the world. Could you hear the other?"

"No."

"There is a fourth. A fourth rider in the world."

"Who is it, Father?"

"Upon hatching of the eggs, corruption will befall them. It must not fall into his hands. The darkened egg is corrupted. It will bring about an era of ashes, then, Hydranok."

"Hydranok?"

"The destruction of all balance. Ultimately leading to… the end of most lives, if not all."

"We must find the egg before the fourth rider."

"The time for that has passed. Listen to me, Isabel. All you must do is save your blood and find your dragon. Are you certain you cannot hear it?" her father faced her, staring blankly at her. Isabel shook her head. *My blood?*

"Impossible. If the first has awoken, all dragon eggs in Emerion would be heard. We still have two dragons versus one. Where is the other egg, the one left unsold? Where is it, Isabel?" his eyes widened like a madman's. Isabel was uncertain if captivity, the loss of his family, or the world itself had plunged him into this horrid state. He reached for her, and Isabel wondered where the thin man's weakness had gone.

"At Accreton, Father. It is safe under my men."

"No. They will never be safe. He will send his minion for it. *He* will scorch the earth until he finds it. Morkath will not stop until he finds it."

"Then we must kill Morkath, once and for all."

"No. Morkath is merely a minion. We must hatch the other egg you have. Your brother must do it. Giles must be found."

"Father. We will prevent the prophecy from fulfilling itself," Isabel replied, unsure of her words.

Her father gazed into the distant side of the cell where Isabel once sat, "Isabel," he paused, "I fear for us. An era of ashes is coming. Hydranok will follow. I fear it may be too late."

The clouds shielded the caravans and dozens of carts riding into the city from the rays of sunshine which rarely reached Accreton. Lucia and Faylinn watched as men, women, and children in ragged clothes entered the city, refugees from the lands their enemies had seized. This was the castle they had seen when they rode to Hillfrey, and Lucia could not help but stare at the magnificent castle as they approached it.

Men had begun to work on the walls and buildings, Lucia catching a glimpse of how they rebuilt the massive exterior wall, a gap she was certain could easily be breached by any force who decided to attack. The wooden bridge had been recently restored, the fresh planks sturdy under their horses' hooves.

At the main gate, a group of guards halted the party arriving at the city's entrance. Amongst them stood Odo, Lucia riding past the people towards them, the guards swiftly raising their spears at the incoming women.

"Halt," the guards yelled, and Odo glanced from the freshly arriving serfs towards Lucia.

"Lady Lucia," he said excitedly, then turned towards the guards. "Let her through. This is Lady Isabel's sister."

"What is happening, Odo?"

"I will explain in a moment, My Lady," Odo replied, turning towards the serfs. "A carpenter you mentioned?"

"Aye," the serf's gaze flickered from Lucia to Odo.

"Down the street we have men cutting logs into planks. Join them. You will be fed and quartered if you lend your services to rebuild the city of Accreton. In a matter of time, you will be allowed to set shop. Any inquiries?"

"No, Lord. Me and the wife will get working right away," and the man departed, Odo redirecting his attention to Lucia.

"Follow me, My Lady," Odo said and instructed one of the men to continue his job.

"Were you not rescuing a damsel in distress?" Lucia watched the city being rebuilt, mesmerized by the population flooding into it.

"We were. In the process, your sister decided to rebuild your ancestral home."

"Ancestral home?"

"Aye. This abandoned city was home to your forefathers. Your sister is more versed on the matter. She may better explain when she returns."

"Returns?"

"Indeed. Your sister departed the city and was en route to find you. It appears as if we will need to dispatch a messenger. I was to oversee the city's affairs while she returned, yet you are her lineage and will inherit the command of it hereon."

Faylinn looked at Lucia. Lucia glanced at her before answering Odo, and with wide eyes, said, "I believe it best if you remain overseeing Accreton. I am certain I am unsuited in rebuilding a city."

"I believe it best if you took command. Nobles should learn to administer their family's cities."

Lucia glanced around, watching the rubble remains of the city being rebuilt steadily with the moving workers. "I would say I would turn this place into rubble under my rule, but I fear it may be difficult to fulfill."

"Much has changed, but it is still an heirloom to your family's lineage. I am certain it will be restored to its former glory."

"For now, resume to oversee what my sister has commanded."

"Very well. Nevertheless, I will summon you if any concerning matter arises."

"Most certainly. Odo," Lucia said, but her thoughts of rebuilding a city fled her. "We are famished and exhausted from our journey. Is there food about the keep?"

"I do not wish to dishearten you, but we have no banquets to please your unexpected visit. Beavis trapped a pair of hares. I am certain he would be willing to share them with you ladies," Odo pointed towards the keep. The ladies trotted away without hesitation, their hunger reigning over their minds with each grumble escaping their bellies.

Beavis sat by a fire near the keep's entrance, dropping the hares into his pot. "M'ladies. Your arrival was unaccounted for."

"Odo has brought that matter to our attention," Faylinn plopped against the wall.

"He may have mentioned that your hunt was quite successful," Lucia's stomach spoke for her, the grumbling increasing, urging her to be fed.

"Of course, My Lady," he handed each a trencher with hare meat.

Lucia's excitement was met with a frown at the taste of the hare meat. After their numerous days on the road, the traveling roads' burden of untasteful meals struck her unfavorably, and she expected a finer meal upon their arrival. The recurring situation was enough to cause her to sigh softly, but Beavis failed to take notice. Nevertheless, custom taught her to be grateful, and the warm meal sufficed to satisfy her after her travels.

"Beavis, thank you for the meal. After all these chilly days, it is good to have a warm meal to fill our stomachs," Faylinn said, then tossed her trencher at a stray dog wandering by the fire.

"Thank you, Beavis. It is quite good indeed," Lucia swallowed the hare meat, and with it, her hopes of a finer meal in the days to come.

Lucia admired from the top of the hill the city her sister had laid eyes upon days ago. The massive towers, the waving banners, and the church kept snatching her attention as she appreciated what may become her new home. The people's labor in rebuilding Accreton was proving efficient, the fresh workers thatching the roofs of the buildings closest to the keep, though she could see there was yet much to be done.

The flow of people flooding into the city like the summer rains was incessant. Lucia wondered how they learned about Accreton's repopulation and why they rushed in these massive groups. Her questions remained unanswered, for Beavis had departed to aid Odo. She remained with Faylinn outside, the long days on the road causing her eyes to close while she admired the working populace from outside the keep's walls.

"My Lady," a voice awoke her from her slumber, Lucia jumping and nearly collapsing onto the ground. The world was gloomy, and Lucia was unsure if night had come or the clouds had seized control of the skies.

"My Lady," the voice repeated, Lucia's vision blurry. She rubbed her eyes and realized it was Odo before her.

"What is it, Odo?"

"We have a newcomer at the gate requesting your presence. He says he knows the lady of the castle and wishes to speak with her. The man is in rags, a serf who must have lost his home."

"I will meet him," Lucia said, the two strolling towards the city's gates, the flooding caravans now diminished. Only a pair of guards remained at the entrance, the occasional cart riding in. Evening was making its way to the city, and the roads had become desolate. Lucia was certain the last of the travelers had arrived, at least for the day.

The man in rags bore a scruffy beard, his dull, wavy hair unkempt. Fair skin escaped from under the torn rags as Lucia drew near, hoping to distinguish him. The ragged man was unrecognizable to Lucia. *Who is this man calling for me?* She got closer, hoping to catch a clearer glimpse of him while remaining behind the guards at the entrance.

"Lucia," he called from behind the guards. It was a voice she could never forget. Veiled behind his beard, the man stared at her. Lucia's jaw fell agape at what appeared to be a ghost, a ghost she believed she would never see again. The guards lowered their spears to impede his passage as he attempted to reach the young noble.

"Let him through," Lucia yelled, the guards stepping aside. The man rushed by them, the distance between the pair diminishing as their footsteps quickened. As he drew near, Lucia recognized the straight nose and chocolate eyes. The man arrived at her side, his eyes in despair.

"Giles?"

"Lucia," her long-lost brother looped his arms around his sister, the two siblings hugging after years of estrangement.

CHAPTER 31: SURVIVORS

Thumping footsteps awoke Isabel from her slumber, her father's arms still enveloping her. Under her heavy eyelids, she watched a guard sit beside her cage, the man honing his sword with a whetstone. Isabel moved from under her father's arm, the man with his back to the cage, unable to see her.

"It is best if you remain where you lay," the man must have heard the shuffling of hay under her. Isabel's eyes widened, her head jerking back at his acute hearing. His ability to identify her movements detained her from approaching him. She glanced around, ensuring it was him, not someone else alerting him of her movements.

"Good." The man continued sharpening his sword. "Now, Lady Isabel. I have been enlisted to aid you both in your escape. You have resourceful friends who wish to see you and your father alive."

"Who sent you?" Isabel leaned closer to him.

"Remain on your side of the cage. We need not raise suspicion." Isabel did as he said, leaning back against the cage beside her father.

"Who sent you?" she watched her surroundings, the idea that they were being observed increasing. Once again, not an eye lay looking in their direction.

"It need not matter. What matters is I have been told you have deep pockets. If you add coin to the pot, I will continue to aid your escape."

"I have no coin."

"You need not lie to me, Lady Isabel. I am aware of the wagon that carried your chests of coins. Morkath mentioned it to us all."

Isabel dropped her gaze onto the hay-filled cage. *Morkath saw us selling the egg.* "I have no coin with me. What is your price?"

"Half a coffer. It would prove to be a formidable ransom."

"That is an excessive amount for our escape. My family could ransom us without the risk of losing our heads."

"To my knowledge, your family is imprisoned, and the rest do not know where you may have vanished. Nevertheless, our endeavor is not solely for your liberation. As I said, your father is in the bargain, and his present condition will hinder our escape. Secondly, do you genuinely believe Morkath would ransom you after all his efforts to locate you?" he paused and glanced over his shoulder, "I would make a quick decision. Your father does not seem to have much time left." The man ceased his sword's upkeep, perusing his surroundings to ensure their conversation had not been compromised.

"I will give you a quarter less of what you have asked. I am certain my anonymous ally is paying you for your work. I will not have you be a rightful pinch purse with me," Isabel saw a creeping smile on the man's lips.

"A hard bargain. Your reputation precedes you," he looked away, continuing to sharpen his blade. "Very well. I accept your offer. We move at dusk with the changing of the guard." He was about to rise when he stopped. "Now, do not believe because these men know you have coin, they will also aid in your escape. Their greed for gold is not as grand as their fear for Morkath."

"And yours is?"

The guard shook his head, "I am no fool. This cult has one purpose, and I would be dispensed if I were the cost to achieve it. I am no blind fanatic as these men. I would rather take my chances." *A cult? This is a cult? An entire cult against us for what our ancestors did?*

"Cult?"

"Cult, kingdoms. Are they not all the same? Following a leader blindly to fulfill what they wish," and the guard rose from the wooden chair and sheathed his sword, leaving Isabel beside her father. She watched him go, unsure if he should be trusted or if his lack of debate proved she had overpaid for her escape. Only one question plagued her more: *Is it a cult, or is it a leader after us?*

"A hard bargain?" her father peeked from under his brow.

"Father, prying? Did you not always say prying into other people's conversations was inappropriate?"

"It is. However, times change, and the rules must change with them too," he smiled. "Now, a hard bargain? Would you care to elaborate on the matter?"

"Nothing grand. It is just that I have bargained with the men at the various towns we have visited."

"Well done so. Taking after your uncle in Zeleciia. Now," his gaze followed the path the guard had taken, "that man, I do not trust."

"Nor do I, yet he will aid in our escape."

"Even so, he is a devious fellow. Best to keep an eye on him. The coin sways his opinions swiftly," he took her hand and pressed it onto the hay. Isabel felt a piercing coldness crash onto her hand, her finger caressing the metal object and its sharp edge.

"A dagger?"

"Indeed. You were one to fancy such an instrument of death. When we leave tonight, take it. If he betrays our trust or the trust of our coin, we must make quick work of him."

The words of killing a man coming from her father were enough to send the hairs on her back spearing into her overshirt, seeking an escape. "Father, I cannot kill him."

"You must not hide the horrors you have seen, let alone done, from me, my dear. I know you are not the little girl I knew in Oakheart," he shut his eyes gently as if seeking to forget all he never saw yet knew.

Isabel gulped, "How can you know father?"

"Once you have taken multiple lives, your body will not hesitate when it spots an opportunity. I noticed how you primed yourself to pounce the man when his back was to us." Deep down, Isabel knew she had been ready to pounce the man like lion on its prey.

"The only lives I have taken had already been deprived of their innocence," Isabel stared at the hay shamefully.

"Of that, I am certain, my dear. Without the deeds you have committed, you nor your sister would have survived, let alone allowed me to have you by my side once more. What we did, it had to be done." There was a darkness in his gaze, and Isabel's skin mimicked a porcupine as she wondered what he may have done in his past. *Could father have done horrid things, all in the name of survival? He would never. Father is kind. We are the heroes, not villains in this story.*

Isabel nodded, the sun descending, night approaching once more. Icas took her chin and said, "Now, if he betrays you, you must strike his armor's weak points. Always strike under his arm, or if the opportunity arises, strike his neck. If you encounter an opponent you must sneak upon, suppress their groans when you slice their throat," he shook his head. She could already imagine herself doing it. Grabbing a man, his muffled groans, his blood flowing over her fingers. An assassin's kill. *Am I able to do this if the time comes?* "All my life, I prayed my daughter would not have to resort to this close level of violence."

"All is well, Father. If it needs to be done, let us remember it is for the sake of our survival."

"Let it not scar you. For violence has a manner of penetrating even into the purest of souls. It, it changes you."

"I will not allow it, Father," yet she knew her words were filled with false hopes, for violence had proven to penetrate within the deepest trenches of her soul, a scar she sensed would never heal.

"Giles," Lucia joined her brother by the crackling fire, "why have you made your way here to Accreton?"

"Our village was raided. If I had not left, my life would have been taken. At times, I only wish it had all ended there," his eyes welled, Lucia's throat tightening at the sight of her brother's sadness.

"You need not plague your mind with such foul thoughts, Giles. Why would you come about and wish for such a ghastly idea?"

"She is dead, Lucia. Beatriz is dead. Those men took her life, and I was not there to protect her," tears escaped him. Giles covered his face, attempting to conceal the pain erupting from his eyes.

Lucia wrapped her arms around him, "Forgive me, Giles."

"She is gone. I am alone."

"You are not alone, Giles. Isabel and I are there for you," she rubbed his back gently.

"I am alone, Lucia. I am certain Father does not want me back. I have failed all those who love me."

"Father," she paused, uncertain if the words were the ones she should let erupt into the pile of pain consuming her brother.

"What about Father?" he turned, and Lucia knew he must have noticed the change in her tone.

"We have not seen Father nor Mother after Oakheart burned."

"What? Who is caring for you then?"

"We have men fighting for us, some of which have left with Isabel."

"Isabel is not here?"

"She went to find me and rally more men to our cause."

"I cannot believe this. I knew our home was burnt to ashes, but when I saw men coming to Accreton, I followed. I hoped you would all be here. Mother and Father, they are not dead, are they?" The thought of it was enough to tense Lucia's back. *No. They are alive. Isabel said so. They must be. I know they are.*

"We have yet to find them. They are alive. They were alive when they helped us escape Oakheart," Lucia answered. *Are we truly alone? Our nearest family members are in Zeleciia, so far from the Midlands.*

"Then you cannot be certain," Giles said. Lucia's throat became dry, and she watched him with wide eyes. He must have seen the expression on her face, for he quickly added, "Perhaps you are not mistaken," and he wrapped an arm around her. "They must be out there somewhere. We will find them, Lucia. We will get our home back."

"We are home," a smile grew as she said this. "Home is where we all are. It is not a place." The great doors opened, Lucia glancing in their direction, Odo striding in their direction.

"Forgive the interruption, My Lady. Your presence is required."

Lucia rose, Giles following her when she halted him. "No, Giles. Stay and rest. Go to the chambers if you must."

The doors closed and Lucia left him alone in front of the fire, the warmth emanating from it dispelling the cold world that had taken the people and places he had come to love most. The silence in the great hall brought solace, the occasional crackle in the fire instilling a sense of peace in his body, his muscles relaxing.

The travels from town to town, sleeping on the ground, had taken a toll on his body. Giles' body weighed upon him like a peasant out on the field, a sensation he had come to learn over the years working them. Escaping with Beatriz had allowed him an opportunity at marriage for love, but the life of a peasant had wearied him. Accreton had proven to be a vital respite, a respite from his travels, a respite from his struggles.

"Giles!"

A whisper echoed within the great hall, Giles swiveling to meet the calling voice. His forehead wrinkled when he found no one behind him, only the hollowness of the great hall, its shadows stretching over the stone floor. *Is it the throne?* The dragon skull stared at him from hollow eyes.

"Giles!" The voice called once more, Giles nearly considering it a figment of his imagination. Yet it was not. *It is not the throne.* The voice repeated, calling out to him, urging him to follow it. His heart banged against his chest, his eyes focused on the steps before him.

Giles left the crackling fire, pursuing the voice. Its sound increased with every step he took toward the throne. After taking the stairs, the voice led him to Isabel's chamber, the candles scattered throughout the chamber casting shadows across it. Giles was mesmerized by the dragon mosaic on the floor, standing at the edge of the painted stones. The voice cared not for the mosaic, interrupting his admiration and drawing him towards the chest beside the bed.

He crouched before it, the voice drowning within the silence, only to be disrupted by the rain's pitter-patter. The water droplets turned into streams, tracing their path down the glass. Giles extended his hand to mimic their journey, his finger lightly tracing the chest and its protruding designs, the ovals and skulls watching him, urging him to open it. The rune-like scriptures were unreadable to him, Giles tilting his head and wrinkling his nose as he stared at the object, his curiosity ignited, reminiscent of the one his sisters had once experienced. *What is this? It looks ancient.*

He did as the chest asked, listened to its plea to open it. Within it, the last egg lay, desperate to be touched. Its azure scales glimmered with the straying rays of light emitted from the candles, strength in every scale, strength in the one who could wield its content's power.

Giles' heart swelled at the sight, his pupils dilating. He reached for the egg, touching the rigid scales, the metal clinging onto him. The egg burned into his skin, his hand scorching. The internal flame spread through his body like a forest fire. It desired to consume him. Giles attempted to pull away, his struggle helpless, incapable of acquiring his freedom as sweat began to bead upon his skin.

His body weakened amidst the struggle. The life within him was draining, a heavy weariness permeating every limb. Overcome by the egg's force, his strength waned as the chamber's shadows expanded, closing in on him. His eyes began to droop as the chamber seemed to spin around him. The egg's power was unable to match his body's pull, Giles plummeting onto the chilly, stone floor, his body entering a deep slumber.

CHAPTER 32: FIRE IN OUR HEARTS

Time waned leisurely, Isabel imagining when the moment for their escape would arrive. She turned to her father, a topic lingering in her mind, uneasiness shifting within her stomach. Hoping to speed up the time of their captivity, she spoke her mind to her father.

"Father."

"Aye?" he remained with his eyes closed.

"Did you and Mother wed out of love?"

His eyelids swung wide open. "Indeed we did. I would call us fortunate."

"Why is that?"

"It is a luxury for nobles to wed out of love."

"I have been told."

"Why the sudden curiosity?"

"Just a thought pestering me." The thoughts of Robion beside her at the lake flooded her mind. "Why did you not offer to wed me as most nobles do with their daughters at such a young age."

Her father cocked an eyebrow, tilting his head, Icas staring at his daughter. "What were those words you always told me?"

Isabel's thoughts flew with the wind, wondering what it was she once expressed to her father. "I cannot recall, Father."

"I always recall you said you desired to become a knight. Am I mistaken?"

"You are not."

"It is a rarity in our realm for a man to wed a knight, for he fears she will cast a shadow upon him, a shadow society will not favor.

That would be if his wife were to be a knight of grandeur," and he squinted at his daughter, holding her soft hands within his callous-filled palms. "I never wished this for you, for I longed to keep you safe from the dangers lurking in this realm. Danger seems to have found us, but seeing as you have escaped Oakheart alive and the stories men around here have spoken of you, I can see I was mistaken. Isabel, you will be a grand knight. That is why you must find a man who will accept you for you. A man worthy of your grandeur, of your ability to be of equal stature to him," he paused, "or perhaps greater."

Isabel's cheeks flustered with happiness, her arms wrapping around his neck. "You were going to make me a knight?"

"No," he watched her pull back, "I *am* going to make you a knight." Isabel's beaming smile could cast a shadow over the sun, its rays unable to compete with the light intensifying endlessly within her.

"Why the sudden change of heart, Father?"

He paused, then looked at her. "Isabel, it is a perilous world. All I have ever wanted was a great future for you, and if you were to wed a powerful house, I believed it would secure your safety. However, those houses frown upon women pursuing the path of a warrior. They prefer their women more versed in politics. I realize now you do not need a mighty house's protection. You, my dear Isabel, are a resilient Beaumont woman. You *are* the powerful house." She could not be more elated, Isabel embracing him with overflowing joy.

"I will make you proud, Father." Then, remembering her journey after leaving Oakheart, she added, "I have restored our family's sword." Her words brought a smile to her father's face, reflecting the happiness within her.

"Such a magnificent sword," he gazed into the air as if he were visualizing it. "Isabel, our great ancestors have carried that sword. It has history, and only the grandest of warriors should wield it. I believe, no, I know, it is your time to wield it. You will, with it, bring honor and justice to our family. I am certain it is meant for you."

Isabel's chest inflated, and for a moment, she believed it might burst. "Thank you, Father. I will do it in our honor." The pair hugged, Isabel imagining her ancestors wielding the sword in the hundreds of battles in their past and the hundred that were to come.

"I believe there was a thought troubling you," Icas said, Isabel's forehead wrinkling as she recalled their conversation.

"I cannot quite recall."

"Is it not about Robion, or have you met another man?"

Her cheeks burned with embarrassment, for she rarely discussed Robion with her father unless they were going to visit him. "There is no other man."

He cupped his chin, "Hmph. Robion then. Have you seen him after Oakheart, or were you merely fawning over him?"

Isabel resumed his game, "We crossed paths in Rivetion, along with his family."

"They were always kind people."

"And that is how they will be remembered," Isabel's face distorted with pain. "Robion misses them dearly."

Icas' eyebrows rose but he quickly understood. He nodded while placing a hand on her knee. There was a brief pause before he continued. "Offer my condolences to him."

"Robion and I were talking while in Accreton. I feel our bond has strengthened since we left Rivetion." Though she rarely spoke with her father about Robion, without Valaenis there, she felt the need to speak to him. After all, a question lurked deep within her mind that she could not push away.

"I would imagine so. Dire times prove who is there to stand by your side. You have also written and seen each other over the years. It was bound to happen. Are your affections matched by his?"

"I believe it may just exceed it," her cheeks burned at the thought of Robion.

Icas closed his eyes and nodded before replying. "My dear. You may be just as fortunate as your mother and I once were."

"If only he were here to hear it."

"Soon. Soon, you will tell Robion. He is fortunate. You are a young woman who knows love. If you were ever to wed, I am certain it would be a worthy union," Icas remarked, lightening her heart with his acceptance of Robion without her asking him.

Heavy footsteps approached, a group of mailed knights following Morkath. He walked towards their cage, pretending to admire the pair. "What a lovely family. I cannot help but imagine how difficult times keep you together."

"A man like you could never understand," Icas glanced at him.

"I do not care for it. All I care about is trust, trust in those who surround me," his words struck Isabel. Her eyes darted towards the guard who had agreed to help her escape, the man amidst the chainmailed soldiers encircling Morkath. "We all have friends in this world, yet are they friends we can trust? Trust with our lives?" Morkath paced in front of the guard who had agreed to help them. "You will never be saved. Your friends, they will not arrive to save you. They have failed. Your end is near."

The guard's eyes were fixed on the cage, watching the pair of Beaumonts he had planned to save for a sizeable fee. "Guards. Do I not treat you well? Do I not feed your bellies, warm your toes during the night with our fires, or fill your coffers?"

"Aye," the men responded in unison.

"You are all men I can trust. Men who would destroy our enemies. *Yet*," a pair of guards joined the group, standing behind the man who had agreed to help Isabel and her father, "there is always one who wants more. Greedy men. They always want more."

Morkath unsheathed his dagger, the evening's late rays glimmering against its blade. "I will give you the shimmering metal you deserved, not the one you desired," and Morkath spun towards the man who had agreed to help Isabel, stabbing the man's stomach. He groaned with the thrust of the knife tearing into his skin, then gasped as Morkath twisted it within. The men behind him snatched his arms, preventing him from retaliating. Morkath stared at the man's grunting face before he removed the dagger. The man's blood gushed onto his hand before he struck him once more, the man groaning in pain. "Your greed has killed you. It will continue to kill you slowly." The guards dropped the man on the floor, "for a wound to the gut is a slow death."

Isabel shielded her eyes at the sight. Her body trembled at the loss of their escape, at their one opportunity for freedom. The man was slumped on the post, coughing blood while his face paled, sluggishly fighting for his life. Icas' grip tightened around Isabel, seeking to comfort her when the world around them only turned dimmer.

"Find a suitable post and tie him. Let our archers practice their aim on his treacherous body," Morkath commanded, a pair of guards rushing to fulfill his bidding.

Morkath watched as the guard's life waned, every trickle of blood causing him to become weaker. He swiveled on his heel, meeting the Beaumonts' gazes. "You believed you would escape my encampment? How naïve. Once you are in my grip, you are nothing but a slithering snake. You may writhe within it, yet escape is unachievable."

"I have powerful allies. You will not keep us reined here forever," Isabel said.

"Their power has such grand reach that I have yet to see them lurking around my encampment," Morkath said, his men snickering behind him. His attention spun to Isabel, "You may meet the day to see them. Your father, however, will not be so fortunate."

Isabel wrapped her father in her arms, shielding him from the perils encircling them. "With you and your purer blood, your father is no longer useful to me. He marks the inception of your lineage's annihilation. Seize him," Morkath pointed at Icas, the guards entering the cage to remove her father from its refuge.

Isabel seized her father, but even she knew it was helpless. "Father, we can take them," he enveloped her within his arms, securing her like a knight's armor. Isabel's heart raced, the men reaching for her father, attempting to cleave their embrace. Her father kissed her forehead, Isabel clinging to his body. Her strength grew, but she could feel her father's grip easing. "Papa, do not let go." The time for grasping onto the past had passed. Icas released her, the guards snatching her arms.

"Protect your sister," he said, Isabel writhing from the guards' grips.

"Leave him," she swung at the guard's face, striking his cheek. The guard spun and elbowed her temple. Kneeing her stomach, Isabel plummeted on the cage's hay. The wind from her lungs abandoned her, Isabel wheezing. She reached within the cage's hay, searching for the dagger, her father catching a glimpse of her.

"It is not the time, Isabel. It cannot be done." The men dragged him away, locking the cage entrance before she had the opportunity to retaliate.

But Isabel would not listen, for her heart would not yield to the men who took all that was dear to her. From behind the bars, Isabel saw the men take her father away. They dragged him to the executioner's block near where she was confined. A group of men encircled her cage. Any hope of escape dwindled when she approached the cage's entrance. But Isabel's determination could not be deterred, and she knocked the first guard off balance with a powerful blow.

"Seize her," Morkath ordered. From under his black hood, the executioner watched his victim being carried towards his head's final resting place.

The guards seized Isabel's arms, Isabel writhing like a snake in Morkath's grasp. Isabel squirmed and struggled, but she was unable to free herself from the three guards restraining her. Her body burned, the fire within her igniting with every step the guards took towards the block with her father.

They pushed Icas to his knees, his weakened body submitting to the defeat that had overtaken his family. The executioner carried his axe over his shoulder, his chainmail's ruby stripes identifying him as one of the men under Morkath's order. Her father glanced at her once more, Isabel reading his lips as he said to her, "Fire in our hearts." With those final words, Icas' head fell upon the executioner's block, yielding to his fate.

Isabel clenched her jaw, Morkath seizing the executioner's axe and standing beside her father. Isabel's face reddened with anger, her body stiff while shouting at Morkath, her eyes welling. A headache overwhelmed her, Isabel's stare as sharp as daggers, wishing to land them on Morkath.

"I will make you burn, Morkath. You will scorch until you are forgotten. Your body nor ashes will remain when I am finished with you!" Isabel called out across the encampment, the vein in her neck throbbing.

Morkath raised the axe, defiance in every move. The sun's rays deflected off its blade, the last rays of light on the horizon illuminating the end of her father's day. Without hesitation, Morkath let the axe fall on her father. Isabel clenched her teeth so tight she believed they would escape her mouth like arrows to eradicate him. The axe fell, slicing swiftly and decapitating her father, his head falling into the basket before him. She screeched, and then, as if she too had been killed, Isabel's body slumped defeatedly, her heart burying away into her stomach.

Isabel cried rivers, a thousand dams incapable of withholding the pain erupting from them. A lifeless dullness replaced the sharp daggers in her gaze. Her hands failed to tussle with the men holding her, her body limp within their grip. She was no longer a snake in Morkath's grip but a rope that lost all hope.

The men threw her into the cage, Isabel collapsing onto her knees. Her arms struggled to support the weight of her body, as if the world's mightiest mountain stood on her back, pressing relentlessly. She longed to awaken from the nightmare that loomed upon her, the sun and all its light vanishing, abandoning her in the shadows.

All her senses died with her father's decapitation. Morkath's heavy footsteps approached her cage. He stood with his axe, the fresh blood dripping down its blade. Morkath stared at her. Then, he said, "You will be consumed in your flame, child. The Valenours are on the verge of meeting their end." He marched away. Isabel had heard nothing, for all she could hear were the streaming rivers of her tears and her father's peaceful voice before he parted.

All that lingered within Isabel was pain and her father's unheard voice saying, "Fire in our hearts."

CHAPTER 33: FORGIVE ME

Time within the cage was a perpetual sentence. It resisted the passing of time, Isabel lying in the hay, her eyes dry after shedding the last of her tears. Night's darkness had wrapped the forest in its blanket, most of the guards leaving their posts for their evening meal. Following their supper, the guards abandoned their logs by the fire, wobbling and yawning as they sought the respite of their straw beds after their long day's work.

Isabel watched them, her chest heaving, heaving with sadness, heaving with pain, heaving with hate. She watched the men drop into their realm of slumbers, her hand reaching under the hay, seeking the dagger her father had left her.

The guard responsible for watching her grew lax in his vigilance, Isabel reaching the cage's entrance while he remained occupied with his meal. Alaehrayne's words echoed in her mind, Isabel's mind mischievous in all its ways.

"Hey," she called out to the guard.

"What do you want?" he said, eating like a rabid hound.

"You are a hungry one," she slid the dagger along her thigh, her grip tight.

"Aye. I cannot quite remember when we last had chicken."

"Hmm. Are you not famished for a fair lady's kiss?" Isabel puckered her lips mockingly.

The man brought his plate towards her cage. "Aye, you think yer slick? I know you are trying to steal me chicken," he laughed hoarsely, coughing when the chicken got caught in his throat.

"What a pity. Cause I was just thirsty," and drew the dagger from her side, thrusting it into his chicken-lodged throat. Without the opportunity to scream for help, his body plummeted silently before her.

Isabel searched his corpse, acquiring the keys to the cell and opening the lock. She hid his body amidst the hay, hoping it would give her the time she needed to escape.

Isabel was well on her way, evading drunk guards and searching for Morkath's tent. The shadows proved to be her ally, although the men's drunken states were enough to prevent them from spotting her in plain firelight. She slipped from shadow to shadow, slithering cautiously until she reached Morkath's tent.

A fireplace in front of his tent crackled, Isabel pouring a pail of water over it, the fire sizzling as its flame was doused. The heat dissipated, and Isabel shivered, her ally returning with the disappearance of the flame. Morkath shuddered while she peeked through the flap, yet he remained in his slumbering slate, unaware of Isabel and her dagger.

Isabel watched nefariously with her curling lip, her skin boiling at his sight, the night's chilliness forgotten. She would remove the man who executed her father, the man who destroyed her home. He had razed her world. Now she would extinguish the flame that kept him alive. *You are dead Morkath.* She glanced around. No soldier was about to witness her deed.

She crept between the flaps, silent as the night. Dagger in hand, her mind was set to slice his throat and escape his gripping hand. In a corner, leaning against his bed, she saw her sword in its sheath, under it, a crown. *Is that the crown, the talon crown I saw in Oakheart's forest? Forget the crown, Isabel.* She would kill Morkath, take her sword, and vanish before she could be caught. Isabel's hand rose over him, her body stiff with hatred for the man who ruined her life. Determined to do it, she admired his vulnerable state, prepared to commit to the task.

One, two, three. But her body did not react accordingly, a sound outside the tent startling her. Isabel's heart leapt to her throat. She glanced over her shoulder. A shadow moved outside the tent, and while she watched, Morkath grumbled. Isabel glanced to and fro from Morkath to the tent's entrance, uncertain of what to do.

If I kill Morkath, I may be caught. If I am caught killing the leader, they may kill me without hesitation. Without Father, Lucia will be alone in the world. The shadow continued to move, getting ever so closer to the entrance. *What do I do? What do I do? I can end this, but if I die, at what cost would it have been to leave Lucia alone? I must kill Morkath. He killed Father. Lucia will understand.* But Isabel hesitated. *Will she?*

In one swift moment, Isabel held her breath and made her decision. Snatching her sword, she rushed towards the edge of the tent, waiting for the man to get closer. When its shadow was by the entrance, she leapt out, pressing a hand to his mouth, her dagger to his throat.

A dagger's ice-cold teeth bit against her neck. Her eyes widened at the sight. She was in disbelief as she saw the familiar gaze.

The man's ebony hair and beard concealed the scars that once littered his face and the many fresh ones he had acquired since they last met. Her glee was met with disappointment, for it was as friendly a face as she could ever hope for, a friendly face who had arrived at an inopportune moment.

"Arot? You survived."

"Lady Isabel, I hoped to find you alive. We must leave." *With him beside me, he can keep watch while I kill Morkath. I will rid Emerion of this pestilence once and for all.*

"No. With you here, I can kill Morkath before I leave this place and take the crown he stole from us," she pulled away from him and spun, her opportune moment nearly crushed by the shouts of men in a fireplace nearby. They remained away, and Isabel prepared to enter the tent.

"Lady Isabel," she heard Arot say behind her, "I hope you may forgive me for this." His words stunned her, Isabel turning to meet the man she hoped would never betray her. To her dismay, she was met by a strike to her head, the world around her crashing as she was knocked out.

The straying rays of the morning sun struck Isabel's eyes as her body bounced up and down, the hoofs trampling the dirt under her. The world around Isabel was bustling with activity, farmers setting out to the fields in search of their harvests, the farmland stretching around a city Isabel had never visited.

She turned, searching for the body crashing onto hers with each of the horse's strides. Her family's most trusted knight, Arot, rode into the city. Isabel recalled the past night's events, the memories reigniting her fury.

"What have you done?" she screamed, Arot reducing his horse's stride.

"I have saved your life, Isabel. That is what I have done," the horse reached a trot.

"Saved me? I was to avenge my father, my family, our home!"

"You were on the verge of destroying yourself. If I had not arrived, those men would have captured you once more. The executioner's block would have awaited you. Your life would have been forfeited. Did you think of Lucia? What would have happened to your sister? Who would have cared for her?"

"If Morkath were dead, my life would have had a purpose."

"Your purpose should not be the end of you. Forgive me for your father, yet if you are to avenge him, you should make certain you live after it has been done. You cannot abandon your sister over a feud. You cannot abandon your people."

Arot brought the horse to a halt, and Isabel dismounted, her insides scorching. "My people are dead," Isabel felt a lump in her throat.

Arot leapt to her side, leading the horse by its reins while trailing after her. "Your people are not dead. Many lost their lives. Others, however, survived. They are here in Goldcrest," he pointed at the city surrounded by fields of wheat, on its far side a dense forest that spread until the mountains met them in the far east.

Isabel's anger dissipated slightly, surveying the city as they approached it. She gulped, "How many live?"

"Many passed, yet many live. One hundred warriors are yours to command."

"How has the Lord of Goldcrest allowed such numbers to dwell within his castle?"

"Lord Entan Faucher was a close friend of your father. He has permitted his people to remain within his walls until they find a new home. However, his alliance was with your father and not that of the family. He will respect you, yet it need not mean *you* are his close friend. Lord Entan does not necessarily believe those who carry the blood will carry the bond. You must prove your worth to him as a friend and ally."

"How will I prove myself?" Isabel asked, her army and friends distant from her, uncertain if one hundred men would suffice to demonstrate her worth as an ally in battle.

Arot stared at the distant city, silence overcoming him. "I believe there is an event which may benefit you."

"How is that?"

"The Faucher family is hosting a tournament. If you can enter and win, your reputation before Lord Faucher will precede you."

"An archery tournament, perhaps?"

Arot shook his head. "You are quite the archer, but archery is not what will impress Lord Entan. The greatest archers of the realm, along with the surplus wheat, stem from Goldcrest. May I add the lord's daughter is one of the finest archers in the land, if not the most remarkable. I would not wager my coin in a tournament versus her. Great archers surround Entan. He needs a different type of warrior. You should joust or join the melee."

A melee did not suit her best skills, yet she understood the importance of participating to secure Entan's support. With her father gone, now more than ever, she needed all the allies she could get. "Then I will join the melee." Arot nodded. "How did you find me?"

"I did not, My Lady. I was in search of your father. I had a man within the encampment who was to aid me in his escape. Then I heard of your arrival and added you to the bargain. Our plan was compromised. Once I heard from the outside guards a guard was killed, and your father executed, I knew you would retaliate. That is why I rushed in, and when I saw you enter Morkath's tent, I went after you."

The words brought Isabel's heart to a halt, and Isabel relived the event. *I could have killed him. Morkath could be dead. Perhaps Arot is correct. If I was killed, who would have cared for Lucia? Who would have cared for our people?*

"How did you survive?" she gulped, Isabel blinking the tears away as her father always managed to do.

"The arrow?" she nodded, and he continued. "It was a mere flesh wound. Your father and I fought off some men after you escaped. Not long after, we were overwhelmed, and amidst the chaos, I lost him. I was fighting multiple men and was wounded. After being wounded, I merely remember waking up in a cottage where a healer removed what remained of the arrow. I could not stay. My duty to your father urged me to get up. I returned to Oakheart, searching for him, but by then, all was burnt to ashes. I heard a couple survivors on the road mention that Morkath captured Icas, and I have followed the enemies' tracks ever since. However, I failed your family, Lady Isabel. I was unable to save your father."

Isabel understood his pain, Arot being one of the most trusted members of the household. He had proven his loyalty throughout the years and deserved the consolation, "You have not, Arot. I would not be alive if it were not for you. My sister is well. If you follow us, we will be glad to have you by our side, as you have been in years past."

"It would be an honor," Arot nodded. "I pledge to serve you and your sister faithfully. Have you any word of your mother?"

"I fear I have no word of her since we fled Oakheart. She was separated from us during our escape. We can only hope she is safe."

"Then she may very yet be alive. Her body was not in Oakheart. She must have escaped. I will not rest until we find her." Isabel watched him reel the horse through its reins, removing an object from the far side. He handed her the lengthy sword with the emerald gem. "I believe your family's heirloom sword will serve us well in our quest."

Her eyes became misty, Isabel blinking rapidly to regain her eyesight. Not long ago, it had been an heirloom sword and a reminder of her brother. Now, it was all that remained of her family.

CHAPTER 34: LOVE OF GOLD

"You will need armor to enter the melee," Arot led Isabel to the smithy. "With that leather armor, you will be annihilated before you even begin."

"I lack the coin to purchase an armor."

"You are blessed, for I collected substantial coins from the footmen we fought. When I scavenged Oakheart, I found some coins as well. They should suffice to get you started."

The pair arrived at the smithy, a flame-haired woman forging a sword at her anvil. An emanating heat crashed onto their bodies, Isabel noticing the sweat dripping down the woman's arms while she hammered down and began to shape the metal into a sword. Arot admired the pieces of armor placed outside of her shop, pieces ranging from shiny pauldrons to a few scattered rusty basinets.

"We are seeking the armorsmith or the overseer of the forge," Arot said to the woman. The woman's hammering ceased with a resounding bang as his words caught her attention.

She peeked at him from the corner of her eye. "You are staring at her. What is it you need?"

"Forgive my knight," Isabel stood before him, removing her hood. "I am in need of an armor for the tournament."

"Huh," the flame-haired woman stared at Isabel. "I have nothing for you here."

"Are you certain? Is there nothing you can forge or sell me before the tourney?"

"If you were a warrior, would you not have an armor? The tourney is for experienced fighters. Assuming you are a beginner, you will be with your behind on the dirt by the end of the first round," the woman continued to shape her metal.

"I will pay the coin. Is that not all you require?"

The woman slammed her hammer, wiping her face with a cloth beside the anvil. "It is not all that I require. My armor must prove its quality in battle, not be hammered down in a simple tournament where it will lose prestige. Are you aware of how troublesome it is for a female smith to maintain her reputation?"

"I will pay double the cost if I do not survive the first round."

The woman cocked an eyebrow, Arot mirroring her as she walked over to Isabel, placing her hand on her hip. "Triple the cost if you do not survive the tourney."

Isabel crossed her arms, "Double the cost if I lose before the third round, and I will pay half the price now."

The woman paused before replying. "Fair enough."

"We have an accord. Where is the armor?"

The woman fetched various pieces of metal and arranged them on a table before Isabel and Arot. Arot moved forward and shook his head at the armor she brought. "This is rubbish. This is no quality armor."

"It is all I possess," said the woman, "the only piece sized to fit you. It is quality metal that I will shape by tomorrow before you start your tournament."

"There is no guarantee this will protect her," Arot picked up the pieces of metal, eyeing them closely, continuing to shake his head before returning them.

"You can settle the payment after the tournament. If you survive two rounds and the armor dents, your winnings should suffice to cover its full price. I will need collateral, should you be defeated and lack the coin to pay me," her gaze shifted onto Isabel's hip. "That sword proves to have been crafted by a worthy smithy."

"No. This is a family heirloom. I cannot place it as collateral."

"It's worth just rose. It will cover your expenses if you do not survive the first two rounds. It is *merely* collateral. If you supply me the coin, I will return it."

Arot pulled her away from the smithy and whispered, "Do not do it, My Lady. You cannot risk losing your family's sword."

Arot is right. This is all I have left from Father. If I lose the tourney, I lose all I have left of him. It is merely a sword. Father does not live in an object. He lives through us and through all he taught us. If anything, he said we must believe in others. Not only believe in others, but believe in ourselves. In the end, he believed I could be a knight. If he believed in me, then I too must believe in myself. I can win this tourney. But at the risk of my heirloom sword? Should I genuinely risk it? Isabel unsheathed her sword and looked at it. *It is merely an instrument for our goal. If it is as great as it is, I must prove I am worthy of it. I know I am. Father believed I was. I will win the tourney.*

"I will not lose it, Arot. We must have faith in others. I have this feeling I must believe in her and me. I will not lose the sword." Arot looked at her, and after sighing, he nodded, stepping aside.

Isabel handed the sword to the woman, the smithy baffled by Isabel's compliance. Remorse crept into Isabel's heart, yet she knew it was her duty to win the tourney for her and her family's sake. The woman gripped the sword, Isabel staring into her eyes. "It would be best if you did not misplace it. I will return for it." The woman nodded, her eyes flashing briefly with fear as she took it from Isabel.

"It is well cared for. You may trust me. I will have the armor repaired and fitted for you by tomorrow."

After measuring Isabel, the pair were ready to leave when a fair-skinned woman with straight golden hair crossed their path. She had a thin nose, her small eyes glancing curiously at Arot, flashing him a smile. The woman wore a silk dress that matched her hair, her petite frame hiding within it.

The golden-haired woman entered the smith's shop, two servants following closely behind her, and the smithy attended to her without hesitation. "My brother has inquired if you sharpened his sword."

Isabel turned to Arot, the pair standing amidst the city street. "She fancies you," Isabel jabbed her elbow against his arm.

Arot scratched his neck, glancing away, "You are mistaken, My Lady. It was just a lost glance."

"That was no lost glance. The lady fancies you. Woo her, Arot," Isabel winked at him, raising her eyebrows playfully.

"It is best if I did not. This is no place to court a lady."

"Now you are brimming with pretexts. You are a knight, and what lady does not love a knight with their share of stories?"

"At a later date. The feast. Aye, the feast," he glanced away.

"I do not think she will wait for the feast," Isabel watched the blonde lady standing by the table, glancing in their direction while waiting for the smithy to fulfill her request.

Isabel nudged him again, Arot bracing himself by holding his sword's pommel while approaching the woman. "Good morning, I am Sir Arot."

The blonde woman flashed him a smile, "I am Lady Atheena. Are you here for the tourney?"

Arot remained silent, Isabel joining the conversation, "Aye. I am Lady Isabel, and I will be participating. Sir Arot is still contemplating if he wishes to join."

"I had given it thought, but I will not be participating in the tourney," Arot said. "I do not wish to confront Lady Isabel in such fierce battle."

"He is merely being modest," Isabel said. "He believes he may be more of aid to me from the outside than within the melee."

"A humble knight, I see," Atheena said, "one who does not wish to dominate in such a tourney and favors to aid his allies over glory," she glanced over him quickly, her eyes lingering momentarily on his arms. "Quite chivalrous."

"Thank you, Lady Atheena. Your words inspire me to enter the tourney."

"I hope they just might, in a future tourney, perhaps. At the least, I pray they may haul you to the festivities." The smithy returned and handed Atheena the sword wrapped in a linen cloth. "I must be on my way. My brother awaits. Good day," and she bowed lightly, vanishing within the crowds.

"Oh, she fancies you," Isabel winked at Arot, Arot shaking his head, a grin on his lips.

Giles did not know what occurred to him on the day he was called into the chamber. His body had blazed with an internal fire, yet no pain had been experienced afterwards, nor was there any mark to bear witness to the fiery sensation. Lucia had found him on the chamber floor, curious and uncertain of why he had fallen asleep instead of clambering upon the bed. Those were the words Giles said to her, for he was unsure of what truly happened, fearful he would be perceived as a lunatic by those who surrounded him.

The events had brought him once more to the chamber, searching it for clues of what occurred, for that day he fled after he awoke, fearful of the true reason. Curiosity, however, had caused him to return, searching within the chest for a sign of the past event.

Within the chest, all that remained were shattered scales, their once-glimmering surfaces now tarnished to a dull cobalt hue. Giles closed the chest, wondering if he had released its contents and if it had escaped within the castle.

A low thud caused Giles to jump, his head turning towards the bed. A slithering tail hid under it. Giles snatched a staff leaning onto the wall and approached the bed. He dropped to his knees, jabbing the staff under the bed until it struck a hard object. He continued to probe until he heard a low whimper, followed by a tug from his staff.

Giles yanked the staff away from under the bed, staring at what remained. The staff was splintered, the shape of teeth marks spread along its length. Giles pressed his cheek onto the chilly stone floor. The shadow under the bed did not let him glimpse what ate his staff.

Giles searched the chamber and snatched an apple from the plate on the wooden table in the corner. He rolled the apple under the bed, disappearing within the shadows. A scraping movement left him pondering, only to have the apple rolled back to him.

Giles brought a chicken thigh and slid it through the floor, falling short of the bed's edge. For a moment, there was no movement. Then, a loud sniff and a pointy snout emerged from under the bed. A wing with talons crept forward and snatched the thigh, swiftly retracting under the bed. Giles stared wide-eyed as the sound of gnawing filled the chamber, and soon thereafter, silence engulfed the chamber, the creature continuing to conceal its identity under the bed.

Giles dropped the last two pieces of meat close to the bed, yet far enough to draw the animal out. The second piece trailed a couple of feet behind, Giles waiting for the animal to reveal itself.

Once more, there was silence. The animal sniffed again, the snout and wings crawling out from under their safety. Giles' face paled, his hands turning clammy as he retreated from the animal's presence, his knees stiff. The horned animal's tongue slithered from its maw, swiftly ensnaring its prey and devouring it in a single gulp. Its bat-like wings allowed it to crawl forward in search of its supper, its arrowhead tail slapping the stone floor. Azure scales ran its entire body, a formidable armor protecting it from Giles as he raised his staff, prepared to strike the animal down.

The dragon's talons scraped the floor, the creature advancing relentlessly towards its supper. Its fiery almond-shaped eyes were aimed at the single object of desire within the chamber: food. Giles blinked rapidly, hoping the mythical dragon would vanish like a troublesome dream. However, the animal, undeterred, consumed the last piece of meat, its eyes pursuing a new source of potential nourishment, Giles.

Giles pointed his staff at the animal, creating distance between the beast and his body, its last food source within the chamber. The dragon waved its tail, its jagged dagger teeth announcing its longing for Giles. Its red-hot, furnace-ignited eyes continued to lust for the one crucial item in the chamber with each step.

Giles retreated until his back met with the wall, the dragon drawing near to the very end of his staff. He prodded at the beast with cautious intent, delivering a gentle jab in the hope of persuading it to withdraw without kindling its ire or arousing its insatiable appetite further. It was helpless, for the dragon halted, and in Giles' swift moment of relaxation, it bolted at him, Giles staff unable to detain it.

The animal's leap brought him face to feet with Giles, its snout at his feet, its wings and hind legs splayed out in eerie symmetry. The fiery eyes watched Giles' stricken gaze. He pondered why it had not come to devour him in that instant. The dragon slithered its tongue, savoring Giles' boots yet restraining from eating him alive.

Giles descended deliberately, his heart pounding as he extended his trembling hand toward the dragon's head. The dragon squinted, stalking his hand. On the verge of touching it, the dragon snapped at Giles. Its body retracted while Giles' hand bolted in the opposite direction. His heart lodged in his throat. The animal settled into stillness, sniffing the fearful human. Giles reached for it again, the dragon squinting at his hand. Then, realizing Giles was harmless, it turned its head to the side. The noble touched its neck, feeling the rigid, overlapping scales beneath his fingertips.

In that instance, he believed he created a connection with the dragon. The dragon closed its eyes, Giles touching its solid scales gently. His moment was swiftly interrupted by a shrill voice erupting within the chamber. "You have a dragon as well?" Lucia screamed, the dragon slithering across the floor before vanishing under the bed's shadows.

CHAPTER 35: FALSE CHIVALRY

The lance crashed against the knight's cuirass, sending him hurtling from his steed. A cloud of dust enveloped him as he crashed onto the ground. His squire raced towards him, the knight on the ground motionless. Spectators roared from the stands, the sight of warfare igniting their bodies.

The knight who won the round rode until he reached Isabel, her newly acquired armor concealing her identity from the man. With his lance, he lobbed a lizard from the ground toward her with remarkable accuracy, the lizard striking her cuirass and falling limply onto the ground.

"You are next, little lizard. You will not survive the first round with your size." He slapped his heels onto the horse's flanks, riding proudly in the opposite direction. The crowd caught sight of his gesture, and a resounding wave of laughter rippled through the air.

"Lord Bardolf," Arot joined her. "He has proven to be an arse, yet the crowd adores him. He is the tournament's favorite."

"Favorite or not, he demonstrates no signs of chivalry."

"Chivalry? You believe this to be a tournament of chivalry? Oh, My Lady, how you have been misled."

"Misled? Tournaments are meant to express your valor and chivalry. That is what Father always said," Isabel turned to face Arot, watching his face from behind the slit of her barbuta helmet's visor. *How can knights see in this?*

"Times have changed and brimming with chivalry, they are not. Men forfeit their lives fighting. They are unseated from their steeds, battered until they can no longer muster the strength to move. Is that meant to imply chivalry? My Lady, you must know they prey on the weak and flee from the strong until the final round."

"Are you implying I am weak, Sir Arot?"

"I would never utter such an idea. These tournament knights perceive your small stature as weakness. You will become the first target they strike," he crossed his arms and tilted his head. "Nevertheless, you have an important ally in the tourney, for I have paid the coin to compete. I will aid you however I may for you to emerge victorious."

"There is a difference between aiding me and wooing a lady with this tourney," Isabel cocked an eyebrow. Realizing he could not see her gesture, she crossed her arms over her chest.

"Then it is fortunate both pursuits can be harmoniously intertwined, is it not?" he mirrored her gesture, watching the men dragging the knight away from the jousting arena.

"I hope proving your fervor to the young lady is a simple task."

"Saving you will suffice to exhibit my chivalrous ways," Arot nudged her with his elbow.

"It will be wise to seek a new way to woo her, for I will not need any saving."

"As for the matter at hand, you would do well to select a lady to champion if you wish to convince the men of your role as a man early on," he gestured at the crowd of ladies gathered beside Lord Entan's galleries, the lined flame-haired family shielding itself from the sun's fiery rays.

"I have just the woman," Isabel said, pointing toward the galleries.

"It would be wise to approach her in your mount. You would not want her to undermine your prowess because of your petite stature." A smug smile spread across his lips, yet Isabel knew his words held truth within them.

Isabel did as Arot suggested. She rode her horse, its colors concealed by a ruby and azure striped caparison. The horse trotted lightly towards the woman standing by the fence. The lady spoke with a noblewoman beside her, but once the horse halted by the fence, she turned her attention to Isabel.

The woman wore a cerulean dress, her sky eyes ensnaring like a nymph any gaze which dared stray towards her. Her mahogany-colored hair met her angular face, a feather that harmonized with her attire intertwined within it. Her dress accentuated her slender figure as the woman reached the fence to meet the valiant knight who had ventured to approach her.

"How may I be of service, Sir Knight?"

Isabel remained silent, well aware a word from her could unveil her concealed identity. The woman cocked her eyebrow, evidently confused at the knight who would not reveal himself.

"A mute one, I see. Most knights who approach me are arrogant men boasting of their exploits. They often require a dose of humility," and she glanced at the noblewoman behind her, who laughed at her remark.

"Are you offering to champion me?" Isabel nodded instantly. "I am not one to be championed, yet your humility may just persuade me to have a change of heart."

The woman's sky eyes admired Isabel's plate armor once more while she contemplated her decision. She removed the feather from her wavy hair, took a handkerchief, and leaned over the fence towards her valiant knight. "Approach me, Sir Knight. I accept your proposal."

Isabel pulled the horse's reins, stepping closer to the fence, allowing the lady to reach over it. She pressed the feather onto the rerebrace, tying it in place with the handkerchief. "Remember the name of the lady you are championing. Lady Alianora. Now ride!"

The first round of the melee tourney was on the verge of commencing, and Isabel's hands began to sweat. Though it was not a real battle, the combat could prove as deadly.

The spectators cheered, the masses lined around the open field behind the fence, the tents peeking over them to catch a glimpse of the fight. The competitors' banners emblazoned the field, waving their coat of arms to the gathering of men assembled in anticipation of the impending melee.

Isabel watched a banner terribly dyed, the same colors as her horse's caparison upon it. The words Barbeau were written over it, a hasty job done by Arot. Few had heard of the name of the minor, northern family, and Arot had suggested she take it to prevent anyone from prying into her identity. Though it was lesser known, she was confident they would not have travelled to Goldcrest.

The first round was a free-for-all, the sixteen men spaced around, each poised to pounce their adversaries. The herald stood at the center, "This is a contest of honor and chivalry. All weapons are blunted, and daggers are not allowed. A fallen man may rise, yet he who lingers on the ground for the aforementioned amount of time will be deemed defeated. Now, knights, you are well-acquainted with the remaining rules."

He jumped over the fence, the men swinging their swords, roaring, and taunting their neighbors. Isabel's heart hammered against her chest, the men surrounding her anxious to fight. Her body was scorching, the blazing sun exhausting her before the battle could begin, her legs weakening. The armor weighed her down. Isabel hoped it would not hinder her agility.

"Melee," the herald announced, sending the men into a frenzy. Arot's assessment had proven accurate, the throng of contenders converging on Isabel, the larger men prowling on her like lions stalking a defenseless lamb. Hiding behind her shield, Isabel could see the tourney ending before it began. Her legs shook, her body unprepared for the hammering defeat coming her way.

The crowd's roars came to life as the clash of swords resounded, yet her sword was no culprit of the sounds. A pair of men arrived to her aid, the first in broken armor, the second in pristine condition. Isabel's legs were stiff, but with the knights' aid, they regained strength, and Isabel joined the tournament melee.

The battle, though brief, felt to Isabel as if it had stretched on for endless days. Within a few strikes, the armor weighed her down. Her agility quickly diminished, her strike's speed reducing with each blow. The sun at her back was of no aid, its blazing rays tearing into her body, draining her with each step. Her sword slipped from her grip, Isabel's sweat antagonizing her.

The horn was blown, marking the conclusion of the first round, Isabel relieved it had ended. Half the men remained standing, the other eight eliminated and dragged out from the melee's field. Amongst the survivors, Isabel spotted the men who aided her. The pair removed their helmets, revealing their faces, Isabel astonished at the sight of them. *Sehan? Baenlorn?*

Isabel fled the field before Sehan and Baenlorn had the opportunity to approach her. Though the pair had been kind to her in Rivetion while she was under the watch of Layne, she did not wish for them to learn of her identity. She sought refuge within her rectangular marquee, its vibrant ruby and ivory stripes beckoning her, Isabel taking shelter within its comforting embrace. Without hesitation, she plummeted to the ground and removed her helmet, thrusting it to the side in hopes of acquiring her breath.

Her chest heaved, Isabel trapped within the armor. She was uncertain if she could fight a second melee bearing the armor's weight. Isabel shut her eyes, pouring wine from the chest beside her and gulping it, its dryness not quenching her parched throat. She sat on the ground, unsure if she should watch Arot's melee or wither away within the tent. She would never come to know what choice she would have made, for a voice from outside the tent called out to her, a familiar voice.

"Sir Knight," the voice repeated, Isabel springing alive and rushing around the tent in search of her helmet.

"I know you are lurking in the marquee," Lady Alianora chuckled, her elongated shadow stretching across the marquee's exterior. Isabel paled at the mere thought of her entering before she could conceal her identity by lowering the helmet upon her head.

Alianora opened the tent's flaps, peeking inside. Isabel was heaving and near to suffocation within the helmet, rising to reach the tent's entrance. Alianora smiled at her, stepping back for Isabel to exit the tent.

"I hope you are not offended by my words, Sir Knight. I had not foreseen such a remarkable fight from your behalf."

Isabel nodded, unsure if to speak to the figure who would undoubtedly identify her if she uttered a word, let alone removed her helmet. Alianora bit her lip, and Isabel was certain she believed she had insulted the knight championing her.

"The words I sought were that I have never observed you in the tourneys, as I am an ardent enthusiast and frequent spectator. Is this your first tournament?'

Isabel nodded, unsure if acknowledging it was the suitable action.

"Considering the circumstances, you have performed admirably in the first round. I am certain you will be victorious in the second round. The first rounds tend to be tumultuous, especially for a newcomer, and I reckon one may feel rather unsettled. Are you feeling well? You appear to be short of breath."

Isabel had been panting, the sun striking her armor and scorching her in the time they had spent outside. Isabel's only strength had her nodding at her remark.

"Would it not be wise if you were to remove your helmet? I reckon a moment to catch your breath might serve you well after your arduous melee," Alianora reached for her helmet, Isabel seizing her hand.

"Oh," she flushed, "strong hands," Alianora smiled. "I understand your desire to keep your identity undisclosed." Isabel released her hands.

Alianora brushed the dirt Isabel's gloves had planted upon her arms, "I will leave you to it then. I would not want my champion fainting like a knight in distress."

A sudden release of tension in Isabel's muscles had her body weaken once more as she let out a huge breath, the warm air crashing onto her helmet and igniting her head like stew in a pot. Alianora had turned to leave, Isabel pushing the tent's flaps, prepared to go in. She suddenly heard Alianora's footsteps come to a halt. Isabel's body stiffened when she realized the lady was not yet leaving.

"If I may say," Isabel swiveled, Alianora standing before her, Isabel's knees buckling, "you have yet to paint your family crest on your shield."

Isabel nodded, turning and hoping Alianora would disappear, allowing her to breathe fresh air once more. That she did not.

"I am a skilled painter," Alianora closed the distance between the two. "Well, I *know* skilled painters," she chuckled, biting her lip. "Would you be pleased if I arranged for your shield to be painted?" she added.

Isabel's gaze remained fixed on the unrelenting young woman, rolling her eyes and relieved her helmet concealed her facial expressions. Alianora stared at the knight, a weak smile lingering on her lips, a smile which faded as Isabel turned away.

Without a reply, she turned, marching away from the abrupt rejection.

The flaps fluttered brusquely, Alianora already making her way down the field. She halted and glanced over her shoulder, the weak smile returning to her lips when she spotted the knight standing before the marquee, wooden shield in hand. Isabel handed the shield to Alianora, whose smile now outshined the sun. She also gave her a cloth bearing the image of a dragon on a mound, a piece from a broken banner she had found in Accreton. She pointed at the words Barbeau on her shield as if crossing it out.

Alianora arched an eyebrow, "You wish to have this on your shield and to do away with your family name?" Isabel nodded, and she could still see Alianora slightly perplexed. Nevertheless, the lady's desire to please the knight was strong enough to deter any further questions. "I will have it ready for your next round. If not, I am certain a second wooden shield should suffice," and she vanished across the field, racing towards the melee, reaching it in time for the second round.

Isabel shook her head. The weight of the armor lingered, yet within her body, she acquired tranquility with Alianora's departure, Isabel entering the marquee, where peace was abundant.

CHAPTER 36: WARRIOR ANGEL

The Lord of Goldcrest and the tournament's knights had come together for a feast at the castle. After supper, the men lingered around the hall, engaging in discussions of city governance, retelling old tales, and the tensive concern of the war lurking amidst the outer cities. As a woman where such gatherings were the realm of lords, Isabel had no privilege to partake in the circles of men. She was to behave as a lady and observe in silence while the men exchanged ideas.

Isabel sipped her wine, standing by a torch beside the wall, watching the scattered groups of people chattering about. She avoided Arot for the time being, hoping to not draw the attention of the castle's occupants, leading to her discovery in the tournament. Standing alone in the outskirts of the chatter, Isabel spotted from the corner of her eye as Bardolf cocked an eyebrow and approached her, Isabel rolling her eyes at the man.

"I had never laid eyes upon such an angel," Bardwolf said, his shaven beard giving way to a long scar on his cheek.

"You have yet to find an angel," Isabel turned. *Leave me be, Bardolf.* But he was persistent.

"Ah, devilish the girl. Some would call it unwise to deal with such a woman, yet I take a liking to that raging energy," he closed the distance behind her.

"Those words stray from the truth as well. If I may say, Sir-"

"Bardolf"

"Sir Bardolf, I am in no need of a champion or courting."

"Ah, you see," he slid his fingers between her arm, grasping her, "I am in no need of courting. Just a-"

"Is there a problem, Lady Isabel?" Arot interjected, the man's fingers lingering on her arm.

"I believe Sir Bardolf is unaware of my courtship situation."

"It would be wise if you allowed the lady her peace," Arot stood towering over him.

"I take what I like," Bardolf gripped her arm.

"Not today," Arot stepped forward. Bardolf's lip twitched at the defiant knight's gaze. After a moment of silent confrontation, he scoffed and allowed his fingers to slide away from Isabel's arm.

"You will remember who I am at the tournament. I swear it," and Bardolf stormed off in the opposite direction.

Isabel sighed, "I am eternally grateful, Arot. However, had we not agreed to stray from each other?"

"I believe I said you would need saving. I was merely going about my duty," Arot leaned onto the wall beside her.

"On the battlefield," Isabel pointed toward the field's direction, "I believe you have more imperative duties to attend to now."

From afar, Atheena smiled at the pair, one of her eyes veiled by a lock of golden hair draped over her face. "Was it not the feast where you had expected to join her, or does my memory not serve me well?"

Arot shook his head, "I will be a knight of my word."

"Are you not always," Isabel grinned, watching him join Atheena.

"Sir Arot. You fought bravely today," Atheena beamed at the sight of him.

"The thought of a beautiful lady watching from the pavilions is certain to inspire any warrior," Arot said, Atheena's cheeks ripe as strawberries.

"Do you pretend to stand away from the masses and admire their interactions all alone by this wall?" A voice caught Isabel off guard, her heart leaping into her throat.

Isabel turned, the sky-eyed woman standing beside her. "I had not imagined I would be joined by someone as lovely as you," Isabel gave her a cheeky smile. "How are you, cousin?"

"It would have brought me joy to know my dear cousin Isabel would be gracing the feast with her presence. When did you arrive?" Alianora embraced her tightly.

"Late this evening. I believed I would not arrive promptly to the feast, and I considered not attending at all," Isabel admitted, hoping to not reveal her identity.

"That is not a matter to ponder about. The numerous dashing knights attending these events attract women from far and wide in search of a formidable suitor," she paused, raising her eyebrows.

"It would justify why you have strayed far from home. I hope everyone is well in Zeleciia."

"They are."

"The years have not taken a toll on your fondness for dashing men," Isabel laughed, "and you have bloomed more beautiful than a prairie flower."

"You have remained equally captivating, cousin," Alianora's brows arched as she cast a fleeting glance over Isabel's figure. "There is news I have not a person to confide in."

"Why is it that your eagerness is giving away your desire to confide in me at this moment?" a playful smile overtook Isabel.

"A knight championed me," Alianora said, their seclusion from the crowds concealing her secret.

"Who would have ever conceived such an idea? You, a noblewoman and so beautiful," Isabel responded, her fingers splaying out like a fan against her chest, her lips slightly parted in apparent astonishment.

"Please, do not jest at my expense, cousin," Alianora crossed her arms and raised her chin regally. "I am more than capable of holding my own in such jests. Needless to say, that is not the matter. Knights have thrown themselves at my feet before. This one, he was quite distinct. He did not speak. Even less so, he did not burden me with his flattery as men habitually do."

"And what, my dear cousin, is the matter of significance?"

"He championed me for the tourney, yet he did not attend the feast. The knight is shrouded in mystery and has chosen to conceal his identity. All I know is he belongs to the Barbeau family, and the knight said it was his first tourney. I believe he is preserving his anonymity to avoid feeling embarrassed before me if he does not fare well. It is quite endearing to have them shy away at times,"

Alianora stared at the chandeliers in the hall's center. "What do you believe? Have you heard of this family?"

"The family name is unfamiliar to me, but I would not be one to fall heels over head over a knight whose true identity remains a mystery."

"Heels over head? I would not, not upon first sight."

"Cousin," Isabel crossed her arms while tilting her head. Alianora rolled her eyes at her. "If I may suggest, keep your distance, at least until he reveals his true identity. There are plenty of other charming men to consider. Why not explore elsewhere?"

Alianora shook her head, "Oh, Isabel. You must understand when a man is different. I just know it."

"I believe the only difference you have seen is that of a man with sowed lips," Isabel laughed, but her thoughts raced beyond, remembering Robion and their tranquil moments before the lake.

"How dare you insult my champion," Alianora's brow furrowed.

"You know my affection for you runs deep, cousin. I merely do not wish to see you hurt." The thought of Baenlorn and Sehan crossed Isabel's mind. *They must know something of Rivetion.* "I must take my leave now. It has been a rather long day. I will see you tomorrow."

"May the gods be with you," Alianora hugged her. For a moment, Isabel held her firmly, missing the warm touch of family. It was rare for them to see the Beaumonts, for they lived all so far away from the Midlands. Perhaps she could have sought their help to save Oakheart if they had lived closer.

Isabel exited the great hall when she could not find Baenlorn and Sehan within. It did not take her long to find the raucous laughter of men, and Baenlorn's laugh was one she could not miss.

The two were sitting by the stairs leading to the battlements. When they saw Isabel, the pair's eyes widened. "You are alive!" Baenlorn said, approaching and hugging her." The man's brute strength was nearly enough to crush her bones, Isabel gasping when her feet left the ground.

"You are going to kill the young lady, you brute," Sehan said, tapping Baenlorn's shoulder. Baenlorn laughed, bringing Isabel to the ground.

"What happened at Rivetion? How did you two escape?"

"After Lord Layne's demise and your escape, the people's spirits plunged," Sehan said.

They were able to hold the city for less than a couple of weeks. Rivetion eventually succumbed, and Cicely was taken captive when the city fell. Cicely hoped her capture would allow her to stall the men while Baenlorn and Sehan rallied more lords to their cause to retake Rivetion.

Isabel attempted to get more out of the fall of Rivetion from them, but the pair hoped to drown the memory of their defeat that night. She decided not to pry much, and by the time they heard how Isabel managed to escape, they were far enough in their cups to carry on a coherent conversation. Not long after, Isabel bid the pair farewell, mindful of the need to rest for the upcoming tournament the following day. They offered little resistance to her departure, and she reckoned they were not very keen on sharing their wine that night.

Isabel tossed and turned within her marquee, reliving the past days in her mind. Certain she would not rest, she lit a candle and sat within her marquee. The raucous laughter of men and giggles of women outside had dwindled. Now, all that could be heard were their loud snores along with the occasional whining of a horse.

After realizing she would not fall asleep, Isabel left her marquee and walked past the knights' tents until the snores of men faded. A cool breeze swept through the land, the golden wheat fields waving like the ocean at her, their waves beating away until she could no longer see them in the darkness.

Isabel sat on a log from which a guard had risen, continuing his patrol through the city's outskirts. He quickly glanced at her before departing, the torch in his hand flickering when he moved abruptly.

"It is best if you return to your home, My Lady. Goldcrest is safe, but no woman should be strolling unattended, for rats can escape even the thickest of nets," the guard said.

"Do not fret for me. I have survived much more than a bandit in my recent days."

The guard shook his head, but he did not ask. He assessed her with a discerning look, and after a moment of contemplation, he caught sight of the dagger in her hip. He replied, "If anything happens, it would be best if you yell for our aid." With those words, he walked away, leaving Isabel amidst the golden sea.

Isabel contemplated her journey and all that she had undertaken to escape Oakheart. She had been compelled to do things she would not imagine she would do so soon. Her mother was lost. Her father dead. She had killed men. She deceived her cousin. What was this world becoming? A profound sorrow weighed on her soul, for though she always yearned to fight and adventure, this was not how she envisioned it. *Will I ever find Mother? How her heart will ache when she hears of Father's murder. And Lucia. What will become of her?* Isabel knew that when Lucia learned of their father, her cries would be heard by even the deafest of men. *How will I tell her?*

The stars in the night twinkled at her as if they sympathized with the young woman. Isabel's eyes twinkled, unable to contain the sea of emotions building in her chest. A tear rolled down her cheek, and without Lucia to see and question her, she felt happy for a moment because she did not need to be strong for her sister.

"They say beauty lies in gold," a voice behind her caused Isabel to leap. The young noble wiped a tear from her cheek before turning. Arot stood a couple of feet away with a hand on his pommel, the other wrapped around a bundled cloth pressed against his hip. "Many do not understand that genuine beauty resides not in the metal, but in all other forms of gold that surround us."

"Those seem like words that must be spoken to your new friend, not me," Isabel said, smiling at him.

Arot mirrored her smile, gazing at the spot beside her, "May I join good company?"

"The company you will find here is in despair," Isabel wiped the other tear which had rolled on the opposite cheek, sniffling. "Joy prospers elsewhere."

"It was not joy I sought this late at night, but friendship." Isabel could not help but smile once more, Arot joining her, the pair staring into the golden sea. They sat for a moment in silence, then he added., "There is no stronger person in this world than the one who holds reins of their emotions."

"Then I must be the weakest the realm has known."

"On the contrary. I know how you have been master of your emotions, particularly regarding your sister." Isabel looked up at him as if he could read her mind, "Lucia is fortunate to have a strong sister like you."

"If not I, then who? I fear it will destroy her when she learns of Father's death."

"A noble man was lost in a dishonorable way."

"I will avenge him," Isabel said, gripping the grass beside her, the veins in her hands pounding.

"Justice will be sought, but you must not let this hatred consume you. Icas, though not with us, lives on. Through your family, through you, through this."

Isabel turned to look at Arot, her heart still pounding with hate at the thought of Morkath. *How could he execute Father? What cruel being could commit such sin? Father had always been kind. Noble.*

Then, Arot unwrapped the cloth, and Isabel's eyes widened. Before her, what she thought she would never see again, now sat on his lap.

Talons protruded from within the cloth, soaring to the sky like towers from a castle. The three most imposing talons rose from the front, Isabel taking the crown, rigid and rough, in her once soft hand, now slightly calloused from using her sword. It was a snowy crown, a row of zigzagged sapphire gems encircling it.

Isabel admired it, and though it seemed ancient and not the grandest of crowns, it felt like it could bring power to any who wore it. A thin yet rigid crown, it did not seem fit for a king.

"Was this the crown in Fleur Forest? Who wore this crown? How did you come to possess it?"

"Aye. As for its previous owner, I am not quite certain. I have my ways to possess the unpossessable," Arot winked at her.

"It seems important, but not that of a king."

"Stories tell it is the crown made from the slayed dragons. A relic. An icon. A symbol of victory against those who believed they could control men through them."

Isabel shook her head. *If it was a symbol of such power, why was it buried?* "There must be a more fascinating story."

"A more fascinating story?" Arot cocked an eyebrow. "Does the story of men defeating dragons not meet your expectations?"

"I can feel it. This crown does not hold such power."

Arot scoffed, then smirked. "Perhaps you are right." He paused, and Isabel stared at him. *Arot believes he is a skillful storyteller, building this suspense. Perhaps he is correct. I always want to know more.*

"Will you tell me the other story?"

"Always curious, our Lady Isabel." He paused, and when Isabel's brows furrowed, he chuckled and continued.

Arot told her of an ancient tale, perhaps as ancient as the sun and wind, perhaps as ancient as Valenoriia. The knight spoke of a dragon rider who fell in love with a beautiful woman, a woman from the heavens. He promised he would do anything to capture her hand in marriage, and with time, he would prove to do just that. The young rider would become one of the most feared men in all Emenoriia's lands and skies, forging the three talon crowns—one for him, one for his heir, and one for the love of his life. Hers bore azure gems, for she came from the sky. A snowy crown encircled with sapphire was not fit for any woman. It was a crown worthy of a talon princess.

"But such crown now possesses more threat than the power it grants. That is why it was buried. Why you should not have it."

"Why is it dangerous?"

"Perhaps with time, you will understand." Arot gripped Isabel's shoulders, gazing deeply into her eyes. The young woman stared back at him, her breath hitching. "Merely understand this now. It must not be worn. To wear it is to defy the realm, to challenge the crown. Perhaps that is why there are two stories. Perhaps one was meant to be forgotten." Isabel remained motionless as Arot looked away abruptly, then began to rise. Still stunned, Isabel watched as Arot started to walk away, his words lingering in her mind.

Isabel escaped the spell, "If it is this dangerous, why do you give it to me?"

Arot halted and remained silent. Without looking back, he added, "Because true power is not about one's capabilities but the wisdom to exercise restraint when you possess it."

The tourney's second day arrived, and Isabel prepared to enter the second round. Alianora had met her at the field, Isabel receiving her newly painted shield. Her cousin had ordered the colors of Isabel's caparisoned horse to be painted in alternating stripes along the length of her shield. Alianora stated the dragon could not be painted, for there was no merchant available to fulfill the task. Isabel admired the colors of her family on the shield, its weight lighter on her arms than the previous day.

The herald announced the start of the round, walking along the center of the field, shouting at the amassed crowds. The anticipation was evident in their faces, their desperation to witness the clash of metal and their hope for the spilling of blood. Isabel's gaze flicked to her adversaries, searching for those most eager to engage her. On the opposing side stood Bardolf, wearing the pale green tunic that represented his team. Sehan had been paired with Isabel and three other men, their group ready to commence the fight.

The melee round began, and Bardolf charged at Isabel without hesitation. Her freshly painted shield intercepted his first sword's strike, Isabel bashing him and commencing the fight. The armor weighed less in her battle with the man. Isabel was unsure if her body was growing accustomed to it or if it was the cloudy day that had befallen the city. The cause's significance was trivial, for Isabel had regained her agility and maneuvered effortlessly around her opponent.

Bardolf's fury increased with each missed strike, unable to take her down. The knight fell into a frenzy, charging Isabel with his entire body and tackling her to the ground. Isabel lost the grip of her shield, Bardolf swinging at her helmet, striking her straight on the visor. His weight pressed against Isabel's chest, her body lacking the strength to knock him off.

Isabel evaded his punch, his body being propelled off her when a second knight struck him with his shield. She sprung to her feet and glanced at Sehan, the knight who had come to her aid. A second opponent charged, and Sehan confronted him. Bardolf stared Isabel down as she grabbed her shield. Then, the two charged each other like an unmounted joust.

Isabel evaded him, and with his back turned to her as he charged by, Isabel seized the opportunity to bash him with her shield, sending him crashing onto the ground. She swung her sword down upon him, but Bardolf, quick with his feet, kicked her shield off her hand. Isabel, relentless with her assault, continued to strike him down, closing the distance between them. With Bardolf under her foot, he resorted to scooping dirt from the ground and thrusting it at her helmet, blinding her. A maniacal laugh followed his deed. Isabel's vision blurred as he knocked her to the ground.

Bardolf rained down blows with his sword, Isabel rolling on the ground to evade his heavy strikes. The dirt scratched her face within the helmet, her mouth dry as she swallowed the gritty soil. Isabel turned and rolled, sending kicks into the air in a blind attempt to push Bardolf away and create distance between them.

Her sight lingered in a blur, the heat within the helm worsening her rapid breaths. The silhouettes of men moved in the haze, beating each other to the ground, much like Bardolf had done to her. Bardolf lifted his sword high over his head, poised to strike her. In a desperate and blind motion, Isabel swung at him, her sword clashing with a vulnerable point of his armor's underarm.

Bardolf gasped for air. Isabel grunted as the herald ended the round, and she was unable to take advantage of his weakness. The remaining men gathered towards their corners. Others were dragged by their squires from the field. The crowd cheered, their gazes pursuing the men being carried away. Isabel blinked away the dirt in her eyes, regaining her vision. The blazon banners came into focus, clear and vivid, a little too clear to her liking.

Sehan turned to meet her, his eyes widening at her sight. Isabel knew why her sight was clearer than the previous day's blue, cloudless sky. She reached for her visor, yanking it to conceal her face, hopeful no other soul had caught sight of her identity. Sehan had stood close to her, Isabel certain the crowd had not managed to identify her as a woman.

The knight approached her, standing wide and breathless before her. He removed his helmet and raked his hair, wiping his face clean while blinking rapidly. *He did not see you, he did not.* But Isabel's hopes incinerated like a book in a flame when the man stepped forward and whispered, "Isabel. Is that you?"

CHAPTER 37: AN OPPORTUNE MOMENT

The flaps fluttered as Isabel entered her marquee, seeking solace after the battle and a much-needed respite. Lobbing her helmet on the ground, she poured wine into a tankard Arot had left on the table. Isabel wiped her face, removing the dirt Bardolf hurled at her, Isabel repeatedly blinking to dispel the scratching sensation from the grains of sand lurking behind her eyelids.

Heavy footsteps and the clanking of metal approached the tent. Isabel lunged for her helmet, prepared to confront the person who was in search of her identity. The person halted, the knight's lengthy, broad back shadow looming over the tarp. The broad back was not one Isabel would easily forget, her body stiffening. A long sigh escaped her after hearing Sehan's voice.

"Lady Isabel. May I enter?"

Isabel peeked through the flaps, grabbing his hand and tugging him inside. "Do not speak my name."

Sehan entered and settled before her on the fur rug, narrowing his eyes as he observed the young woman. "Why are you so mindful of your identity?"

"I prefer to not be revealed, not until the tournament has concluded," Isabel searched for a tankard, unable to find one to share the wine. Sehan's brow rose, the perplexed expression lingering.

"What purpose will it serve?"

"Since we escaped Rivetion, my ability to lead men has been questioned. The tournament is the moment when I can build a reputation, and hopefully, men will come to view me as a leader worth following," she refilled her tankard and pressed it against his hands. Sehan shook his head, yet after a slight hesitation, he took it and gulped the wine.

"This tournament does not make a leader. It is merely a spectacle of strength and swordsmanship. Since when did you wish to become a leader? Did you not wish to be a knight?"

"I did, but with the fall of Rivetion, I learned I need to be a leader to save Rivetion, and a leader for House Beaumont after my father's murder." Sehan's eyes widened at the word murder, and he reached for Isabel's hand. She looked down at it, and her heart skipped a quick beat when she saw the compassionate look in his eyes. "And you are right, the tourney is a spectacle, but it is a spectacle which exhibits and forges warriors of renown. A win in this tournament will inspire men to stand with me, and with time, I may demonstrate that a woman is worthy of being followed into battle. If I can inspire enough men, we may amass the troops we require to retake Rivetion."

"There is truth in your words. The only challenge standing in your path is winning and Bardolf. I noticed it has become a personal melee for the both of you." He placed his other hand over hers, holding it gently between his. "I am sorry to hear about your father." Isabel nodded, quickly removing her hand from between his.

"Not as personal as it may appear. Nevertheless, defeating him would prove an interesting victory."

"He is one of the tournament's favorites, if you were not aware."

"Who is the other?"

"He sits before you," Sehan raised the tankard. "I have fought many a tourney. Bardolf, I can outmatch."

"Any weaknesses you would share?"

"My weaknesses? None," he let out a chuckle, Isabel rolling her eyes. "He can easily parry strikes to his right side. His left side is vulnerable to a swift attack. Your agility may serve you well. You would have only one problem."

"That would be?"

"You would have to outmatch me, which is a challenge."

Isabel laughed, "Quite humble."

"My distinctive attribute," he grinned from behind the tankard, spilling its contents upon his surcoat.

"May we add sloppiness to your attributes?" she leaned in with a cloth to wipe his surcoat.

"That attribute would strike horror upon the ladies of the court." Isabel leaned close to him as she began to wipe the wine's stain, Sehan grabbing her hand. The warmth emanating from Sehan's body enveloped her, and even though the tent shielded them from the sun, it was insufficient to cool the rising temperature inside. The heat within the tent spread like a plague. Isabel's heart raced, Sehan's lake eyes unable to cool her swiftly burning body. For a moment, she was so close she could see the stubbles growing on his jawline, where they ended around his lips. His finger slipped into her hand, gently unraveling the cloth from her grip, snapping Isabel from her lingering gaze. She leaned away, Sehan continuing to clean his surcoat. *What is the matter with me? Why this sudden rush of energy?*

"How did you manage to survive the siege of Rivetion?" Isabel turned her gaze away, raking her fingers through her hair, seeking to shift the conversation.

"We escaped through one of Cicely's tunnels and rode out to Goldcrest," he said while scrubbing away the stain.

"And Cicely. When did you last see her?" Isabel glanced from the corner of her eye, hoping to calm her racing heart.

"We lost her within the castle when we were overwhelmed. She was a difficult one to lure away from her burning city. We always knew she would stay, and she told us we should go on without her if anything happened. She led the men until its final moments."

"Just like her husband," Isabel shook away the thoughts of Layne seeping into her mind like an overflowing river. "We must return to save her."

"It has always been our intention. We arrived to acquire Entan's aid. He has sent a messenger to gather his armies. I only pray Cicely is alive when we return."

"She will be alive. They would not dare to kill her. She is worth a formidable ransom to them."

"A ransom I am not certain her sister would lay the coin down for."

"She will be alive. I will fight for her. *We* will fight for her."

His gaze rose to meet hers, his surcoat's stain hidden by the cloth planted upon it. "You have the heart of a warrior. I would fight beside you in battle if the time were to come, Isabel. Never forget that. No tournament victory can define nor change that."

"I long for the day we fight side by side, Sehan. I hope these words are spoken from the heart and not merely words used to woo a lady." *What am I saying?*

"Do you believe me to be unchivalrous?" Sehan pulled away, shaking his head vigorously, and for a moment, Isabel believed there was a hint of nervosity in the typically confident man.

"Time will tell," and she shrugged, looking away.

The tent's flaps swung open, and a frustrated Arot dropped his shield inside the tent. Disregarding Sehan's presence, he spoke away, spilling the anger boiling within him.

"Oh, Isabel. You best send that weasel on his arse. Men, I tell you, they fight dirty. Used the oldest trick in the book."

"Bardolf?" Isabel took the tankard from Sehan and poured wine into it. Arot snatched it from her grasp, continuing to spill his fury.

"He flung dirt at my face. I was blindsided, and the weasel was certain to eliminate me from the tourney. Oh, you must defeat that cheating bastard."

"A wise man once told me tournaments are not filled with chivalry," Isabel refilled the tankard. Arot hastily gulped away the wine as if it had angered him.

"I hope you are as quick on your feet as you are quick-witted," he pushed the tankard towards her, Isabel refilling it. "You must beat him to the ground. It need not matter how it is done, as long as it is done."

Arot turned towards the man glancing at him, but continued to speak to Isabel, "Was your presence not to be undisclosed?"

"This is Sehan—a friend from Rivetion. My visor swung open, and he caught a glimpse. He is informed of my intentions and is a friend. He can be trusted."

"Ah. I see. You bear no resemblance to a weasel. I may yet trust you," Arot opened the chest, taking a hearty bite from a loaf of bread.

"I must return to the tourney. My round is bound to start soon," Sehan rose, Isabel following.

"I will join you," Isabel said, Arot squinting at her while Sehan exited the tent. "If I am to win, I must study my opponents."

Isabel and Sehan arrived at the melee, the crowd's enthusiasm bursting through the field, the herald prepared to announce the next round's contestants. Rustplate caught sight of Sehan, bolting to join him and Isabel. Rustplate eyed her, as if contemplating the familiar sight.

"You are the knight we fought alongside in the first round. Is that not so?" Rustplate leaned onto the fence.

"He is so. He expressed his gratitude for our aid," Sehan replied, staring at Bardolf as he crossed through the opposite side of the field.

"We have no fondness for intimidators," Rustplate closed his eyes while shaking his head, "'less it is us," and he let out a hearty laugh, slapping Isabel's pauldron. "It is not customary to form teams in tourneys, but if it means we will rid ourselves of that man, then I am more than willing to do it."

The herald announced the next two contestants. "Sir Sehan will be in the eagle team while Sir Bardolf will be in the bear team, each joining a surviving contestant from the previous round."

"Wish me good fortune," Sehan vaulted over the fence.

"Crush them," Rustplate said. Sehan turned for their goodwill ritual, their arms meeting in a cross-forearm handshake, the pair remaining in a prolonged clasp unlike any Isabel had ever seen.

Isabel nodded as Sehan joined the melee, both pairs of warriors standing on opposing sides. Sehan's confidence in the tournament made Isabel believe she would not confront Bardolf and that Sehan would be her final opponent. He would be the one to avenge Arot, and her skillful friend would challenge her.

The fight commenced, Sehan bashing through Bardolf's ally, Bardolf returning the favor. The crowd chanted, the clanging sound of the knights' swords erupting their wine-induced bodies into a frenzy. Sehan's movements were a graceful dance on the field, his steps exuding poise, and every swing and block displaying his exceptional balance and skill.

Bardolf's temper rose as he roared, searching for an inexistent opening in his opponent's defense. His strikes, unlike Sehan's graceful moves, were reckless. Sehan had indicated his left side was his weak side, and Bardolf's recklessness had only accentuated it.

Sehan evaded his strikes and landed a blow with his arm on his face, stunting Bardolf, his footsteps receding.

Sehan was to crush Bardolf, walking towards him, his eyes catching a glimpse of Isabel before swinging his sword. Isabel's heart desired his victory, yet her eyes lusted for her challenge, her moment to defeat Bardolf. With each passing day, her desire to be respected by men, to be followed by them, to be seen as an equal, grew. As Sehan looked at her, there was a hesitation in his strike, and she wondered for a moment if he was listening to her desire.

The distraction in her gaze had allowed Bardolf's ally to rise, the man wrapping his arms around Sehan's neck. Sehan responded with a sharp elbow jab, causing the man to grunt and loosen his grip on him. Swiveling, Sehan's forearm connected with the man's helmet, sending him sprawling to the ground, dust rising around them.

In that instant, Bardolf struck an unwary Sehan across his helmet, causing him to lose his balance. Bardolf hit him once more before he could recover. He smashed an unsteady Sehan again, Sehan falling on one knee. Bardolf's enthusiasm turned into recklessness. He exposed his left side, leaving him weak, allowing Sehan to strike him from his kneeling position. Except he did not commit to his tactic. Sehan glanced at Isabel. *What are you doing?* Bardolf swung at Sehan, but he quickly parried the blow.

Bardolf committed to his second strike, delivering a powerful blow from above and kicking Sehan onto his back. Sehan lay sprawled out as the herald ended the round, preventing any bloodshed. The crowd groaned in disappointment, leaving Isabel to wonder if the discontent was on the absence of blood or the unexpected loss of a tournament favorite. Despite the crowd's reaction, Isabel's focus was on the challenges that lay ahead.

It was evident Sehan had deliberately taken his defeat and missed an opportune moment to secure victory. He had selflessly paved the path for Isabel. The reasons behind his decision remained a mystery to her.

Her mind was fixed on the fight that was to follow. If she won that fight, she would enter the finale versus Bardolf. It would all then rest on that final fight. Her tournament victory, it all hinged on that decisive round, it all hinged on defeating Bardolf.

CHAPTER 38: FIGHT OF THE WEASEL

There had been one more round before Isabel had to face off Bardolf in the final round, and now that she had won, it was time to face him. Each round had been progressively more difficult than the last, but Isabel knew the true challenge lay now against Bardolf.

"When you get that weasel, beat him to the ground. Let him pay for his devious ways," Arot said, following Isabel towards the field.

"Arot, calm yourself. I do not need any more pressure in this final round," Isabel lowered her visor, concealing her identity from a band of men walking in their direction.

"Forgive me, My Lady. It was not my intention to burden you."

"Fear not, he will taste my steel," Isabel entered the field. The crowd in the galleries and around the fence shouted at her arrival. Their adoration for her had grown throughout the tournament, more and more cheering for her with every round she triumphed.

Bardolf received an ovation that exceeded hers, for the crowd roared and cheered his name as he vaulted over the fenced field, swinging his sword and taunting Isabel. He raised his arms at the public, calling for their voices, their shouts igniting the life within him. Isabel could see Bardolf lusted for their energy and all of the tourney's glory.

Sehan sneaked upon Isabel, dropping his hand on her pauldron. "Take heed of his vulnerability, for it will serve you well when the time comes. The sun is approaching the horizon, and the heat will not be a burden." Sehan's words were undoubtedly accurate, for the nearby forest's gusts howled, their crispness invigorating her, much like the crowd's fervor did for Bardolf.

"I will bear it in mind. Thank you, Sehan," she whispered, hoping the surrounding onlookers would not hear her. She thought of asking him why he had lost the last round, but with the herald's approach, there was no time to speak.

"The final round has arrived," the herald's voice was nearly inaudible, the crowd's cheering consuming his words. The crowd eased, and he continued. "Our last two opponents will now fight, the victor being declared the tournament champion."

"He is not the most captivating speaker," Arot said to Isabel, Sehan overhearing him and chuckling. Arot turned to him, "You know I do not lie. They merely scream because the tournament has lifted their spirits, for his words would not be able to swoon a lady into his arms."

"Now our combatants will face," Isabel vaulted over the fence after the herald's words. "Combatants," he turned to each of them individually, signaling them, "ready?" When they both nodded, he said, "Begin."

The crowd cheered, their excitement never ceasing, for the tournament had sprouted with life like a seed germinating with spring's rains. No drought in Emerion would dare desiccate their spirits, for they would receive the battle they longed for. Isabel glanced at her cousin standing by the lord's galleries, her eyes fixed upon the fight that had begun.

Bardolf came alive, charging at Isabel, not allowing her to strike first. His initial blow struck hard against her shield, causing the fresh paint to crack, yet the shield withstood his attack. Isabel pushed his sword away, then retaliated, Bardolf easily parrying it. Bardolf's relentless energy granted him the advantage. Isabel had no choice except to fend him off, hoping for the moment he wearied himself.

But his energies were everlasting, the effect of the battle burdening only Isabel, Bardolf fresh from the fighting. In the eyes of the crowd, Bardolf brought about the impression that it was his first round in the tournament. Isabel withheld his attacks, the evening breeze breathing life within her, its chilliness allowing her to slip around him, the wind carrying her with ease.

A lethargic lizard dragged itself across the field. Isabel was certain it was the lizard Bardolf had thrust her way. Her mild distraction allowed Bardolf to overwhelm her, sending her off balance, and Isabel collapsed. The dirt around her shot off into the sky, and the lizard arrived to her aid, its wide eyes watching her intently. Isabel reached for her sword, but Bardolf stepped on her wrist, preventing her from grasping it. "Ah!" a shooting pain ran up her arm.

Bardolf lunged for her sword, Isabel attempting to grasp the lizard by her side. "Oh, knight. You sought yourself to be so grand," Bardolf seized her sword, laughing while committing a reckless act. With his body exposed to her, Isabel swung her shield at his arm, Bardolf groaning in pain and releasing her wrist. Isabel struck her shield once more at his leg. Bardolf crumbled to the ground.

With Bardolf on his back, Isabel leapt over him, her legs trapping his waist. Isabel bashed her shield a third time, striking his helmet, Bardolf's visor swinging open. With his face exposed and his body stunned, she reached for the lizard and thrust it into his helmet, slapping the visor closed. She struck it with her shield, damaging its hinges, Bardolf unable to open it.

"There is your little lizard."

Isabel snatched her sword, Bardolf rising frantically while the lizard bolted within his helmet. He grabbed his sword, and Isabel charged, prepared to strike him down. Bardolf's attempts failed, his blows missing his target, Isabel swiftly evading the anxious man's attacks. She swung at him, Bardolf parrying her blow, Isabel retaliating with her shield, crashing its edge against the side of his head. An unbalanced Bardolf wobbled around the field, Isabel's swift attacks strong enough to dent his armor, his defense failing him with the lizard rushing through his helmet.

Bardolf swung his visor open, the lizard escaping the madman's cage. He roared furiously, his blazing gaze aimed at his target, Isabel, who played his foul game. Intending to end her and win the tournament, he raised his sword, yet his time had passed, for it only remained as an intention. Isabel's foot struck the center of his cuirass, and an already stunned Bardolf dropped on the ground. Isabel sprinted towards him, kicking his shield, stepping on his wrist, and pressing the tip of her sword onto his neck.

Bardolf stared at her, bewildered, as the crowd roared and the herald announced her victory. His eyes ignited with fury, Bardolf dazed from the rapid turn of events. What could have been his potential victory had transformed into an awful defeat.

Arot vaulted over the fence, embracing Isabel as she achieved the victory she longed for. Isabel's gaze shifted to Sehan, watching over Arot's shoulder as he nodded at her, her victory lighting his sky eyes. Isabel's cheeks flustered at the sensation of triumph, her skin burning amidst the breeze, overwhelmed with the crowd's cheering. Arot released her, the herald leading her towards the lord of the tournament.

Rising from his wooden chair, Lord Entan watched the tournament's victor approach him. His wavy, fiery hair could not outmatch Isabel's skin, the blood rushing under it building an energy within her she could hardly contain. The man's fair skin was unblemished by scars of war, his robust body signaling grand strength within him. As a renowned warrior, his face bore no scars from the battlefield, a characteristic seldom seen in warriors of his age.

"Welcome, knight," Entan began, "who of House Barbeau may I have the opportunity to crown as the melee champion in this tournament?"

"He is a little lizard," Bardolf rose, spitting blood on the field.

Entan narrowed his eyes at the man, then turned to Isabel. "A little lizard indeed," the crowd laughed. Entan raised his hand, and the laughter subsided, the respect they held for him eclipsing that of the herald. "A little lizard you entered this tournament. A little lizard you are no more," he paused.

"From an unknown man in this tournament, you have demonstrated valor and won the affection of these people. Your development is truly admirable. You entered a little lizard, and you have become a dragon," he raised his arms, the crowd roaring. *If you only knew.*

One of the guards led a horse by its reins and presented it to Isabel, the young noble stroking the animal's mane. It was a snowy beast, its hair glimmering as it caught the evening sun's final rays. Isabel mounted it, riding it bareback while grasping the reins.

Entan continued, "Hand this man the crown for him to crown his queen of the tournament." The herald handed Isabel the crown, and Isabel trotted by the galleries, searching for her cousin.

Alianora beamed at the sight of her champion knight, Isabel, carrying the crown in her blunt sword's grip. She saw Alianora effortlessly upon the crowd, Isabel's mount allowing her to catch the sky eyes gazing at her. Riding her steed towards the edge of the fence, she halted before her cousin. Alianora bowed her head while Isabel extended her sword, placing the crown upon her chocolate hair.

The crowd cheered at the tournament queen, Isabel returning to Entan upon her steed. "As is customary, you may acquire your spoils of war. The coin, the steed, and the glory are your prizes. Who is the man I name the champion of this tournament?"

"I do not desire your coin," Isabel's heart drummed against her chest, the pressure building the closer her hands reached for her helmet. Removing the barbuta, the crowd gasped and susurrated at the sight of a woman amidst the tournament. "I am no man," Isabel said, placing the helmet on her lap.

"She must be disqualified," voices erupted.

"No woman must fight in the melee."

"This is a place for men and nobles," voices continued, Lord Entan's daughters murmuring to each other at the sight of a woman fighting amidst the tournament.

Alianora's skin paled, her eyes avoiding Isabel's gaze. She blinked rapidly, leaning against the fence, her body slumping forward. Her champion was unreal, and it was evident Isabel's deceptions had left her devastated.

"Silence," he raised his hand, the crowd's murmur dissipating. "What is your title?"

Isabel gulped, her dry throat scratching like the sands of the distant beaches in Emerion's borderlands. "I am Lady Isabel Beaumont of Oakheart, now Lady Isabel Valenour of Accreton, daughter of Lord Icas Beaumont and Lady Valaenis Beaumont of Oakheart."

"Accreton," the crowd erupted in murmurs, the sounds of a world plotting against her, fear glimmering in their eyes.

"Valenour," said others. Had she made a mistake?

"Valenour," Entan repeated, then whispered, "you are indeed a dragon. Though I hope not a fool." His eyes held a blank expression.

Entan continued in his normal tone, "Your father is one of my dearest friends. Why do you, a woman, seek my tournament if not for the coin?"

Isabel licked her lips, unsure if her throat's desiccation was due to the words she was to deliver or the tournament that had come to drain the life from her for the burden it carried with it. She knew it was both. "Lord Entan, I have come to seek your assistance in retaking the city of Rivetion."

Lord Entan sat upon his wooden chair, leaning back while cupping his chin. "You speak of assistance, yet how many men are under your command? Do you even have an army?"

"Four hundred men, My Lord."

"Rivetion has fallen. The men that have ravaged our lands are certainly dwelling within its walls, seeking warmth in its hearths. With winter coming, I will not risk my army," Isabel's heart sank. "Nevertheless, I will match your men, for you have proven yourself a brave warrior. During the past days, I have been dispatching messengers to gather my men here at Goldcrest."

Isabel's heart filled with hope, the hope brimming up to her cheeks. "Thank you, Lord Entan."

"Now let us celebrate," Lord Entan announced, sipping wine from his goblet, the spectators roaring once more. He came down and met Isabel, the crowd dispersing to enjoy the evening's festivities.

"Your father, as I mentioned, was a close friend, and you have proven yourself during this tournament. For this, I will allow you to lead my men. If by the beginning of winter you have not reclaimed Rivetion, you must not stay. I will not have my men starve and freeze."

"Aye, My Lord. I will not allow their lives to be forfeited unnecessarily."

"Good fortune, Lady Isabel. May you instill dread into our foes' hearts." He paused, glanced around, and then continued, "Were you aware that employing another family's name in a tourney is an offense punishable by law? It is my duty to report such transgressions to King Ulron." Isabel's eyes widened, her heart coming to a halt. Entan regarded her with a stern expression. "It is good fortune my herald seems to have misheard Barbeau instead of Beaumont during the crowd's screams," and he smiled at Isabel. Entan turned, then vanished while escorted by his guards.

Sehan joined Isabel by the fence, admiring her steed. "A fine steed. Imported from Aroonshire, where the plains reach the horizon, and the horse rides last until you meet the Serene Sea."

"It sounds like a place one must visit."

"A place to vanish and enjoy the last days of one's life," he stroked the horse's mane, his eyes meeting hers. "You have done it, My Lady. You won the respect of men and exhibited the woman's strength found within you."

"If not for your aid, I would not be holding these reins," she raked her fingers through her hair, Sehan extending his hand towards her, assisting Isabel in dismounting her prized horse.

"You were the fighter, Lady Isabel. I did not fight for you. The victory and all its glory is yours."

Isabel glanced away before meeting his gaze, pressing the reins into his hands, "This horse, I wish for you to have it."

"I cannot, My Lady. It is yours to ride."

"I insist."

"You need not. I do not desire such a horse, for it is not such a good horse," he pushed the reins into her hands, Isabel rolling her eyes.

"Why did you lose the tournament?"

"I was outmatched, My Lady."

"Sir Sehan, you fiddle with words," Isabel caressed her horse's back.

"I have won many tournaments. There have been many, and many are yet to come. Tournaments serve a purpose, and today its purpose was grander if it served you."

Isabel's cheeks burned, a sea of blooming roses forming at his words. She shook her head and remembered her father. He would have been so proud after seeing her win the tourney, for she was becoming a warrior. Between Sehan before her and her father's memory, a glint of joy appeared in one eye and a flash of sadness in the other. "You are a noble man, Sir Sehan."

"Have I not been told," they laughed in unison. *Why have you been so kind? After leaving Oakheart, so few have shown such kindness. Why would Sehan, a champion of tourneys and grand knight, give up such a prize for me? Could he truly be that noble? Is Sehan a good friend or…*

"Isabel," the words interrupted her thoughts. She turned to meet the figure. A cascade of unbearable pain encumbered her, remembering how they had last been separated.

"Robion?" she managed to find her words. Confronted with marshes of intertwined emotions, Isabel's stomach clenched like a fist. "You are alive. I thought the worst had come upon you."

But before he could answer, the world around her became alive with chatter. The words uttered in the distance would once more turn her world upside down. They were words which disrupted all she searched for, words that could bring pain into her world once more. The words echoed through her head, a man dashing and yelling gibberish at Lord Entan.

"It is true," a second man confirmed the news as the first gasped for air.

"Are you certain?" Entan awaited the man's response.

"I saw them with my own eyes, My Lord. Enemy riders, on the horizon!"

CHAPTER 39: THE VAST ARCHIVES

Isabel embraced Robion, the crowd dispersing as Entan ordered the people to enter the city, the church bells tolling. Entan ordered his men, and they trailed after him, Sehan nodding at Isabel while following Entan on his horse. Robion closed in on her, cupping Isabel's face in his rough hands.

"I believed the worst of fates had come upon you. Since our night at the lake, we have tracked you down around Montanar. It was not until we spotted a group of horse tracks and carts riding towards Broonwood that we could find you. We found an abandoned encampment and heard from a local traveler that nobles of House Beaumont were there. We saw an army marching this way after that and believed you could be amongst them. Tell me, were you harmed?"

"No," Isabel embraced him once more, wishing she could momentarily forget the world around her. "Thanks for never giving up the search."

"My Lady," Arot joined them, "we must enter the city. The gates will close briefly."

Isabel nodded, mounting her snowy steed, the three riding into the city. Soldiers had begun to man the walls, guards standing by the entrance as the masses flooded the city. Men led their families on foot and carts, seeking safety within the city's thick walls. Columns of smoke in the distance became one with the sky, the outlying villages burning with the army closing in on Goldcrest. Desperate screams and the shouts of guards filled the air like a pot of franticness being poured into Goldcrest.

The smith woman moved swiftly around her forge when the group arrived, her gaze darting towards Isabel. "The news has spread like a plague. My armor has served you well, and I believe it will do so with the passing of time."

Isabel had yet to receive her coin and was unsure how to repay the woman, for she was certain a horse was not what she desired in exchange for her silver. Arot stepped forward, handing the woman a purse, "Your coin."

Isabel spun wide-eyed at him, his generosity unsurmountable. Arot shook his head, "Do not fret, Isabel, it is not my coin. That is your prize from the tournament," he shot her a light grin, Isabel shaking her head unbelievingly.

"Paid by the weight," the smithy bounced the purse in her palm. "I have taken the liberty to sharpen your sword," she returned it to Isabel, a novel scabbard concealing the blade. "Word has reached me that you are a Beaumont of Oakheart, or perhaps a Valenour of Accreton. So it lives." Isabel cocked an eyebrow, but the rushing masses reminded her there was no time to question her words.

The scabbard had a lengthy dragon carved onto its leather, showcasing exquisite craftsmanship that attested to its value. "What is its weight in silver?"

"It is invaluable. A worthy possession for the Lady of Accreton," the smithy offering a slight bow, to which Isabel gracefully mirrored, conveying her deep appreciation.

"Thank you," and Isabel was about to ride away toward the castle when she crashed into a soft body.

"Alianora?" she stepped away from her cousin.

"You fooled me," Alianora frowned. "My cousin deceived me. Why had you not told me it was you?"

"Forgive me, Alianora. If I had told you, your expressions would not have been as genuine."

"Here I believed you were a noble knight who had come to champion me. You manipulated me."

"It was not my intention to inflict suffering. Did I not warn you during the feast?"

Alianora crossed her arms, her chin held high, her eyes in contemplation. "It does not matter if you warned me. You knew how invested I was." She shook her head, "Are you willing to do anything just to achieve your desires?"

"No, I would not," Isabel stepped forward, attempting to grab her hand, but Alianora stepped back.

"I had hoped for better from my own family," Alianora shook her head.

"Alianora," Isabel lowered her gaze.

"There is no time, Isabel. I must go to the castle," and Alianora left. *Am I truly willing to do anything for my ambitions? I have manipulated my own cousin, my own blood. What is becoming of me? I had to. There was no other way. I hope with time she forgives me. I have done her wrong, but I did not wish to ruin our bond.*

Alianora was right, for she had manipulated an entire tournament to gain the favor of warriors and lords who surrounded her. At that moment, it seemed like the only viable path. Their ascent in this realm would only begin by regaining control of influential men, if they were to exert any sway on the world confining them like a horse's corral.

The resounding clamor of galloping horses grew louder, prompting the group to swiftly disperse from the streets, making way for their thunderous advance. The leading horse came to a halt, and Entan gazed at Isabel. His numerous fiery-haired daughters and their guards trailed him, the common folk evading contact while continuing their retreat.

"Lady Isabel, join us at the castle. Your safety will be assured. My men are limited and have yet to arrive from the outlying lands. Our numbers may not suffice to defend the city if they do not arrive imminently."

"I will not stand by and witness your city meet the same fiery fate as my home. My men and I are prepared to lend our aid to defend Goldcrest," she turned towards Robion. "Our men are prepared, are they not?"

"They are," Robion replied. "Half of Barda's troops are camped not far west of Goldcrest."

"And we have the warriors from Oakheart already positioned within the city," Arot reminded her, Isabel stealing a sidelong glance in his direction.

"And Alaehrayne and her men?"

"Alaehrayne's men returned to Viakaven," Robion began, "yet she remained with us in our search to find you. She is at the encampment." *Alaehrayne stayed to find me? King Ulron's daughter?*

Isabel looked at Entan, "I will grant you my support if you are willing to receive it."

"You Beaumonts have never faltered in coming to the aid of an ailing friend. Very well, Lady Isabel. Ensure your men are prepared at the walls. We will stand our ground until reinforcements arrive. I never envisioned the day when our two houses would unite in battle once more," he glanced in the direction of the castle, contemplative. "I must prepare for the battle to come. We will meet at the walls," and Entan spurred his mount, the flaming riders scorching through the city like an unending inferno.

"Robion, summon our forces. We will need their swift arrival if we are to emerge victorious in this battle."

"I will dispatch a messenger," and Robion left, the group watching as the masses continued to pour into the city, their lives depending on the few soldiers preparing deep within the city's walls.

"Do not stray, Erratia," Lucia chased after her dragon, slithering and bouncing through the dimly lit passageways. The castle lay shrouded in sleep, its tranquility shattered by the dragon's tail skimming and crashing, reverberating through the vast passageways.

Erratia turned a corner, and Lucia persisted with her pursuit. Her dragon had doubled in size in a short span of time, Lucia wondering where she was to conceal it from the others. Its appetite, however, outmatched its size, for Erratia ate all the meat in sight with little desire to share with her neighbors. Lucia was unsure how she would come to feed the beast if it doubled in size once more, all the more so if its appetite continued to expand at a similar pace.

Upon turning the corner, Erratia had vanished, a colossal door standing before Lucia, one of them ajar. This area of the castle was gloomier than the rest, not a candle lit in these passageways to dispel the shadows, the walls adorned with draping cobwebs. Only one torch staved off the sprawling shadows shrouding the floor between Lucia and the door, Lucia plucking it from the wall. As she raised the torch, its flame unveiled the carvings on the wooden door. Two imposing figures, cloaked in robes, emerged from the carved surface. The first man wore spectacles and clutched a pile of books. The second man's gaze was directed away from the passageway as if searching within the room, a pile of scrolls tucked beneath his arm.

Lucia pushed the door, its elephant weight groaning as she opened it. An earthy smell greeted her as if the woods had been placed within the room. Lucia could sense the vastness of her discovered room, the door's groaning reverberating through its walls as if it were reaching out to her in a haunting echo. The room's smell was all too familiar to her, a pleasant scent, one that brought serenity to her life.

Lucia's torch did not expose the room's vastness, for its rays died within a short distance. Unlit candles were scattered about, Lucia lighting them while navigating the room. Upon her entrance, she stumbled upon a wooden table that had tumbled to the floor, its legs splayed out in all directions, like a hound seeking affection from its master.

By the entrance, a cartwheel chandelier was dangling near the floor, its chain rising and disappearing within the shroud of darkness that obscured the ceiling from plain sight. Lucia lit the candles with her torch and tugged the chain, its rings rattling with its ascension. It broke what must have been years of silence, its sound vanishing before reemerging behind her. She followed the sound while it faded, leading her to a windlass and crank. She turned the crank, the rattling sound reemerging and the cartwheel chandelier ascending with every turn, gradually illuminating the room until it finally came to a halt, the windlass tensing.

A whooshing sound rattled the chains, Lucia searching the air for its origin. The ignited candles set aflame the candles around it, spreading like wildfire, the vast archives coming alive after years in the shadows. Massive bookshelves reached for the ceiling and descended into the dungeons, the windows concealed by large cloths blocking the entry of exterior light. Lucia paced across the bridge to the far side of the archives, staring with her lips parted at the towering bookshelves and down into the abyss where thousands of books lurked. At the far end, a colossal astrolabe was affixed to the ceiling, with a balcony that once allowed the ancient studious men to admire and study the stars.

This is unlike anything I have ever seen. House Valenour must have had riches beyond that of Royalty. How else could they have afforded a library so vast?

A swooshing sound regained her attention upon the far end of the bridge. Erratia sat alone, the intense sky eyes watching her. Her face turned, Erratia's eyes splitting in opposite directions as her long neck craned. She sneezed, and a ball of ice shot forward from her snout, aimed helplessly at Lucia. Lucia ducked, the ball of ice crashing onto the wall behind her before shattering into a thousand pieces.

Lucia hurried over to Erratia, excitement lighting up her eyes at the sight of her first ball of ice. Accustomed to Lucia's touch, Erratia awaited it calmly, shutting her eyes as Lucia ran her hand through her scales. The moment was short-lived, for speedy, stuttering footsteps and a pair of voices echoed near the entrance, Erratia fleeing.

Lucia watched a pair of men enter. A rosy-skinned man with pince-nez glasses strapped to his ears approached her swiftly, his magnified eyes curious at the sight of the young girl. "Hello. Who may you be?"

"Lady Lucia and you?"

"I am the archivist Dunstan. You are familiar. Are we acquainted?" but before she could answer, he continued, "I cannot place it. If you are searching for Lady Isabel, she is not within the city."

"No. My sister has not been seen here since I arrived."

"Your sister? You are *the* Lady Lucia. At first, I reckoned you were lost. I was certain there was a familiarity about you. Your sister, she was the one who allowed me to serve as the archivist. I must be grateful for her and Priest Aubrey," he said speedily.

"Priest Aubrey? He is alive?"

"Indeed, and in excellent health, if I may say. Your sister, I fear, was captured."

"Captured?" Lucia's eyes widened, her heart stopping. "How? When?"

"Late at night outside Montanar. She was ambushed while she was with Lord Robion. Her captor is a dreadful man. The men said he was a knight in ebony armor."

No. The knight from Oakheart. Can it be? Did he capture Isabel? "I must find her."

"You must remain here, Lady Lucia. The men personally requested your presence in Accreton for your safety." Dunstan folded his hands together and offered a weak smile, though there was more trepidation than weakness in his expression.

"I cannot abandon my sister to face that man alone. I must search for her," Lucia said, on the verge of turning away. But Dunstan shook his head firmly.

"My Lady, you must not. Remain here. Keep yourself safe. I hear he may be looking for you as well."

"And leave my sister to fend for herself?"

"She is not alone. Robion and the others will find her. I am certain of it." *What do they want from us? Why are they constantly following us? What have we done?*

An acrid smell caused Dunstan to swivel on his heel, turning to be met by a bookshelf lit ablaze. "Fire," he screamed, nearly dropping his glasses. Erratia descended beside the bookshelf, flapping her wings, the fire intensifying with the air she fed it. Dunstan's legs wobbled at the sight, for there was a dragon amidst his archives. Beside the bookshelf, a candle had fallen.

Erratia ejected a ball of ice, the bookshelf's flame vanishing, its last breath remaining in the smoke and ashes left behind. Dunstan's young apprentice, a slender man with straw hair and pale skin, his body concealed by buttery robes, shrieked in horror. "The books, they are burning."

Dunstan turned to meet the young man, "You care over trivial books when there is a dragon in our midst?"

"It is going to devour us," the young man fled the archives, his voice echoing and rebounding off the walls.

"Erratia," Lucia called out to the dragon, Erratia turning to meet her with a dumbfounded gaze.

"You command it? Is it yours?" Dunstan approached the creature cautiously, Erratia extending her sharp dagger claws at him, Dunstan retreating.

"We have traveled for some time now," Lucia closed the gap between her and Erratia. Erratia's tail perked up, her wings poised before her, ready to pounce Dunstan at a moment's notice, should Lucia command it or if such a desire crossed her mind.

"I know the tales of your family. The Valenours were renowned dragon riders in the past and the last family to retain their pure blood. After the Houses changed names, many believed House Beaumont to be their descendants. It was true. You are one. All this is in the forbidden books. I reckon they must be here, yet these archives lack the books the tales tell of them."

"Lacks books. Are the shelves not stacked?" Lucia gazed upon them once more.

"No, Lady Lucia. These are not the books we are searching for. The forbidden books are unique books and scrolls. Men say they date back to the time Accreton was built and beyond. Many were burned in the last era, history erased. But rumors persist. Rumors of there being one last hidden set. Some believe they are hidden in Accreton, others in Viakaven. I have heard whispers they could be scattered throughout the realm."

"And where do you believe they are?" Lucia crossed her arms, tilting her head at the thought of the missing books.

"I do not know, but I intend to find them. I have heard tales, tales where the books remain hidden within the deepest dungeons of Accreton. If this is true, I have yet to know. If this is true, then history may yet be saved." His mind appeared to drift with his words, but Lucia's interest lurked in his previous remarks.

"Do you know of my ancestors? The past of Accreton?" Lucia sat on the ground before he answered, like a child prepared to hear stories of past adventures.

"Of your family. Indeed. Your true family crest is the dragon. Did you know it is yours to bear if you choose so?" Dunstan stared at the dragon, and Lucia could see he was mesmerized by it. She knew Erratia could swallow him in an instant, and her narrowed eyes fixed on him revealed that thoughts of hunger still lingered in her mind.

"Is our crest not the Pegasus?"

"That is your *new* family crest, for every family's coat of arms changed after the Fall of Fire Era."

"Why?"

"Your family lineage, they were overcome with greed and lust for power, a strong desire to take over the land. With their dragons, they set the land aflame. During these times, the wars had almost driven the noble houses to the brink of extinction. Their deep-seated animosity toward each other had driven them to resort to extreme measures to eradicate their enemies.

"It fails to justify the coat of arms change," Lucia frowned, pulling on her braid.

"Ah, you see, the animosity boiling within them was so profound, they could scarcely stand to gaze upon each other. It was the alteration of their coat of arms which marked the start of a new era, for them to feign ignorance to the death and treachery that had befallen them. In these times, family names were forgotten. With a scarcity of scribes, this time in history went largely unrecorded. Only banners and visual depictions endured, a coat of arm change essential to eliminate the odium consuming the noble families, particularly regarding the Valenours."

"The banner of our ancestors is the dragon," Lucia said to herself, Dunstan listening intently.

"Indeed. It is a banner you may adopt," Dunstan kept his eye on the dragon, his forehead creasing as he said, "yet be forewarned, repercussions may arise."

CHAPTER 40: THE GOLDEN TOWER

"All of the messengers?" Entan's voice boomed, the guard handing him a stained sack.

"All of them, My Lord. No one is coming for us," the guard shook his head helplessly.

"Are you certain these were the men sent to the outlying villages?" Entan peeked within the sack, his head snapping back at the foul sight of his messengers' decapitated heads. Their faces were frozen in time, their expressions reliving their last moments of pain.

"Aye. All the men we sent were returned," the guard could not bear to watch the bag, his eyes averting it while Entan spoke to him.

"Very well," Entan returned the sack, the guard leaving the despaired lord within his great hall.

Isabel could not help but notice the commotion. She approached Entan, the lord sitting upon his wooden throne pondering. His throne was elegantly adorned with tree carvings. A ruby banner hung on the wall behind him, a golden tower in the center, flanked by a pair of archers aiming their bows at those who dared stare at it. The banner bore the embroidered words "Faucher," one of the wealthiest cities in eastern Emerion.

"What troubles you, Lord?" Isabel stepped before the man, Entan shaking his head as she shattered his thoughts.

"You need not worry, Lady Isabel. It is of no concern," he avoided her gaze.

"When a man utters those words and is unable to meet his ally's gaze, it is a matter of concern." Her words seemed to strike him, Entan raising his head to meet her gaze.

"My men will not arrive. Our troops will not suffice to defend the city," he said, lowering his head into his hand. "My messengers were intercepted."

"Victory lies not in numbers but in strategy. We can defend the city," Isabel stepped forward, Entan looking from under his brow at the young, hopeful eyes staring back at him.

"You are your father's daughter. There was not a battle he would yield. Always managed to strategize and bring us to victory."

"He knew we must not admit defeat. All is not lost, not until the last man has fallen."

"I could not have said it better," Entan rose from his throne. "I can still remember the first time your father and I fought side by side," he walked down the stairs, meeting Isabel.

"We were young and fought for the king, tasked to assault a band of enemy raiders laying waste to an outlying village. What we encountered that day was not a band of raiders. Nay. It was an army of savage men who stopped at nothing to shed the blood of their foes. I was young, and if I may confess, I was frightened. Your father stood beside me, and though fearful of our first battle, he stood strong. He would not yield to the enemy's roars. Nay. He stood within our lines, his courage instilling valor within me. My sword drew its first blood that day. I met your father, and beside him, I met my courage."

The pair paced within the great hall, "Was that the day the two of you became friends?"

"Friends we became, but the day your father saved me from certain doom, that was the day he proved to be a worthy ally. He was relentless and demonstrated the odds were always surmountable. This I learned on the day of the Battle of the Golden Tower."

"My father never mentioned this battle."

"Ha! He was humble. Let me show you," he led her to a spiral staircase. Entan led the way up the stairs until they reached the top of the tower. Outside, the wind caressed her cheeks, splitting as it encountered the tower's crenellations. The fires from the enemy encampment lit the castle's surroundings, Entan ignoring their sight and pointing at the courtyard below.

"This was where the Battle of the Golden Tower unraveled. We were outnumbered, yet your father devised a plan which led us to victory. I had my doubts, but the enemy fell into your father's trap. As you can see, the courtyard has a pair of portcullises. Your father told me to hold the enemy, that a last-gasp retreat would lure them into our courtyard. I did as he commanded, my men retreating, the enemy pursuing them directly into the courtyard, just as your father predicted. We entered the castle, and once the leaders entered the courtyard, we dropped that portcullis right there," he pointed at the main portcullis, now closed. "Once trapped, my men exited this tower and surrounded the enemy from the ramparts. Our arrows rained upon them, your father charging and flanking the remaining men outside. Deprived of their leader, the frantic soldiers desperately fought for their lives. When they saw the dire state which had befallen their leaders, they routed."

"You made history."

"History? I would have become history myself if not for your father. I believed that day would be my last. Your father came to our rescue and saved us from certain doom." Lord Entan cleared his throat. He hesitated but asked, "Your father, he did not survive the attack on Oakheart, did he?"

"He did," the thought of her father weighed upon her chest. "He was captured, and I was imprisoned with him shortly before arriving at Goldcrest. They killed him. His death was not an honorable one. They took his life like a criminal."

Lord Entan shifted his gaze, meeting Isabel's, "You must remember, your father did not require an honorable death. He lived a life filled with honor, and that is what matters most. He will be etched into the annals of history through the songs of bards as an impressive man, a skillful warrior, but above all, a remarkable friend. He deserved to die in peace," and there was a moment of silence, as if Entan had gone once more into the dungeons of his thoughts.

Isabel nodded.

"It is in you," Entan continued, "you must keep him alive, in your memories and in your heart. For if he lives there, he lives forever."

"I will," Isabel stared at the enemy's lines. "We will honor him by saving Goldcrest once more. Goldcrest will not fall, I swear it."

"Your family's spirit is strong," he smiled weakly, "I must prepare my men for the night ahead," and Entan vanished within the tower.

Isabel and Entan joined the guards at the castle's battlements, Isabel drifting towards Alianora while she watched the distant campfires flickering, worry in her eyes. Isabel remained silent, patiently waiting for the words that her cousin yearned to share with the nearest soul. The anticipation continued to mount, and not a word was uttered by Alianora. Few guards patrolled the battlements, Isabel wondering if they were the only men who stood to defend Goldcrest.

"What troubles you, cousin?" Isabel followed Alianora's distant gaze.

"Do you ever wonder how it is you might die?" her voice was solemn.

"It is not a thought which has crossed my mind. Yet the brushes with death, they do seem to occur with an alarming frequency in my life."

Alianora was silent for a moment. "I always hoped it would be beside my future dashing, noble husband, becoming old by his side and withering away in our beds peacefully within our sleep." She paused, pressing her hands on the stone crenellations. "In our lives, that is an event which seldom happens. Our people are ravaged by wars, disease, and many fall to greed by poison. I never believed I would die in a siege. Who knows what these warriors will do to us. Isabel… I have heard the tales of these warriors… lustful… forcing themselves…"

"Do not poison your mind with such thoughts," Isabel turned to her cousin, who continued staring at the horizon.

"I am a lady, not a fool," she spun to meet Isabel. "Lord Entan was struck at the sight of the sack tainted in blood. I overheard his messengers were intercepted. There is no help coming our way, and we are outnumbered."

"We will survive," Isabel said. Then, after a moment of silence, she continued. "I know I did not act accordingly before, but Alianora, you are my cousin. I can understand if you will not forgive me for what I have done... and even if you do not, I will still not allow these men to capture you."

Alianora remained silent for a moment. "There are only so many you may fight at once."

"We will not lose. Have hope, cousin."

"How can you be so certain?" she said, lowering her voice to a whisper, the glimmer that once shined in her eyes now absent.

"Because if hope is gone, then all is lost."

"Sometimes I wish I had seen less of the world so I may yet see it as you do," Alianora glanced away, her hands tensing upon the crenellation as if she were to demolish the castle before the enemy's attack. "If the worst is to come, I wish to ensure your vow."

"What vow?"

"Vow that you will end my life swiftly, with a dagger to the chest."

Isabel stepped back, the words penetrating her chest like the dagger her cousin requested. "I cannot, cousin."

"I am not one to beg, but I will not become a prize to be passed around the warm fire of our captors. Swear this to me, Isabel. I could not bear to live through that pain," the glimmer in her eyes returned, the light shimmer of the stars reflecting off her moist eyes.

Isabel could not bear the thought of ending her cousin's life. She spoke of such pain, a pain beyond that of any dagger that could penetrate her heart. Man's cruel intentions after war were not to be taken lightly by the women of the realm. It struck Alianora in a manner her cousin never imagined she would see. She was not one to take the life of a friend, but this was not taking her life away. Instead, it was allowing her to become free of the shackles of man's lustful ways.

"I-I swear it," Isabel let the words slip through her lips, Alianora's eyes going up, looking heavenward, her relief falling like a burden upon Isabel's heart. She hoped the day would never come, for Isabel was unsure she could bring her cousin's plea for help to fruition. Her cousin embraced her, Alianora's heaving chest crashing onto Isabel's. Alianora's light sniffles were enough to awaken a jabbing pain in Isabel's chest.

"May the gods watch over you," Alianora said as she left, Robion replacing her among the battlements.

"Would it not be best if you rested for the battle to come," Isabel turned to meet Robion. She hugged him unexpectedly, seeking comfort as Robion's arms wrapped around her.

"It appears as if our last moment together met an abrupt interruption," she receded, their gazes meeting.

"It never ended as I hoped. I should have been more aware of our surroundings. I swore to myself to find the men who did this and save you," his brows furrowed, Isabel recalling their moment at the lake.

"Do not burden your heart with such thoughts," Isabel touched his chest lightly. "You could have never foreseen what was to transpire. If only all moments were as peaceful as that night at the lake, and I would not have needed saving."

"It appears as if you need not to be saved. But know this: I will not lose you as I lost my family, Isabel. I will protect you, even if it means giving my dying breath for you to see another day," Robion stepped back. Isabel had never heard a man express such passionate words in her favor. *How chivalrous of you. But I wish for you to live by me, fight with me, not die for me.*

"How noble of you, Robion. I must confess I received some aid in my escape. If not for Arot, I may have met my father's fate."

"My condolences. Your father was a great man. Wars have a cruel way of claiming all those we hold dear. We should not live daily wondering who of those we love are at risk, let alone have death creeping at their door. I could not bear the thought of you-" and he paused, keeping his thoughts to himself.

Isabel's eyes widened, his statement left unfinished, his silence concluding the sentiments his heart carried. Isabel leaned in, sharing his sentiments with a kiss, a kiss that took her back to the lake.

"I could not bear to see the worst come about you either," Isabel leaned back, avoiding his gaze. "When morning comes, I am certain it will not be our last morning."

"It will not. Goldcrest will not meet the fate of Rivetion. I will not allow it. Lord Entan's messengers may have been killed, but I saw their heads, and my messengers were not amongst them." He turned to look at her, Isabel turning her head slightly as he cupped her face, "Your men will come."

"Then there may yet be hope," she shot him a half-hearted smile,

Isabel certain reinforcements would arrive. *Goldcrest will not fall.* She merely hoped that when the day drew to a close, and their reinforcements arrived, they would all still be there to witness it.

CHAPTER 41: COURAGE

The siege ladders dropping against the walls were never-ending, the men vaulting over the crenellations, overwhelming the defenders. Arot fought off the attackers while Isabel pushed one of the incoming ladders away from the castle's walls. The men yelled as they plummeted to the ground. Entan wielded his sword with ease, cutting through the groups of men and pushing the enemy lines back.

Hordes of enemy troops gathered by the castle's entrance, their ram splintering the wooden door. Entan glanced over the crenellations. The enemy troops crowded the entrance, prepared to charge through the doors once the battering ram fulfilled its task.

Men dropped oils and stones over the gatehouse. Their relentless efforts were matched by the enemy's fervor to destroy the wooden door. The door's end was near. Time was of the essence if they were to stall the enemy while the men below mended it. Entan pushed one of the men with his shield, the man falling off the ramparts. He turned swiftly, searching for Isabel in the battlements.

"Isabel," he began amidst strikes when he spotted her, "take your men to the main gatehouse! They are on the verge of breaking through."

Isabel nodded and turned to find Arot amidst the men from Oakheart he had assembled. She spotted Arot and, seizing his chainmail armor, she said, "We must make for the gate."

"Men! To the gates," he ordered, Isabel leading them down the stairs.

The walls would not hold long, as their forces were inadequate to repel the enemies surging over them. Their troops continued to diminish as they held the entrance. The area they were defending was too extensive. Isabel was certain it was only a matter of time before the walls succumbed to their enemy's assault.

"My Lady, I fear we will not hold off the enemy. Our forces are dwindling."

"Arot, your words do little to bolster the troops' morale," Isabel said to Arot between breaths, making sure to keep her voice low so as not to be overheard by the soldiers.

"They should not be led into a slaughter. When will your mercenaries arrive?"

"They will not. My men should be here soon." *I hope.* Norman had arrived after the messenger was sent, informing them the troops would come. Without them, the enemy's extensive numbers would overwhelm their defenses swiftly, leading to the city's downfall. Their contingency plan was a remedy, and Isabel was uncertain if it would be successful without her mercenaries.

Their arrival at the gatehouse had been timed perfectly. The ram shattered through the wooden door, splinters flying in their direction. The men raised their shields. Clouds of smoke concealed the air by the entrance, the men holding back, awaiting their opponents' charge. They stood around the entrance, their feet steady, their shields heavy, their spears at the ready.

A moment of stillness was followed by charging men and their roars. The first line of attackers met the spears of the castle's defenders, the second wave pushing the spears away and crashing into the defenders' lines. Isabel's men joined the group, pinned behind the masses of soldiers holding the line, a bottleneck forming by the main gate.

Peeking over the line of defenders before her, Isabel saw as men charged and jumped over the frontal spearmen. The men of Goldcrest thrust their swords over their shields, pushing back the attackers and closing the gap between them and the gatehouse. Their spurt was short-lived, for a second wave of enemy men crashed their shields onto the defenders' shields, their numbers pushing Isabel's men back.

A fresh wave of defenders surged in behind her, enclosing Isabel within their ranks. The force of her enemies moved the defenders back, their movement dragging Isabel, her body incapable of pressing forward. Men before her began to fall, their enemies overpowering them with every step they took through the gatehouse.

A sudden push overwhelmed them, and Isabel lost her balance as her men retaliated, a retaliation that met quick failure. The enemy eased and hastily pushed back, men around Isabel slipping, dragging her along to the ground. The energy shift broke the defenders' line, the men falling back, stomping Isabel. The world around Isabel eclipsed, the men continuing to crush her, Isabel raising her arms to shield her face. A foot crashed onto her stomach, and Isabel let out an abrupt, painful exhale as the air was forcibly expelled from her body. She gasped within her helmet, desperately searching for air, but the men continued to step over her. It was as if the weight of a thousand castles descended upon her, leaving Isabel immobilized and unable to free herself. The helmet seemed to constrict around her face, its metal seemingly stealing the very air from her lungs.

"Fall back! To the keep!" voices around her shouted, bringing dismay to a nearly fainting Isabel. *Do not abandon me. They will kill me.*

The weight upon her eased, yet she remained constricted by the speeding steps trampling over her armor. The defenders receded, the attackers advancing rapidly toward the keep. In the distance, the pounding hoofbeats grew louder, prompting men to scream in panic. If a thousand men trampled her, she might survive. If one hundred horseshoes landed upon her body, she would be squashed like ripe tomatoes during the harvest season. Isabel struggled to rise, the weight burdening her, the pounding hoofbeats drawing nearer and nearer. Her breathing accelerated, and Isabel felt unprepared to meet her impending fate.

Men shouted and scrambled to evade the charging horses, Isabel sensing the number of feet trampling her diminishing. The earth beneath her trembled, and Isabel shut her eyes for what was to come. The end was not how she hoped it would come to be.

"Get up," a hand gripped her forearm, the cacophony of clashing metal and groaning men still ringing in her ears. She opened her eyes, Arot hoisting her back onto her feet.

The air around her was thick. Isabel panted and searched for a path to safety, her men fleeing toward the keep. The pounding hoofbeats surrounded her, pounding rhythmically with her head. The horses charged and crashed into the men encircling her. Isabel sensed an object pushed into her hand, and she looked down to catch sight of her sword. Arot seized her arm and dragged her away from the oncoming soldiers, forcefully shoving those who crossed their path. He guided her off the street and towards the shelter of the nearby buildings. Once they reached the side, Arot lifted her visor, staring into her face.

"If you want to live, you best mount your horse. Robion cannot fend the enemy for much longer," and he pointed towards the snowy horse. He snatched the reins from one of the cavalrymen who had arrived with Robion to confront the enemy. Isabel took the reins and looked towards the center of the road. Robion was on horseback, slashing away at the enemies by his feet, Sehan and Baenlorn by his flanks.

She quickly mounted her one hope, glancing back at Robion and her men, the source of the hoofbeats that had come to her aid when she had feared she would be trampled. Robion spotted her on the horse and redirected his men away from the gatehouse, with Isabel leading the group back to the keep.

Upon arrival at the keep, Isabel dismounted her horse, one of the squires taking the reins. She turned towards the portcullis, watching men pour within, searching for refuge from the overwhelming enemy forces. Isabel searched for Entan. His imminent arrival was critical for the second phase of their plan.

The men above the gatehouse shot their arrows, defending the incoming soldiers, the last group of men returning from the outer walls. Amongst them, Entan appeared, panting from the lengthy retreat to the castle.

He removed his great helm as he reached Isabel, "Are you certain this will work?"

"It is our only opportunity for survival," she replied, watching the men hail a volley of arrows at the incoming attackers.

"I hope your strategies are as successful as your father's. Where are your mercenaries?"

"Lord Entan, they will be here."

"For both our sakes, it would be best if they arrived soon. Our lives rest on it, and the time for our opportune moment is waning."

"They will be here," Isabel rested her hand on his pauldron, "have faith in me."

"Only because you are your father's daughter."

Isabel nodded appreciatively. "Is your daughter prepared?"

"Ysmay is inside the tower."

"I will join her," and Isabel left, the men around the courtyard retreating within the keep, the portcullis open for the enemy to enter.

By the time Isabel reached the top of the tower, the enemy had begun to pour through the gatehouse, the men of Goldcrest hidden within the keep's walls. Entan's flame-haired daughter glanced at Isabel. Her hood concealed her face, the chain mail under her receding cloak meeting her leather gloves, bow in hand.

"If your plan fails, you will not live to feel the remorse of our people meeting a swift death on your behalf," Ysmay said. The pair hid behind the crenellations, peeking at the men gathering within the courtyard below.

Ysmay's gaze remained fixed on the men gathering below, a battering ram splitting the crowd as they carried it towards the courtyard. Isabel stared beyond them, searching the horizon for men who did not appear. *They will be here when the time arrives.* The time had come, and they were nowhere in sight.

"When will we give the order?" Ysmay whispered.

"Wait. We must wait for their leader to enter." Isabel searched for the general, a group of horses trotting into the courtyard, the helmet of her opponent familiar. The figure entered, its bellow face helmet with spines reminding her of her days in the tent with Odo during the siege of Rivetion. It was the man who had entered with his prisoners into the tent, the man Wolfax had called Crow.

Crow sat on his horse at the center of the courtyard, the leader of the men holding his position. They slammed the battering ram against the keep's door, ramming it without any retaliation as the defenders had abandoned the courtyard. The courtyard was brimming with enemies, Entan's army trapped within the keep's walls. Isabel nodded at Ysmay, Entan's daughter igniting an arrow with the torch beside them and shooting it high into the sky.

At the sight of the arrow, the portcullis in the courtyard dropped, and Crow's men were trapped. The enemy's trebuchets continued to bombard the city. A line of men outside the portcullis continued their efforts to batter down the gate, hoping to rescue their trapped leader. Men streamed from the castle onto the battlements, encircling Crow's men from above.

"Yield or die," Entan ordered Crow.

Crow shook his head and laughed grimly, pointing his sword at the man. "You think I will yield? You are outnumbered, and your castle will be mine. Your daughters will be mine. Your *head* will be *mine*."

Isabel shuddered, thoughts of her cousin's words echoing in her mind. Entan's daughter was infuriated. She pulled her bowstring and aimed it at Crow, releasing the arrow with a cry. However, it was too late, for he had ordered his men into a testudo formation. The men's shields went high, concealing them from Entan's daughter.

"Fire," Entan ordered, his archers' arrows raining upon Crow's men's shield formation.

It was a futile attempt. With their shields protecting them, their reinforcements would soon batter the portcullis, pouring into the courtyard and overwhelming Entan's army. Entan rushed into his castle, leaving Crow to his fate in the rain of arrows. Isabel searched the horizon, but her men were not arriving as anticipated. *It must be done.* She ignited her arrow, pulled the bowstring, and sent it high into the sky in the same manner Ysmay had done.

A tintinnabulation echoed through the city, signaling the second phase of Isabel's plan.

Below the city, within its tunnels, Robion and Norman stood ready with their cavalrymen. Now rarely used, this area was designated for habitation and storage when dragons roamed Emerion, a haven for the people of Montanar. The tunnels were expansive and spacious, causing builders to erect columns in certain areas to bear the weight of the city above. Now, they served a new purpose, and Robion and Norman charged through them. They rushed under the portcullis and the path beyond it, which led towards the city's main gatehouse. Leading the horsemen with their war hammers, they smashed the tunnel's columns as they charged by them. They evaded the falling stones, the tunnel plummeting around them until they reached the end.

From above, Isabel watched as the stone road leading towards the keep's portcullis began to crumble, men wobbling and plummeting into the city's forgotten tunnels. Isabel and Ysmay ignited their arrows, aiming at the firepots within the tunnels. These pots held a specially prepared mixture designed by the locals to ignite rapidly when struck with fire. A group of pigs squealing from below bolted towards the sprawled enemy troops. The pair continued to shoot arrows, igniting the men as a pair of catapults hurled oil pots over them. The flames intensified as the animals caught fire, spreading the flames rapidly through their enemies' ranks. With the giant fire spreading swiftly from the portcullis and beyond the road, the enemy withdrew in a feeble attempt to avoid incineration. Robion and Norman exited the crumbling tunnels, their cavalry slaughtering the fleeing troops.

A giant boulder hurtled through the sky, leaving Isabel's mouth agape as it struck the portcullis, shattering it into pieces. The enemy within the courtyard scattered in disarray, the archers' volley bringing their fleeing efforts to a halt. Crow mounted his horse and fled through the portcullis, retreating in hopes of not becoming a vulture's banquet.

The castle's doors swung open, Entan and his cavalry guard pouring from within, charging at the men. Entan noticed Crow and pressed his spurs on his horse's flanks, sending the steed in pursuit of the enemy leader. Isabel's body stiffened, fearful of Entan's quest to bring to justice his opponent.

Isabel rushed after him, descending the stairs and mounting her steed. Her heart raced at the thought of Entan meeting with the enemies' fleeing troops and an unforeseen reformation of their lines. With a significant portion of their army remaining, they could end their rout, and Entan would be trapped as they regrouped.

As she rode alongside the collapsed road, Isabel evaded the fires, the stench of burning flesh permeating the air. The men's moans had faded, their bodies motionless and ashy from the fire which brought an end to their lives.

A horn in the distance brought Isabel to a halt at the end of the road. She recognized the horn, her heart swelling with hope. *Henry's horn.* The horn resounded a second time, fear striking her enemies as they fled and dared not glance back. They recognized that the battle was lost, and the sounding of the horn was a grim and disheartening signal to their troops. Entan dismounted his horse and battled the few lingering enemy troops who displayed unwavering morale in the face of their defeat. A shirtless, blond-bearded man towered over Entan and swung his axe at him. Lord Entan's smaller size allowed him to move nimbly around him, fending his attacker's strikes.

Isabel felt a tug at her leg, one of the footmen attempting to dismount her. She kicked the man, then swung her sword at his shoulder, cutting through him with ease, the man plummeting to the ground screaming. Her gaze returned to Entan, who had managed to disarm the man, pushing him on the ground and stepping over him. He was on the brink of bringing his sword down upon him when his body suddenly receded, Isabel's heart aching at the sight.

"No!" she yelled, watching Crow from the distance as he loaded a bolt onto his crossbow. Isabel urged her horse forward by pressing her heels into its flanks, but a pair of men grabbed at her feet. She pushed them away, but it was to no avail, as they seized her wrist before she could swing at them. Isabel held her reins to avoid falling. Her steed reared at her tug, the men losing their grip. Isabel's gaze met Entan's as a second bolt from Crow's crossbow struck him, the man's knees buckling.

Isabel charged at the shirtless man, who had risen and taken his axe, prepared to swing it down on Entan's head. She intercepted his strike by crashing her horse into the man, hurling his body onto the stone road. She pulled the reins and rode to his side just as an enemy horseman charged at her. Parrying the man, the clanging of their swords echoed through the dying battlefield. Isabel thrust her sword through his chest, the man's body plummeting from the horse as Isabel spun to kill the shirtless man. But the shirtless man and Crow had vanished, leaving her in the battlefield's ruins amidst the burning men.

With the battle over and Crow having retreated, Isabel dismounted her horse. She knelt beside Entan, holding his weak body. The two bolts penetrated his chest, blood from his armor mixing with her bloodied chainmail and gauntlets. Entan eyed her weakly, his lips parting as he uttered faintly, "We saved Goldcrest, like The Battle of the Golden Tower." He reached for her cheek, his bloodied hand blemishing her face. "You are like your father," he paused, searching for the strength to mutter the few words that lingered within his weakened body. Entan stared at her and completed his sentence with a weak smile, "You gave me courage."

CHAPTER 42: THE KING, JEST, AND FLAME

Isabel's eyes welled as the men lifted Entan and placed him gently on a cart drawn by a pair of chestnut horses. Entan lay unconscious with the bolts sticking out of his chest, deliberately left untouched to prevent excessive bleeding. His daughter walked beside the cart, urging her men to search the city for their most skilled physicians.

With the battle ending, Isabel's reinforcements had arrived at a critical moment. Nevertheless, their arrival had not permitted them to capture Crow. Most of his men were now charred, only a few of them escaping the gruesome ending. Arot had ridden down and reached Isabel, his eyes on the horizon, watching the second army which had come to their aid.

"Your men arrived as you ordered," Arot dismounted. "I believe a second army has come to our aid. I cannot discern their banner. They are too far."

Isabel's gaze remained fixed on the cart, Arot's words not eliciting a reaction from her. He followed her gaze, Entan disappearing from the markets as the men hauled him to the keep. Arot turned to Isabel, resting his hand on her pauldron.

"He is a strong man," he paused, "do not carry the burden of his injury. Your actions are not to blame for what has happened. To some it may have been a foolish decision, yet it was an act of valor which brought him to pursue his opponent."

"How was it the suitable decision if his life hangs by a thread?" Isabel walked toward the gates, her men entering.

"If it were not for your plan and his attack, the men may not have routed. If their ranks had reformed, more lives would have been lost," Arot quickened his stride to walk beside her.

"I only hoped I had saved more."

"War, it comes at a cost. Not all can be saved." He grabbed her arm, Isabel turning to look at him. "If it were not for you, this city would be burning under Crow's regime." Isabel's eyes softened, the young noble lowering her head.

"You do not always babble senselessly, Arot, except when you are drunk," she met his gaze.

Arot smiled at her, "It is my babbling that keeps you entertained, is it not?"

She smiled and turned, watching her men enter, the hoofbeats of their horses followed by the banner of the second army that had stood on the edge of the field. The jade banner was raised over the cavalry that entered, a phoenix with a flame surrounding it, its beak reaching for the sky. The knights rode in, their surcoats matching the banner while they protected the man in the center. Engraved upon his steel cuirass was his family crest, the engravings hardly visible because of the heavy wolf fur robe covering it. His straw, ashy hair fell limply upon his shoulders, his goatee and lengthy beard concealing his cheeks. A spiked crown with dragon talons rose from his head, a crown worthy of a dragon slayer. *Arot, now I understand. Now I understand why it is a threat.* There was no qualm about who this grey-eyed man was. Isabel now understood why it was a threat to wear the talon crown.

A hand pulled her away from the streets, and Isabel turned to meet Arot. "King Ulron," but Isabel had come to realize it the moment she saw his hair and remembered Alaehrayne.

Ulron glanced around the city, his knights detaining anyone who dared approach him. They led him toward the keep, away from the masses which had begun to pour into the city streets. The warriors cleared the roads of the bodies, looting their treasures and paving the way for Ulron's guard to ride through.

"What is the king's business in Goldcrest?" Isabel whispered, one of the guards glancing at her.

"I believe they may have requested reinforcements from the king himself, though his arrival was long overdue," the pair watched as the king and his men vanished in the keep's direction.

Henry, Lunet, and Barda trotted towards the pair. "Lady Isabel. It is good to see you alive and in good health," Henry nodded at the lady.

"I would not have been alive if not for your timely arrival. Your horn brought delight to my ears. I was beginning to lose hope," Isabel said as Henry dismounted.

"They did not disappoint," Henry said.

"The best men you could have paid for, in gold and blood," Barda added, his tone rough as he finished his statement, Isabel's stomach quivering at his words.

"They have proven themselves well, Barda," she nodded.

"The coin motivates their efforts," he added, turning to watch the ruins Isabel had made of the city.

Isabel walked outside the city walls, hoping to admire her freshly gathered army. The men looted the bodies, hoping to increase their greedy pockets beyond her payments. Jarin and his friend from the stocks sat beside one of the dead bodies.

"You need to fight. You will receive no coin from Isabel if you do not fight. I told her you were a warrior, not a slump drunk," Jarin shook his friend.

"I did not ask to be saved. I will not lift a sword, I will not pull a bowstring, I will not fight again," his friend slouched beside a shattered cart, its cartwheel mimicking his slouch.

"You will be released from her ranks. No man will hire your sword in your lifetime."

"Good," the friend said, "I do not wish to fight under anyone's name. I merely wish to be left in peace," and he rose, abandoning his friend.

"Is there a problem here?" Isabel asked as she approached Jarin, pulling her horse's reins.

"Nay, My Lady. No problem at all. I-we- merely wish to thank you for taking us under your command," and Jarin nodded, then rushed after his friend.

Isabel turned towards her men, "Is there a situation I am unaware of?"

Henry and Barda glanced at each other, "It is your problem, not mine," Barda blurted.

Henry cleared his throat, "It appears as if Jarin's friend does not desire to fight. I am unaware of why this may be. He has not received any coin."

"Men who abandon the sword tend to have troubled pasts," Barda muttered, his gaze upon the battlefield, "or they wish to live off your charity.

Isabel's brows furrowed, "Henry, see if you can encourage him to practice. We may need him if he is as good a fighter as his friend said. If all fails, toss a couple of coins his way. It may sway his decision to not pick up a sword again." Isabel wondered what would drive a man to abandon his warrior life in the past and never wield a sword once more.

After exploiting their defeated enemies' riches that evening, the men gathered in the keep. The great hall was filled with murmurs, the men fearful that their voices would wither away what remained of Lord Entan's life. The clattering of men placing tankards was the only loud sound echoing through the hall, the men filling their bellies with warm food, keeping their mouths full to prevent their lips from liberating cheerful words amidst the solemn ambience. The firepits in the hall's center did not suffice to warm the hearts of the family whose bedridden father's health deteriorated with each passing moment.

King Ulron sat upon the throne of the great hall, his belly filled with wine, his lips upturned and brimming with content. The heaviness weighing the hall did not burden him. Isabel watched as men entered the hall, among them an old family friend. She raced to the opposite side of the hall and embraced the man, his bushy beard scratching her neck.

"Odo. I had not been informed you were in Goldcrest," she leaned back, the man healthy as ever. "I see our remedy did you well."

"If not for you, My Lady, I may not have been alive today. I joined the men shortly after your disappearance. When we learned of your request, I knew we must quickly come to your aid."

"It was a timely arrival I must say," Isabel walked with Odo to one of the lengthy wooden tables.

"It was the least we could do, My Lady. How did you manage to escape?"

"Arot, he saved me whilst I was trapped by Morkath."

Odo sat beside Isabel, gripping her forearm gently. "I heard of your father. He was the greatest man I served. How have you been?"

Isabel felt a lump in her throat, and she swallowed it with a gulp of her wine. "It is just so cruel. Why would they decapitate..." she paused, regaining her composure, "decapitate him?"

"It is a cruel way to go. It was a swift death, painless if I may say, but of no honor. This man-"

"He will burn," Isabel dropped her tankard on the table, the silence in the hall causing the reverberation of the tankard to be amplified. She remained still, sensing glances shooting her way.

Odo squeezed her arm, "The pain you endure, it is a pain and sight no child should witness of their parents." He paused as she exhaled, the anger within her body escaping before it could build within her. Odo stared at the candles before them in silence before he continued. "In times like these, one must guard against hasty decisions driven by passion. Your quest for justice is a noble one, and your father deserves it, but remember, rashness can lead to undesirable outcomes. I want you to know I am always here to support you, Lady Isabel. I always will be."

Odo met Isabel's unwavering gaze, her eyes burning with a fury more incredible than all the flames combined within the hall. "I am your sworn sword and guidance, if you ever should need it or want it."

A weak smile spread across her lips, "Thank you, Odo. Your loyalty will be rewarded."

"I seek no reward. If I may say, the honor of guiding you is the reward itself," he squeezed her arm gently before pulling away. "Accreton. You must see it. It has expanded greatly in your absence. You would not recognize it. I entrusted its stewardship to loyal hands. Your family's hands."

Isabel's eyes widened, "Lucia has returned? When?"

"She rode with Faylinn one day as the masses entered the city, and I have advised her in rebuilding the city."

Isabel dropped her tankard, her wine spilling out from the sides and upon the table, nearly staining her jade dress. "You entrusted my sister with an entire city?" she laughed.

"Your siblings will do well. I am most certain."

Isabel cocked her head, certain she had misunderstood. "My siblings?"

Odo nodded, "Indeed. Your brother has arrived at Accreton."

"Do not jest with me, Odo."

"It is no jest, My Lady," he chuckled, Isabel's thoughts wandering to her father's words. *I fear for us. An era of ashes is coming. Hydranok will follow. I fear it may be too late.* "What troubles you, Lady Isabel?"

Isabel shook her head, pushing the words to the back of her head, a second taking their place. *Giles is back. This is good. It is great. We are together after so many years. It cannot be true. Is it? Did Odo mistake another man for him?*

"Are you certain, Odo?"

"Aye, your sister recognized him. What troubles you?"

"Nothing. I simply fear they will burn the city to the ground."

"If anyone is burning cities to the ground, I fear it is you," Odo sipped his wine. "I hear they call you the Lady of Fire."

"Men and their jests of warfare."

"I fear it is your title now, yours to bear. Lady Isabel, Lady of Fire," he raised his hand. "It is a title worth carrying, My Lady."

Fire will incinerate it, or the flame will be its salvation. The old lady's words ran through her mind. *Could the prophecy be real? Prophecies cannot be real.* But now it seemed more likely. The words continued to race through her mind as Isabel recalled the woman's prophecy, engrained within her thoughts and never vanishing, not then, and not now as events appeared to prove it.

CHAPTER 43: DRAGON'S FLAME

Within the great keep, a movement toward the chambers caught Isabel's attention. She rose and followed the group of nobles until they entered a dimly lit chamber, the servants replacing the previous day's candles. Silky, vibrant curtains cascaded around the chamber, concealing the walls and preventing the moon's light from entering the chilly ambiance chamber, a chilliness created by the low murmurs of the men surrounding the bed. A pile of pillows had been placed in the corner, cleared from the bed to allow the lord of the castle space to rest.

Entan was propped on a pillow, a pair of trousers concealing his waist, his bare chest wrapped in blood-stained linen cloths. The bolts no longer protruded from his chest, yet the blood loss had paled his face. Few circular marks were scattered around his torso, testimony of past battle scars where arrows or bolts had pierced him. *He is a veteran of these injuries.*

As Isabel entered the bedchamber, Ysmay, who had stood at the tower with her igniting their enemies, now squinted at her. She weaved through the crowd, reaching Isabel, her brows furrowed. "If not for you, my father would not be in this state. They say you brought this war onto us. You should have never sought reinforcements from my father," she attempted to whisper, the crowd of nobles glancing at her when her tone surpassed their murmurs.

"Ysmay," her father groaned from the bed as he attempted to sit upright. The men rushed to his side, aiding him in hopes of easing his pain, the lord wincing. "Bring Isabel to my side."

Isabel joined him, glancing at Ysmay, her nostrils flaring. Her fiery hair appeared to carry her emotions. Underneath it, a circlet with a sapphire at its center was intertwined with the strands of her hair. Her family, although of pale skin, did not resemble her father's ill state. With rosy, freckled cheeks, Isabel was uncertain if it was their natural state or if they had ripened with her emotions. Ysmay's full lips rested on a narrow face, a narrowness that extended along her slender body. A brooch around her neck fastened a wool cloak, a brooch made of gold, upon it, an archer engraved. One of the servants entered the chamber, and becoming aware of Ysmay's arrival, promptly moved to take her lady's cloak.

"Isabel," he held her hand, Ysmay standing on the opposite side of his bed. "It burdens me to say I must rescind my offer. I will not be able to supply the men I assured."

"I presumed, Lord Entan," she held his hand, her gaze falling upon his chest.

"A man is as good as his word," he said feebly, coughing, Isabel's gaze turning to the stained bed around him. "I will supply you with one hundred men."

"Father," Ysmay interjected. "We have lost men as it is. A second attack will endanger Goldcrest."

"I am aware," he turned to his daughter. "That is why this has been a difficult decision for me. Nevertheless, a second attack is not bound to happen."

"I will not permit our city to be exposed," Ysmay leaned into the bed.

"The decision is not yours to make. It is mine. Goldcrest would not be standing as it is if not for this young woman. It is the least we may do to repay her," his eyes narrowed, his words silencing Ysmay. "You will keep my word, Ysmay. Give your word."

Ysmay resisted, her gaze dropping, her lip curling. Entan reached out to her, grasping her hand gently. "Ysmay, swear you will not break my word."

Ysmay raised his hand, kissing it while staring at Isabel from under her brow. "I swear it, Father."

He nodded, "Thank you, Ysmay. Never forget, we are as strong as the man who stands beside us."

"Thank you, Lord Entan. Your men will serve well," Isabel glanced at his wound.

Entan followed her glance to his wound, "Worry not, My Lady. It is not the first bolt to pierce my flesh," he laughed, coughing and blood filling his mouth. "All will be right," he spat on a bucket a servant held by his side. "Now, if you two will grant me leave to rest, I must rest."

One of the servants stood beside Isabel. "M'lady. The Lord has requested your stay in the castle. If I may, I will lead you to your chamber."

Isabel glanced at Entan, nodding, then following the servant. She heard Ysmay rise from her father's bed and reach them by the chamber's entrance before the servant took her away. The slender fingers slipped through her arm, and Isabel spun to meet her.

"Our families may have been allies, but bear in mind, I am not my father," and she left the chamber, vanishing towards the great hall.

Isabel followed the servant in the opposite direction until they reached her temporary chambers. The servant opened the door and said, "If there is anything you may need, M'lady, do not hesitate to summon us." With those words, she departed, Isabel remaining alone within the chambers.

A bed lavishly adorned with an abundance of pillows dominated the chamber's far end. To the right, a pile of vibrant pillows lay strewn upon the floor, forming a more modest resting place where nobles would convene and sit. On the left side of the chamber, a wooden table stood alongside a pair of chairs, a solitary candle casting its flickering glow. The lord's heraldic tapestries hung upon the wall, serving as a constant reminder of whose castle it was. A hearth warmed the bedchamber, yet its warmth did not reach deep into Isabel's body as she rubbed her arms to stave off the chill.

The distance from home and the solitude in the chamber served to heighten her sense, keeping her acutely aware of her surroundings as she continued her restless pacing. *Why do they harbor such disdain for me? It was but men before, and now Ysmay? I did not stir these men to come and fight me. Did I? Was positioning myself as a leader their reason to find me? Do they dread I may gather the resources to liberate Rivetion?*

Isabel retrieved the flagon from the table and poured the wine into her goblet, sipping at the wine while she contemplated deeply.

With Entan's men, she was to leave Goldcrest at dawn. She sat on the bed, staring at the wall, when a rap on the door snapped her from her thoughts.

"Enter," she said, expecting the return of the servant. Except it was not the servant, and her heart warmed at the sight of the man who entered. The walls and fireplace may not have been sufficient in making her feel at home, but Robion had made certain his presence brought peace to her.

"Lady Isabel."

"Robion," she placed the goblet on the table, attempting to maintain her composure, but her legs betrayed her as she approached him.

"The servants led me to your chamber. I hope I have not interrupted," he said, Isabel wrapping her arms around his neck.

"You have not. The chambers, they felt lonely, cold without any company."

"I will stay as long as you need," Isabel led him to the pile of pillows in the corner of the bedchamber, the pair sinking upon them.

"I am troubled," she said, tracing her finger down his arm, "I fear Lord Entan will not survive what is to come."

"We can only pray," he paused. "The same thoughts plagued my mind while we were on the battlefield."

"You saw Lord Entan ride after Crow?"

"Aye. No," he turned his gaze away. "I was concerned for you, Isabel. After you rushed after him, I worried for you and any danger that could come upon you. At times, I wonder if you will not continue to put yourself in the way of harm." With his wandering gaze, Isabel could see he spoke from the deepness of his heart, her cheeks burning. She had thought the same, hoping she would not lose him during the battle where their fates appeared to be destined for the worse.

"The sentiments are shared. I prayed that the worst did not befall you upon the battlefield. Yet here we are, our prayers answered. Danger follows me, regardless of my actions. If it will chase me, then I must face it head-on, even if only as an attempt to push it away."

"Isabel, forgive my blunt words. It is just… I am uncertain if I could endure your loss should the worst befall you."

"Do not speak so ill. We are here together."

"Indeed," he took hold of her hands, rubbing them with his thumb as they leaned upon the pillows, side by side.

"As long as we remain by each other's side, all will be well," she grabbed his face, their gazes locking. The thought of Ysmay crashed her thoughts. Robion's forehead wrinkled as he noticed her change in expression.

"What is the matter?"

"Trivial memories," the thoughts continued to drown her. "We would not have survived this battle if you had not found me. Without our men, we may not be sitting here together." She paused, cherishing the moment, cherishing his loving gaze. Her thought transported her back to her days with her father, her days with her mother and sister, moments which may have been her last, Isabel unaware of them. Then, the moment at the lake with Robion flooded her mind once more. "We must cherish every moment as if it is our last."

Their gazes locked. Isabel was certain life must not wait, for the world could shift as swiftly as the wind changes its course. As if their minds were one, they closed the gap between them. Their lips locked in a passionate kiss, Isabel wrapping her arms around Robion's neck. His body fell over hers, Robion's hands racing up and down her body, unfastening her leather armor. Isabel pulled away his tunic, exposing Robion's chest. As if the fire sensed their passion, its flame warmed tenfold, their bodies perspiring with the heat of the moment.

Isabel had never been in a position like this with a man, and she halted Robion, panting heavily. "I have… never done this...." Isabel dropped her gaze, embarrassment flushing her cheeks.

Robion smiled upon her, his chest bare as he held his body straight over hers. "Neither have I… it gladdens me you will be my first."

"What if this is a mistake?" she placed a hand on his chest, her chest heaving as she struggled to catch her breath after their passionate kiss.

"If it is," he replied, a mischievous smile dancing on his lips, "let us make certain it is one we will cherish for a lifetime." Isabel giggled while shaking her head, Robion leaning in, planting kisses along her neck.

"You are a mischievous one, Lord Robion. Is this a façade to ease the burden of your first time?"

Robion receded, his cheeks flushing, "It most certainly is not."

"I do not care for what you conceal. In our few moments, we have always been true to each other, and I am certain this will not be a mistake," she said, Robion leaning down to kiss her.

Robion's lips caressed her smooth body, a body pure in all its wake. He slipped her leather clothing away, revealing areas no man had laid eyes upon, Robion admiring it with all its beauty. At first, Isabel turned, concealing herself from the man as her cheeks ripened, but in his gaze, in his gentle touch, she opened herself to Robion.

Their quest to conquer each other's bodies, for their hearts were a conquest that had only been recently exchanged in words, but their true surrender had occurred ages ago, now unfolded before the watchful gaze of the fires surrounding them, observing while the world remained oblivious.

Isabel raked her hands through her hair as Robion made love to her, forgetting the world and pain pursuing them. She had left herself vulnerable to his sight, to his touch. Her vulnerability brought life to her, for she accepted giving herself to him, confident he would never inflict pain upon her. Isabel's insides fluttered, the feeling of love burning within her body, an ardor she would yearn for in the years to come. It was a night Isabel could soon not forget, a night that must remain in silence, for the world would look down upon them for sharing their carnal passions outside of marriage. That night, candles burned out, and their bodies remained close, the approaching winter unable to cool their bodies from the passion burning like a dragon's flame within the two lovers.

CHAPTER 44: ARMY OF PEACE

Lucia hid herself from the world, isolated within the highest tower in Accreton. Usually, Lucia's nose was dug deep in her books, especially with the few books Dunstan had managed to lend her, Lucia spending her days engrossed in the nature-scented pages. Unlike the archives, the days within the tower's utmost reach were discernible, the limited rays of sunlight penetrating the dense clouds and illuminating her books' pages. Lucia read of the past, the present, the future, the existent, and the non-existent. Knowledge seeped through her like water through a rock's crack, yet unlike it, it seldom departed. She hoped one of the scrolls or books would help her understand the book her mother had left her, but as she continued to read from Accreton's archives, she found nothing. *Why did you leave this to me, Mother?*

The noises of the working men in the city below were insufficient to grasp her attention. With the working day's end approaching, the men left for the taverns, joy filling their lips as the imported ale had finally made its arrival to Accreton.

However, the clinking of armor near the main gate snapped her focus, and Lucia redirected her attention to the fresh group of arrivals. People had seeped into the town since Lucia's arrival and the spreading news of Accreton's rise from the ashes. This lot's banner waved in the air, Lucia unable to identify its family's crest as the gust of wind vanished, the banner concealing its identity. Armed men rode alongside the leading rider, turning towards the keep, making their way as if they were the Lords of Accreton. One of the guards brought the group to a halt. He soon waved off another of the guards as he exchanged words with the group's leader, allowing them to continue their march.

A heavy grunt caused Lucia to close her book, spinning to meet the figure reaching the top of the tower. His friendly smile vanished, the man panting, the scar running along the length of his face bouncing. He remained silent for a moment, attempting to regain his breath. A pile of books stood between him and Lucia, the man's large ears holding tightly onto his glasses in case he collapsed.

"Dunstan, what is the matter with you?"

"Oh," he gasped, dropping the books at the top of the stairs, raising his hand at her.

"Dunstan, please do not collapse. There is no physician to cure you if the worst were to come."

"I will be all right, My Lady. I found these books and thought they may interest you."

"Oh," Lucia beamed at the sight of the towering books he carried to the top of the tower. "I will bury my nose within them soon," Lucia said, her attention trailing in the direction of the band of men reaching the castle entrance.

"I have no doubt," Dunstan said, nearly regaining his breath.

"Nevertheless, now is not the moment. I have visitors I must attend to," she rushed past him. "Would you mind taking those books to my chamber?" she asked, but a reply never came, for Lucia had descended the tower hastily, leaving poor Dunstan behind.

Dunstan's eyes widened, the man mumbling, "How will I ever make it down this tower without carving a new scar upon my face?"

At the great hall, Lucia sat upon the throne, a throne that appeared to swallow her petite body, Giles standing beside her while the guards spoke with the men outside the castle. Her brother cleared his throat, watching as one of the guards proceeded their way.

"We should only allow a pair of the guards to enter, Lucia. With our available forces thinned out, it would not be wise to allow many men to gather within our hall while we are unguarded," Giles whispered to her.

"Indeed."

"Lady Lucia," one of the guards approached her. "A man outside the castle wishes to speak to you. It is no time for visitors, but he continues to press on that he must have an audience with the Lady of Accreton."

Lucia nodded, "Let him enter. Only a pair of his men may join him inside."

The guard nodded and returned to the entrance. Soon after, three men entered the great hall, their bodies protected with scaled armor hiding within their thick robes. A fur lining adorned the center figure's robe, his once chocolate hair and beard now tainted as if winter had fallen upon it. His presence had Lucia's mind running around the hall, searching for its recognition.

The man approached the base of the stairs, and his eyes widened as he recognized the pair at the top. "Giles? Lucia?" he watched the pair, the man smiling.

Giles' hand fell upon Lucia's shoulder limply, an incredulous stare escaping him at the man's sight. It had been years since they had last seen the man, let alone heard of him. Giles recognized him immediately, and though Lucia recognized his voice, she could not remember who he was. Lucia remained confused, her thoughts not gathering swift enough.

"Uncle," Giles said, the words igniting Lucia's head like a flame, the memories of her uncle coming alive.

"Uncle Beridon," Lucia added, watching the man before them.

"I had not believed the news and had to come for myself," he opened his arms, glancing around the great hall in amazement. Giles descended the stairs, Lucia's body becoming one with the seat as her legs became weak, unable to accept they were amongst family.

Beridon Beaumont embraced his nephew as he made his way down. The sight of the two brought the blood back to Lucia's legs, and Lucia rose to meet her uncle. Beridon glanced at the young woman approaching him and enfolded her in his arms, bestowing a gentle kiss upon her brow.

"It fills me with joy to see the two of you alive. I heard about your estate, and claims spread that the Beaumont children had settled down in Accreton. I would not believe it. I had to travel to the mountain," he embraced the pair. "You are alive and well. That is all one may hope. Why did you do it?" he turned towards Giles. "Why did you regain control of Accreton?"

Giles shook his head, "It was not me, Uncle. It was my sisters."

Beridon's head cocked back, bewilderment flashing from his eyes. "Little Lucia? You did this?"

Lucia, although honored, shook her head, unable to accept the acknowledgement for such a deed. "No, Uncle. It was Isabel. She is the true leader of Accreton. It was her decision to rebuild it."

"Where is Isabel?" he turned, searching for her as if she lurked within the castle's shadows.

"At the moment, she is away from the castle. She entrusted me with the city, to be the Lady of Accreton," Lucia beamed at him.

Beridon remained bewildered, but he shook it away. "I am overwhelmed. Ladies in control of a castle. Who would have imagined?"

The great hall's doors barged open, and a group of men followed a chestnut-haired woman with a golden leaf comb. Her bright eyes were darkened with her slanted eyebrows, the shadow cast upon them powerful enough to swallow the hall into its obscurity. The castle guard moved in to surround the incoming men. Giles pushed Lucia away, Lucia retreating to the top of the stairs, seeking the safety of her dragon throne.

"Where is this Lady of Accreton?" Katinee snarled like the wolf on her banners.

"In what temerarious manner do you intrude our great hall?" Giles reached for his sword.

"Silent peasant. I have come for the Lady of Accreton, and only with her will I speak," Katinee's gaze shot up at Lucia.

"Yield your weapons, and I will grant you my protection," Lucia called out to her from the throne.

"Protection?" Katinee's words boomed over the castle's walls. "*Protection?* From you? It was I who protected you, and now your sister snatched my own away. She was to find and return her, but instead, she has taken her as her captive."

"The Ladies of Accreton would never commit such a crime," Beridon stood before her fearlessly.

"If they would not, then where is she? Where is my sister?" She glanced around, "Nowhere. I should have your head on a pike.

Justice should be served for kidnapping a noble," Katinee's men snatched the grips of their swords.

Lucia caught sight of a slithering figure within the crowd. It was a figure she knew all too well. With Katinee glancing backwards at her men, she lost sight of the figure. She was swiftly met by its sword's biting edge kissing lightly against her throat.

"There will be no bloodshed today," Faylinn said to Katinee, her eyes narrowed. Lucia hoped this would provide a respite from the dispute.

"The thief's accomplice," she said, Faylinn replying with her sword, inching it deeper into her skin.

"Have them stand down," Lucia said from her throne. Her blood pumped within her veins. She could feel it boiling into her skin, on the verge of exploding within the great hall.

Katinee lowered her hand, and her men released their swords, the guards inching closer towards them. "Hand your weapons to my guards. Let us not spill blood this evening."

Katinee did not comply. She glanced over her shoulder, one of the men within her group aiming a bow at Faylinn. "If I die, so will you."

"I do not fear death any more than I would fear you," Faylinn's lips curled. Lucia's heart throbbed at the thought of Faylinn being injured. She could not bear the thought of her friend being taken away. Her eyes glanced back and forth at the clashing parties below, and a quick decision was made.

"Leave her, Faylinn," Lucia said, Faylinn glancing incredulously at Lucia.

"She will not stand back," Faylinn retaliated, but Lucia did not give in.

"Leave her, *Faylinn*," she emphasized. Faylinn removed her sword from Katinee's throat and grunted.

"The lady always has a dog," Katinee murmured with a smug smile, Faylinn glowering at her, prepared to strike her down. Lucia would not allow unnecessary bloodshed. She knew, however, that if peace did not come soon, Faylinn would remove Katinee's head from her body.

"Let us end this dispute," Katinee said as she gazed towards Lucia. "I have word your sister captured Seraphina and drags her around like a trophy. Tell me where she is, and I will allow you to live."

"My sister did not capture her. She freed her from her previous captors. I have no knowledge of their whereabouts."

"It is not freedom if she remains in captivity. I will not allow my sister to remain in your sister's claws. She will be free, and if you will not comply, then I will do what I must," the tension had risen once more. Lucia was unsure she could keep the men within the hall from spilling unnecessary blood. Her uncle grasped the grip of his sword, and all the men mimicked his behavior. Lucia was helpless. She did not choose this position of power, of power to end life or bring the death of humanity's discords. She looked at her brother, but he remained gazing at the woman who entered their great hall. Faylinn did the same. No one who would utter a word of guidance. She was alone, the curtain removed and unveiling her fears. The decision of life or death remained in her hands. The air thickened, and her body prepared to scream for help.

The great hall's doors groaned, allowing her to inhale as the attention spun in the opposite direction. Lucia's chest heaved, the young woman gazing into the sky. She thanked the gods for bringing peace into her life once more, or at least removing the decision from her hands.

From the door, a voice boomed along the length of the great hall, "My claws do not grip her. My claws have merely freed her." Lucia's smile was weak, but it was present as she saw who had emitted those words. *Thank you, Isabel!*

There they stood before the great doors, Isabel side by side with Seraphina, and an army of peace breathing down her back.

CHAPTER 45: FRIEND OR FOE

"Come, Seraphina," Katinee said, her arms outstretched. "Be their prisoner no more."

Seraphina cocked her head back, "I am no one's prisoner. They saved me from my imprisonment, from those barbarians."

"Then come, let us go home," Katinee stepped forward. However, her sister remained motionless, her stance resolute.

Taking notice of Seraphina's unmoving stance, Giles watched as Isabel intercepted. "You and your men should stay the night. Take a respite from your travels and continue your journey tomorrow."

Katinee's eyes narrowed at her words but eased instantly. Isabel knew her men needed rest for the travels ahead, for the roads were swarming with enemies. Katinee lowered her head slightly and met Isabel's gaze, "Only for the one night. Tomorrow we resume our journey."

"It is settled. My people will spare what we have to feed the men, and I am certain we may settle any disputes during supper, if there are any that remain," Isabel's posture was stiff, waiting for an answer.

"Very well," Katinee's reply was short but not sweet, turning her back to Isabel as one of the castle's servants led her to her chambers.

Isabel's gaze fell upon her sister and Giles, her eyes widening at the family reunion unfolding in her hall. Not too distant was Beridon, yet it was the sight of her brother in Accreton that brought her the most joy. Beridon, the nearest to her, approached Isabel and embraced her.

"My niece. It is good to see you with health," his lips curved into a smile, a smile that was not the most earnest she had seen from him. She was quick to disregard it when her sister bolted towards her.

"Oh, Isabel, you have not the slightest idea how good it is to see you," she said while wrapping her arms around Isabel's neck.

"You held Katinee off while I arrived. You have managed the castle better than I expected," Isabel winked at her.

"I do not believe I would have held them much longer if not for your timely arrival," Lucia's cheeky smile soothed Isabel from her challenging travels. "Uncle and Giles aided in keeping them at bay. Uncle had just arrived. The gods have a way of perfectly orchestrating their world."

"Is that so, Uncle?" Isabel glanced at him, still perplexed from seeing him in Accreton.

"It is as if the gods themselves premeditated this," he tilted his head and shrugged.

Giles came forward, joining his family. Upon seeing him, Isabel mimicked Lucia's behavior at the sight of him, wrapping her arms around his neck.

"You have grown since I last saw you," Giles returned the embrace.

"Stronger and more agile too. You would certainly meet defeat if you sparred with me."

Giles retreated from her, pretending to be fearful of her words, then stepped forward, "We have yet to see about that."

"Where is Beatriz?" Isabel looked around, not seeing her within the great hall.

Giles glanced down, then replied, "I fear she did not survive the attack in our village." There was a dullness in his eyes as he rubbed his arm, a dullness she had never seen.

"That is terrible!" Isabel leaned in to hug him. "I cannot imagine what you must be feeling," she said while holding him close, his hand wrapping limply around her. They were silent for a moment. *I cannot tell him about Father. To know Beatriz is dead, and Father as well. It would devastate him, even if their last encounter was not the best. Father and Giles were always so close. I cannot. Not now.*

Taking a step back, Isabel said. "How were you able to find us here in Accreton?" but she did not wait for a reply. "You must tell us of your journey, certainly, in due time. For now, there is a supper we must attend." She walked away, urging Lucia to walk beside her as she nudged her toward the throne. *Giles is back. Is this truly happening? Is it because he decided? Or did the egg somehow lure him back? No. Impossible. The egg has no such power. Why did he come back? Did they lose everything?*

Left amidst the hall, Giles and Beridon walked out into one of the dimly lit halls, reminiscing about moments of times past.

"I take it you have yet to see your father," Beridon turned to look at his nephew.

Giles remained silent, his mind swept with thoughts of the past, reliving their last moment together.

Father, I will be marrying Beatriz.

What?

Those were the words that came crashing into his mind, words that were nearly the last ones the pair had shared. His life had been spared, the father's heirloom sword left shattered, a sword he believed now hung by Isabel's waist. All he could remember was his father's struck eyes when he nearly sliced him down, horror beckoning from them with the near-death experience of his eldest son, a son he had soon lost to Beatriz when he abandoned the estate for her.

"Do not allow the past to trouble you," Beridon placed his hand on his shoulder. "As you can see, times have changed."

Giles' gaze rose to meet Beridon's. "Illuminate me, Uncle."

"War, money, power. It is altering the course of history," Beridon did not blink.

"Is that not all subject to change."

"It should not. War has lost you your family home, for are you not here?"

"That is bound to happen in this life or the next."

"Money, I reckon you are short of it after leaving all behind."

"I have never desired wealth. I will leave Emerion as I entered it," Giles replied, Beridon's eyes reflecting the dimly lit flame from the chandelier.

"Power. It is not for women to wield." At those final words, Giles remained still, unsure of his uncle's intentions. The air around them became dense, Giles' breath hitching.

"It need not matter who holds power, so long as it is controlled."

"Power corrupts people, especially those who have never wielded it within their lifetime. Did you not see Lady Katinee out there? She was not a woman of power. She was a docile child, if I may say. Do your eyes not see what it has brought upon her, this feeling of an iron boot?"

"She was raised differently. She may not have been the child my sister was. Isabel has a deeper understanding. She is virtuous. She would not inflict harm upon a soul without just cause. Such is the wisdom our father instilled within us."

"Oh, blinded by the sun you have been. You did not learn that you could not shield its light with your hand," Beridon shook his head, clicking his tongue.

"How could you say that of her? You have seen her and are familiar with our father's ways."

"Giles, that girl you knew. That girl who entered the great hall, she has changed. It is power itself, corrupting her to do its bidding. There is a gleam in her eyes, a gleam I have beheld in far too many souls led astray by corruption. I feel she has been contaminated by its poison, and time is escaping us, for soon we will be unable to rescue her from its clutches."

Giles remembered her gaze just moments ago, nodding as he replied. "If what you speak is true, what can we do?"

A small smile crept upon the corner of his lips, but he wiggled it away while his nephew glanced around them, hoping no one was watching. "Only what is righteous."

Supper came, and the nobles gathered around the great hall, a once dusty place coming alive with the freshly lit candles standing tall upon the chandeliers. The wooden chairs were not of the finest craftsmanship, differing in forms and stature. The table was bare, adorned only with a smattering of candles and a bowl of imported fruits.

Isabel watched from the corner of the hall, waiting for her guests' arrival as the scant servants who had come to the castle bustled about the table. Maple entered the hall, a loyal servant to her family ever since they left Rivetion.

"M'lady. There is a man who just arrived. He states he has come here to join you upon hearing your plea for help," Maple finished saying as Robion joined the pair.

"My plea for help? Have him enter," Isabel continued watching the servants, wondering who the man might be.

Robion's eyes widened when the man Maple had spoken of entered the hall. Isabel and Robion became mirror images of each other before taking notice of the other's expression. Before them, the man came to a halt, smiling, a smile Isabel would not forget.

"Osbert," Robion murmured to himself.

"Lord Osbert. To what may I owe this unannounced visit?"

Osbert cleared his throat and began, "Lady Isabel. I hope you forgive our encounter in Rivetion. The ale and wine, they do not coalesce amicably within myself."

"No harm has been done, nor blood been spilt over drunken words. Now, what has brought you to Accreton?" Isabel's mind continued searching for the plea for help.

"Aye, swift to the matter at hand. Upon hearing of your tournament victory and how you and your men managed to aid the city of Goldcrest, I have come to join Lord Robion," he turned to meet Robion's widened eyes.

"Me?" Robion jabbed his chest, evidently confused.

"Indeed. If you believe following Lady Isabel is wise, then I will join under your banner. As Lady Isabel has said, I hope we may put the past behind us. I am aware this will not absolve our transgressions, but I merely wish to assist you in shedding the blood of those who spilt your family's blood."

Robion remained stiff for a moment, a reaction Isabel believed would be characteristic of such a situation. "Forget the past? After all you have done to those who I love?" Robion began to step forward, Isabel snatching his wrist. Robion looked at her, fury evident in his gaze. "You insulted Lady Isabel in Rivetion."

Osbert shook his head, "Lord, I only hope we may put all that is in the past to rest. Perhaps this will aid in your decision," Osbert stretched out his hand, but a guard rapidly interposed himself between them, creating a gap between Osbert and the Lady of Accreton. Osbert looked at the guard, and after a brief pause, opened his palm, revealing a minute scroll. The guard accepted the scroll and presented it to Isabel, who then walked away, accompanied by Robion. The pair ascended the stairs to the throne, creating a formidable distance between Osbert and themselves.

Osbert continued to talk, "This is from Lord Courbet. After hearing of your recent victory, he said if I would be willing to set aside our differences and join your cause, then he too would be willing to join you in the fight for Rivetion."

Odo had entered the great hall and stood watching from the side, Isabel tearing at the raven seal and opening the scroll.

Lady Isabel,

Our last encounter may not have been one which I can take pride in. I commend you on your tournament victory and on leading such fierce men in the defense of Goldcrest. My men are at your disposal and will follow you to liberate Rivetion from its captors, should you still need my aid. Should you require it, Osbert will dispatch a messenger unto me, and we will join you at the battlefield to vanquish our true common foe.

Warm regards,
Lord Rulf Courbet

Isabel, now sitting on the throne, pulled Robion to her side. She reread the letter, then looked up at him. "Robion, we must gather all the forces at our disposal to liberate Rivetion."

"You would allow this man to join us after all he has done?" Robion's eyes ignited, a fire she had yet to see in him.

"I do not trust him either," she said while shaking her head lightly, hoping Osbert could not overhear their conversation from afar. "Nevertheless, there is a greater menace in our midst. We cannot change the past, but we can still rescue Rivetion's people." Robion looked at her, Isabel holding his hand in hers, rubbing it gently, "I do not suggest we forget his transgressions. I merely propose we accept their military support. With them by our side, we can keep a closer look on those who may attempt to deceive us."

Robion inhaled, shutting his eyes. "I believe that is in the past," he said while turning towards Osbert, "We must unite now to serve a common enemy. What would you ask in return?"

"All I desire is for the past to be put to rest. Liberating the fallen city of Rivetion is all I seek now." *Now. All I seek now. Why would he do such a thing after bringing down his own brother? I know it was him.*

But amidst the chaos, did Robion notice too? With Layne gone, will the city be his, or will Cicely remain governing it? If she remains alive.

"Thank you for this message, Osbert. I will see to it that Lord Rulf receives his reply. My messengers will contact him. Join us for supper, and we will discuss the remaining matters in our war room."

Osbert nodded, "Thank you, Lady Isabel," and walked away.

Am I truly becoming what Alianora said? Is it right for us to set aside our differences? For Robion to forget all Osbert has done? I am not doing what I do merely for myself. No. There is a grander purpose at hand. This is not for me. This is for the people of Rivetion. It must be done.

Odo joined the pair as they descended the stairs, "Lady Isabel, do you believe it wise to accept his aid? Rulf had a feud with your father."

"I am not my father. Feuds are lost in the past. We can never move forward if we continue to dwell upon it. We must gather every man at our disposal. Troublesome feuds burn out when a common enemy is present."

Odo sighed and was interrupted from counseling the young Beaumont girl when Lady Katinee joined them. As if she had been listening from the shadows, she began, "Lady Isabel. On behalf of saving my sister, I believe your intentions are pure." *This woman has succumbed to madness. One moment she is attacking us, the next, diffusing her aggressions?*

"I only went about what I believed was most noble."

"Your nobleness may be your greatest attribute. I have decided I will aid you in your journey to save my dear sister, Cicely," she gave a light nod.

"A sudden change of heart?" Isabel watched as Katinee held her chin high.

"It is only fair after you saved Seraphina from those bandits. I will arrange for us to join you for the attack."

"I will have my messengers prepared for when your troops are underway. Thank you."

Lady Katinee remained silent, choosing to take a seat at the table where supper would not be as lavish as her castle, for Accreton had only begun to import supplies into the city. Isabel observed as her people and the assembled guests came together at the table, uniting as one, regardless of their previous allegiances, now bound by a common foe. Her training under Norman and her recent actions had brought about renown, the lords of the realm taking notice and pursuing her directly or indirectly in their quest to rescue her old friends in Rivetion. The pieces were falling into place. The world would soon recognize she was the leader who would deliver them from their plight. The world would soon realize *she* was a warrior.

CHAPTER 46: REFLECTIONS

As if her days had not taught her enough, Lucia proceeded with her old ways. Concealed within the deeper shadows in the castle, Lucia slipped amongst them, standing outside the great door separating her and Katinee. Moments earlier, Katinee and Nalthok had vanished within the chamber, joined shortly after by Seraphina. With her ear pressed onto the door, she listened intently, hoping to find more answers than questions.

"We leave tomorrow," Katinee's voice was the first to make its way through the dense wood.

"I have thought it best if I joined Isabel, at least until we free Cicely," Seraphina refuted while stepping back.

"You do not know what is best. What is best is for you to join me before you bring along more turmoil to this family," Katinee's voice strengthened.

"I am a free woman to do as I please. I will go where I see fit," Seraphina stepped forward, reducing the space that separated the two, as if the proximity between the pair would facilitate the transmission of her words to her sister.

"You may be as free as you believe, but I will make certain no turmoil comes along your way, not as long as I live," Katinee said, Nalthok watching the pair from across the bedchamber, his curious gaze bouncing back and forth between the sisters.

"This family is the reason for such turmoils. We live in a sea of them and flourish within them. Is that not how it is, Katinee?"

"I will not have you speak ill of our family."

"Is that a turmoil you will prevent as well?"

"If need be, I will make certain of it," their voices boomed inside the chambers.

"If you are so keen on preventing such turmoils, where were you when our sister needed you most? Why is Cicely amid such troubles? I did not see you rush to aid her, to rescue her from all this chaos you wish to prevent. Or is this your reason for controlling me, for keeping me by your side?"

"After all I have aided you, you presume I am controlling you? You dare say I have not shielded you from being dragged into this realm of chaos?"

"You have not. If you had, I would never have been taken away. I would have never needed to be rescued," Seraphina raised her head, mimicking the Loup stance.

"You will lead this family to its downfall. That is what you will do, Seraphina."

"If you have not yet done that yourself."

"I have not. Dare your arrogance not impede you from remembering I was the one who kept the world at bay when you last needed it."

Seraphina turned her back to her sister, Nalthok watching with devious eyes and a crooked smile. "I did not need saving then."

"You did not?" Katinee's voice softened, yet enough strength lingered to instill authority. "You did not need saving when your husband came to pass?"

Seraphina swallowed hard, unable to turn and meet her sister's piercing gaze.

"Or, dare I say, his *regrettable* loss of life?"

"You are cognizant of the sort of man he was," Seraphina's voice choked.

"I was well aware," her voice softened, Katinee stepping deliberately towards her sister.

"You know it was for the best," her voice broke, her eyes brimming with tears.

"That is why I needed to keep you safe."

"The memories, they still linger," Seraphina could no longer hold the tears, the tiny teardrops rushing down her cheeks, sobs replacing her words.

"It is bound to happen. Let the past escape in tears and sobs. It is your best remedy," Katinee placed her hand on Seraphina's shoulder, Seraphina's back still turned towards her. "Do not let it turn to words, for they will haunt you like a ghost in the twilight."

"I would never," she gulped, no words of the past escaping her. Katinee turned her, Seraphina staring blankly at the ground.

"Now you know why you must leave with me. It is for the best," Katinee said as Seraphina rose to meet her gaze, squinting as she took a step back.

"I will not. You merely wish for me to leave with you so you remain safe from our past. You will not keep me caged like the thoughts that I am burdened to carry and bury within me for all eternity."

Katinee's voice strength returned, her eyes narrowing as she stepped forward, her words burning into her sister's face like a dragon's breath. "You *will* leave with me. If you stay, your world will burn with the truth of your past, and this time, I will not be there to save you."

Seraphina's voice hitched as words attempted to escape her lips, yet they were held prisoner by her body. "I-I," she stammered, but that was all that escaped her lips.

"You what?" Katinee's voice bore down upon her sister without laying a finger on her.

"You sicken me," Seraphina turned, receding from her sister. The stomping and cries drew closer to the door, Lucia tapping her finger restlessly on her thigh. Her body froze, then came alive. She retreated down the hall, avoiding any further confrontation for lurking and eavesdropping on the conversations of nobles.

The giant wooden doors swung open, and Seraphina emerged. Her sobs escaped her and echoed down the vast passageway as if in pursuit of Lucia, but she was nowhere to be found. Lucia hurriedly reached her sister's chamber and collided with Isabel in her desperation to flee.

"Ouch!" Isabel turned to meet her. "Watch where you are running, Lucia."

"Forgive me, Isabel," and Lucia was well on her way, vanishing down the shadowy passageway.

"I wonder what she is up to," Isabel turned to Odo. Noticing his gaze elsewhere, she asked, "What is troubling you, Odo?"

"I am uncertain if we have enough men."

"Strength does not always lie in numbers, Odo. We possess skilled men and exceptional leaders, both seasoned and newly forged," she looked at him, her gaze sweeping over him from head to toe. Odo nodded and offered her a gentle smile. "Remember Montanar."

"As your advisor, it is my duty to worry, Lady Isabel. Perhaps you are correct, and I am fretting without cause. I merely pray I can serve you well in the coming battles."

"You have proven yourself a great advisor so far. I trust your judgement."

"I am pleased to hear you say so," he said, his hands crossed behind his back, his gaze briefly falling to the ground. "During your absence, I dispatched a party to scout Oakheart."

Isabel's heart hitched. After seeing Arot and her father, she had not thought much of returning. The only person missing was her mother, and there had been no word of her. "What did you discover, Odo?" she asked, uncertain whether she desired to uncover the truth.

Odo was silent, then looked at her while shaking his head. "I fear quite the opposite. I discovered nothing. Oakheart is deserted. Anyone who lived escaped or lost their life there."

Isabel gulped. Though Arot said he had returned to Oakheart and only heard word of her father, she decided to ask the question that lingered. Arot stated he did not find her mother, but she needed to know once more, one more time for confirmation, just to be certain. Perhaps he had not seen Valaenis amidst his rush. Perhaps she was there, dead, and that is why none had heard of her. With a heavy heart, she asked, "Was my mother amongst them?"

Odo shook his head, "I fear not. I made certain to instruct the men to be thorough in their search. I reckon she is alive if she was not captured." Isabel sighed. *Mother is out there. I know it.*

"Thank you, Odo. For going back in search of my family," she said, thanking the gods there was still hope for her mother. "There is no pressing cause to return now. After we liberate Rivetion, I look forward to returning to Oakheart. Perhaps there lies a clue to where she might have gone."

"Perhaps," he said. After a brief pause, Odo said, "Now, My Lady, if your attack goes askew, do you have a plan? One as you did in Goldcrest? The men say you were quite prepared."

"I do, Odo. I do."

"You have grown much since Rivetion, My Lady. The world has changed you, but you have changed even blind men."

Isabel was silent. "There comes a time when great deeds bestow sight upon those who were once blind. I believe the world has finally regained its vision, and it will soon witness a grander deed set to befall it."

"Your family always brought light to this world. I hope you will do the same. I will follow you until my end, My Lady," and Odo left her chambers, leaving Isabel alone with the flickering light of the candles near her bed.

The monumental mirror discovered within one of the chambers in the castle had been moved to her chamber, a mirror so grand her reflection was like a mere fish in the vast sea. Her reflection moved as she did, watching her intently, as if gazing into each other's souls. Within the mirror, in the far reaches, the bedchamber appeared darker than hers as if night had fallen upon it and not a candle in the world could revive its gloomy state.

Her thoughts wandered and were shared with only the figure before her, a figure that resembled her exterior, yet she was uncertain if they were indeed the same person within.

Odo had been a great advisor in her journey. She could see why her father fought beside him. Odo's counsel had steered her along a straight path, and when she had strayed off her course, his voice had been one of the reasons she found her way back to her intended path. The path walking forward was often misty, but she could always see farther by his side, like a lamp in the night.

Odo had led her this far, but now it was time for her to take the lamp and illuminate her path with the wisdom acquired. The moment she had prepared for had finally arrived. Isabel was poised to lead the army that stood steadfast behind her into a battle that would soon determine the fate of her imprisoned friends, the realm, and perhaps even her future.

Isabel raised her dress as she sat by the fountain in the courtyard beside the great hall. Guards stared silently towards the city from the crenellations above. Their torches flickered in the night, a gentle breeze caressing her cheeks, cold, like death taunting her visage.

She looked at the cloth beside her and removed the talon crown from within. The stars in the night caused it to shimmer, but before she could further admire it, an eerie feeling enveloped Isabel. The hairs on her nape stood on end, and she knew she was being watched.

Gazing slowly from the corner of her eye, she saw a gowned figure appear from the shadows under the archways. The figure approached ever so gently, and her shoulders relaxed when she saw the friendly face.

"You should be resting, My Lady," Father Aubrey said, his arms across his chest, his hands concealed within his sleeves.

"I cannot. There is much on my mind," she said, holding the crown firmly.

"Hmph." He looked at it, then at her, "Will you wear the crown?"

Isabel's eyes widened as she looked up at him, shaking her head. "I am no queen, nor a princess." *Why would I wear a crown?*

"Neither were your ancestors when they first wore it, yet wear it they did," Father Aubrey said, shrugging while sitting beside her. He took the cloth and placed it on his lap, Isabel looking at him worriedly.

"Can you tell me the true story of the crown?"

Aubrey shook his head and gazed at her hand, taking it within his own before meeting her gaze again. "I fear I do not know the story well. Perhaps Dunstan knows, or there is a scroll in the archives which tells the tale."

A lost story of a lost age. Forgotten. What is the story behind the crown? "Why would I wear it then? It is merely a crown with a forgotten story."

"The only stories left forgotten are the ones we do not recount nor strive to uncover. The story of the crown endures. I assure you it is not lost. As is your story. Yours will not be long forgotten."

"How can you be certain?" *What if my story ends tomorrow? What if my story does not continue? What if Rivetion is where I drop the sword? Am I ready?* "Father Aubrey, I fear what is to come."

"The crown will give you power as it has done your ancestors. I heard your father speak of it long ago, how all who wore it acquired much fortitude, and how it kindled inspiration in the hearts of those who followed them. Do you not see, My Lady?" he squeezed her hands, "the gods wished for you to find it. You are destined to wear it."

But Isabel could not reconcile herself with the idea. She sensed great perils awaited if she wore it. It was an act of defiance. "What will the other nobles think if I wear it? What will King Ulron believe? It will be an act of defiance to the realm."

Aubrey patted her hand, "This crown is no symbolism of king hierarchy. It is a symbol of inspiration, courage, and of the tradition the Valenour's Dragon Riders lineage." Father Aubrey, however, looked her straight in the eyes, "I will be forthright with you. It may cause strife between you and the crown, but if you knew the stories these crowns carry, you would not hesitate to wear it."

Father Aubrey, you tell me it is a danger to wear it, yet you wish for me to wear it. You can be quite complicated. Isabel looked down at the crown, its sapphires calm in the night. *How can one crown sow such strife without instigating defiance yet kindle this inspiration?* She murmured to herself, "I am no princess."

"No," Father Aubrey whispered, "you are no princess. You are The Talon Princess." Isabel glanced up at him, the priest smiling softly at her.

She stared at the crown. *Why are the gods so unjust? I have been nothing but forgotten by them. My home was raided. I lost this crown. Father is dead. Mother has disappeared. Oakheart is nothing but deserted. A battle's fate looms in my hands. I am not yet a woman, I am merely a child.*

The darkness in the courtyard vanished, the moon escaping from behind the shadowy clouds. The crown came alive, and Isabel glanced up at the sky, then back at the silver claws.

But I found Arot. I found Aubrey. Lucia is safe with me. I won a battle. Men have followed me. I have survived these tumultuous lands. Though I believed it to be lost, the crown has returned to me. Why would something lost return if it did not serve a purpose? Perhaps the gods are watching over us. Perhaps I am fated to wear the crown. All this has forced me to tread a path no person would have survived. Many have fallen in my journey, but I have endured at every turn. Perhaps I started as a child, but a child would not have survived this path. I am changed. I am no longer Isabel Beaumont of Oakheart. I am now Isabel Valenour of Accreton. I am no longer a child. The thoughts in her mind fell silent for a moment as she watched the crown, tracing the sapphire line embedded within the silver with her finger. *I am a Valenour, but am I truly a talon princess?*

CHAPTER 47: WAR'S PAYMENT

Rivetion, once ablaze with flames that reached like fingers into the sky, now lay extinguished. All that remained were ruins of the battle that took place within it. Smoked-out buildings, stained with the blood and ashes of its past siege, were unwelcoming to the approaching army. Isabel watched the city they would attack from the woods where she once hid, yearning to free her friends from their captors.

The army had come to a halt and awaited their allies' arrival, hopeful that in the strength of their union, they could bring the siege to an end before winter set about them. The winter winds had begun to strike the incoming forces, Isabel shivering within her fur-lined cloak. Her thoughts returned to a few nights prior, when she had seen her sister for the last time.

"I wish to go with you," Lucia had said, crossing her arms over her chest.

"You must stay and watch over our new home, Accreton. The people need a leader. You must take the throne while I am gone," Isabel's eyelids were heavy, the travels still taking their toll on her.

"I am no leader. You saw how men were at each other's throats when you arrived. I was nearly unable to bring them to a halt."

"Even then, you managed to do it. No man was killed, and it was all due to your swift thinking. I understand what you are feeling. We will not always be prepared for what life hurls our way, yet that does not imply we should not confront it as best we can. Not all knowledge is acquired through books. Experience is, at times, our greatest teacher," Isabel closed the distance between the two.

"Isabel, I am not made to govern," Lucia's eyes glimmered, and Isabel knew it was not governance that concerned her.

"You have, and you can. I believe in you. I trust in you to keep what our family holds dear together. When I am done, I will return swiftly to you," Isabel's weak smile was enough to be mirrored by her sister. Lucia blinked away a tear forming in her eyes, and Isabel took her hand, squeezing it tightly. "All will be as it should be."

Lucia took a stride forward and embraced her sister, Isabel wrapping her arms around her. The two shared a heartfelt hug, recognizing it would be their last moment together before the impending battle, a future fraught with risks and uncertainty awaiting them.

"You take care of Giles," Lucia moved her head back from Isabel's chest, gazing at her. "I do not wish to lose him again."

"I will. We will not lose him," Isabel's arms tightened around Lucia, her hand wrapping around her head as her eyes welled with fear of what lay ahead.

The tears were the same she had felt that night, for her eyes began to well as they watched Rivetion. The winds were enough to dry them before they rushed down her cheeks, and Isabel blinked them away, mirroring Lucia's action in their last moment together.

Beside her, Odo and Robion were the closest to her, sitting idly upon their steeds.

"The men's morale is elevated," Odo leaned into her. "There were murmurs as we broke camp this morning of the 'Talon Princess,'" he said while glancing at her head, the talon crown sitting firmly upon it. "I never believed the tales of the fortitude and inspiration it had on men in the past. It seems the tales are true." After much deliberation, Isabel had considered wearing the crown. Though some nobles had eyed her dubiously, Odo's words filled her with hope.

"Never had I thought I would find myself on a battlefield beside my sister," Giles said from the rear.

"It is not the best of circumstances to be beside those we love," Robion added, his eyes fixed on Rivetion.

"It may not be, but at the very least, I may watch over her if the worse were to come."

Isabel glanced over her shoulder at her brother, grinning at him. *Family. Always there to protect us. Now I must protect these men as if they are my own, for I have rallied them under my banner.* "Are you well, My Lady?" Odo snapped her from her thoughts.

"Aye," she gulped, "I never believed I would see so many men fighting by me, let alone die because of me."

"They will not die because of you. They will die for you and for the cause you have led them to. They will be remembered, not for their deaths, but for their great deeds."

In the rear of the party, Uthred stood ready with his men. "I fear this is suicide. We should leave."

"I always took you for a frightened child," Fulk roared, watching the army amassed around them.

"It is not worth dying over."

"Aye, it is not. It is worth the coin, the hefty coin and glory we will get for it. Have you not seen our army? We will be unstoppable," Beavis pointed around him. "These men are skilled men."

"It has been a while since I bloodied my axe," Merek stroked the edge with the tip of his fingers. "She needs to drink off of these men."

The bells within the city rang, and with their tintinnabulation, the drawbridge descended, swarms of men erupting from within its walls. Isabel squinted, the army forming along the outside wall.

"That is peculiar," Odo watched the banners aligning and rising within the enemies' ranks. "Why would they leave the city?"

"Barbarians," Merek said, "do not know how to fight from a wall. Blood is all they seek, and fields are what they yearn for." *Perhaps. Perhaps that is true. They have proven victorious in every battle on the field against our people.*

"Where are our men? Lady Katinee assured us she would be here," Robion said, searching the hill for their aid.

The army that erupted from within the castle's walls stretched farther than the one she encountered outside the city in the tent encampment. Their numbers had grown vastly, and without their promised aid, Isabel was uncertain whether her men could withstand and decimate the enemy forces without suffering heavy casualties.

"Look," Giles said, pointing toward the hill on the horizon. Indigo banners flapped with the wind, a giant wolf and a pair of swords at its center, the silhouette only visible to a keen eye at such a distance.

"Katinee has arrived." Isabel sighed, certain their numbers should suffice until Lord Rulf made his appearance.

A party of three broke from their enemies' line, riding in their direction. Isabel broke her line, riding with Odo and Robion to meet their opponents halfway down the battlefield. They were three men she would never forget: Wolfax, Horn, and Crow, once her captors, today her rivals.

Horn looked at her crown, and a solemn expression overtook him. He shook it away and said, "If it was not the pretty girl you carried upon your lap." Horn laughed.

"Lass, who is your master today?" Wolfax's hoarse voice challenged her. Crow was silent, his helmet turning to watch Robion and Odo.

"I have never had a master, and at the end of this battle, Rivetion will have a new one. Hand over Rivetion, and I will spare your lives for what little they are worth."

"More than yours will ever be when you return to be my slave, impudent child." Wolfax's confidence had never mellowed, and today their blades would clash.

"I will make certain to be the first one to have fun with this girl," Horn laughed, Wolfax's gaze narrowing as his brows furrowed, his head spinning towards Horn. "What? You had your turn."

Wolfax's lip curled as he turned his horse and left, Horn wiggling his eyebrows at Isabel. Crow's gaze remained deadly as ever, yet he never let a word slip through his lips, not after his defeat at Goldcrest. The groups galloped away, the dust from their horses setting the battlefield air's ambience, an air that felt much heavier after they reached their army.

The men watched Isabel intently, awaiting their orders and watching as Wolfax ran down his army's line. Isabel had many thoughts and few words. She must speak, for her men's uneasiness was seen in the silence amongst their ranks.

"Today," she began, "we fight not just for glory or the loot we will gain from killing our enemies, but for freedom, the freedom of our allies and our people. I do not ask you to join me, to fight for me, but to fight for those you love, those who could meet a similar fate if we do not crush the tyrants who instill these chains upon us. Fight by my side so that we may step upon our foes. After today, after liberating these people, the world will call you one thing, the one thing I have always known you to be: heroes!"

Silence befell her, the men unsheathing their weapons. After a brief pause, they bashed their swords against their shields in unison. Their roars spread through their ranks, energy clashing onto the ground with every step as they marched in place.

"What will you bring?" Isabel raised her sword.

"Freedom," the reply came forward, spreading along the battlefield.

"And what are you?"

"Heroes!" The men roared as Isabel turned her horse, swinging her sword down, the men marching by her. Wolfax's army had now begun to march towards her, prepared to meet them in the center and spill their blood upon the land.

"Archers," Isabel said, the men Entan had granted her nocking their arrows onto their bows. Her heart drummed against her chest, Isabel prepared to give the first command to her amassed army.

"Ready," she watched as Wolfax's battle-hungry men charged at her line, her heart thumping loud enough she could sense it in her ears.

"Loose," she screamed when they met the adequate distance for their arrows to have an effect. The sky over Wolfax's men darkened, the day's clouds concealed by a barrage of arrows raining upon them. Isabel saw as scattered groups of men fell swiftly to her arrows, breaking down the near-uniform charge.

"Ready!" she repeated, "loose!" and a second barrage of arrows rained down upon her enemies. Their numbers were spared as their round shields took to the sky, preventing an adequate number of arrows from piercing their bodies. However, not all their shields provided the protection needed, for many still fell to her archers' volley.

Isabel's men charged at the incoming soldiers, the barbarians' shields lined beside each other, forming a wall. The crashing of metal against metal erupted along the battlefield as both armies collided.

It was not long before the shield wall affected her center line, causing it to break. "Robion and Osbert, reinforce the center." Robion nodded and rode away with Osbert's army towards the center.

Her men reinforced the center, Isabel watching the battle as it ensued. She searched for weaknesses, urging men to cover the areas where they were losing ground, hoping to maintain formation.

From the forest north of Rivetion, a barbarian cavalry burst forth. *Was this the reason they wished for a battle outside the city?* A stalemate would not endure if these men reached the infantry soldiers below and flanked her forces. It was her turn to save them. "Cavalry, on me,"

Isabel led her cavalry in a charge, prepared to intercept the opposing forces' cavalry unit. She knew she must make haste, or the enemy would flank her men and force them to rout. As the battlefield darkened, she glanced to her side, observing Jarin charging beside her. His friend from the stocks was still reluctant to fight and remained back with the few battalions prepared to reinforce their troops.

Hoofbeats were met with her men's shouts, followed by the thumping and crashing of horses. Men were flung from their steeds, crashing onto the ground, while others collided with the enemies' ranks. Isabel swung her sword at the opposing cavalrymen, slashing at their armor and tearing away rivets. She raised her shield to block one of her opponent's strikes, bashing him with her shield, then slashing at the man. Finding an opening, she sent him off his chestnut horse, the man plummeting to the ground.

A tug at her leg had her turning, one of the infantrymen attempting to dismount her. She kicked and sent him back. A pair of men snatched her from behind and knocked her to the ground. Her body slammed into the dirt, and she remained down momentarily until one of the men swung at her. Isabel lifted her sword to parry his strike, then thrust her sword deep into his stomach. He grunted, and she pushed him away, the man falling beside her. A horse reared, and Isabel quickly rose, avoiding being crushed.

The battle raged on. Being at the center of the field, Isabel could not determine in whose favor the tide of the battle was swinging. Until now, all the remaining forces had joined the fight. All that remained were Lord Rulf's forces, who had yet to arrive. As the battle raged, Isabel's sword swings slackened, heaviness overtaking her body. But weariness would not deter her. She continued to fight for her life and those of her friends.

A pair of horns from a helmet protruded from the battlefield, and Isabel saw the figure turn towards her. It charged euphorically before she could turn to face him. He sifted through the men, reaching her, and struck down upon her sword as Isabel attempted to halt his crushing force.

"Lady, I will feast with your body once this battle is over," Horn yelled over the sounds of metals clashing, pushing her down. Isabel rolled on the ground, preventing his swing from tearing her in half. The weariness of the battle did not aid her in her fight against Horn. Her remaining energy came from the desire to prevent his words from becoming a prophecy.

"I would have never taken you for a warrior," he said, shoving her arm away with his axe and snatching her by the throat, choking Isabel before hurling her away.

Isabel coughed and reached for her neck, losing grip of her sword and shield. Horn walked over to her, his shadow looming over Isabel as she seized her shield, stopping his strike. Wood splintered, and the shield tore in half. Horn's sword came to a stop at Isabel's wrist, the edge of his axe denting her armor. She flung it away and kicked Horn, rolling over to regain her sword.

"Now you are starting to prick my patience," Horn wobbled before charging once more at her. Isabel rolled on the dirt and bounced off her back, the sword clashing onto metal, followed by a deep groan.

Horn turned to meet her, a horn sounding in the distance as he held onto his stomach. Rulf's banner waved in the air, Isabel certain her forces were being crushed. His aid elated her heart, for Isabel was surrounded by more opponents than allies within the scattered battlefield. "It is over now," and Horn swung his axe at her, Isabel sidestepping, a second groan escaping him when Isabel's sword trespassed his body.

"It *is* over now," she said, pushing him back. The thud of his body caused the dust around him to rise, a smile still lingering on his lips.

With one leader out of her path and Rulf's men rushing down the hill, Isabel was certain victory was closer than she could imagine. Never had she been more wrong, for Horn's smile and Rulf's arrival carried a significance that would be etched into her mind for as long as she lived.

Isabel turned to see the field around her, her own men meeting their end by an allied sword, or a sword she had once trusted would allow her this victory. Osbert's men had now come to stab her people in the back, Katinee's forces joining in the slaughter. Jarin, who now stood beside her, was met by the spear of one of Osbert's men at arms. The young man groaned as he sunk to his knees.

The world around Isabel slowed, witnessing what once would be a decisive victory now turning into a bloodbath of traitorous slaughter. A roar came from the distance from the only man who had yet to join the battlefield. Jarin's comrade, who had vowed to not fight again, now raced into the field, prepared to avenge his friend's death. Unarmed and unarmored, he crashed into one of Osbert's men, launching him into the ground and beating the life out of him. Disarming him, he took the man's sword and ended his life.

With the fall of her closest allies, Isabel's gaze swiveled in search of those she cared for most. Her heart ached, watching the men who she thought would fight alongside her joining the enemies' ranks, taking with them the scanty hope that remained for victory. Arot fought men from both sides, Merek confronting Barda, swinging his axe at him in hopes of terminating his contract. Barda struck Merek in his stomach, trespassing him, the veteran warrior grunting. Merek, overtaken by his frenzy, punched Barda, sending him flying back. He removed the sword from his stomach, grasping for his life in pain as Fulk and Beavis rushed to his aid. *Even the mercenaries are betraying us. It cannot be. Barda, that traitor.* Uthred was nowhere to be found, and Isabel's mind forgot him when she set eyes on one of her most loyal friends, one who, with time, had turned to become her lover.

Robion fought Wolfax's men, unaware of the situation razing Isabel's world to the ground. Behind him, Osbert approached, his helmet gone amidst the heat of battle. With a sword in his hands, his eyes were set on Robion as his next target. The distance between the two was shortening with every step he took. Isabel's time was running out.

"Robion," she shouted from the top of her lungs, certain she would not reach him in time. Robion sliced the man's neck and turned to see the world around him, catching sight of the betrayal. His gaze met Osbert's, Robion parrying the man's sword at the nick of time. Except, it was not the nick of time. Robion might have deflected Osbert's sword, but Osbert's dagger met Robion's chest. Robion grunted, and a pain seared through Isabel's body as if her own had been stabbed. Robion panted, life expelling from him with each breath.

"Noooo!" Isabel's heart continued to burn, from fury, from seeing him stabbed in this betrayal. The burning sensation rushing through her was as if a thousand dragons had exhaled their fiery breath onto her body, the fire so potent it would not allow her to die at that moment until she sensed the last flame. Her entire body burned from the inside, the piercing pain in her heart causing her to sink to her knees. Isabel's eyes welled, attempting to flush her body from the fire, yet the flame was so vast it burned within her like the sun.

"No," she murmured, watching Osbert retreat from the battlefield, searching to flee from the wrath that would erupt from her. Except it did not. Isabel felt as if death had come for her as well. Her world had burst into flames, blood spilling over the battlefield, blood she was uncertain if it was friend, foe, or a traitor's. In a time now distant, clarity once reigned, but the present was a realm where distinctions blurred into one. Pain. Death. Hopelessness.

As if the gods had given her a breath of life, she managed to reach his body, Robion's fluttering eyes staring up at her. His dying gaze was enough to shatter what was left within Isabel, life spilling from his body onto her armor, her arms, her legs, and her face as he touched her cheek gently, his blood's warmth planting upon it like one last kiss.

"F-Forgive me," Robion sputtered, life escaping from his lips in a ruby fashion.

"No. You are not to blame. None of it is," rivers erupted from Isabel's eyes, rivers filled with pain, hoping to wash away all sin that had brought her to receive such punishment.

"I should have trusted your judgement," she said.

"You did what you thought be-best," he gasped, scavenging for energy for his words.

"No. Please do not abandon me. Not you too, Rob," she dropped her head against his.

"You have my heart, Isabel. You always have," he said, Isabel retreating, catching a glimpse of his face. It was painless, as if the world had not managed to betray him as well. His pale face became still, his eyes wide open as his hand slipped down her cheek, caressed her chest, and died at her stomach one last time, the life once in him vanishing into Isabel's body.

His memory was all that remained to Isabel, for she would never ride by him. He was gone, just as all those who had deserted her by means of her enemies' swords. Isabel cried, the world around her coming to a halt as the battle ended for her, for she would not be able to lift her hand to strike another soul. Her body was weak, what little strength remained within her pouring out of her in tears.

A horn in the distance blared, emitted from the far reaches of Rivetion, a horn familiar to her. Henry's horn indicated Cicely had been saved, their alternate plan succeeding, but at the expense of the many lives she led and the one she loved. Her long quest had failed, and it had proven costly. The city remained lost. War's principal payment was due, and it was to be paid in blood.

CHAPTER 48: A WORLD'S SHADOW

Lucia watched the battlefield from the hilltop, her heart tearing in half. Dropping her hand onto her chest as it heaved, she hoped the pain would not knock her off her horse. The winter's wind blew past her, its coldness carrying the loss of life from the battlefield. She could not understand why the onslaught had occurred, why betrayal was taking over their ranks. *Were men not supposed to be creatures who kept their word, particularly knights and nobles?*

It appeared not. The sword which was supposed to aid them at one moment, was now being thrust into their backs. Men on the field fell and scattered, the few who remained loyal to her sister meeting a terrifying end. Her sister bid her to defend Accreton, yet a nagging thought burrowed into her mind, and she decided to follow Isabel. She had not brought the necessary numbers to turn the tide of battle, for it was only Faylinn beside her with a dozen guards who came to escort her.

"I must save Isabel," Lucia said heartbrokenly.

"It is slaughter down there," Faylinn said, Lucia watching the men continuing to meet their end upon their foes and false friends' swords. "We cannot join them. If we rush down there, our fates will be no different than theirs."

"I cannot leave them to die. They are my friends, my family," Lucia pointed, her finger wavering.

"I am not asking you to do that. I am merely saying we will not change the tide of battle."

"What will you have me do? Watch as all those I hold dear perish under my gaze?"

Faylinn gulped, Lucia certain there were no words to console her soul. "Forgive me. Your sister said we must defend Accreton."

"No. That is what Isabel ordered *me* to do. I cannot save Accreton on my own. I need my family. She said I must protect our new home. What is a home without them? If I am to save Accreton, then I must save them first."

"I will not watch you die amongst them," Faylinn gave Lucia a stern look, her eyes no longer pleading.

"Then you better remain close. I have my duties, and you have been given yours. Is that not your duty, to protect me?"

Faylinn shook her head, her eyes brimming with doubt, Lucia disregarding if their men were enough to protect her in her mission to save those she loved. Lucia descended towards the few survivors, and her party was left without a choice but to chase after her, ensuring her protection. Lucia glanced at the castle as a horn blared from it, unsure of its meaning.

From the battlefield below, Isabel watched a descending party without a banner approaching her. She waved it off as the remnants of the treacherous forces that were to destroy what remained of her army. Her bloodied cheek was pressed hard against Robion's body, losing warmth with every sand that descended the hourglass.

The horn in the distance had proven that the sacrifice on the field was worthy of their alternate plan, except that saving those had proven to cost more than she bargained for. *All this death. Is this what rescuing friends entails? The death of others? Of more friends and lovers?* All around, her men began to flee, understanding their lives would not be spared if they remained to fight for what many believed a lost cause.

All those she had come to know in her travels were no longer to be found amidst the battlefield, the few men remaining dragging their bodies along the ground. Many groaned in pain as their enemies stabbed them, culminating their agony. Others pretended to be silent and motionless in hopes of avoiding capture. Soon they would realize their fates would be sealed by the same blade that met the injured.

A pair of men raced in her direction, their plated armors dented and stained in the blood of their opponents. She recognized them, her face numb, Isabel unsure of their survival if they were to remain by her side. She was certain they were aware of their fates, their loyalty driving them to her side.

"Isabel, we must leave," Arot said, turning to defend her against the remaining men rushing towards them.

"Your friend speaks the truth," Odo knelt beside her, his eyes fixed on Robion's lifeless form. He took her hand, his gaze meeting the reddened and pain-filled eyes gazing back at him. "He is gone. There is nothing we can do."

"I will not leave him. Not after being guilty of his death," Isabel sobbed.

"You must not carry guilt over his death. He joined you willingly. He knew the perils of his decision."

"I should not have trusted these people. I should not have brought us here. Why have they all betrayed me? What have we done for them to wish to kill us?"

"I cannot answer that, Lady Isabel. The minds of many men are disturbing. One cannot know what they are always thinking. The city may still be lost, but Cicely is free. You were a true strategist, always having an alternate plan. You have not failed," he squeezed her hand.

"I failed every man who lies dead beside me. Is one person worth so much death?"

"Cicely would be grateful-"

"Odo, it is I, not Cicely. I am the cause of this death…" she gazed back at Robion.

"I would like to live today," Arot yelled as he took a man down, slashing his chest.

"I should have known, Odo. Now I must live with my decision and the deaths I have caused. They are a heavy burden to carry," Isabel's gaze remained fixed upon Robion's pale face, gently stroking his face with her finger.

A group of men began to rush towards them, and Arot said, "There is no escape now. We are at the mercy of our enemies." Odo glanced over his shoulder, his eyes widening. "Their numbers are overwhelming, but they will not capture us until more succumb to their fate," Arot declared, steadfast in battle. There was no escape now.

Lucia and her retinue of horsemen reached them, confronted by an array of spears jutted from the earth and a formidable assembly of men barring their path to Isabel. Tugging on her reins, Lucia cried out to her sister, hoping to lead her away from the field in a desperate bid to secure their survival.

"Isabel, get up. Fight," Lucia called, her voice laden with fear and anguish. Though a wave of relief swept over her upon spotting her sister, Isabel remained fixated on Robion. *They killed him!*

"Isabel, you are a warrior. Do not yield to them," Lucia cried, her voice teetering on the edge of tears. The encroaching men formed a tightening circle, akin to a hungry wolf's maw surrounding its prey, teeth poised to snap and claim the kill.

Isabel turned towards her sister, looking across the field, her tired, soaked eyes looking at Lucia. Her heart sank, a feeling she seldom experienced, a feeling which ached when she saw Isabel's defeated eyes.

"Please," Lucia said weakly, Isabel unmoved by her sister's words.

"Leave. Go!" Isabel's voice boomed over the field, the only energy remaining being emitted from her lips.

"You must fight, Isabel," Lucia's chin trembled, Isabel still on her knees.

"Go, Lucia. Save what remains," Isabel's voice waned, fading away with the wolf's bite enveloping them.

"Please, Isabel," Lucia wept. "They will kill you," her heart fracturing into myriad shards, watching her sister kneeling defeatedly.

"I said go! Save yourself, save what is left of us." She rose, as if Lucia's words had breathed one last air into her. "I will take every last one of them before they lay a hand on me," Isabel shrieked, her cry tearing through the battlefield. She snatched her sword, her hair disheveled. "Go, Lucia!" Isabel turned her gaze towards Faylinn. "Take her, Faylinn, *I beg you.*"

"No! I cannot watch you die. Please! I cannot," Lucia cried as Faylinn seized her horse's reins, leading her away while she continued to sob, staring back. *Isabel, I cannot survive without you. You cannot die.* And her heart sank evermore when she saw her sister succumbing to the unforgiving ground, the fleeting strength within her dissipating. *She yielded.*

"I cannot do this," she cried, her shrieks vanishing along the tree line with her party as the wolf's mouth met Isabel, the spears surrounding them, Odo and Arot fighting off as many as they could, as long as they could.

Sheltered by her loyal men, Lucia vanished into the refuge of the trees. Deep in contemplation, she buried her head in her horse's mane. Isabel had changed. She was no longer who she once was. She was no longer the sister she had grown beside.

Living with Isabel her entire life had given her an insight into Isabel that all those around them could never see. Isabel was strong, determined, and faithful to all those she loved, but life had changed for her. Those darkening eyes, that weak voice, that attempting command. It was not her. Within those wet eyes, something had changed. Lucia could see it. Something deep inside had cracked.

Was it her soul? Was it her heart? Was it her spirit? Was it one thing, or was it everything? Lucia would never forget those eyes, for they had torn into her being like a predatory beast, preying upon her while life still coursed through her veins. Lucia's mind escaped to the past, remembering the active child Isabel had always been, running amongst trees, sword fighting against the boys, shooting arrows as fast as she could flash a smile.

Today, all had changed. Perhaps it had been changing, but Lucia had failed to see it. Today, nevertheless, it snapped. Deep within her, it all tore away, gnawing like a monster from her inside and finally making its way to her exterior, an exterior once hard as a knight's armor, now torn and exploited by man's treachery.

Isabel had always ensured Lucia's safety, from soft gestures such as finding her food and shelter during their journeys to snapping at her and apologizing because she had been wrong. She had never hoped to destroy her sister, only to protect Lucia from the cruel world they had been thrust upon, to fend for themselves like cubs in the jungle. Without a family to protect them, Isabel had been all Lucia needed, staying by her side, teaching her of the world they had encountered, naïve to a world they once thought so beautiful. A world that was no longer about festivities, about gorgeous dresses, about dancing, or lords who sought women to marry. No. The world was not as they once thought it to be.

This world, this new world, it was harsh. It was treacherous, it was greedy, it only hoped to gain all that which benefitted itself. This world would tear through anyone like a raging sea, breaking all in its path like a crashing wave, unstoppable. Nor the loftiest walls nor the deepest trench could detain this wave, for its tide surged with irresistible strength, reaching towering heights and plunging into unfathomable depths.

This world had shattered her sister, and she had changed. Lucia could still see Isabel's eyes, her voice urging her to leave, but her eyes pleading for help. Lucia knew from this moment forward she would never be the same, for the world had changed Isabel, and with it, herself. Her heart ached with the thought of her sister becoming one of them, one who had been so different, yet one who would follow the teachings of a world so cruel.

It did not matter. Lucia knew the world could tear her down, but it would never change Isabel. Impossible. Even if the world attempted to alter who her sister was, Lucia would stop it. Lucia would save her from its cruelness. Lucia would save her from its shadow.

CHAPTER 49: A WORLD ON FIRE

Have you ever been inside a house set aflame, pieces of timber falling upon you? They drop on the ground, the flames further igniting the wood around it, spitting its horrid heat in your direction as you attempt to breathe. With each breath, it feels as though the world's weight presses down upon your chest, like a dragon seated upon it, refusing to lift. The air you breathe is toxic and burns, for it is not air but poison, the poison of all that has fallen out of place, the poison of all this failure.

Isabel's sensations were such as she was sequestered in a cage and carried away once more. Her gaze fell upon the few remaining men who had been captured, witnessing them being rounded up and bound with ropes. Most were destined to be transported to Rivetion, their fate distinct from hers. Isabel was hauled off in the caravan riding in the opposite direction, imprisoned for what could be all eternity. It did not matter, for the world around her had ceased to exist at this moment. She was trapped within a cage, trapped within its flames.

The men who betrayed her cheered, a victory not well earned but gained through the fangs of a slithering snake, like venom traversing your body as you sleep. Isabel was unsure how such men could endure the weight of their deeds, living with such a profound absence of honor. It mattered not, for the deed had been done, and she had come to realize that not all men were created equal. Within their differences, a crucial lesson emerged: one must learn to navigate life with a keen awareness of their surroundings, for a traitor could lurk in any shadow.

All that did not matter as the loyal pair trailed behind her, bound to the metal bars confining her within the cage. The bars granted her a view of the freedom lying beyond, yet they cruelly denied her the ability to escape and feel its touch. The soft grass below, once so near her feet, now became a distant memory of sensation. As if the world knew her pain, it did not breathe the breeze that once caressed her skin, the air reeking with burning flesh.

Her gaze set once more upon Odo and Arot, the men with their heads bowed and maintaining their pace behind her. A pair of guards paced closely behind them, maintaining a calculated distance to avert any potential mishaps. The guards watched their surroundings, victory crawling within their skin, Isabel sensing their glee in their walk and laughter.

"Where will you take us now?" Odo turned to watch the guards.

The first laughed and delivered a blow to his back. "Turn around, prisoner. Do not get any ideas to flee."

"It was merely a passing thought ravaging my mind."

"I care little for your trivial thoughts. Keep walking forward and forget where we are going. It need not matter, for you will spend the remainder of your days there."

The pair exchanged glances and laughed, giving Odo another shove to hasten his pace.

"Strike him again, and I will bash your faces," Arot turned, glowering at the pair.

"How are ya going to do that, huh?" the first guard said.

"It appears as if you have got those hands bound," the second added, the first one cackling to his remark.

"Now keep moving," the guard shoved Arot. He turned and attempted to kick him, but a third guard swiftly intervened, delivering a powerful blow to his stomach. Arot crumpled to his knees, the cart dragging him along by his bound hands.

"Get up. We have a schedule to maintain," the guard kicked him. Isabel snatched Arot's bound hands and assisted him in rising to his feet.

A pair of horses rode and reached the guards shoving the prisoners, Isabel noticing the figures riding. Katinee, Nalthok, and Osbert rode high and mighty, Katinee being the first to speak.

"Do not rough them up, not just yet. I want her to reach *him* in a decent condition."

"The Crimson King will revel in delight when he sees her," Nalthok played with his fingers and cackled, his gaze shifting between the prisoners. "A shame for you two not to meet him. He yearns solely for the Valenour's purest bloodline."

"Silence, Nalthok. He will be pleased. It is best if they await the surprise."

Crimson King? Why is he still after us? What does he seek with my family?

These questions would remain unanswered, for few knew of the Crimson King, and even fewer had the opportunity to meet him. Isabel was destined to meet him, yet a meeting with this king was not one all longed for.

Then, a hooded horseman approached her side, and all those who stood nearby instinctively withdrew from his presence. He tugged on his horse's reins, the nightlike horse neighing and whinnying. The figure looked at her from under the hood. The last time she saw him, she wanted to kill him. Now, Isabel merely sat staring at the cage.

A soldier handed him a sack and rushed away before the rider could look at him. Morkath took the talon crown from within it, dropping the sack on the ground, his horse trampling it. He stared at the crown, then scoffed. "Valenours. Fools of fate. You believed this crown would save you." He looked at Isabel, but she did not meet his gaze. "It does not matter if you wear the crown. One fate befalls all Valenours who bear it. Death."

But Isabel had already perished. A piece of her had shattered. Perhaps it was the crown. Perhaps it was not. Discerning between each was of no significance to her.

With no response from her, Morkath scoffed. Slapping his reins, he galloped away towards a pair of hooded riders further ahead.

An eerie sensation struck Isabel, the world warping, a vision that was not a vision, for she could not see it, or so she believed. Within a dimly lit hall, within its murky shadows, there it lay, scaled plating placed upon one another. An ebony egg, an egg she had once touched, still connected to her in a manner she could not well understand. It did not glow, for its darkness consumed all light, a gloominess instilled within it that appeared to take life at a glance.

Cracking open, a reptilian figure emerged, its wings unfurling high into the air, stretching as far as they could reach, for they still had much growth ahead. Ruby eyes burned within its gaze, igniting all who dared seek its vision, its power. With the flap of its wings, the room's dimly lit candles would vanish as if stealing all hope from the world, all life from the hall. The beast knew of only one thing. It knew only one desire in this already burning world. It desired to consume it. Its shadowy maw sprang open, dagger teeth reaching for all and none that stood before it, for it was alone and not alone.

Behind the creature stood a figure so shadowy Isabel believed it to be a ghost, planting its hands on the ebony dragon. They were one and the same. Their touch appeared to join them in harmony, bringing to life the dragon's roar, a creature Isabel had been unable to spring to life with her touch yet somehow remained connected to it. It was like a curse, such as the one carried by all who bore the name Valenour. The wings spread wide, flame eyes fixed forward, their burning gaze locked onto Isabel as if she were staring into oblivion. The fire erupted and tore through the vision, akin to a banner caught aflame, sizzling and then becoming lifeless.

Isabel panted, clutching her chest, gripped by the fear of what was to come. Countless horrors had been set loose upon the world, and she was certain she had yet to encounter them all. They would surpass anything she had witnessed thus far. Terrible things were yet to be unleashed.

While one captured Beaumont was to be sent to meet the Crimson King, another stood high upon the towers of Accreton, watching the world as it was set on fire.

From the high towers of Accreton, Lucia watched the city surrounded by a sea of flames, a sea without waves but with living creatures ready to pounce upon their walls. Accreton now lay under siege, an army gathering outside its walls, preparing to steal it from the family who had hoped to rebuild it to its former glory. *Why are the Loup so determined on our destruction?* Terrowin, Katinee's brother, now stood leading an army under their indigo banner, ready to annihilate what remained of the Beaumonts in Accreton.

"It has been ages since I had seen such a vast army encircling a city," Faylinn joined Lucia by the crenellations.

"We must defend it, for it is all that remains of my family," Lucia hid behind the merlon, the solid wall frosty against her touch, as if the flames gathered outside had stolen the life within it. The first snowflakes had begun to descend, touching lightly upon her skin. Lucia hoped it would suffice and dowse the sea of fire staring at her, yet the first snowflakes served as a mere reminder of the icy world she had been thrust into.

"A wall, a castle, that is not what remains of your family," Faylinn said, "this is merely a demonstration of what they had. What truly remains is that which lives within your heart. Your family still lives. They are out there."

"Is it not amusing how this world is? It gives us nobles a silver platter with one hand and swipes it away with the other."

Lucia could not help but remember how repetitive life had proven to be. It did not matter how much they fled. The past always caught up with them. Their journey to flee its horrors had begun with them running away from their burning home. Throughout their travels, they had met many friends, some whom they had lost, others who still remained. In the end, upon these battlements, she stood with those who endured, prepared to defend it until her last breath. Her new home was to meet a similar fate to her old home, for the past had come to breathe fire upon it, ready to incinerate it.

The fire was prepared to ignite Accreton, yet Lucia was firm in confronting it this second time. From the battlements, she saw all that had pursued her to this place, but she now saw it with a new perspective. The world had taught her many lessons. Today she would use these lessons to protect those she loved. With the world aflame, she was the water that yearned to extinguish it. As long as she breathed, she was confident she could save it.

"How could she stay behind?" Giles joined his sister.

"I fear they killed her by now," Lucia blinked rapidly to hold back the tears welling in her eyes, determined to keep them from flowing.

"Isabel is alive. I know that much," he reassured. "Those men would not kill her. They want her alive, but for what purpose?" Giles looped his arm around his sister and planted a gentle kiss on her forehead. He lifted her chin, their gazes locking. "We will find her. I promise."

Lucia flashed him a weak smile. "I know we will. Even if we must travel to the world's end, we will save her." Giles smiled as they turned to watch the sea of flames.

Lucia stared blankly, her eyes fixed on the fires, yet her mind could only conjure the image of the extinguished flame within her sister's eyes. It was as if her body had turned cold, as if she had lost all the warmth which kept her alive. The world, it had come to change her, it had burrowed itself deep into her skin and attempted to destroy the warrior she was from within. For now, Isabel had turned cold like a corpse. Lucia knew that would not last forever, for deeper within those eyes, Isabel's true warrior self was buried under the ashes of a thousand betrayals, a thousand heartaches. Lucia was certain that as long as she lived, she would dig away, dig until she uncovered her sister's lost self. The old Isabel was merely dormant, and as long as it was dormant, Lucia could save her, for there sleeping, deep within, lay hope.

ABOUT THE AUTHOR

J.C. Rose's passion for writing ignited at the age of 12 with his first short story, and since then, he has eagerly whisked anyone willing to embark on adventures beyond this realm. Currently, a nomad navigating the eastern coast of the USA for graduate studies, he is accompanied by his Siberian Husky, Akira. When not immersed in academia, J.C. can be found engaging in sports or other athletic pursuits, exploring new locales with friends in his current state of residence, crafting novels or poems, and unwinding in bookstores and cafes. You can follow J.C. Rose and stay updated with his new releases on Instagram: jcrose_official and Facebook: J.C. Rose.

Check World Anvil: J.C. Rose for Maps, Wiki, and Family Trees

www.ingramcontent.com/pod-product-compliance
Lightning Source LLC
Chambersburg PA
CBHW060413030726
47495CB00003B/558